BROKEN SHADOWS

SORREL PITTS

BLOODHOUND
— BOOKS —

www.bloodhoundbooks.com

Print ISBN: 978-1-916978-25-6

For Mum, Claudia and Adrian

For my grandmother, Margaret Crotty, who left Ireland for the love of an Englishman

And for Michael. I hope it all worked out.

You only had to look
Into the nearest face of a metaphor
Picked out of your wardrobe or off your plate
Or out of the sun or the moon or the yew tree
To see your father, your mother, or me
Bringing you your whole Fate.

Horoscope by Ted Hughes, *Birthday Letters*

* * *

TOM

Years later, when I tried to explain to Anna how I found you, I realised how crazy it all sounded. Like a bad scene in a film. But that's how it was.

It happened on the hottest night of that year. I'd not been sleeping well for obvious reasons, but that night was particularly unsettled – thrashing around on the bed like a landed fish with the sheets kicked down to my thighs. I was aware of Dad's harsh snores coming from the other end of the house as I slipped in and out of a muddled slumber.

It was no surprise. During those months I never really knew what was wakefulness and what was sleep. I kept asking myself if what had happened was just some terrifying dream I was about to wake up from, or something I could close out with my eyes and make disappear forever.

They'd wrapped up the searches by then, but I was still looking. *Where are you?* I'd ask as I skived school to plod across Marlborough Common and Savernake Forest, because by then we'd covered every square piece of earth around Fawley so I'd guessed you must have gone further afield, were maybe hiding out somewhere inside the hollow trunks of one of Savernake's huge, dead oak trees, where you loved to loiter during games of hide-and-seek. It would make sense – even if it had been six months since you'd gone. I'd have done the same, except I'd never grown to fear our father as much as you had – or as much as I now realised you had.

Yeah, I was still searching for you, every day, every night, chewing over the reasons you'd decided to go. So it came as no surprise to suddenly find myself in my dream amid that string of locals and police with dogs, our row of faces, in the chilled winter sun, gazing hopelessly across the bleak hillside. We were making our way forward with slow, heavy steps, Dad directly to my left, and next to him, our mother, walking with her red hair fallen across her face, her lips sucked between her teeth and her eyes heavy with spent anguish. She had her arms folded across her chest as if trying to prevent the truth from seeping in – the same truth I was also fighting to keep at a distance – and I was just ruminating on this when I heard you.

Your voice was distant at first, soft but insistent, drifting up behind me. You called my name and I turned abruptly in response, but there was nothing, just our many footprints in the snow fanning back down the valley like a discarded bead curtain, and at the end of its long swathe, that arch of stones.

'Tom... Tom... Tom... I'm here, Tom...'

I glanced at Dad, but he showed no sign of having heard you. He plodded forward with his hands in his pockets, those inscrutable black eyes fixed to the hillside as condensation rose with his heavy breaths. My mother, catching my shocked face from the corner of her eye, turned, and her lips broke into a small, questioning smile.

'Tom, Tom, I'm here. Tom, I'm here, I'm here.'

This time there was no mistaking your voice. It rose, anguished and fraught, from the valley, rising in decibels until it became one long, endless 'Tooooooooooommmmmmmmmm!'

2

'Hey, can you hear that?' I said, turning to the faces around me, but no one looked at me or even lifted their head.

'Dad! Listen! Can't you hear him?' I yelled, reaching out to grasp my father's arm, only to find my hand involuntarily slicing through the darkness. The next moment I was sitting upright, my skin wet with sweat, my heart pumping like a piston.

Minutes passed. The window next to my bed was open. I put an arm on its ledge and stared out into the darkness. The silhouetted gables of the Victorian school opposite rose against a star-filled sky. As I waited for my heart to slow, I was aware of nocturnal scuttling from the garden below, the darting of bats in front of the village's only street lamp as my father's snores continued to rip through the house. I'd no idea what time it was.

Eventually I lay back down and closed my eyes, only to open them once more and stare into the darkness. I couldn't shake off the feeling that this dream was actually something tangible and defined after the blur of the last six months. The terror in your voice, the way it had come to me – it had felt as real as a knife slitting skin.

What's more, I knew that place. I'd gone up there last year with my mates because someone had told us about these stones near Milbury which were really spooky. We didn't have the guts to go there at night, but we'd headed up one Saturday last autumn and dared each other to climb them and jump down to the turf below. Except that two jumps in, Justin Lockley had sprained his ankle and we'd had to hoist him home on our shoulders and his mum had been furious because they were about to go on holiday over half term and had to cancel the trip.

I sat up, then reached over and turned on the lamp. The alarm clock beneath it read 4am. Lying back against the pillows, I stared at the opposite wall, oblivious to its coating of Bowie posters and the Swindon Town scarf pinned above them. I was thinking about you and how you couldn't have known about those stones, because you hadn't been with us that day.

Abruptly I rose and started to dress. Not that I needed much in the heat, just a T-shirt and jeans. Turning off the light, I crept out into the hallway and approached my parents' bedroom, its door left ajar. The curtains were half open and the street lamp's light poured in between them, illuminating the bed. My father was on his back with his mouth open. My mother was turned away from him, from me, with her red hair spread across the pillow.

I turned and crept down the narrow stairs, then made my way through to the small utility room to pull on my trainers.

Lifting the latch, I let myself outside before moving round to the front of the house. I could have gone out the front door of course, but that was right under my parents' bedroom and my mother would've shot upright no matter how gently I closed the door – that's how on edge she was.

Tramping quietly over the gravel, I made my way up the village's high street, towards Ivy Lane. I'd not brought a torch but I didn't need one. The moon was full, casting its milky light over the silent village, the chimneys of the cottages rising around me. No lights lingered behind curtains, no movement came from the gardens – the only sound was my hurried footsteps.

I remembered how to get there from that last trip, only that time we'd been on bikes, riding out of the village in a gang along the back road towards Milbury. At Milbury crossroads, you take a left and cross the main road, where there's a lay-by and a gate, beyond which runs a long track. Confronted by the latter's deep, water-filled ruts, we'd left the bikes chained to the fence and walked the rest of the way.

I'd never been out at that time by myself before. I expected to feel scared as I left the houses behind me and found myself on the deserted lane with just the occasional lone tree thrown up against the moon and the ghost-like presence of sheep moving around the field to my left. But I didn't feel scared, I felt the opposite; empowered, driven, and despite everything, enjoying the sensation that, just for this short time, the night belonged entirely to me.

The main road was dead when I got to it. It felt strange, like the street of a city under curfew. I had a compulsion to lie down in its middle, and if you'd been with me I might have done that, and you'd have giggled and said, 'Come on, Tommy, don't be daft. What if a car comes?' But you weren't with me; I wouldn't have been there if you were, and suddenly I missed your presence like a huge hole in my gut.

As I closed the gate and began walking up the track, I noticed the sky to the east was turning red, even though, far to the west, the paper-thin moon still hung above the horizon. The ground beneath my trainers was becoming visible, no longer water-filled but dusty, sun-hardened clay ruts, and between them a narrow belt of dried grass laced with weeds and thistle. To the left and right of me, tall verges emerged, thick with bramble and wild wheat.

I'd never known the majesty of dawn before and for a moment I forgot why I was there as I saw the emerging cornfields on each side covered in long swathes of mist and the sky becoming a flaming, mottled orange and red, with cumulus clouds like gold-capped mountains rising before me. I walked forward filled with a sense of wonder as the track slowly bore to the left, the hedgerow finally petering out to reveal a henge of three stones rising out of the mist, their base surrounded by a sea of red poppies.

I came to a halt, the dawn forgotten.

Last autumn, I'd not really given this place much thought, even though we'd come up here specially to see it. On a November afternoon in the company of the other boys, it had just been a bunch of stones to have fun around. But for me at that moment, that henge looked like something apart, like some angry living, breathing thing.

A noise made me jump. I turned to see a hare racing over the field to my right. It disappeared into the tall corn. The song of curlews, muted, almost imperceptible, could suddenly be heard coming from the hedgerows. I began to wonder if I was still dreaming. The sense of unreality brought about by the extraordinary scene around me – it was like being in an Oz of my own design.

I carried on walking, going on for another twenty yards or so until I reached a stile. Beyond it lay the small, triangular meadow that was home to those strange stones. As it reached the stile, the track bulged to the right where a Wiltshire gate – a barrier made of posts and barbed wire – was strung across the entrance to a derelict barn, its doors barred by two crisscrossed splintered planks, above which sat a metal, gridded window. The barn's slate roof was broken and scarred with gaping cracks, some roughly patched with green tarpaulin. I stopped for a moment. I didn't recall this barn from our visit but then I guess we'd been too taken up with Justin Lockley's swollen ankle. Otherwise we'd have been in there, building tunnels under hay bales or messing around with whatever else was kept inside. The barn's single window stared back at me like a cyclops' eye.

I moved on, crossing the stile as if in a trance, and started making my way through the poppies, their scarlet heads becoming a river which seemed to carry my unwilling feet towards the stones. I wasn't in control anymore, had maybe never been in control.

Whether dream or reality, a force had brought me there that, even all these years later, I can't explain beyond hearing the call of your voice – but when I reached the stones you were silent, as if you'd already bowed your head and made a retreat, your work done.

As I looked down beneath the dolmen, I exhaled a long breath and felt my body slump with relief. Apart from a scattering of flints, nettles and larger boulders, its base was empty. Not that I'd really expected to find anything, but still.

The sun continued its slow ascent, its rays breaking through the mist. The birdsong rose several decibels and I became aware of the faint cries of sheep echoing up from the long valley which fanned out behind the stones. Putting my hands in my pockets I smiled, allowing myself for the first time, to feel some amusement about my situation and the vivid boy's imagination which had driven me up here. I was turning to head home – I wanted to get back before Mum woke up and noticed I was gone – when I suddenly became aware of a smell.

I turned back to face the stones, my brow furrowing. Then I lifted my hand and ran it across the flaky lichen which clung to the sarsens' surface. In most places it was a greyish yellow, as it should be, but as it reached the base of the stones it turned a dirty brown, and then, right at the bottom, charcoal black. As I squatted lower, my fingers following the lichen right down to the clay, that smell became unmistakable, even to a fourteen-year-old boy who didn't drive.

It was petrol.

I sank to my knees, staring hard at those lichen walls, then directing my gaze to the clay base beneath them. That too, in places, looked burnt, and there was a visible basin of grey ash. I reached out, my fingers trailing over its powdery surface. I wasn't particularly perturbed, just curious really. People lit fires all the time – it's something me and my mates might have done if it hadn't been for Justin's ankle – but this one had scorched the entire insides of the stones.

My stomach's rumbling told me it was breakfast time.

Through the dolmen, I could see sunlight pouring across the valley. My parents would be getting up and very soon they'd be wondering where I was. I tried to remember if I'd closed my bedroom door when I left, and realised I probably hadn't. Mum would look in there, see I wasn't in my bed, and she'd immediately think I'd run away too.

As I placed a hand on the stone to push myself up, my eye caught something at my feet. I paused, reaching down to pick up a scrap of red wool. I lifted it gingerly, my heart, once again, beginning to accelerate. It was part of a pullover sleeve, scorched at the edges, but its intricate diamond shapes were clearly visible.

I dropped it as if my hand were stung.

The next thing I remember was the world spiralling, and then blackness, and suddenly I was over by the stile throwing up my guts and at the same time praying that this was still a dream and the next moment you'd be calling my name again but this time you'd be laughing and pointing your finger and shouting, 'Got you, Tommy! Got you!'

But as I finally raised my head there was just the cries of the sheep and the muted birdsong. Slowly I rose to my feet and made my way back towards the stones. The piece of jumper lay where I'd dropped it. Picking it up once more, I let my eye wander around the base, but could only see more of the same blackened clay and white ash among the flint and thistle. I began walking in small circles, pushing the poppies aside with my trainers as I studied the ground for more clues. But the sea of heads made it impossible, their petals falling as I traipsed through them, leaving splinters of red wherever I looked.

Eventually I sighed and gave up. Pushing the scrap of wool into my jeans pocket, I turned one last time, trying to understand what this find meant, but despite the evidence I still couldn't quite accept it. Yeah, you'd been up here, I decided, no doubt with some of your friends and you'd lit a fire and maybe it had got out of hand or you'd got into trouble with the farmer who owned this place, and you'd scarpered because you were ashamed. Because shame came easily to you, didn't it? You were always a kid who liked to please, especially when it came to our father.

Yeah, that must be it, I told myself as I headed back towards the stile. I tried to ignore the fact it was strange no incident had been reported back to us, either by your mates or whoever had caught you, because there had been enough media appeals for your whereabouts and everyone – even Dad – had made it very clear you weren't in any trouble.

The sun was high in the sky now and a restless breeze swept across the valley, making the surface of the unripe corn ripple like a khaki sea. Swallows shot across the tops of the trees and ahead of me two muntjac deer bounded along the track. I jumped down from the stile and as I did, shivered and released a sigh of relief that I was finally getting away from this place which, despite the sun's warmth, emanated a coldness which seemed to have crawled into my bone marrow.

And that's when I saw it.

Sliding to a halt, I turned slowly before taking a reluctant step towards the Wiltshire gate which protected the entrance to the barn, my gaze fixed to its two rows of barbed wire. As I slowly made my way towards them, my heart rang up its denial. Even though I already knew what I was looking at – a long piece of rotting red wool dangling from one of its lower barbs – I was still telling myself that it was just one big hideous coincidence.

Pulling out the scrap from my pocket and, holding it in front of me, I squatted down. It was the same wool – thick and deep scarlet. I remembered it well because I'd once sat impatiently with it wrapped around my wrists while my mother wound it into a tight ball. That was followed by days of alternatively knitting then stopping to pore with frustration over the pattern. 'But I've done that,' she'd said to herself with her eyes closed together. 'Knit two, purl three? No, I'm *sure* that's what I did.'

I raised my gaze towards the barn.

And to this day I've never understood why I chose to do what I did next. Even though every reflex in my body was telling me *to get out get out* of this place, to get straight home and tell Mum and Dad what I'd found so the adults could take over, I remained squatted, my eyes locked onto that piece of wool. Then I rose to my feet and calmly pushed the wire down under my palm, swinging one leg over it and then the other, making my way over the heaps of rubble and bits of machinery until I reached those tall wooden doors with their crucifix of planks.

My heart was no longer racing. I felt instead, a strange calm as I quickly assessed there was no way in at this end of the barn. A moment later, I was circling around the side, navigating my way around piles of rubble and bushes of bramble and thistle, picking my feet over rolls of rusted barbed wire and bits of rubbish. At the other end I found another set of doors which were also closed but there was a small gap between them and no bolt or lock that I could see. I grabbed the right-hand one and hauled it open.

The smell hit me even before I'd stepped inside. No doubt made worse by the warm weather, acrid and thick with offence, it greeted me in a putrid stench that made my guts heave. I immediately stuffed my hand inside my T-shirt and pushed it up across my face before stepping into the dull light.

It was pretty obvious that no one had used this place for a very long time. To my right stood a rusted tractor, its driver's seat covered with mouldy straw. Bits of broken machinery and old farming equipment littered the floor. A length of rope hung from one of the beams in a long loop and rolls of barbed wire were flung here and there. In the far corner rested an old plough, its teeth choked with clay. A heap of straw bales was stacked under the gridded window and near the doors rested a navy-blue builder's skip with *Clear it, Skip it* written on its side in white writing.

I guessed that the latter was where the smell was coming from, yet as I took another step forward my heartbeat remained steady in my chest and my breathing was slow and controlled. I made my way towards the skip, picking my feet over the debris. The smell increased, greeting me like some awful, pulsating, living thing and at the same time I became aware of a low-level buzzing. It reminded me of the hum of beehives; only this sound was much thicker and darker, like a low, monotone growl.

When I reached the skip, I stood still for what seemed like ages – though it was probably just a second or two. Images tumbled through my head, of you six months ago, the last time I saw you, coming into my bedroom bristling with excitement because it was snowing and you wanted to go sledging; of my anguished mother standing day after day at the sitting-room window watching the road; of Dad slumped against the bar of the Catherine Wheel after his seventh or eighth double, his eyes turning to you filled with suppressed fury because you'd yet again dared to ask when we were going home.

I was shaking, yet at the same time my palms felt clammy and hot. Sucking a lungful of air through the shirt, I placed my elbows on the edge of the skip, hauling myself up. Immediately that buzzing became a roar as a million black flies swarmed up from its insides, rushing past me in a panic and choking the air around me. I pinched my eyes shut and screwed up my face, waited until their angry flight had waned.

'You've just run away,' I told myself again. 'You ran away because you were scared of Dad but you'll be back soon and then people can stop pointing fingers at us and the police will stop asking him questions and Mum will wear make-up again and she'll laugh, and everything will be back to how it was,' before slowly opening my eyes once more to gaze into the bottom of the *Clear it, Skip it* skip, and as I heard myself scream, I realised finally that this was no nightmare from which I could suddenly wake up to find you sitting on my bed laughing and asking when we were going out into the snow, because I was already awake and you were dead, and this shit was really happening.

1

TOM

22 DECEMBER 2022

Who in the hell would want to live in England? It's the most miserable, godforsaken dump on this earth. And it's freezing. I'd forgotten what real winter – *English* winter – feels like. It's nearly half-past three in the afternoon and the patches of ground the sun hasn't reached are still numb and frozen.

I promised myself I'd pull in here and pay my respects. I've been thinking about it ever since deciding to make the trip – even had a notion about walking up to the stones and laying some flowers for him. Only I was so bushed when I got to Heathrow that I forgot to buy any. So I reckon I'll leave it for the moment. But that's okay. I'm going to be here for a while and, to tell the truth, I'm just not ready to go up there yet. Not this afternoon, anyway.

They are called the Shadowing Stones because archaeologists believe ancient man once used them to determine the time of the year. The story goes that, one day after the midwinter solstice, their shadow points directly east, but in midsummer, it points to the south.

I can just about make out the stones from where I'm standing – a distant fleck in the middle of a sheep-dotted valley.

They've always looked a bit out of place to me, an arch of stones plonked in the middle of a field like it kind of got abandoned, as if the people who built it were practising for bigger, more impressive monuments like nearby Avebury or Stonehenge. The Shadowing Stones belong to the National Trust but there's no sign to let you know about them – at least there's not where I'm standing.

A couple of cars pass along the road behind me. Then it's silent again. I don't know whether it's being back in this place, jetlag from the trip, or that double espresso I had at the airport, but my heart's started to race and suddenly I'm feeling a bit sick.

Need to get on – Dad'll be waiting. I try to imagine how he's going to look now he's in his late sixties. He used to have wide shoulders, a dark scowl and brooding black eyes that could beam at you unexpectedly. He was a big, unpredictable fucker and I really don't know what I feel about seeing him again.

Am I nervous? Excited in spite of everything? I reckon I am a bit. I wonder, how's he feeling about seeing me? I guess he might be angry too – and maybe he deserves to be. I dunno. I've never known – that's the problem, and right at this moment I just can't conjure up anything about anything. My head's all over the place and I'm missing my family already, even though soon I may be missing them a whole lot more. But that's another thing I don't want to think about.

Because I have another reason for leaving Australia.

* * *

It only takes five minutes to reach Fawley from the stones. It's a quick, uphill drive along the A4 towards Avebury before you turn left into a narrow road which, after half a mile or so, brings you down over a bridge. I notice the meadow to my left is flooded, just as it always did every winter, a wide overspill from the River Kennett forming a frozen lake in its middle. Its far end rises into Angel Hill where we used to sledge when it snowed, but I guess the kids can't do that anymore because some farmer has strung a barbed wire fence across it.

The meadow's deserted, bar a few miserable-looking ponies which stand huddled in one corner. It's strange to see it empty in the Christmas holidays. When me and Callum were little we'd be skating on that ice along with all the other kids, or at least we'd be sliding about on our boots as our father couldn't afford to buy us skates.

I've given a lot of thought to the stones and seeing Dad again, but I'd not reckoned with how I'd feel about the village. Fawley rests beneath the Marlborough Down, the latter's dark spine casting a permanent shadow across its clutch of slate and thatched roofs. Driving in right now, it doesn't look like much has changed; same latticed windows and lintels on the larger cottages on your left. Same low, grey sarsen walls, same post box and bus stop. There's a couple of new, posh-looking detached houses where the Jacobs' paddock used to be. A narrow, muddy public footpath still runs between the last of them and the chapel up to the back of Fawley House. The Catherine Wheel pub is still there. I try to recall the name of the couple who ran it but I was only seventeen when I left so not even old enough to drink alcohol – yet old enough to travel to the other side of the world.

My father's cottage lies halfway along the village's short high street, on the left-hand side, opposite the primary school. I pull up in front of it but don't get out of the car right away. I'm putting it off, and knowing I'm doing it isn't helping my mood.

For the past twenty-four years I'd been assuming I'd never have to look at his face ever again, which suited me just fine. And even when I did make the decision to come, egged on by Stella's, 'If you don't, you could regret it for the rest of your life,' and Ray Curtis's voice echoing from the other side of the planet, 'He's been asking for you, Tom. He asks for you all the time...' – well I don't suppose I totally took in the fact I'd actually have to face the bastard.

I just need a minute to prepare myself, that's all. I know he's inside that house, waiting for me. He's probably already watching from one of the windows, but I'm refusing to turn round and look. Instead, I get out of the car and, rolling a cigarette, stare across the road at the school's empty playground. Outside its wrought-iron gate, a blue sign reads *Fawley Vale Primary School*.

I light up and take a long drag before reaching into the car and hauling the large holdall off the back seat. I've not brought anywhere near enough warm clothes but I guess I've only got myself to blame. After all, Stella offered to help me pack but I said no and then I made it clear I didn't want her involved in this trip in any way. And when I told her that, she knew something was wrong besides Dad's illness. She knows me too well, and I know her too well.

It's nearly dark now. I can't put it off any longer, so I take a few hurried drags then crush the cigarette under my boot and turn to stare at the small, 1950s end-of-terrace where I grew up – the 'council cottages' as they were known back then. My childhood home looks back at me with equal mistrust, its two storeys rising above me in the frozen dusk, a thin trail of smoke ascending from its single chimney. I always thought the place was small when I was a kid, but it seems a whole lot smaller now. Its decrepit condition stands out shamefully against the two tidy and well-maintained cottages it adjoins, its render cracked and flaking. Rotting window frames look out over what used to be a flower-filled front garden but is now just a muddy yard filled with logs covered in tarpaulin and corralled by a low brick wall which is topped with rotting trellis, its splintered slats overrun with ivy. Outside on the road stands an old Ford pick-up truck which I guess must belong to Dad. From the look of its deflated wheels and mould-edged windows, it's not been driven for some time.

Jesus, Ray Curtis warned me he'd let things go – but I wasn't expecting this.

Pulling the holdall over my shoulder, I plod across the weed-pocked drive and make my way round the side of the house, just as I did every day as a kid when I finished school. And now, as then, I lift the latch to find the back door unlocked. But as I step through into the dim hallway, I'm aware my heart's started to pound.

'Tom ... That you?' The voice is thin, shaky.

'Yeah, Dad. It's me. Come at last.'

I drop the holdall in the hallway. Making my way towards the sitting room, I realise not much has changed inside the house. The place smells strongly of damp, each room hosting ancient Dimplex storage heaters which are no doubt switched off for the sake of economy. The same worn, yellowing-cream linoleum runs from the floor of the utility room to the back of the narrow kitchen; that row of brass coat hooks still adorning its far wall. Now a single donkey jacket hangs from them but when I was a kid you'd not be able to see those hooks for everyone's coats and scarves.

The kitchen's sliding chip wood door opens out into a cramped hallway, on the other side of which is the door to a small office where Dad kept his accounts, and after that a small toilet. And finally, at the hall's far end, the low door frame that leads into the dingy sitting room with its familiar floral wallpaper, now faded and peeling; beneath it the same green carpet; and at its back, the brown settee I remember Dad buying with great pride 'almost from new'. The two matching armchairs are pushed forward, a pine tea table sitting between them. On the latter stands a small reading lamp, a bottle of Bells whisky and two tumblers.

He sits in the furthest armchair with his back to me in front of a lit fire, *The Mirror* resting in his lap. A basket of logs lies within his reach and above him stands a stainless-steel drip holder, its plastic line snaking down the pole and disappearing under his pyjamas sleeve. A thick red blanket covers his legs, from under which poke a pair of frayed, chequered slippers.

'Hello, Dad.'

At the sound of my voice he turns, his small eyes straining to see me over the top of the chair. I smile back at him in a pathetic attempt to hide my shock. Because even though Ray Curtis tried to warn me, I'm in no way prepared for what I'm seeing. He's almost unrecognisable; the goliath of my memory reduced to a shrivelled gremlin – or at least, that's the cruel thought that comes to me as I stare down at his atrophied features, the pallid, almost translucent skin aged way beyond his years. The thick, black hair I've inherited has now all gone bar a few white wisps which clutch at his mottled scalp.

Only those black eyes, pushed deep in their sockets, assure me that this man is still my father. They glower at me now behind the steel-framed glasses before he presses his lips together and says, 'You took your time...'

I kind of laugh, and it's a bit too loud and obvious, and then I go to say something, but instead remain silent, overwhelmed. Then I step towards him, surprising myself by the impulse, and press his shoulder. His bones feel sharp and brittle under my fingers.

There's a long silence. I can see tears in his eyes and I've a dryness in my throat I wasn't expecting.

I step back and let myself down into the other armchair. He looks at me then. Properly looks at me. His eyes travel over my face and body, starting with my long black hair and moving down over the wool jacket to my jeans and leather boots. Then he slowly turns back to the fire.

'Aye. They won't know what to make of you ... down the Catherine. How's er... er...?'

'Stella.'

His voice, like his body, has leaked most of its power and his words now arrive in breathless, ragged sentences. As I've never completely lost my Wiltshire accent so he's never lost his Irish one, but there's nothing left of the thundering tones he once used to subjugate his sons. As a boy, I remember how often he used to bellow at us in Fawley Wood after he'd sent me and Callum to pick up the windfall wood. We'd hear his truck pulling up at the entrance followed by his summons. Like cowed dogs, we'd emerge from under the trees with our wheelbarrow to find him leaning against the driver's door with a cigarette dangling from his lips, his black gaze checking out our haul.

'Stella,' he says now. He extends a purple-veined, bird's-claw hand and pinches the worn velvet at the end of the chair's arm. 'Been married a while now ... haven't you?'

'Nine years. But we were together for four before that.'

Though I've not seen Dad since leaving England, I never completely let the contact go – as Stella said, how could I when I couldn't be sure? Plus, he was still my dad and our kids' grandfather. So after our second son Noah was born seven years ago, I'd submitted to her nagging and made the effort to keep more in touch. Since then, I've made the odd phone call to him, always at Christmas and sometimes around his birthday, if I remembered. And him the same with me. But it wasn't him who told me about the cancer, even though I phoned him in November for his sixty-seventh. He'd already had it for six months by then but didn't say a thing. I don't think he would've done either. It was Ray Curtis who let the cat out of the bag – he got hold of Dad's address book and phoned to give me the news. 'A couple of months at the most, Tom,' he'd said. 'If you have any desire to sort out your differences then you'll need to get back here as soon as you can.'

'Would have liked to ... come to the wedding.'

'I know, Dad,' I say slowly. 'We should have invited you. But Stella wanted to keep it small and simple – we didn't want any fuss. And we'd been together so long by then, anyway...'

'Small and ... simple?' He coughs before wiping his mouth with the back of his wrist. 'Too small and simple to ... have your father there?'

I reach forward and place a log on the fire, knowing that more of the same is likely to follow in these coming weeks. But I don't want to get into it right at this moment. Now that I'm finally at the end of this journey and sitting in front of these warm flames in this sitting room which, in spite of everything, still feels so safe and familiar, the fatigue's beginning to take hold and I can feel my eyelids starting to drop.

'You're done in,' he says. It's the same steady tone he always used when we were kids, just before bedtime – or he did if he was sober. 'Go and get some sleep, son. The bed's made up ... in your old room. Ray did it this morning when ... he brought in the wood.'

But I shake my head and straighten in the chair. 'I'm not ready to sleep yet.'

And then I find myself staring at him and he at me, and it's as if we're seeing each other properly for the first time. But it's so hard to know what he thinks with so little flesh left on his face – like trying to read the thoughts of a skull. Those shrunken eyes examine me from the depth of their sockets and I think I can see a pensiveness there, and a melancholy, but I'm not quite sure if that's what I want to see and at the same time I'm aware of my gut tightening as the stabbings of anger and suspicion I've been feeling all these years threaten to break apart the old power he's somehow managing to exert over me in just a matter of minutes. But I'm not saying anything yet. It's too early and I'm too fucked. I need to feel my way into this thing.

'So I guess Ray comes round a lot?' I say finally. 'Did he sort out the wifi?'

He nods, then looks towards the mantelpiece. I follow his gaze and see the router with its steady blue light – an anachronism next to the old-fashioned corded telephone.

Above the router hangs the picture that was always kept there in my childhood – of Dad and Mum on their wedding day, arm-in-arm in the sunshine outside Soweton Church. Next to it stand two smaller framed school photos of me and Callum.

He slumps back in the chair and pulls the blanket up towards his chin.

'Aye,' he says. 'He's been good – especially in these past few years, which have been ... difficult ... to say the least. Does the shopping for me and brings me wood. Comes down most evenings to check on me and get the fire going – or at least he did until today. He'll be relieved you've come.'

'It's good of him.'

'Aye so. Good of me to hand him ... my half of the business. Would've preferred to give it ... to you.'

I wait for him to pursue this, but he goes silent for a moment. Then he says, 'Four children ... that right?'

'That's right.'

'How old are they now?'

'Reef's eleven, Noah's seven. Then there's Indiana, she's five, and Georgia's three. Got photos of them on my phone. I'll have to show you later.'

He nods. 'Two boys and two girls. Always thought that ... was tidy. And what about work? How's that going?'

'It's going well. You wouldn't know there's been a global pandemic, hey.'

'How many are you employing now?'

'Forty-two on the last payroll.' I've often talked to him about my business, but I know his old man's memory means he usually forgets the figures, or pretends to. I also know that he judges my success by the number of people I employ, and each time I tell him this it seems to make him proud.

And now I'm confused – confused because I realise I'm glad to see that pride burning in the back of his eyes. What is this father–son thing? I see the same feelings in Noah and Reef each time they score a goal or get a good mark for their school work – their first instinct is to come to me to check their victory has been witnessed and approved. It's as if their success means nothing without my validation.

'You've built up ... quite an operation then. Who's looking after it while ... you're ... here?'

'Stella. We're partners now. But I can still do a lot from here. That's why I needed the router putting in, hey. Gives me access to the internet so I can still have Zoom meetings and send emails.'

'Aye. Well that's ... all a bit ... above my head ... but glad ... it's of help.' He lifts a hand to scratch his chin. 'You must have a ... big house. All those children.'

I nod. Again, I've told him all this before but he seems to enjoy hearing it each time. 'Seven-bedroom place in the suburbs. Got a bloody great terrace and a garden with a small lake at the end. There's a swimming pool as well, but that's pretty normal in Australia.'

'You've done well, son.'

The lack of any perceptible bitterness or resentment at his permanent exclusion from my life isn't helping the way I'm feeling right now. I turn away to stare out of the window because I'm finding all this a bit hard to handle and I wasn't expecting to feel so... I dunno – moved, I guess.

It's pretty dark outside but the road is lit by a street lamp that stands to the left of our driveway. Its orange glow illuminates two large white flakes which float down and disappear behind the trellis.

'It's snowing,' I say.

I turn to the bottle of Bells. I'm guessing Ray Curtis has left it there for us, that there will be a lot of this now, the two of us, father and son, drinking and talking. And I'm glad. Because this is what I came for. This is what I want.

'Okay to have one?' I say, pointing to the bottle. Then I add, 'It's been one hell of a journey.'

He nods. 'You don't have to ask, son, it's what it's there for. Aye, I'll have a wee one myself ... while you're at it.'

I pour whisky into the tumblers, then rise and place one of them between his shaking fingers.

'You can smoke,' he says suddenly. 'I know, I saw you out there. Ashtray's up there.' He raises his eyes towards the mantelpiece. 'Don't worry about me. I'm dying. Bit of cigarette smoke ... won't make any difference now.'

I stare at him doubtfully but his eyes flash his insistence. As I rise from the chair to pick up the ashtray, I find my gaze coming to rest on those three photos, moving from my mother's animated blue eyes to the more reserved expression of the red-haired boy who was her youngest son. As I stare at the latter, I feel Dad's gaze gripping my back. I'm waiting for him to make a comment, but he remains silent.

I carry the ashtray towards the window before taking out my tobacco and rolling myself a fag. The flakes are spiralling down in droves now. Shit, when did I last see snow? Have I ever seen it in Australia? Have my kids ever seen it? Outside, a middle-aged woman walks slowly along the pavement under the lamplight, face ducked against a spiral of flakes, her hair tucked under a woollen hat. She looks vaguely familiar; most likely the mother of one of the kids I went to school with. She would have been in her twenties or early thirties then. Now she must be in her fifties. Guess I'd better get used to this – a whole bunch of familiar faces but a quarter-of-a-century older.

'So how was the last scan?' I say, lighting the fag and turning, finally, to acknowledge the first of the two elephants in the room. 'You hadn't had the results when we spoke last week.'

He nods and rubs his chin. 'No change.' Sliding the glass across his chest, he sips at the whisky. I realise he's tired too, is probably always tired and the anticipation of my arrival has wearied him even further. 'I'm riddled with it, son. Maybe a couple of months at most,' he continues, answering the question I can't bring myself to ask, though Ray Curtis has already given me the answer. 'Maybe just a few weeks. Things can change ... quickly. They don't really know. Been in and out ... of hospital ... this last month. All depends on the pain. The nurses want me at home ... as much as possible. It will be better ... now you're here. Plus they've finished with the chemo. This helps–' he points to the drip. 'The nurse will show you how to change it.'

After that, he turns his face slowly back towards the fire, as if done with the subject. Then he pushes the tumbler of whisky away from him along the arm of the chair. He yawns and his head falls forward, his eyelids fluttering and closing.

I wait for a minute, two minutes, the warmth of our union slowly receding and being replaced suddenly with another, very different memory, of hearing Dad's voice yelling mine and Callum's names after a visit from our local shopkeeper. We were hiding upstairs because she'd just caught us playing with a ball we'd stolen from her shop the day before. Within a matter of minutes, Dad was stood above me in my bedroom tearing off his belt and pulling me by my hair onto my back. I'd stared up into those eyes and seen a rage and savage determination burning in them brought on, Mum told me later, by too much whisky. But I wasn't sure. Was never sure. And there were all the other times, rushing up the stairs like frightened rabbits at the slam of the door when he came in from The Catherine after a session, never knowing what kind of mood he'd be in.

And then his face, a month or so after the episode with the belt, when I'd entered this sitting room on a baking June day and told him what I'd discovered up at the Shadowing Stones. The immediate sense that, just for a moment, he wasn't completely surprised as he stared back at me. A few seconds passed, and then slowly the tears began spilling down his cheeks, the grief sending him sliding down the wall, his hand clutching the mantelpiece for support.

He'd screamed, *'Eileen! Eileen! Eileen!'* until Mum appeared from outside, tearing off her gardening gloves and going to hold him, and though she reached out for me with her other hand and pulled me to her, she didn't ask me anything. She was a mother and she didn't need to be told.

2

ANNA

Last night I dreamt I was back in Istanbul. It was summer and I was standing on the Eminönü ferry port staring out across the Bosphorus.

Before me, the twin supports of 15 Temmuz Köprüsü – the first of Istanbul's two great suspension bridges – rose like the soaring wings of a great bird as the water splashed and dazzled against the dockside. Above my head, the gulls were streaking and shrieking, open beaked, their quest the silver-scaled fish that flapped, hopeless eyed, in the brightly coloured plastic bowls laid out along the quay. Soon the fishermen would be grilling them to sell as *balik ekmek* – fish kebab – to the street traders and tourists.

And behind me, the usual din of the city; the horns of a hundred yellow taxis greeting the tourists arriving off the boats; the grubby-faced shoeshine boys and the ever-present *Lotto Lotto Lotto* sellers – their voices all fusing together to form Istanbul's complex aural landscape.

The sudden blast of a horn jerked me out of my musings, prompting my gaze to drop from the majesty of the bridge to the ferry which belched black smoke as it steamed its way from

Üsküdar, bearing him towards me. I strained my eyes and felt my blood charge, because I could already see him in his dark suit. He was standing on the port-side, his hand resting on the rail, his face turning from left to right along the quayside as he searched the crowds.

When the ferry finally docked, everyone, even the taxi drivers, went silent, their eyes following his tall figure as it clambered unsteadily down the wooden ramp, and pushed its way through the barrier's rotating steel arms.

He turned and smiled, his black hair lifting in the breeze, his brown eyes behind the small glasses beaming apologetically before striding towards me, arms outstretched, only to walk on past to embrace her instead, the young, veiled figure who had been standing behind me but, until this moment, I'd not noticed. I turned to watch him take her in his arms, picking her up and swinging her around.

There were admiring whistles from the street vendors as he pushed back her black abaya to reveal her naked body – she could not be more than twenty years to his thirty-five. They were laughing and kissing, and it was only then, as I sank to my knees, my heart imploding, that a voice in my head assured me this had to be a dream, that such a scene could never occur on the conservative streets of Istanbul, and I woke with relief because I realised the girl in the abaya does not exist, and Kerem is still mine.

* * *

It snowed last night. I pull back the curtain to see it banked up against the window sill; frost flowers coating the diamond-latticed panes. It lies a foot deep on my mother's lawn and beds, its brilliant white surface flawed here and there by a shallow trail of bird feet and the prowling paws of Zola, her arthritic black cat. I can't remember when I last saw snow like this; the hedges and the smaller branches of the apple tree sag like the shoulders of old women beneath its weight and the chestnuts on Soweton Road rear like black skeletons against a yellow sky.

This is the snow I remember from my childhood before global warming left its drab stamp on our winters; snow that used to stop the school buses and was difficult to walk through because its splinters spilled over the edges of our wellington boots and slipped inside the rims of our socks.

It's the same snow that used to collect into huge drifts on Angel Hill and that, as children, we carved tunnels into before sailing through them on our sledges. Or we'd go down on our backsides on the blue plastic fertilizer bags that, in those non-environmentally challenged days, the farmers seemed happy to leave lying around everywhere.

At least the snow's beautiful to look at – because looking at stuff is pretty much all I can do at the moment. When the hospital discharged me two days ago, the nurses told me to keep moving around for the sake of my circulation, but I've been avoiding it as much as possible because, to be honest, just sitting upright's agony.

I'd never admit it to anyone but apart from the pain, I quite like being stuck here in my childhood bedroom recuperating with nothing to do but lie curled under the duvet or sit and stare out of the window at the white gardens.

It's even nice being nursed by my elderly mother, especially because she wants to nurse me and feels a sense of purpose in doing this, so I don't feel too much guilt though I'm sure being trapped here in this room in this silent, dreary village, will soon start to drive me nuts. It doesn't help that there's no internet connection – my mother hasn't embraced the digital age – and the mobile signal in the village is weak at best.

My mother's house stands behind the village primary

school, and over the tall dividing hedge I can see how thickly the snow has settled over its playground and encircling black railings, whitening the roofs of the cottages beyond. Everything's completely still and there's that deep, dreamy silence you only get with snow. There's nobody around – not even the sound of children playing.

My bedroom's on the far corner of the house and partially set in the eaves. Its ceiling slopes down to a set of three small latticed windows, two at the front and one on the far wall overlooking next door's garden. It's warm, yet light and spacious, with a thick white carpet, wooden beams and clean cream walls (my mother had it decorated when she heard of my impending return and recuperation).

My bed lies in the corner of the room, next to the furthest of the front-facing windows, the one which overlooks the school grounds and the high street beyond. At the other end there's a small alcove which is home to a hand basin and mirror.

This room used to be my father's office and I asked to have it after he left us. I've always loved it – probably because I feel close to him here. Daddy was a successful publisher and my earliest memories are of coming in here to find him sitting at a pile of papers, his lips clenched around a cigarette; or leaning back on the chair with phone in hand, heatedly discussing a manuscript with one of his authors.

But now, apart from a shelf full of my old books, the room could be anyone's – my teenage pop posters long-removed and the walls bare apart from one or two neutral pastoral scenes and a couple of Degas' ballerinas. They're the kind of prints you see in spare bedrooms all over the country.

I dread these nights when the dreams come. My rational mind knows Kerem has called every day. He keeps saying he misses me, that the apartment feels empty without me. I try to ignore a voice in my head that warns me he's telling me this too often. We do not talk specifically about what the operation will mean for our future – we never have before so why should we now? My mother tells me he sounds charming. But I know that all Turkish men are charming.

After a few more days I'm feeling stronger, more clear-headed. I can pad along the landing to the toilet without help and pee without buckling over with pain. Sometimes I hobble downstairs and watch a few hours of daytime television, but in general I prefer to spend these long hours propped up in bed, alone with my thoughts, my hands wrapped around the endless mugs of tea my mother brings me.

I'm tired though. Really tired. In addition to the dreams, I've started waking up in the night feeling clammy and hot, even though it's mid-winter. I throw off the duvet and two minutes later I'm shivering again. They warned this might happen, and that it would resolve. It still feels like a slap in my forty-one-year-old face.

The hospital discharged me on the twenty-second of December. They don't celebrate Christmas in Turkey so I'd not given the festive season much thought until I found myself lying in that ward, drip and catheter in place, staring at a string of plastic snowflakes and a tree already shedding its needles.

In recent years, I've managed to avoid Christmas in England and have done so quite deliberately and much to the chagrin of my family. Ever since our father walked out on us on Boxing Day when I was eight, there always seemed to be a patriarchal hole in the proceedings and, at the back of mine and my sister Isabel's minds, the painful image of him in his red Santa hat, passing presents to his new children, as he once had to us. It was never spoken about, but I suspect our mother used to suffer terribly at Christmas and, after she'd gone to bed, the teenage Isabel and I would invariably down illicit bottles of wine and go into an inebriated rant about his betrayal. But we always kept our feelings from our mother.

And though he had his fatal heart-attack more than ten years ago, and so many years have now passed since we laid him to rest, I still find Christmas brings associations I'd prefer to avoid.

Since the birth of my niece and nephews, my mother usually goes to Isabel's on Christmas Day but this year, because of my convalescence, my sister and her family have decided to come here, to Fawley House, instead. And even though Isabel will be doing the lion's share of the cooking, this swapping of venue has put my mother into an unprecedented state of worry.

Each morning, she creeps into my bedroom bearing a mug of tea, whispering my name, her grey eyes peering down at me through her varifocals. Then, once wakefulness is established, she backs away from the bed and, twiddling her hair, commences with mention of about a dozen issues over which she has lost sleep – which crackers to buy, how *expensive* everything has got this year and should we all take covid tests given my vulnerable state, and what to do with all the left-over wrapping paper and food once everyone's gone.

As I stare up at her anxious face I realise it's not just her body which has grown noticeably frailer since I last visited. She was never an outgoing woman but she always possessed a certain maternal determination to take care of family occasions, and Christmas has been her forte. But it seems to me with her growing age that this determination has become increasingly beaten down by a baying pack of petty concerns.

And after all her anxiety, Christmas Day turns out to be a bit of an anti-climax. I wake up in a great deal of pain and only make it down to the dining room for a couple of hours; but it's enough to watch Isabel's children open my presents (cards with money and some Turkish Delight – there was no time for

Christmas shopping with preparing for the journey and the pressure of the coming operation) and appreciate the heat thrown by the fire that Bill, my brother-in-law, has built in the room's huge hearth.

The atmosphere's warm and jolly, with Bill and Isabel opening several bottles of wine – I am under strict instructions to abstain – and the children shrieking and laughing with excitement. I do my best to join in with the festive spirit, grinning over at my niece, Ella, who occasionally breaks off from teasing her brothers to eye her errant aunt with suspicion.

I'm not strong enough to pull my cracker so I let her and Nathaniel pull it for me, reading out the joke to them as they fit the yellow paper crown on my head. At the age of five, Ella is a tiny version of her mother, with long blonde hair and an unconscious pout. Her eight-year-old brother, sandy-haired, blue-eyed Nathaniel, who sits next to her, looked more like his father while the youngest, Ben, with his dark curls, takes after his grandfather and therefore looks more like me.

I try to impress on the three of them how special it is to have a white Christmas but it's tiring to try and act cheerful with hundreds of stitches tugging at my abdomen. The children aren't fools and they know something's wrong – they can see it in my face and the way I hobble around, my hands gripping items of furniture for support. They're also not about to be charmed into forgiving my absence from their lives with a bit of money and Turkish Delight. It's true that I never forget their birthdays; I always send them presents and they're usually generous ones. It's the same at Christmas. But my physical presence in their lives to date has been fairly minimal, consisting of a handful of short summer holidays and – since EasyJet started flying into Istanbul – the occasional weekend break. As a result, they eye me over the candles and holly-lined silver serving plates as if I'm little more than an eccentric vagabond that's been brought in from the street out of pity.

But it's not just the tiredness and pain or those curious stares which make me want to retreat to the privacy of my bedroom. Maybe it's paranoia, but I feel I'm under constant surveillance by my mother and Isabel, as if they're watching me in order to monitor how well I'm adjusting to this most domestic of scenes. As they clear the lunch plates and go to prepare the dessert, I'm imagining their whispered updates in the kitchen – 'How do you think she seems? Do you think she's all right with the children? – it must be terribly hard... She is being *awfully* quiet...' and I want to shout at them because it's this attitude I've sensed right from the beginning when I first walked into the *Arrivals* hall at Heathrow and saw them both waiting there with their pained smiles.

'Bill, would you pour me a glass of wine, please? I can't reach it from here,' I say as soon as they've disappeared behind the kitchen door, turning to Isabel's husband who's busy wiping bread sauce from Ben's chin with a piece of kitchen roll.

My brother-in-law raises an eyebrow, his hand hovering over his son's mouth. We stare at each other for a few moments, and I know he's aware we're alone, that I'm taking advantage of the fact. 'Are you really sure you should be drinking, Anna?' he says eventually.

I stare back at him, trying to gauge if he's humouring me. Despite his being married to Isabel for almost a decade, I still find him difficult to read, although I appreciate it's my own fault for not being around very much. Tall, and in his early fifties, he's handsome in a chiselled sort of way, with expensive-looking rimless glasses, a sweep of grey hair, high cheekbones and a wide, determined mouth which tends to fill with spit when he talks. On the dozen or so occasions I've met him, he's always struck me as a typical businessman with a no-nonsense approach to life and an entitled manner.

The son of an army captain, he went to Eton and spent an appropriate amount of time in the RAF before starting up a successful software company. Ten years ago, Isabel got a job as his PA and within twelve months they were married.

I bite down on my thumbnail and stare at him from beneath my hair. 'Come on, Bill, cut me some slack.'

He attempts one more swipe at Ben's cheek before his son shoves his hand away with an indignant howl. Then he takes a glass from the cabinet, half-filling it with Rioja and placing it on my coaster.

'Thank you,' I say, feeling a surge of irritation at his air of reluctant disapproval.

As far as I can see, Bill and my sister have the kind of situation that every middle-class woman and man aspire to. Financially secure, with their children at private school and a beautiful house in several acres of grounds in nearby Devizes, they also own a seemingly endless fleet of top-of-the-range vehicles including the brand-new black hybrid Jeep which Isabel used to pick me up from the airport and the silver Mercedes in which Bill drove his family here this morning. It's not that I'm jealous – unlike my sister I've never been one to bother about cars or the size of houses and I've never believed that money makes anyone happy – but what I don't like about wealth is the confidence that usually accompanies it; confidence that comes not just with the security it offers, or with the level of education it affords; but which seems to pour straight from the money itself.

'Oh Anna...' my mother says despairingly, returning from the kitchen with a stack of dessert plates in her hands and catching Bill pushing the cork back in the bottle. 'You'll be ill if you drink that. Have some juice instead. Or coffee. I'll make you some.'

'For Christ's sake, can't I just have one *fucking* drink?'

The expletives result in a stunned silence. My mother lifts her palm to her mouth as the children gawp at me saucer-eyed over their vegetable-strewn mats. Bill coughs awkwardly. 'Come on, Anna. There's no–'

'What did they say, Mummy?' I interrupt. 'Not to lift a kettle until the fourth week but no one told me how long it would be before I could pick up a glass of wine. Feels pretty easy to me. Cheers, everyone, Happy Christmas!' I raise the glass to my lips and knock back the Rioja in one gulp.

At this moment, Isabel enters the room balancing an ignited homemade plum and walnut Christmas pudding between two oven gloves, the sight of its blue flames drawing loud '*oooohs*' from the children and briefly distracting their attention from the drama. I watch her place it carefully in the centre of the table then step back and stare around at my mother's and Bill's faces.

'What's happened?' she asks.

'*I've* happened,' I say, to save them the trouble. 'Your soak of a sister dared to ask for a glass of wine on Christmas Day. And what's more, she used the F-word in front of the children... Well, I'm sure it's not first time their little ears have encountered it, and it won't be the last – not if *I'm* their aunt.' I push the glass back towards Bill, who stares back at me with an expression which lies somewhere between affected concern and suppressed irritation. 'Could I have another one, please – thank you, but that wasn't really enough for a growing girl.'

Isabel straightens and stares at me, her long blonde hair falling around her face, the latter which, shadowed and softened by the glow of the fire, looks as unlined and gorgeous as ever.

My beautiful sister – always turned out to perfection no matter what the occasion. Today she's wearing a low-necked velvet purple dress over black, high-heeled leather boots – her appearance, as ever, hinting at a seemingly bottomless purse and generous time allocated for grooming. She's the elder by two years, and probably the more sensible-minded – at least, she's certainly the one my mother considers to have carried out her true vocation in marrying a well-heeled man and having a brood of healthy children.

It's quite ironic really, considering Isabel was the more successful at school and managed to get herself a place at Oxford to study history, while I only just scraped my A-levels and ended up graduating from The University of North London before doing an MA in cultural studies at UCL.

But Isabel only stayed at Oxford for two terms. The pressure of studying alongside other highflyers led to a series of severe panic attacks. Eventually she decided the academic life was not for her and took a position as a secretary for a small firm in the City before moving back home and landing the PA job with Bill.

I press my thumb and forefinger against the base of the glass. 'Honestly. Isn't it my decision what I put in my body?' I ask sullenly. 'I'm not a child.'

The pudding's blue flames have petered out and my tense rejoinder has regained the children's attention. My mother places the plates on the table and backs slowly towards the Christmas tree. Her shoulders, beneath the pale mauve of her cashmere jumper, look frail, and she nervously threads her gold glasses chain between her fingers.

Bill leans across the table and pours me another half a glass of wine before placing the bottle safely out of reach. 'Drink this one slowly,' he says, as if I'm ten years old. Then more gently he adds, 'Anna, we all know it's Christmas, and no one is saying you can't have a drink – but you're on a lot of painkillers and we simply don't want you to do yourself any damage.'

His pseudo fatherly tone irritates me – the assumed closeness to somebody he barely knows because he happened to marry into their family – but the sight of my mother fingering that chain has softened me, reminding me of all the stress and worry I've brought to her this Christmas.

I sip the wine. Across the table, those three pairs of eyes watch me reluctantly return the glass to its coaster then raise their gazes to Isabel to gauge her reaction. But she's spooning out the Christmas pudding with a rigid expression and taking no notice of me or them.

My mother returns cautiously to the table, sitting between Nathaniel and Bill who, as the only man present, has claimed his position at its head. She reaches out to take the plate from Isabel. 'Darling, that's really far too much – half would be enough.'

'I'll have it, Nanna,' chirps Nathaniel. 'Here, put it on my plate.'

'No, Nanna won't put it on your plate...' Isabel interjects. 'Wait until she's finished, then you can have her leftovers.'

'But then it'll be covered in her spit!'

'Nathaniel,' Bill says through closed teeth. 'We won't have language like that spoken at the dinner table.'

'But Auntie Anna said...'

'We know what Auntie Anna said, but Auntie Anna isn't very well at the moment and that means she's allowed to say things that you are not.'

A silence follows as we start eating, though the pudding's much too rich for me. Spooning a small amount into my mouth, I watch Nathaniel trying to make sense of his father's logic, his confused gaze passing from me to Bill, and back again. Eventually I wrinkle up my nose and wink at him, then slide my eyes in the direction of his father and pull a face. Nathaniel grins and pulls one back, his lips lined with brandy butter.

'So how's life in Istanbul, Anna? Are you still teaching?' Bill says between mouthfuls, unaware of my silent mickey-taking.

I turn my gaze from Nathaniel to his father, letting my chin fall into my hand, the other playing with the cream on my plate. 'Yes,' I say, suddenly serious. 'But I've only got a handful of private students now. Most of my time's spent writing for the *Lonely Traveller*.'

'The Turkish edition?' he says, waving his spoon up and down in the air, impatient to swallow the food and move to his next sentence. 'Of course, Isabel said – that must make a change from teaching our marvellous language. How long have you been in Turkey now?'

'Six years.'

He drops the spoon into his empty dessert bowl. 'And how does it compare to Oman?'

I shake my head. 'You mean Egypt. I was in Egypt before Istanbul. Oman before that. I was living in Oman when you two got married.'

'Sorry, yes. Egypt. You have rather a penchant for Muslim countries, don't you?' he adds, wiping his mouth with a napkin.

I shrug, not understanding his point but sensing a slightly unpleasant inference. 'Not particularly. I've lived in Italy as well – and Spain. But I'd say Turkey's a lot more tolerant than Egypt – to women, I mean...'

'What, even under this present fellow. What's he called?'

'Erdoğan.'

'That's right, President Erdoğan. Seems to like pushing his weight around, that one. And what about your Turkish chap? Why's he not here looking after you?'

Out of the corner of my eye I see Isabel glance at my mother with something close to alarm. Neither of them has dared ask why Kerem has stayed in Turkey.

'He wanted to come,' I reply after a moment, pushing a

thumb into my palm and not looking at Bill. 'But I asked him not to.'

A silence follows, punctuated now and then by the scraping of spoons on plates. I turn to watch my nephews and niece as they cram the last of the brandy butter and cream into their mouths, their ears clearly glued to my conversation with their father. Then I let my gaze travel over their shoulders, taking in the Persian carpets and various paintings and ornaments that lie around our large dining room, the latter items Daddy had brought back from his various business trips abroad and my mother felt unable to throw away after he left. Very little has changed in this room since I was a child – wide and light with beams on the ceiling and a wooden conservatory overlooking the garden, it's only ever been used at Christmas or when Daddy had important clients to entertain from London.

'I see...' Bill says finally, swallowing a mouthful of wine.

'It's not Christmas over there. He has to work.'

'Well if it were me I'd...'

'Would you make us some coffee now, Bill?' Isabel narrows her eyes at her husband, her hand playing with the gold pendant that lies in the V of her dress. 'It would be nice if you made the coffee...' she repeats in a low tone. 'You know where Mummy keeps it – in the cupboard above the kettle.'

Bill stares hard at his wife, his jaw moving slowly from side to side. There's another silence, and I'm aware of the children sitting up, their heads, like a row of meerkats, turning from one parent to the other. Their father slowly rises to his feet, his focus fixing itself on some unseen enemy in the distance as he walks across the room and goes through to the kitchen, the door closing quietly behind him.

Isabel turns and smiles at me. I attempt a small smile in return, sipping the rest of the wine, suddenly feeling desperately hot and tired, and in need of escaping this tension.

'Your auntie needs to go back to bed now,' I say, smiling at the children. 'But she's looking forward to getting to know you all properly once she's back on her feet.'

Isabel puts her arm around me and helps me up the stairs. 'Anna, I'm sorry. Bill can be so bloody tactless at times,' she says, closing the bedroom door behind us. 'He really should mind his own business.'

'He's all right...' I say, without conviction, then I shrug and let her remove the jogging trousers and sweatshirt I've been wearing over my pyjamas to save the discomfort of undressing. 'Things are all right between you both, though?' I add, at the same time not quite knowing why I'm asking the question.

'Of course,' is her reply, offered too quickly. She turns on the bedside lamp, then hangs my jogging trousers over the dressing table stool, smoothing them with her hand. And in the silence that follows I suddenly realise something's *not* been right with Isabel, ever since she picked me up from Heathrow and drove me back down the motorway to Fawley. In the Jeep that day, and a week later when she collected me from the hospital, I thought I could sense a tension in her which, until this moment, I'd put down to awkwardness at not having seen me for a while, and possibly out of pity at my situation. But watching her face right at this moment, I'm wondering if I've misread things.

Only I'm too exhausted to probe further right now and instead, lower myself slowly back down on the bed with her arms supporting me. I feel her hands tucking the duvet around my shoulders, her face and hair leaning over me so I can smell her perfume.

'I'm really sorry I haven't been over to see you since the operation, Anna,' she says, pulling me forward and placing the pillows under me though I'm quite capable of doing this for myself. 'There's been so much to do with Christmas. But I'll be over more often now.' She straightens, then smiles. 'I'll even sneak you in a bottle of red as long as you promise to hide it.'

I smile back at her, knowing this is her way of excusing my earlier behaviour. At the same time, I realise I should be also be saying sorry for swearing in front of her children and generally behaving petulantly, but I can't muster the energy right now and there's a part of me that isn't ready to. So instead I turn away and stare out of the window.

I expect her to leave, but instead feel the mattress dip as she lets herself down on its far end, then presses her hand across her mouth and yawns. In the soft light thrown from the bedside lamp, I notice the shadows criss-crossing her eyes.

'So what's it like to be back here with Mummy?' she says. 'It must feel strange after so long away, especially at Christmas.'

I curl a hand under my head and rest my face against my forearm. 'You know, it's probably the remains of the anaesthetic, and the drugs... But sometimes I feel like I'm in some kind of surreal dream where I've suddenly become a child and my life's about to start all over again.'

'Well Mummy's very happy having you around. I know she gets lonely.'

'She worries all the time... About everything. Have you noticed? She never used to be like that.'

Isabel slides her fingers down a strand of blonde hair. 'It's just her age,' she says, studying its non-existent split end. And it's *you* she worries about mostly, Anna. I do too. I mean today, that wasn't like you. Mummy says you... well, you spend pretty much all your time up here and that you're terribly quiet and withdrawn.'

'I've just had major surgery. What does she expect?'

'I know. But it's not just that. We think you seem depressed. We think...'

'I know what you think.'

At this my sister falls silent, but I sense her watching me as I turn back to the window, wiping its condensation away with my palm. We seem to have reached an impasse, neither of us willing to talk about that which most troubles us. What on earth is this? Why can't we speak to each other? Does the fact that I live abroad mean we can no longer be close? We used to be when we were small, and I still feel close to her now, in spite of living so far away for so many years. We suffered the departure and death of our father together; we shared our mother's pain at his betrayal and supported her through their divorce as best we could; we grew up in this house and played together and experienced the same child's world. But now, as we're reaching middle age, we seem to be incapable of seeking empathy or support from each other just when we probably need it the most.

There's a sudden crash from downstairs followed by Bill's voice yelling Nathaniel's name. I expect Isabel to rise at the commotion but she pushes a hand through her hair and remains on the bed. A few seconds later, there's the sound of the dining room door opening, then our mother's voice calling.

'For Christ's sake *can't anybody* get a few moments peace around here?' my sister mutters as she rises to her feet. 'I'd better go back. Try to get some sleep. I'll tell the kids to keep it down.' She stares down at me for several moments before turning and padding light-limbed across the bedroom, closing the door softly behind her.

I turn and press my forehead against the cold of the window pane, my eyes following a blackbird as it lands under the apple tree and pecks futilely at the snow. On the other side of the hedge, the school playground shimmers inside its protective railings.

Minutes pass but I continue to sit and watch as large flakes begin drifting down once more and the street lamp flickers on to illuminate the white roofs of the three terraced cottages behind it, the smoke from their chimneys forming vertical grey smudges against the dusk.

Then, closing my eyes, I try to remember Kerem's face as he'd dropped me off at Istanbul Airport amidst the usual hullaballoo of shouting and taxi horns. He'd yanked up the boot and lifted out my suitcase, passing its handle to me before going still and running the tips of his fingers down my cheek in a way that said something more than I wanted to hear. I'd given him a small smile before leaning across the suitcase to embrace him.

'I hope it goes well, *canim*,' he'd murmured into my ear, his voice just audible above the din. I'd expected him to follow it with, *I'll try to come and see you soon,* or *You'll be back before you know it.* But he'd said nothing. Just stood there in front of the terminal's glass doors holding me in that awkward position, the top part of our bodies close, our pelvises divided by the suitcase.

The silence is broken by a flapping of wings. I open my eyes once more to see that blackbird land on one of the garden's snow-covered sarsen walls and perch there for several moments, a precious grub clutched in its orange beak. It pauses and turns its head from left to right, then launches itself violently back into the air and ascends westwards over the treetops, its shape gradually reducing to a tiny speck, and finally, to nothing.

3

TOM

I didn't give the date much thought when I made the decision to fly over, but Christmas Day without my family feels like shit – and not just because I'm spending it on the other side of the world in this dilapidated cottage with only my dying father for company.

I keep imagining the scene back home. Stella will have the barbeque going and the sun will be beating down.

Her folks will have come up from Sydney and I'm glad about that because I reckon she can't get up to much while they're around. I picture Tony, her round, red-faced father, carving the turkey in my absence. Stella and her mum are drinking wine and laughing.

Underneath the table our two heelers will be whining for scraps and Stella will probably let the kids give them some because it's Christmas Day for the dogs too.

Indiana and Georgia are in the pool – Indiana's already swimming. She's leaping star-shaped from the diving board and little Georgia, in the red bands I bought her just before I left, is bobbing about in the shallow end.

Now Stella's calling them to dry off and come to the table.

There's more room than usual for the plates, crackers and other Christmas paraphernalia because I'm not there. I assume my absence may be commented on once or twice and the kids will say they miss me. Stella will occasionally look at the place I usually sit and I know what's going through her mind. It's the same shit that's going through mine.

I got up in the early hours to Zoom them – I'm still jetlagged so it was no trouble. But it felt strange, seeing their faces and listening to their excited voices with the garden's bright sunshine behind them, knowing it was midday and high summer in Adelaide as I stared out of my old bedroom's window into the darkness to see that blanket of snow under the lamplight covering everything. I turned the iPad round to show them, and to explain how rare it is to have a white Christmas in England, but it was too dark for them to see, and they didn't really get the concept anyway.

I spoke to each of the kids in turn but they were too excited to take much notice of their dad though each one remembered to thank me for their present as they had obviously been told to do by Stella. Then she came on and we talked about the obvious shit. She asked after Dad, England, the weather. She wished me Happy Christmas.

Once we would have spent hours going over it all, me and her. I would have told her about how foreign and rural this place feels after Adelaide. I would have told her how strange it is to look over at the old school where me and Callum went as kids, and about my father's altered appearance; how he's the shadow of the man he once was and how muddled and fucked up I feel because I came back wanting to hate him, only I don't.

And she'd have asked me how he'd seemed – whether I could sense any guilt or remorse. And I'd have replied, *No, if I'm honest, all I can feel is sadness. Just sadness – and I don't know what it means, Stel. Does it mean he feels bad about*

something he did, or just sad for the way everything turned out?
And then I'd go on to tell her about remembering our
Christmases as kids, how mine and Callum's homemade foil
decorations used to twinkle on the Christmas tree and the fire
would be crackling in the small hearth as Mum leaned over the
pull-out table to serve the turkey, her long red hair tumbling
over her arms. Only I didn't tell her any of it.

Because she didn't ask.

Fuck, I know I'm overreacting. She was a bit drunk and
surrounded by the children and her folks so she could hardly
have gone there, could she? The kids still haven't got any idea
about Callum and what happened at the Shadowing Stones all
those years ago and I'm not planning to tell them about that
until they're in their twenties at least. But still I just got the
feeling that all she really cared about was how long I was going
to be away. She asked me it twice, those blue eyes narrowing
between the curtain of blonde hair, and not for the first time I
felt a swelling in my veins.

'Jesus wept. How am I supposed to answer that, Stella?' –
that's what I said to her. I only use her full name when I'm
cross. 'I'll be back just as soon as Dad pegs it, I promise.'

It wasn't the best of Christmas conversations between
spouses and I was relieved to close down the call. Relieved,
suddenly, to be thousands of miles away from her.

Though I kept my voice low, I reckon when I bring Dad his
morning cup of tea that he's overheard my side of our
conversation because he keeps looking at me like he's kind of
troubled.

Still, it's his last Christmas Day on this earth and despite
everything, I've done my best to make it good for him. I went
into Marlborough yesterday and got the very last tree from the
market. Then I bought some cheap lights and a Christmas
pudding from the One-Stop shop, and was amazed to find some

of mine and Callum's old decorations in the back of the cupboard under the stairs – those very same, ancient foil paper chains and snowflakes. So I hung them on the tree and around the sitting room, at the same time remembering Mum making them with us and how I'd sat back bored and a bit embarrassed because I thought it was girlie stuff, but Callum had piled right in with the scissors and the glue and had a right old time of it.

This morning, after Dad had drunk his tea and eaten a bit of toast, I shaved him and then did his bedpan and wiped his arse before helping him over to the armchair. It's strange but the toilet stuff doesn't feel as weird as you'd expect – at least no different from doing it for my own kids.

When that was done, I tramped through the snow to chop several baskets of wood before building a fire in the small hearth. After that I poured him an early whisky and roasted a couple of chicken legs, boiling up some peas and carrots and even making some gravy. I'm no Jamie Oliver, but I reckon I haven't done too bad a job of it and he manages to eat a bit of everything I put before him.

We speak little and about not very much – most of the time he seems lost in his thoughts, only it takes me a while to realise that, maybe as with me, the occasion's been making him reflect, because after another long silence he suddenly slides his plate onto the arm of the chair and says, 'Do you think ... about ... your mother much?'

The question takes me by surprise.

'Yeah, of course.' Then I shrug. 'She's still kind of everywhere, isn't she?'

He nods, and his eyes swerve away towards two large bluebell paintings which hang on either side of the room's small window. I've been studying them myself these past two days. With their bold colours they don't seem right somehow, spring scenes in a dingy room.

'That's Fawley Wood, isn't it?' I say.

I hear him cough. 'Aye.'

'Mum painted them?'

'Aye.' There's a silence. 'She was a good painter, but of course that's ... how we met ... you ... remember how we met?' and I suddenly know what's coming because I've heard it many times before, though not for a very long while.

As I turn back towards him he smiles to himself and closes his eyes. 'Flame-haired thing ... she was. Sitting there ... painting Lough Swilly in her little book.'

It's something my folks often used to reminisce about, how Dad had met my mother on his family's sheep farm in Ireland. He'd been sent down to see her off by his father who'd spotted her walking across his land, sketchbook under her arm and clothed in all her bohemian garb.

The middle-class daughter of an architect, my mother had been a talented painter and fiercely free-spirited and independent. After completing her final year at Birmingham School of Art, she'd decided to take several months off to travel around Ireland in a VW camper van, heading up through Connemara to Donegal, where her artist's eye had immediately fallen in love with the wild shoreline and dramatic, rugged landscape. As a result she'd decided to settle on the Inishowen Peninsula for a few weeks, and not long after that she'd run into Dad on that fated summer afternoon.

According to his version of events, she'd sat herself down with her sketch book and had been painting for some time when he'd suddenly appeared over the hillside looking as she'd later described it, 'tall, dark and impossibly, romantically Irish'. He'd stopped to admire her work, and then informed her she was trespassing, to which she'd suggested flirtatiously that he immediately guide her away from her precarious situation to the safety of the nearest public house (she always argued with this –

'Oh no. Be in no doubt it was *him* who asked me out, and within two seconds of speaking to me'). They'd both laughed and found themselves staring into each other's eyes, and that had pretty much been that.

Despite everything that had happened to my family, if there was one thing I was sure, it was my parents' love for each other. Years into their marriage, their deep connection was still obvious for all to see, especially us boys. 'Ee-yuk!' Callum used to cry, screwing up his eyes as Dad would grab my mother around the waist while she was in the middle of cooking and give her a full-on kiss. And she'd laugh and playfully shove him away. 'Get away wid' ya now yer bawdy old Irishman,' she'd tease.

I remember one particular beautiful mid-summer afternoon when they ordered me and Callum to join them on a walk in Fawley Wood. We ran off into the trees for a while to play war games.

Then, once we'd exhausted ourselves and our imaginary ammunition, we'd tiptoed up on the path behind them, intending to jump ahead and surprise them. The earth on the path was damp from recent rain so our stealthy approach was made easy. A golden light filtered between the branches, illuminating my mother's thick red hair as it bounced down her slim back. They were clasping hands and her body was leaning towards Dad's.

'Remember the day when we went up to Malin Head,' he was saying, unaware of our eavesdropping, and Mum had nodded. At the same time, he'd dropped her hand and slipped his arm around her waist.

'You wrote my name on the hillside with rocks.' She laughed.

'Aye, so. That's what you do there,' he replied, kissing the top of her head. 'Who would have thought it, Eileen? That ten years later we'd be together here with our boys, and still in love.'

She'd turned to stare at him with a smile on her face. 'Do you think it's still there?' she mused, and Dad replied, 'Is what still there?' and she'd said, 'My name, at Malin Head? Do you think it's still there written in stones?'

'Things I ... gave up for ... that woman,' Dad says now, his gaze still fixed on those paintings.

My father's family: rough, rural working-class farmers, staunchly Roman Catholic, had been livid when they'd found out about the relationship. Meeting an English girl had been bad enough, but a Protestant at that... My grandparents promptly ordered Dad to give her up or forget inheriting the farm – which was his right as the oldest child – and with very little hesitation, he'd chosen the second option. A short time later, he and Mum had driven the camper van to the Belfast–Liverpool ferry docks and come over to England, staying with her parents in Marlborough for a short time before getting married and buying, the small ex-council house in which, more than forty years later, we are now sitting.

A few months after coming to Fawley, Dad had started the wood business with Ray Curtis, and Mum had mainly devoted herself to bringing us up, although she also cleaned part-time and sold the odd painting. As far as I know there'd been very little contact with the Donnelly family – in fact I can only remember one incident of their involvement. It happened on a dull Sunday afternoon, sometime in the mid-eighties, when I was around seven years old. I'd been helping Dad rake up some autumn leaves when Mum had stuck her head outside the back door and said wonderingly, 'There's someone here to see you, Jim...'

I'd followed Dad into the sitting room to see a man standing by the window. I remember my surprise at those coal-black eyes and thick dark hair. Apart from his shorter height he was the spit of Dad, right down to his chin's shallow dimple and the arching eyebrows that met in the middle of his forehead.

'How're you doin', Jim?' he'd said. I sensed Dad's shock and found myself wondering at the long silence which followed, the room's charged atmosphere.

'Patrick,' my father suddenly exclaimed, then he kind of fell towards the man. 'Pat, Jesus,' and the next thing their arms were around each other and for several minutes neither of them spoke as my mother busied herself around them giving the room a hasty tidy up in preparation for our unexpected visitor.

I sidled next to Callum. My brother was sitting cross-legged on the carpet, happily scribbling a picture and oblivious to the stranger in our midst – and waited until Dad finally turned towards me. 'Tom,' he said, 'meet your Uncle Patrick. Pat, these are your nephews – Tom and Callum.'

A strange evening followed. Mum cooked a big meal and after we'd finished eating our uncle entertained me and Callum with stories about our family back home – our grandfather and grandmother and our many aunts and uncles who still lived there. He then accompanied my father as he put us to bed, and I remember him holding my shoulders to stare into my face, 'Aye,' he said to me, 'you've the Donnelly blood in you all right, Tom,' and then he'd turned to Callum but of course, with my brother's red hair and blue eyes so like my mother's, Patrick couldn't say the same thing, so instead he just grinned at him.

Though I was only five, I still remember noticing throughout the evening that Patrick's behaviour to my mother was different to the rest of us. He was polite but distant, hostile even, despite her obvious efforts to welcome him, and later, as I lay in bed listening to the goings-on below, I became aware of the laughter fading and being replaced by more serious, hushed tones.

And then suddenly my father's voice raising sharply

followed by Mum's '*sssshhhh*', only I couldn't make out what was being said so eventually I got up and tiptoed down the stairs. I stuck my ear to the door but all I could hear was heated murmurings and a man's name I didn't recognise being repeated several times, and then Dad suddenly shouting that he would never *ever* regret marrying my mother and to hell with all of them back in Donegal, and at the same time Mum started crying hysterically.

This was followed, a few seconds later, by the hard slam of the front door and the sound of footsteps heading off down the road. An hour later I heard them return, then a car starting up with a screech of wheels and accelerating down the high street.

When I got up the following morning, Patrick had gone and Dad was distant and subdued. My uncle's visit was never mentioned again.

Funny what comes back to you. I stare at Dad now and think about that tense conversation, the terrible disappointment he must have felt that the Donnellys still hadn't forgiven him for choosing my mother over them, and then I think how sad and stupid it is that religion can cause one whole arm of a family to simply be dismissed and forgotten – children, nephews and nieces, grandchildren and great grandchildren.

'Gave up my home,' Dad says now, shifting his body in the chair. 'Gave up everything... Where you ... grow up, lad... The soil's in your blood. It's what you ... are. I gave that up because ... of your ... mother. That's how much I ... loved her.'

After that he goes quiet, as if so much talking has exhausted him, but those eyes continue to blink heavily and occasionally he turns to stare at me as if still trying to take in the fact I'm really here.

I put the Christmas pudding on a bit late and we don't get to eat it until early evening. The rest of the time we sip whisky and watch films on his small TV. At times I can tell he's tired, and in pain – but in general he seems comfortable enough and I hope I've made the day as good as it can be.

By eight o clock he's fast asleep, his white face pressed against the side of the chair, his breathing shallow and wheezy. I sit watching him for a long time, trying to assimilate the hollowed cheeks and stringy arms into the man who used to be my father.

The minutes tick by and I'm beginning to feel restless and in need of some air. I also want a fag and though he says it's okay to smoke in here, I really don't want to while he's having a kip. So I roll one and bung a couple of logs on the fire before placing the guard in front of it. Then I take my jacket off its peg and let myself out the back door. It's still snowing heavily, the flakes settling onto my shoulders like duck feathers as I trudge round to the front of the house and come to a halt under the street lamp. I light the roll-up, cursing at the same time because I've still not got round to buying any gloves. There's not a sound out here on the road, the snow absorbing everything.

It snowed that day too. I woke up to see it lying like thick dandruff on the pavement and thinking it was a pisser because it was no way deep enough to stop the school bus from getting through – I was at the comprehensive by then so I had to catch it into Marlborough every morning.

Of course I tried it on, staying in bed until Mum put her head around the door. She was in her green dressing gown with her hair wound up in a matching towel, and she said, 'Come on, Tom. It's just a bit of snow. Get up now.'

And then Callum had appeared behind her with that easy smile of his. He was wearing the red diamond-stitched jumper she'd knitted him for his birthday the previous month and he looked like Santa's little helper, and when she'd gone he'd said, 'Guess what? Dad reckons it's going to snow really heavily later on. He says he'll make us a sledge to take up Angel Hill,' and I remember thinking, *About time because I'm fucked off with going down on plastic fertilizer bags and finishing up with my arse covered in bruises,* but for some reason I replied, even though I'd no plan until that moment, 'Tell him not to bother. I'll make us one myself,' and Callum's smile had stretched from ear to ear as he exclaimed, 'Oh *ace,* Tom. Let's make it together. Let's make it tonight,' but because it was a Friday I'd replied, 'No, not tonight, it'll be too dark – we'll do it tomorrow morning when it's light,' only to spend the rest of my life wondering how much might have been different if I'd just said, 'Yeah tonight, we'll do it tonight so make sure you come straight home and wait for me.'

There's no one around, but at the end of the high street I'm surprised to see The Catherine Wheel's lights on and the thought of a pint and company suddenly appeals. I push my hand into my pocket, my fingers closing around a ball of notes and coins.

It's only a hundred or so metres away, but it still takes me several minutes to flounder through the deep snow which is now banked in heavy drifts against the pavements and hedges. When I finally reach the pub's red-brick Victorian porch, I pause, because it's just occurred to me that there will probably be people in here I've not seen for a very long time and those people are likely to remember about Callum.

I stall for a moment, fumbling around in my pockets and rolling another cigarette. Do I really want that on Christmas Day of all days? Despite the long hours I've spent in Dad's company, Callum's not been mentioned even though we both know he's going to be, even though his baby-elephant shape sits between us in the room every passing second.

I light the cigarette. Fuck it, I'm being a dickhead. Dad looks like he's still got a good few weeks left in him at least. The nurse said as much. I'm not going to be able to avoid people in a village of this size and besides, now the thought's entered my head, I'd kill for a pint of lager. So I enter the pub's hallway, which is pretty much as I remember from back in those childhood days when Dad used to bring us here, its walls lined with old photographs of barrel makers and hunting scenes, its worn red carpet scattered with lumps of snow thrown from the stamping feet of other Christmas-Day escapees.

But once inside, the lounge bar feels different from how I remember and it takes me a while to work out what's changed. The carpet's been replaced with pale laminate which looks cheap and out of place in an old Victorian building like this, and a modern extension's been slapped on the side to make a dining area, though the tables aren't made up. A blackboard stands at its end, wiped clean of its menu. At the same time, the management are clearly attempting to keep the original character of the place – all the old paraphernalia I remember from my childhood is still here; the Yard-of-Ale above the bar, and the line of upturned horseshoes.

There's only five or six punters present. A group of men sit around the bar, and at first glance I don't recognise any of their faces. On the right side of the room, halfway towards the bar and the arched opening to what used to be the games room, there's a fire burning in the same wide stone hearth that Callum and I used to warm ourselves next to as kids.

I remember how on Saturday afternoons Dad used to bring us in here after we'd finished helping him deliver the wood. In the winter he'd sit us in front of that fire and buy our silence with a glass of Coke and a packet of Walkers crisps each. Only in his hurry to get alcohol down his neck, he'd usually buy two different flavours without asking which ones we wanted and then hand them to us without discussion, turning his broad back on the inevitable squabble that followed because one of us would end up with a flavour we didn't like – usually bacon. The bastard always forgot we both hated bacon.

Then he'd go and prop himself up at the bar and down double whiskies with the regulars and, for a while, Callum and I would listen into their conversations and sometimes we'd go into the games room and play billiards or darts, but it was always freezing and eventually we'd slope back and ask if we could go home but he'd never let us until he was ready because Mum used to clean at Forest Manor on Saturdays and she thought we were too young to be in the house on our own. So we'd sit there next to that fire, our hands stained with moss and dirt from helping with the wood, getting increasingly bored as we watched Dad getting more and more pissed.

'You mind smokin' that outside? Sorry.'

It's the barman who speaks – or most likely he's the landlord as I don't suppose anyone else would be working in a pub on Christmas Day. He's staring up at my roll-up as he pulls a pint of bitter and I can see from his incredulous expression that it's a long time since somebody last smoked a fag in this place.

After Callum's death Dad mostly stopped drinking down here – I reckon it was because he couldn't handle the gossip and speculation, the silent finger-pointing he imagined was taking place behind his back. But he carried on with the wood business and had been kept informed over the years about the goings on in the Catherine. He said he'd heard the brewery had been getting younger people to manage the place in recent years and the village wasn't very happy about it, though this new chap was apparently giving it a go with discos, special theme nights and the like – stuff that would have been unthinkable thirty years ago when the customers were predominantly farmers and land workers.

Of course I knew about the UK's smoking ban but hadn't really taken it in even though they have the same shit going down in Australia. But I guess it just seems unbelievable in the Catherine where all my memories are of the farmers puffing cigarettes and pipes around the bar and the landlady constantly emptying and wiping ashtrays with an old beer cloth. Dad always had an open packet of Rothmans lined up next to his glass of whisky and another sealed one in his pocket as back-up. Sometimes Callum and I would be close to choking there was so much smoke in the place, but there was something we liked about it too. It was weirdly comforting, that bar with its warm fire, filled with animated conversation and the smell of beer.

I go outside and chuck the cigarette into the snow.

'Thanks,' the landlord says as I approach the bar for a second time. He's a youngish bloke with sandy-red hair and a goatee. His hands grip the pump handles while his eyes move slowly down my body, pausing at the wide belt with its brass buckle. At the same time I'm becoming aware of a hush settling on the place, the simultaneous turning of heads.

'Sorry, mate,' I say. 'Failed to make the leap. Haven't been in England for donkey's years and in my last memories of this place it was packed with smokers.'

He smiles and the beard tilts upwards, like it's been stuck on. 'That's all right,' he says. 'We'll forgive you this once seeing as it's Christmas. What can I get you?'

My eyes move along the long row of bitter pumps with their unfamiliar names. 'Jesus, I wouldn't know where to start with these fellas. Guess I'll play it safe and have a Carlsberg.'

As he pulls down the handle and concentrates on pouring my pint, I prop myself on a stool, my boot heel curling over its bar, and take another look around. On the other side of the room, in the window alcove, stands a small, plastic Christmas tree, its coloured tinsel gleaming in the fire light. Sprigs of holly litter the mantelpiece and a stereo system over the bar's playing *White Christmas*, but that's about the sum of the festive cheer.

I turn and look at the other drinkers. A teenage couple sit at one of the tables. She's bleached blonde, over-made-up, and ranting at her partner between urgent mouthfuls of cider. The lad opposite her wears a baseball cap over his head and stares wearily at her with half-closed eyes.

Two middle-aged men sit at the bar next to me conversing about the issues of rewilding hedgerows. Another, younger man sits alone next to the fire in the corner, fingering a whisky tumbler and staring morosely into the flames. Probably in his late thirties, he's got thick brown hair and wears a brooding expression under his too-big glasses. A black-and-white collie lies at his feet, its chin resting between its paws.

'That'll be five pounds twenty,' says the landlord, placing the pint of lager in front of me. I pass him six bucks and he hands me the change. 'Interesting accent you've got there. Australian is it?'

I nod. 'That's where I live now, but I grew up here in the village.' I swallow a mouthful of the Carlsberg and it tastes even better than I'd imagined.

'You're from Fawley?'

There's a scraping of stool legs, and I'm aware those men to my right have gone quiet.

I nod. 'That's right. Went down under when I was seventeen and stayed there. This is my first time back.'

He goes quiet, absorbing this information and I expect him to ask me more, but instead he sucks in his cheeks and starts slowly wiping the bar.

Scratching the back of my neck, I stare down at the laminate under my stool, feeling suddenly uncomfortable. The scene's feeling a bit surreal and I wonder why the pub's even open at this time on Christmas Day. When I was a kid it always opened for a few hours at lunchtime so the landlord could give his regulars free drinks, but never in the evening. What's worse, the

CD's finished, adding to the you-could-hear-a-pin-drop atmosphere, and the two blokes to my right still haven't resumed their conversation. Out of the corner of my eye, I notice the nearest one turning towards me.

'Tom?'

I slowly twist round. He's leaning back on his bar stool with one hand pushed in the pocket of his coat.

'Ray,' I exclaim, reaching out to clasp his free hand because I'm actually pleased to see him. 'Bloody hell, mate. The old man said you still drank in here.' At the same time he rises from the stool, stocky and bow-legged, like I remember.

Jesus, Ray Curtis. He must be in his late fifties now and still looks damned handsome with shoulder-length, grey-peppered wavy hair falling over the collar of his buckskin coat. Funny how some folk don't change, because I now recognise those magnetic blue eyes, and as I stare back at him, hear my mother's voice echoing inside my head like it was yesterday. I was about ten and she and Dad were watching Ray loading wood outside our house. Dad, not aware I was listening, made a comment about not knowing how Ray pulled so many women, to which Mum replied, 'Well, Jim, it's because Ray Curtis has eyes people never forget.'

'Tom Donnelly, look at you, all grown-up...' He pauses, his mouth spreading into a smile, his expression kind of emotional, but then I guess I'm feeling that way too because I've known Ray Curtis since I was in nappies. 'So glad I persuaded you to come over. Lord, but you're the spit of Jim when he was your age.'

I grin and bow my head. I'd forgotten how middle-class he is, how his perfect enunciation had always sounded out of place in our home among the Irish and the Wiltshire. 'That's how you two should be speaking,' was what Mum always said when me and Callum took the piss out of him. Ray had grown up in

Fawley in one of the detached houses along the Soweton Road, and wouldn't normally have had anything to do with a working-class family like ours except that he developed a taste for alcohol which inevitably led him to the Catherine and the company of Dad. His own father had been a civil engineer, his mother a teacher at Marlborough College, and he'd had the best of upbringings.

There were two attractive sisters who'd done well – Dad told me that one was now a university lecturer and the other a BBC producer. But something had gone a bit wrong with Ray. Despite having the best of private educations, he seemed to lack the drive to succeed. It wasn't that he did badly at school – he was far from stupid – but he hadn't wanted to go to university, choosing instead, in that way some people do, to stick around the place where they were born.

Ray had always been a bit of an anomaly really: an intelligent and knowledgeable man who used to sit in our front room reading the broadsheets, yet he never seemed to want to do much with his life.

His lack of motivation probably wasn't helped by coming into money at a young age. His parents both died in a car accident when he was in his twenties, leaving him and his sisters a substantial pile which he'd used to buy a large cottage on the village's back lane. It had a number of outhouses he wasn't sure what to do with and eventually a conversation held at this bar had led to him starting up wood deliveries with Dad. The business did better than either had expected, keeping the wolf from both their doors and ensuring Ray was occupied enough to prevent him from becoming an out-and-out alcoholic. But his career as a wood seller must have been a far cry from what his folks had once envisaged for him.

'And hopefully without your dad's blarney,' he adds with a smile. 'Came back last Tuesday, didn't you? I've been meaning to come round but thought you'd want some time alone together. How's Jim doing?'

He doesn't seem drunk right at this moment. Too in control somehow, too smooth – but I'm aware of that stale, beery smell people have on their breath when they've been on a long session and reckon he's been putting it away most of the day.

I shrug and swallow a mouthful of lager. 'He's dropped half his body-weight... It's like looking at a stranger.'

Those fingers drum the surface of the bar for a moment, and then go still. 'The old spirit's still there though.' He turns his head sideways and looks at me. 'You can see it in his eyes.'

I nod, and at the same time notice the landlord's listening intently to our conversation as he lifts glasses from the washer and dries them. On the other side of Ray an elderly man with a wide, ruddy face and short grey hair watches and listens with the same muted curiosity. And then I suddenly recognise him too. Len Combstone... He had a cottage up by the village green and used to be a dairy farmer but got put out of business after the foot and mouth crisis. Callum had been friends with his oldest boy.

'Len,' I say, nodding to him and at the same time noticing the fat brown spaniel lying at his feet. Combstone nods back, then says, 'Evenin', Tom. Good to see you. I was sorry to hear about yer dad.' But he doesn't smile and I watch him absorbing my strange dress and air of 'foreignness' – or maybe it's more than that. Len Combstone was around when all the shit went down – he liaised with the police and, knowing the land as he did, and also knowing Callum, had been one of the chief organisers of the searches.

I turn away from their curiosity and find my eyes travelling along the ceiling's central beam, feeling oddly comforted as my eyes take in those familiar curios handed down from one landlord to the next.

'So how's life in Adelaide?' Ray asks eventually, ordering himself another pint of bitter. He offers to buy me another lager but I shake my head and lift my half-full glass.

'Still got this, mate. Should get back soon – need to keep the fire going.'

But I end up staying for another half an hour as I fill him in on the business, Stella and my ever-expanding family, though of course I don't mention the shit that's been going down with my wife these last couple of months. Then Ray tells me about the two long-term childless relationships he's had that didn't work out and the problems he's having getting building materials for the extension on his cottage. Then he starts banging on about Putin and the war in Ukraine and I'm aware of the pub slowly beginning to lose interest. Len Combstone finishes his pint and says goodnight, patting my shoulder as he passes and sending his best to Dad. The landlord puts on a different Christmas-medley then disappears through the door into the kitchen. Behind me, that girl's drunken ranting starts up again.

Ray goes outside for a cigarette but I can't face the cold right at this moment. I'm almost through my Carlsberg by now and wondering if those logs I put on the fire will last a second pint, when the bang of the bar door announces Ray's return. 'By the way, Tom, has Jim talked to you about going back to Ireland?' he says, swiping the snow off his shoulders and climbing back onto his stool.

I stare at him in surprise. 'Not really. He was saying earlier that he misses it, but he's not mentioned anything about moving back there.'

'Too late now of course. But these last few years he's been talking about it a lot – saying it's where his roots are and he should never have left.'

Maybe it's the booze, or tiredness from the long day, but I'm suddenly feeling a bit pissed off that Ray should know more about my father than I do. At the same time I'm wondering what this irritation's really about and if it's actually me I'm feeling cross with. Because it's only just starting to occur to me that Ray might consider me to be a bit of a wanker for fucking off and leaving Dad on his own soon after his wife and child had died – not that I'm getting any sense of it at this moment. But even so... I don't know, but this man's been a loyal friend to him all these years while I went as far away as I could get. Even at the time when Callum disappeared, I remember Ray coming round each day to help. Reckon I never thought about it at the time, but it's pretty clear to me that Ray Curtis doesn't suspect Dad of anything, and never did.

I place my pint back on the bar. 'No, mate,' I add for emphasis. 'He's not said anything.'

The CD's got stuck on Live Aid, the constant *having fun having fun having fun having fun having fun having fun* in the background beginning to irritate like hell. I'm about to reach up and punch the thing when the landlord finally reappears through the kitchen door and flicks it onto the next track before glancing round to see if anyone needs serving. At this moment, the brown-haired bloke rises unsteadily from his table in the corner and sways towards us, coming to rest unsteadily against the bar between myself and Ray. The collie sits up and wags its tail, its eyes following him.

The man orders a Scotch but then changes his mind. 'Actually I'm fucking ... sick ... of whisky,' he says. His voice, beneath the slurring, is well-spoken. 'Let's make it a pint... of Stella.'

The landlord stares at him. 'Don't you think you've 'ad enough, Alex?'

'Fuck off, Mike. It's Christmas.'

A few seconds pass as the two size each other up. Then the landlord sighs loudly and places a glass under the tap. At the same time, Ray lowers himself wearily from his stool, walking round behind me and reaching out to put his hand on the man's shoulder. 'Listen to Mike and go home, Alex,' he says, his voice lowering. 'You're hammered. Go home and get some sleep.'

In the background the CD's 'Here it is, Merry Christmas... Here it is, Merry Christmas...

But the younger man wrestles his arm free, almost falling backwards on me in the process. 'Get your hands off me ... Ray. You have your Christmas and I'll ... fucking have mine.'

Mike puts the pint on the bar and the man picks it up wordlessly before staggering back towards his dog, banging into furniture, his hand clutching the mantelpiece for support as the beer spills onto the carpet. We watch him lower himself onto his chair then tip forwards, his forehead pressing against his palm as he mutters something incomprehensible under his breath.

'Been like this all week,' Mike says. 'In 'ere every night getting plastered and rubbin' everyone up the wrong way. Don't know what's got into him. Ee's not usually like this.'

A minute or so passes, then I place my empty glass on the bar and rise from my stool. 'Good to see you, Ray. Guess I'll catch you down here again soon – or at the house?'

Ray nods and stares at the floor. 'I'll be down to see you both,' he says. 'Tomorrow or the day after. Give my best to Jim.'

It's still snowing heavily when I leave the pub. I suck hard on the roll-up as I trudge along the pavement back towards to the house, my head bowed against the snow. The only sound is the slow *splat splat* from the gutters and the sucking of my boot heels. When I finally get inside I find Dad as I left him, fast asleep in the armchair, his head pressed against the cushion. Small flames lick at what's left of the wood and along the mantelpiece the single string of fairy lights twinkle between mine and Callum's foil snowflakes.

Jesus, it's like something out of *The Swiss Family Robinson*.

Looking at the scene before me, I've suddenly got this really fucked-up sensation – like I'm feeling two things at the same time. On the one hand, it's a kind of pleasure because it's good to see him looking so comfortable and at peace and I guess there's a sense of warmth and security in being here with him in my childhood home. But on the other I've got this rush of dismay that I've gone to so much trouble. It's like, simultaneously, I'm happy because I've managed to give him this last Christmas Day and made it nice for him, but I also feel totally wound up.

Nothing makes any sense and it's just too easy to forget. Too easy. I don't owe him anything. I don't owe Ray Curtis or anyone else in this village anything. I had my reasons – I've still got my reasons – for leaving this place, even if it was easier to be sure of them when I was twelve thousand miles away.

But something's been bothering me and it's taken me a bit of time to work out what it is. Why did Len Combstone pat my shoulder like that and send his regards to Dad? Hadn't Combstone been one of the people who most suspected him at the time? So what's changed now – is it just because the bastard has cancer and a lot of water has flowed under the bridge? Or does Len know something – do *they all* know something – that I don't?

Jesus. I need to distract myself from all those chattering demons in my head. Moving noisily across the room to that small table, I pour myself a large whisky before putting on the television and hiking up the volume.

Behind me, I hear Dad stir, then cough wetly. I turn to look at him but his eyes are fixed on the screen. It's showing an old Christmas edition of *Morecombe and Wise* and he's smiling at something Eric Morecambe's saying to a fat woman in a green silk dress, the skin under my father's eyes creasing and reminding me of those dark laughter lines he used to have when he was younger. He'd had a hard, stern face much of the time, but he used to laugh a lot with my mother and those features would suddenly soften and the eyes would crease and twinkle, just as they are now. He was the same with the guys down the Catherine. He'd be telling them some implausible story that would end in an expertly timed punchline, and you'd hear them all falling about before whoever's turn it was ordered the next round.

'All right, Dad,' I say softly, taking a mouthful of whisky. 'How're you going?'

He turns his head slowly towards me. 'Hello ... son. S'pose I'm not ... too bad – for a dying man.' There's a silence. I can hear his breathing, laboured and shallow. Then he lifts a hand and stretches it towards me, his eyes holding mine.

Despite myself, I take a step in his direction, then another, until he wraps his papery fingers around my wrist.

'Happy Christmas, son,' he whispers, then smiles up at me. 'It's good to finally ... have you home.'

4

ANNA

New Year's Eve comes and goes. My mother and I don't wait for the chimes. Instead we go to bed early and lie in the darkness thinking our separate thoughts.

I listen to the village's silence which is occasionally interrupted with the shouts of drunken revellers leaving The Catherine Wheel. Then I imagine how Istanbul would be this night, if I were there. The Turks really know how to do *Yil Başa*. I would be standing hand-in-hand with Kerem among the crowds outside Guneş Bar in Arnevutkoy, watching fireworks soaring over the suspension bridge. The air would be rich with the smell of roasting chestnuts from the late-night food stalls and there'd be party boats travelling up and down the Bosphorus, their flashing neon lights reflected in the water. Once the chimes were over, we'd head back inside the bar and carry on dancing to reggae until three or four in the morning. That's what we would be doing tonight if we were together and none of this had happened.

But we're not together because it has happened and instead I'm stuck here, a prisoner in this frozen morgue of a village, my stomach full of stitches, my sheets soaked in my sweat. And

Kerem is God knows where. Probably at Güneş Bar with his mates. All I know is that, wherever he is, he can't be thinking much about me because it's New Year's Eve and he hasn't bothered to call.

* * *

A few days later, the children return to school for the winter term. Each morning, their shouting and laughter drifts into my dreams before the heavy iron bell is rung and they're called inside. After that, I usually sink into that strange, lucid sleep one only earns after a restless night, to be woken again when the bell rings for a second time and the children charge out for first break. This is when I usually roll myself awkwardly from the bed, using my elbows and knees to propel me as the physiotherapists taught me to do. Then I slowly ease myself down the stairs to make a cup of coffee before coming back to watch the children through the window as their bodies, half-hidden beneath coats, hats and scarves, charge between the piles of slush, their boundless energy fuelled and sharpened by the cold as they throw snowballs at each other and build snowmen.

When I was nine, and Isabel eleven, we attended the village school for a term. There was a fire at St Anne's – the all-girls' private primary school in Marlborough we usually went to – and the main building was unusable so we had to go to Fawley instead. It was a memorable period in our lives; the unfamiliar presence of boys unnerved me and I suspected the local children considered me a snob.

To them, we were the posh London family who, until I was eight, had only used Fawley House at weekends and for holidays. The rest of the time we'd stayed in our large house in

Mornington Crescent until my father left my mother and the necessary division of property had ensued.

I've never quite been sure why my mother chose to live in Fawley rather than London, but I assume the decision must have been made for us, her children, to give us the best childhood she could. Moreover, even though we were 'weekenders' she'd got to know people in the village over the years – it had a local shop back then and she liked to spend time there chatting to Mrs Bussle, the shopkeeper and the other housewives. I suspect she could see, and already felt part of, an immediate, visible community here, a community which in London had, to all purposes, ceased to exist once her marriage was over.

There, she had a few friends of her own, and her sister and mother, but her social life had mainly been spent in Daddy's circle, usually authors and arty types who were very different to her. The move to Wiltshire also enabled her to distance herself from my father and his glamorous new girlfriend.

Isabel comes over most days now that Nathaniel and Ella are back at school, but she rarely stays very long, joking that she needs to get back to Ben before the nanny poisons him or gives him broken glass to play with. But there's something about the way she says these things that doesn't convince me, though I'm not sure why.

Usually she knocks on my door around mid-morning and brings me a cup of tea before sitting on the end of my bed. But apart from asking how I'm feeling she says little, and most of the time seems a bit distracted, her gaze turned to the garden, her hand reaching out to absently stroke Zola.

I remember how she was at Christmas when I asked her

about Bill, the way she'd shrugged off the question. This quiet, agitated Isabel is not the sister I remember but I've been away so long I'm having to get to know her again and I remind myself that her pensiveness may well now be normal, brought about by the responsibilities of marriage and three children. But somehow I doubt it. I want to ask more, to find out what's on her mind, but it's the same thing going on between her and me that's going on between me and my mother, this stupid situation of being unable to speak about anything that matters.

But one afternoon as I'm curled up under my duvet watching Isabel staring out of the window and absently running her fingers down strands of her hair, I'm reminded of another time, many years ago, when she behaved in a similar way.

It was during the summer following that term at Fawley Primary. I was seeing little of her by then, losing her to her new school friends, puberty and boys. I remember how, as each hot evening stretched before us, Isabel would go off with some of the village kids to play rounders on The Green or swim in the Kennett. I would sometimes join her – especially when I knew that other, younger children were going – but mostly I'd simply let them get on with it because I sensed I was unwanted and my hanging around was a bit of an embarrassment to my sister.

So that was why I wasn't with her the evening she came back from the river barefoot, in just her swimming costume and without her towel. She ran through the house and upstairs to her bedroom without a word.

Fortunately, our mother was busy weeding the flower beds, her head ducked behind some dahlias, so she didn't see Isabel come in, but I did and quickly followed her upstairs to ask what was wrong. When I knocked on her bedroom door there was nothing but silence. Then I opened it, only to glimpse Isabel, pale and red eyed, marching towards me across the carpet before slamming the door in my face and yelling, 'Fuck off, will you? Just fuck off!'

After that, she became increasingly withdrawn, coming straight home from school and going up to her room without a word. My mother was oddly oblivious to her older daughter's troubled behaviour, but she and Daddy were going through their divorce at the time so I suppose her mind was elsewhere.

The sight of my forty-three-year-old sister sitting here on the end of my bed each day looking pale and pensive as she stares out of the window, reminds me now of that summer. The twelve-year-old Isabel *had* opened the door to me eventually, and in my childish incomprehension of what might have happened to upset her, and my inability to penetrate the wall of silence she'd built around herself, I took to sitting on the end of her bed for long hours simply to offer her the comfort of my presence, rather as she's doing with me now.

In the days that followed, we spent many hours sitting together, both of us staring out of the open window and watching my mother in the garden, always obsessively weeding and clipping and mowing.

Then, one evening, Isabel had burst into tears and confessed what happened, making me swear at the same time not to tell a soul. She'd left the river with the other boys, she said, but when she was almost home realised she'd forgotten her towel, so she'd gone back on her own to find it. When she was halfway across the field a man had come up behind her. He'd grabbed her from behind, his hand landing on one of her breasts, and told her she was beautiful in breath which reeked of beer and cigarettes. At this point Isabel had screamed and the man had let go of her. She shot away so fast her flip-flops were torn from her feet.

She didn't get to see his face. All she noticed was a tattoo on his hand. The word 'ZEN' was written across his three middle fingers, and a swirly flesh and black circle – which she would later realise was Yin-Yang, or the anti-apartheid sign – had been drawn just below his knuckles.

The silly part was – and I guess it's the way children's minds work – but the thing she seemed most worried about was the lost towel. It was one of our mother's 'best towels' and Isabel had been expressly warned not to use it for swimming. She was fretting that Mummy would notice it was missing and start asking questions, that she would force Isabel to go back to the river on her own where the man would be waiting for her. So the day after she'd confessed to what happened, Isabel begged me to come with her to help her find it and I remember how I'd relished the renewed feeling of togetherness as the two of us had walked through the long grass towards the water, her hand nervously clutching mine. It was a thrill to know I was still her sister and she needed me.

Fortunately the towel was still where she'd left it – spread out on the grass, damp and now smelling of mildew. We took it home, retrieving the broken flip-flops on the way, and put it in the washing basket. In those days we had a housekeeper and I sometimes wondered if she ever noticed the state it was in when she did the next wash. If she did, then she chose not to say anything to us or our mother.

It was an unpleasant incident, but in hindsight not a serious one though we both wondered what might have happened if Isabel hadn't screamed. She recovered quickly, though she made sure she was never again alone on those evening swimming trips. I kept my promise and told no one, and in time I forgot about it. I assumed she had done the same.

* * *

I've decided to go out for a bit.

My mother's not at all happy about this. 'Anna, darling, are you sure it's wise?' she says, following me through the house into the utility room. 'You know what the nurses said. They said...'

I reach up and extract my maroon parka from its peg then extend an arm towards her, my other hand dangling the coat over my back. 'Could you?'

Her eyes blink hard behind the varifocals and she clasps her hands together.

'All right, fine,' I say, simultaneously hating myself for being so sharp. 'I'll just die of cold then.'

That does it. The next moment she's taking each of my arms and threading them into the coat's sleeves. Then her fingers drop to the buttons, climbing slowly from one to the next until they reach the collar, which she fastens tightly under my chin.

I feel like a three-year-old.

'And you'll need something around your neck,' she says, opening the door to the pantry and dragging a large, stale-smelling cardboard box across the floor. As she kneels down in front of it I notice for the first time the exaggerated arch of her spine, the brittle points of her shoulders pressing through her cardigan and suddenly I'm filled with a queasy mortification as I find myself imagining her in the not-so-distant future bowed over a Zimmer frame in the corridor of some soulless nursing home.

'Mummy, please don't worry. I'll...'

'There it is, right at the bottom as usual,' she exclaims triumphantly, her hands pulling out various bits of old clothing and redundant equipment: a tennis racket with broken strings, a torn skiing jacket, various sizes and types of umbrellas, Daddy's ancient studded golfing shoes. Eventually she rises, one hand clutching the edge of the fridge-freezer for support, her faced flushed with pleasure at her victory. The other grips a black-and-red woollen scarf I recognise from my youth. It reeks of dust and damp cardboard.

'Thanks,' I say, taking it from her and winding it round my neck, but she's already knelt back down and is burrowing even deeper into the box. She hands me a black bobble hat and matching woolly gloves.

'There's still lots of snow on the ground so you'd better borrow my wellies.' She twists round and lifts a pair of boots from the rack. I stare down at the top of her head, watching as she dutifully puts a hand around each ankle in turn and raises each of my socked feet, placing them in one after the other.

'I promise I won't go far,' I say. 'Just up to The Green and back.'

I can't describe how good it feels to inhale real, fresh air tinged with ivy and wood-smoke, holding it inside for several long seconds before slowly exhaling.

The path from the house is short but it still takes me ages to get to the end because I'm moving so slowly. When I reach the road, I hobble over to the far pavement and step onto its snow-heaped curb before moving in the direction of the school.

I become aware of the languid clop of horses' hooves and turn to see two chestnut rumps moving past The Catherine Wheel in the direction of Marlborough Down, their riders' heads turned towards each other in conversation, the taller one on the right resting a hand casually on her jodhpured thigh. I pause for a moment to watch them, recalling the many hours I used to spend on horseback in this village.

It was inevitable I suppose, given our gender and class, that Isabel and I would come to love horses, so Daddy paid for riding lessons and bought us a Connemara mare to share. But when Isabel was in her early teens she'd had a fall and lost her nerve. She wasn't terribly heartbroken about this as her focus had already shifted towards boys, so the mare, Bella, quietly became mine by default.

Looking back at it now, I realise that the Bella situation was really an extension of that same separation between my sister and myself that had started during the term at Fawley Primary. Most of my friends boarded at St Anne's and were spread out all over the country during the holidays – I couldn't just walk into the village to meet them. As a result, I was lonely and often at a loose end so Bella slowly became my main focus and most of my early teens were spent exploring Fawley's surrounding countryside on her back.

When I finally reach the school, I find myself shuffling across the road once more and wrapping my hands around its wrought-iron railings. My eyes move over those arched windows, the slate-tiled roof with its single chimney and huge bell. The classrooms at St Anne's were always an oasis of order and calm, rows of green-clad girls sat in silent obedience as the teacher explained the Latin rule for the infinitive or wrote complicated mathematical formulae on the board. Whereas Fawley's huge single classroom was a place of anarchy, with different groups of boys and girls taking lessons in anything from joined-up handwriting to arts and crafts, with the flustered teacher rushing between their tables as the boys pinged rubber bands at his back and the girls stuffed their hands over their mouths and sniggered.

Today is Saturday and the playground is silent and empty. My gaze lowers towards its white netball markings before moving across to the muddy grass which, in summer, became the sports track, its faded lines now obscured here and there by heaps of grubby snow. Beside it runs the same long hedge that the older children – including Isabel – would hide behind when they were playing kiss-chase; we younger ones looking on with coy amusement.

It had been an education, that term.

A slate-bellied cloud rises slowly over the school's roof, casting the playground in a gloomy darkness and threatening rain. It's much colder than I thought. I've been duped by my mother's central heating and I'm glad now, as I tighten the scarf around my neck, that she wasn't so easily fooled.

Becoming aware of the sound of sawing coming from behind me, I turn round to notice a man in front of one of the terraced cottages which stand opposite the school. He's in the front driveway, his jeaned backside bent over a sawhorse behind a piece of trellis. His arm moves back and forward in fast swiping motions, a pile of freshly sawn logs scattered at his feet.

I shuffle on, smiling a little to myself as I consider how ridiculous I must look in my maroon parka, woolly hat, and over-large green wellington boots.

As I pass the turning to Ivy Lane, the wound in my belly's beginning to ache but I'm determined to reach The Green where I'm hoping that empty bench will still be waiting for me under the tall beech tree; the same bench where I used to sit watching Isabel and the older kids play rounders all those years ago. From the village's back road I can hear the grumble of a tractor's engine and behind me the slam of a car door from someone's drive, but apart from the bloke sawing and an old man in a garden to my right tending a bonfire, there's no one around.

I keep taking those small steps, aware that the latter has raised his head to watch me through the smoke.

I can see The Green now. It's not far, but I'm finding this journey much harder than I'd imagined. Somehow the warmth of my mother's house and the ease of the short walk from bedroom to kitchen to bathroom, has masked the seriousness of my injury.

But I struggle on until I come to the familiar triangle of grass. The play equipment has been updated and modernised, with black rubber bases beneath the swings instead of the old, lethal concrete, but otherwise it's as I remember. At its furthest point that old metal bench still sits under the branches of the beech tree and opposite it, on the other side of the road, stands the Combstones' whitewashed cottage, its sunken windows frowning at me beneath their dark brow of thatch.

At last I step off the road and onto The Green, pausing for breath because the action of climbing its shallow bank has strained me. Then I shuffle over the sodden grass and gratefully lower myself onto the bench, feeling surprised there's no children here today given it's Saturday – there would have been when I was young but I suppose they're being kept inside, no doubt, because of the cold weather and the draw of social media, computer games and a multitude of digital television channels.

From somewhere comes the slightest of breezes. It stirs the naked branches above my head and from the sarsen-scattered field behind me I hear the cries of sheep. I turn for a moment to watch their fleeces moving over the grass, their mouths tearing scrawny blades from drenched soil. Before me, the swings hang, silent and un-played on under their iron rail.

To the left of the swings stands the climbing frame. As I stare at its steel bars, I find myself recalling how on one of those hot evenings, I'd once climbed up and hung my legs over them, then slowly lowered myself until I was hanging upside down, the cold metal biting into the crooks of my knees and my hair dragging on the ground. And then the feeling of utter mortification as my skirt suddenly fell up my bare thighs. With one hand still gripping the bar and the other pushing at the skirt, I'd struggled frantically to cover my knickers, terrified there might be a skid-mark on them and imagining the taunts that would follow. I still remember the sound of the boys' laughter and their high-pitched wolf whistles.

Isabel had come to my rescue in the end, taking hold of my shoulders with a long-suffering expression and slowly lowering me down to the ground.

That huge dark cloud has been joined by others. I look up through the branches to see a fearsome grey blanket weighing heavily over the village. Still I prevaricate and allow myself a few more precious minutes. But I'm getting cold and it's clearly going to rain at any moment. So reluctantly I place a hand on the bench's metal arm and push myself into a standing position.

The walk back seems to take a lifetime. My steps are getting shorter and more exaggerated; it feels like I'm walking through tar. Halfway down the road I'm hit by a wave of dizziness and have to stop to take several deep breaths, my hand pressing a wall for support. But as sleet smatters my cheek, I force myself forward once more. That old man has wisely gone indoors, leaving the white smoke from his fire swirling around me. I shuffle through it, inhaling its woody fumes, before propelling myself past the turning to Ivy Lane and around the slight bend in the road towards the school. As I step onto the pavement opposite its railings, I can't believe this journey, which would normally last no more than five minutes, is taking so long, but my steps seem to be slowing and slowing, the throbbing in my pelvis exploding into a blaze of pain, and just as I'm realising something's very wrong there's a movement to my right and I hear a voice say,

'Anna?'

I turn to see him on the other side of the low brick wall, his slow eyes watching me through the trellis. He's leaning across that pile of wood, the saw dangling from his hand, and he's half-smiling at me under his curtain of black hair. I attempt to smile back, raising my hand weakly in greeting, and at the same time my foot comes down on thin air then, inexplicably, I'm falling, my hand instinctively reaching out and gripping the trellis for support. I let out a cry and simultaneously feel a panel coming away under my hand before my body crumples and my head smacks against the pavement.

I'm only out for a few seconds, if I'm out at all. Immediately I try to sit up, but my vision's blurred and the molten pain shooting through my pelvis makes movement impossible.

Like a beaten animal resigned to the kill, my head sinks slowly back to the ground. I'm aware, dimly, of the sound of something being dropped, of boots rushing across gravel, then I feel his hand under my cheek and something soft and leathery – it must be his jacket – is being pushed beneath my head. I open my eyes to see him staring down at me.

There's a sudden gust of wind then a fresh surge of sleet thrashes down, heavier now, more persistent. It splatters against my nose and cheeks. He leans forward to protect me from its force and he's saying something to me but it's hard to hear him over the sleet's fierce racket. I pick up the words, 'face' and 'cut' and, several times, my name.

Then I say, 'I've had an operation, Tom...' and with horror realise I've begun to cry. His eyes retreat under his brow and I think I hear him say, 'What operation?' so I reply, 'a hysterectomy' and then, 'I think I'm bleeding,' before I feel the press of his palm across my forehead, a dark concern in his eyes as his other hand withdraws a phone from his shirt pocket and starts, urgently, to dial.

5

TOM

I guess I should take the path which runs up by the chapel to the back of Fawley House. It's a public right-of-way and we often used it as a shortcut to Soweton Road when I was a kid, even though we knew it wound up Mr Carmichael because he hated people walking through his land. So I walk up the high street and hang around the path's entrance for a couple of minutes, but it just feels too informal somehow, like only people who really know the Carmichaels ought to go this way, and I don't really know them, even though I've kind of known Anna since we were kids.

So instead, I take the official route, heading up the tree-lined Soweton Road until I arrive at a white-painted five-bar gate which I push open before heading down the Carmichaels' drive, my boots crunching in the cream gravel. It runs for a hundred metres or so alongside a long, well-kept lawn before reaching a large white house with a thatched roof and criss-crossing black lintels. Here the gravel broadens into a wide circle, to the left of which there's a low garage next to the large wooden shed where me and Callum would stack Liz Carmichael's logs before the start of each winter. To the right of the shed stand a pair of sarsen walls divided by a narrow metal gate which takes you through to the front of the house with its wooden porch and solid oak door.

In front of the house lies a private, enclosed half acre or so of lawn, its surrounding hedges and walls banked by clumps of snowdrops. The dirty remains of a snowman stand slumped in its centre; carrot, hat and stones slid halfway towards its belly. I wonder briefly whose children built it.

There were just the two girls – Anna was my age and Isabel was a couple of years older. Sometimes I'd hung around with them while Dad was fixing stuff around the house for their mother – he helped her out a bit after Stephen Carmichael left.

In the middle of the lawn stands the large apple tree I remember climbing one hot summer day with Anna when we were kids, and behind it some flower beds which on that day had been full of colour but now lie dank and bare.

I open the gate and follow the narrow paved path round to the porch. I'm about to lift the iron knocker but the door's already falling away beneath my hand and Mrs Carmichael's stood there peering at me anxiously through her glasses.

For a second I'm shocked into silence. The last time I saw Anna's old lady, she must have been in her mid-forties. I remember her being very good-looking in a buttoned up sort of way, and there were rumours she'd been a model in the past but Dad always said that was bollocks – he reckoned she was much too classy for that kind of game.

Most of what I remember I'd picked up from eavesdropping on my parents' conversations. Liz Carmichael had been the focus of village gossip for a bit because she'd been deserted by her husband for another woman at a time when things like that didn't happen so much – particularly to upper-class people like them. In fact, thinking about it now, she was probably the only single mother I knew at that age. Even when I started going to the comprehensive in Marlborough – well it wasn't common and I remember people in Fawley feeling sorry for Anna and Isabel and talking about 'those poor girls coming from a broken home' though personally I reckoned being rich made up for a lot.

'Afternoon, Mrs Carmichael.'

She nods, and I can tell she doesn't recognise me. I look down and notice her hand gripping the edge of the door, the white points of swollen, arthritic knuckles pressing through the liver-spotted skin. She seems uptight, agitated, like she's got something on her mind and hasn't got time to talk right now, but she's too polite to say it.

'Yes?' she says. Then realising how brusque she sounds, 'Sorry. Hello er...?'

'I don't expect you remember me, Mrs Carmichael. It's been a long time. But I'm Tom, Jim's son.'

'Jim?'

'Jim Donnelly. He used to deliver your wood.'

'Oh *Jim*... Yes that's right.' She attempts a smile. Her voice is as I remember; gentle and contained, full of cash and private education, but thinner now with the reedy tone which comes with age. Then she repeats distractedly, 'Jim Donnelly. Yes, Tom, of course. You emigrated to Australia, didn't you?'

Did she wear glasses in the old days? I don't remember. Behind the small lenses her eyes are over-made up with pale-blue eye shadow and her papery skin's coated in a thick dusting of powder. She seems smaller and the once carefully coiffed blonde hair is now cut to her collar line and mousey-grey.

'That's right. I came back just before Christmas – for the first time.' I smile, and I'm about to add, 'To look after Dad,' but I don't know if she's aware of Dad's cancer and don't want to burden her with that right at this moment.

'For the first time since you emigrated?' she echoes, her eyes flitting over my shoulder as if she's watching out for something. 'I don't expect much has changed...'

'No, I guess it hasn't.' I smile quickly then decide to cut to the chase. 'Listen, Mrs Carmichael. I came to tell you that Anna just collapsed outside our house. She's been taken to hospital in an ambulance. I would have gone with her but she wanted me to come here to let you know.'

There's a short silence as Liz Carmichael absorbs this news, her lips pressing together in a kind of grimace and her eyes closing.

'I see...' she says finally, opening them once more and blinking hard. 'I was wondering why she'd been so long. Is she all right? Well no, I don't suppose she is if an ambulance had to come.' Then her hands rise to her face. 'Oh that *silly* girl. I tried to stop her from going out. The doctors said that she wasn't to do anything physical for the first two weeks. There were some complications during the operation, you see, so she was supposed to take it very easy...'

I reach out and cup her elbow to steady her. 'I'm not sure what happened. She kind of passed out for a bit but she was conscious when the ambulance came. Do you want me to drive you to the hospital?'

Her mouth opens and I'm immediately cursing myself.

'She passed out you say?'

'Yeah, she did. But it was only for a second or two and she was...'

'Oh Lord, oh dear...' And now those hands are pressed against her face and suddenly she looks a bit unsteady so I grip that elbow more tightly and shove the door to one side with my shoulder, propelling her inside and letting it swing shut with a bang. Then, half carrying her towards the large oak table which sits in the centre of the kitchen, I lower her down onto a chair before moving over to the draining board and picking up a glass. Filling it with water, I place it on the table before her.

After that I go to the window and lean back against the sink, feeling a bit uncomfortable as she pulls a handkerchief from her cardigan pocket and starts dabbing it around her mouth. There's a long silence and I don't know if she's trying not to cry or feeling faint – or both.

'Mrs Carmichael? Are you all right?'

But she shakes her head then blows her nose into the handkerchief. 'Just give me a moment, Tom, will you?'

I cross my arms and wait patiently, my gaze moving around the large room in which we stand. It looks pretty much the same as I remember it; from the iron plant holders in the corner to the tall dresser with its display of family photos and the large hunting print over the Aga. It's a world away from Dad's narrow, unfitted kitchen with its ancient Calor gas stove and chipped MFI units – only now I'm thinking how stupid it is I'm comparing it to his place and not my own – if I have to compare them at all. Because back in Adelaide I own a house even bigger than this one, but standing here right at this moment, well it's like I've never been to Australia, never made a life there. And you know, maybe that's it. Maybe we don't ever really escape the class we're born into because, right now, I've still got that same feeling of, well *awe* I guess, that I used to feel standing in this kitchen as a kid and I'm starting to wonder what this shit in my head's all about.

I glance down at Liz Carmichael. She's crushing the handkerchief in her fist and holding it against her chest, her face turning towards me. 'I'm so sorry, Tom. I suppose it's the shock. I... I've been so worried about her, you see. She said she was only going to The Green, so when she didn't come back... Well, I'm not sure if you know but...'

'She told me about the operation,' I say to help her out. 'That's a pretty major deal, hey.'

I hear her sniff, then she blows her nose once more before taking a sip of the water. 'Yes,' she says finally, and I can tell she's a bit taken aback by my directness. 'It is. Especially at her age and having no children. She's only forty-one – but of course, you two were the same age, weren't you?'

I nod and smile, then turn away, not knowing how to respond, and find myself walking over to stare at those family photos on the dresser. Most of them are school photos of the girls sitting next to each other looking grave and serious in their green St Anne's uniforms. There's another photo of a thirty-something Isabel in front of a church in Devizes. She's wearing a long, strapless white wedding dress and standing next to a tall, haughty-looking bloke. In a second shot she's on the lawn outside this house with the same man, only now there's three small children sitting crossed-legged at their feet.

There's only one adult photo of Anna, probably taken in her twenties. She's wearing jeans and a blue T-shirt, and sitting on a wall in blazing sunshine. There's water behind her, and beyond that, glinting glass office blocks and ancient minarets. It looks like Dubai, or Cairo maybe. She's smiling out at the camera and looking relaxed, her wavy brown hair swept back behind her shoulders.

I hear chair legs scraping on stone and turn to see Liz Carmichael rising slowly from the table. Immediately I move towards her. 'Let me drive you to the hospital, Mrs Carmichael.'

But she shakes her head with sudden determination. 'No. It's very kind of you, Tom, but you've done more than enough already. I'll call Isabel and ask her to take me.'

'Well okay. No worries – if you're sure.' I go to open the door. 'I'll be off then. Tell Anna I'll drop by in a few days to see how she's going.'

'Yes, yes I will... Thank you very much for letting me know, Tom.'

But as I'm stepping into the porch she calls me back. I pause and turn back towards her, one hand still on the latch.

'Tom, I was terribly sorry to hear about Jim – I assume that's why you're back? I've been meaning to pop round and see him. Do give him my best.'

My immediate reaction is to think, *Pop round my arse. When have you ever* popped round *to see Dad? You wouldn't be seen dead in a house like his.* But then I check myself because I can see something in her eyes and Jesus, who am I to know what her relationship is with him after all these years? And yeah, maybe it's my class, and that pound of chips still sitting on my shoulder because despite all her worry over Anna I reckon I can sense real empathy coming from her right at this second. Liz Carmichael's known Dad for a long time; she knew Callum and Mum as well, and I guess that means something to me. So I nod, then say, 'I appreciate that, Mrs Carmichael. And thanks. I'm sorry about him, too.'

* * *

I don't go straight home. Dad knows where I've gone and that I might be away for a bit. So I decide to use the opportunity to go for a drive because, apart from a few visits to the pub and the occasional shop for provisions in Marlborough or Devizes, I've not really had much time to myself these last few weeks and, if I'm completely honest, could do with some headspace.

I consider driving up to the Marlborough Down, then decide against it. Sure, it's easy enough to avoid the Shadowing Stones but I'm really not ready to face the place yet. So instead I decide to head out of the western end of Fawley, driving past the village green and onwards, ascending through open farmland for five or six miles until I come to a wide concrete parking area. When I reach this point I turn and pull up, switching off the engine but keeping the radio on as I roll myself a cigarette.

The DJ's playing 'Let's Dance' by David Bowie – Christ, it's a while since I've heard this one and it takes me back to those teenage years. Bowie had been my thing then, my idol. I liked the enigma of the guy, the way he wouldn't let anyone else influence him. I wanted to be like that.

Outside, it's starting to sleet again. White Horse Hill – yeah, this is headspace all right. One of the best views in England, Dad always said. He used to bring me and Callum here sometimes to fly kites. Sitting here and staring out through the sleet-battered windscreen, the view's even more mind-blowing than I remember; the land before me dropping abruptly away into a deep escarpment; long flanks of ridged, grass-covered chalk stretching away on either side and, before me, a watery patchwork of brown-and-green squares stretching far into the distance.

The Bowie song ends and something trashy and dancy comes on. I finish the cigarette and stub it out in the ashtray, then switch off the ignition and get out of the car, making my way out of the car park through a small gate. The afternoon's getting on now – it must be three at least and there's not much daylight left but I'm suddenly feeling determined to walk up to that great chalk horse even though dark clouds are ganging up on the horizon and it's getting really cold. A cruel wind roars over the hillside, bringing with it a charge of suffocating sleet and whipped up snow. I push forward with my head lowered.

Anna Carmichael left a bloodstain on the pavement. After the ambulance took her away, I bent down to pick up my jacket and saw it there, a patch of snow soaked with red. I tried not to look at it because it made me feel uncomfortable. But as my strides grow more laboured and the wind rages around me, that stain keeps coming back into my mind. I close my eyes, trying to wipe it away. But it just seems to get wider and brighter, until it's not Anna's blood I'm seeing but a meadow full of poppies in the dawn.

The memory hits me, abrupt and unprovoked. Shit. It's been years since I thought about those poppies and suddenly I'm struggling over clumps of earth, my legs stumbling over molehills, gorse and thistle as I try to escape a rush of adrenalin, my breath rasping in my throat. Fuck, I'm just not ready to think about this at the moment.

Anna Carmichael. I'd had a bit of a thing for her when we were kids. She and her sister attended Fawley school for a term because there was a problem with the private place they usually went to. Anna must have been about nine, and Isabel eleven. It was springtime, and I remember Anna on her first day in a yellow dress, looking awkward next to the other kids in their jeans and T-shirts. She stood at the edge of the playground, her head fallen slightly to the side, her long dark hair half-masking her face. I remember her smiling at me because she most likely recognised me from the times I'd helped Dad deliver the wood; she maybe even remembered that afternoon we'd climbed her apple tree together. But she didn't come over to speak to me and I didn't go to speak to her.

I try to recall other occasions I'd been with her, or spoken to her. There were the searches. I remember her staring down the row of volunteers towards me on that afternoon as we'd trudged across a ploughed field; the intense sympathy of her stare and how it moved me to see her standing there in her thick duffle coat and mud-caked wellies. But I don't want to think about that either. A better memory was that late autumn day in the woods, not long before Callum disappeared. Me and him had been up in the woods collecting the windfall wood when she'd suddenly cantered around the corner on her bay mare. The mare had shied at the wheelbarrow and as she'd steadied her, Anna had laughed, then shouted, 'Don't tell Mummy you saw me without a hat, Tom. She'd kill me.'

And without waiting for my reply, she'd kicked the mare and cantered on.

I clamber over a ridge and approach the summit of the hill. About a hundred yards below me, that great white carving finally appears, its chalk legs outstretched across the flank of hillside. I'm scrambling towards it, my arse and thighs sliding over the grass because it's so steep and I'm blinded by the wind and sleet, my hands clutching at those narrow chalk ledges until I'm finally stepping over that horse's chalk brow and squatting down like an Indian on the single, grass dot of its eye.

I turn my back against the wind, at the same time wondering how Anna feels about not having children. As someone who's got four of them, I really couldn't imagine life without my kids. I think of little Georgia the last time I saw her as I stood with my suitcases waiting for the taxi to take me to the airport, bouncing around the pool with an ecstatic smile on her plump, sunlit face. And on the evening before I left, Reef, my eldest, kicking his first football past me into a goal made from two traffic bollards we'd stolen together on our way back from his youth club. Jesus, I love those kids more than anything in this world.

But then the picture's ripped away to be replaced by Stella's face, her marble-blue eyes studying me through the taxi's window as I left for the airport; a brief wave before she wraps her arms around herself and takes a step back. We stare at each other with an unspoken query to which only she holds the answer, and suddenly those priceless family images take on a different aspect, reminding me that my love for those kids is also the chain holding me to a woman who's probably been screwing someone behind my back.

Anna doesn't know it, but she'll never feel the weight of that chain and for that at least I envy her, because she's free. She can wake up tomorrow and make a decision to change the course of her life without having to consider any of the repercussions. She can get on a plane or in a car and go where ever she wants; she can change her job, she can stay in bed all day watching crap TV and drinking beer and put off until tomorrow anything that doesn't need to be done today. Not that she will – it's just that *she can*. If she'd wanted children then I guess she might feel sad and maybe a bit cheated, and yeah, rightfully so, because my kids have brought out in me a capacity to love, and be loved, that can't be surpassed. But she'll never know the other side of having them; the weight of responsibility, the self-accusation and guilt and feeling that you're always fucking up as a parent; the no-getting-back the life you once knew and the freedom you took for granted, right up to the moment you lost it for good.

I turn round once more to look at the view but it's impossible to see anything with the sleet coming straight at me from a forty-five degree angle, slamming straight into my eyes like a sheet of ball bearings, my face and neck rapidly turning numb under their relentless charge. Walking up here on a day like this was crazy; my shirt and jeans are soaked through and I'm shivering from the cold yet I still don't want to leave; don't want to go back to that dark room with its stench of helplessness and sickness; don't want to go back and sit with a man whose presence fills me with so many conflicting emotions.

But as I picture him sitting there in that chair, his eyes gloomily studying the fire's dying embers, I reckon I've got no choice. Turning reluctantly, I start trudging back towards the car.

* * *

I arrive home to find him awake and in pain.

'You've ... been ages,' he says as I enter. The room is in shadow, a troubled dusk fallen outside the window, the last of the sleet still faintly rattling its panes. Dad shifts his body towards me but the effort makes him wince, and whatever colour is in his face drains away, leaving him paler than a cadaver.

I go to the table's small lamp and switch it on with a hand that's blue with cold.

'The fire's gone out and my bag's ... empty,' he adds with muted accusation, and I feel his frustration and self-castigation at his inability to help himself.

'Hey sorry, Dad,' I say quickly, immediately fetching a fresh bag of morphine from the fridge and attaching it to his cannula, noticing as I do the spread of purpled skin around its red plastic hood. Then I go to check the room's storage heater, because it feels so damned cold in here, but its sides are molten under my palm.

'Need the loo?' I ask, and he nods, so I bring his bedpan and help him out with that, too, placing another blanket over him when he's finished. I empty the pan in the toilet, then start to rebuild the fire.

'How ... was Liz?' he asks.

'She was okay. I...'

But his body suddenly convulses into a cough and at the same time he moans loudly.

'Dad?' I say, rising to my feet. But he twists away.

'Need more morphine?' I venture, but my thumb's already pressing the dispenser. I feel bad now that I've been out for so long, leaving him without any pain relief, but I was too preoccupied with Anna to check it before I left. 'It's on its way,' I say. 'You'll feel better soon.'

I press a hand briefly on his shoulder before turning back to the fire. It takes me a few minutes to get it going. Sleet has come down the chimney, dampening the wood beneath. I decide to start again, laying down a firelighter and covering it with kindling. Eventually the flames lick up and fill the room with their welcome glow.

'We played ... mazes,' Dad suddenly murmurs.

I twist around on my haunches. He's staring up at the ceiling, his eyes open. The morphine has hit home.

'What's that?' I say, rising to my feet and moving towards him.

'At the beach in Buncrana. She took me ... in her van.'

Then his lips stretch into a smile. He's talking about Mum again. I realise, at the same time feeling mild irritation at the stuck record of his mind, the frustration of listening to those who exist in the past because they have no life remaining in the present. I think about telling him I need to get on with work stuff – the business with Anna and my walk up the White Horse has used up a lot of the day – but I don't want to offend him even though I know this story well because he was telling me it yet again last night, how after he'd come across Mum painting on the farm, they'd agreed to go for a drink on the harbour at the local town.

He'd bought them both fish and chips, which they'd eaten on the rocks before walking onto the beach where she'd shown him this game –you created a maze in the sand with a stick, and then timed your opponent as they found their way out of it. Whoever escaped the other's maze in the shortest time, won.

'Aye but she was no good ... at it.'

A blind man could have found his way out of that one, I think.

'A blind man could have found his way ... out of that one,' he says. 'But she couldn't work mine out ... at all. Round and round ... she went. Back and forward. "You've cheated," she kept saying. "There's no way out." "Aye, there is," I told her. "And I'll promise you a surprise, when you finally ... find it." "What's that then?" she said. "You'll have to ... wait and see," I told her.

'In the end I had to go in ... and lead her out ... of my maze. She didn't believe there was a way. But there was and I led her ... through it. "Damn you, Jim Donnelly," she said. "That was *my* game. Now what's ... my surprise?"'

And that's when I kissed her, I think.

'And that's when ... I kissed her,' he says, and he closes his eyes, then chuckles. 'And then I took her to see *A Star is Born* at the Limerick ... Palace. She said it was her favourite film.'

Behind me I hear the flames devouring that kindling, their welcome heat rising up the back of my sleet-soaked jeans. I go to hang my jacket on the door, then return to the fire and place some heavier logs on the blaze.

'Aye, but it took ... guts,' he goes on suddenly, opening his eyes.

I pick up the poker and blow hard on the kindling. 'What took guts?' I ask vaguely.

'Going to Ireland ... on her own like that.'

'Yeah,' I say. 'Must've done.'

'It wasn't an easy country ... back then ... not for a single woman like Eileen. She was meant to go with Sheelagh, one of her ... art school friends. Dublin girl. But Sheelagh cancelled at the last minute because her mother was ill. Just like ... your mother not to let that ... stop her.'

I'm wondering what's in the fridge and whether he'll be able to eat anything after that hit of morphine as it sometimes makes him sick. I'm also thinking that it's been a few days since I last Zoomed Stella and maybe I should go upstairs and do that now because there's a big delivery scheduled this week with a new client, and I need to check she's handling it okay.

'They all thought she was a whore ... in Buncrana.'

I rest the poker down and slowly turn towards him.

'Aye. Pretty English girl on her own ... going into the ... bars. That's what it was like ... in those days.' He grimaces. 'She got the locals stirred up ... all right. Men and women, only for ... different reasons. We had to keep it very secret.'

'Seriously? They thought Mum was a prostitute?'

Outside, evening is drawing in and the sleet has ceased its urgent patter. As I move over to the window and stare out onto the empty street, I realise my irritation has morphed into a sudden interest. This story of their meeting had previously been told by both parties with a sense of rose-tinted wonder, so much so that it seemed like it had happened to two other people in a film rather than the hard-drinking man and effervescent woman who were my parents.

I lower myself into the armchair.

'Aye,' my father says, but his eyes are beginning to close and I realise I may have pushed it with the morphine. 'Aye,' he says again. 'She had to move the van. Farmer was told not to let her stay. We took it to a field ... owned ... by an English couple and I'd ride my bike over there every day ... to see her.'

Whenever my mother had talked about Ireland, it was usually to describe the stunning Donegal landscape and the tumultuous rush of passion between the two of them which had swept both of them off their feet and into a new life together. She'd always referred to their meeting there in earnest, breathy tones, a poignant look in her eye. I'd found it all a bit embarrassing, as teenage boys do, the thought of my parents actually having romantic physical relations making me squirm.

But this other, grittier, side of their union is news to me. I'd known about his family's hostility of course, but not the reaction of the wider community. Listening to him now, I remind myself that people elope for a reason, and those reasons are not often good.

'The men fancied her and the women ... were jealous of her. It all went over her head, of course. You know what your mother ... was like. I didn't care. One look at those eyes of hers.' He smiles softly. 'Those dancing ... eyes.'

'What brought her there anyway?' I say after a short silence. 'I mean, *that* town particularly.'

The sound of my voice makes him jolt, as if he's forgotten I'm here.

'Buncrana?' he says, his pupils sliding towards me. He shrugs, then stares back up at the ceiling. 'The friend that didn't come ... she told her to go there. It's a good base for Donegal ... if you want to travel around.' He's silent for a moment. Then, 'Aye, but it was a one-horse town back then. Like most of them in Ireland. A lot of unemployment. Most of the young people ... had to leave.'

'To look for work?'

He nods. 'To look ... for work. There was a lot of anger and religion.' He shakes his head suddenly. 'Aye, the religion was terrible. The priests controlled ... everything.'

'They didn't control you.'

Just for a moment, he fully opens his eyes. We stare at each other and I know he realises I'm paying him a rare compliment. 'No, son,' he says in response. 'No, you're right. They didn't control me. There was only one person ... who did that.'

'Mum?' I say with a smile.

He looks back at me for a moment and his face suddenly darkens as he slowly shakes his head.

'What do you mean then? Who was controlling you? Your parents?'

But he turns away and stares vacantly towards the wall. Then his eyes suddenly close.

'Dad?' I say, after some minutes. Because suddenly I want to know more and it's beginning to hit me that there isn't much time left for any of this, that when my father dies all his stories will follow him; and by that I don't just mean the stories of my brother's death, but of his courtship with my mother; his memories of me and Callum as children before it all went wrong; his parents; Mum's parents – now dead. There's so much stuff I don't know and he's about to carry it all with him to his lonely grave.

'Dad?' I say again, a little insistently now. But he's silent, his breathing slow and heavy. I remind myself that I've got stuff to do, yet I remain sitting on the arm of that chair for a very long time, my eyes fixed to my father's sleeping face.

6

ANNA

The surgeons stitch me back up and put me on a course of antibiotics, then send me home with a stern warning to do as little as possible for the next two weeks. So I'm back to convalescing in my single bed. Outside, it's grown milder and the last of the snow has thawed, but somehow the warmer temperature seems to add to the slow, interminability of these days which plod damply forward towards the bleak horizon of February, that most crushing of months.

I try to remind myself that after February comes March, and with it the slow warming of the earth. So my eyes are constantly seeking small changes and though not obvious, they do exist. The chestnut trees which line Soweton Road still rise dark and naked, but around the edges of my mother's lawn, snowdrops are raising their heads and I know that in a few weeks the tips of daffodil and crocus leaves will appear at the foot of the sarsen wall.

The disturbed sleep, mood swings and flushes have begun to abate as the HRT, which I'd started taking on the day after the operation, finally kicks in, but the dose of the latter isn't quite right, I know it. My breasts are tender and I feel bloated. I'm also craving sugar and am relieved that my mother does not have a sweet tooth, or I'd soon be turning into a heffalump. Of course I know that I'm lucky I had endometriosis rather than cancer, and that I was able to get such good medical treatment, but I can't help resenting going through menopause ten years earlier than planned.

To take my mind off it, I've started to reread some of the novels which line my bookshelves like comforting old teddy bears. I tend towards the lighter, younger stuff – Frances Hodgson Burnett's *The Secret Garden*, Walter Farley's *The Black Stallion* and *The Hobbit*. It's not just my body I want to escape, but the fact that Kerem has started calling less and less, resulting in a feeling of foreboding about our relationship which keeps me awake in the early hours, my heart now full of a black fear for my future.

As I sit back against the pillows reading those old novels, my eye occasionally gets drawn over the top of the page towards the Donnellys' place, beyond the school playground. It's never occurred to me before, but I've actually got a pretty good view of their cottage from here in the winter when the sycamore trees lining the railings are bare of leaves. Not that there's much sign of life, but I know there's people at home because lights are on at night and a trail of smoke ascends from its single chimney.

Tom Donnelly. When had I last seen him? When I was fourteen? Fifteen, maybe? He used to come round to the house to help his father deliver the logs and we'd been in the same year during that term at Fawley Primary.

As I stare over at their cottage, it occurs to me how concealing the houses are in Britain, especially when you know flesh-and-blood lives are being lived out behind their walls. In Turkey, those lives are usually on display for all to see: the women yell down from their apartments as they lower baskets on strings containing shopping lists and lira to the corner shop below. Outside on the streets, men bash the tops of cars and shout *merhaba* to each other and on the pavements outside the cafes, the old men sit together on low, cushioned stools and smoke their *şiş* pipes. There are always gangs of excited children kicking footballs around in the streets who yell 'Hello, Lady' as I pass and ask me my name in English. And whenever I'm visiting my Turkish friends, the doorbell will be rung ceaselessly with neighbours asking for or offering favours, or guests popping in for a glass of *çay*. I know that life is the same in the villages, because this is simply the way the Turks are. There's little price put on privacy in their culture, but a large one put on friendship, hospitality and community, and I know which of the two I prefer. I do not believe my mother would be so lonely if she'd been born in Turkey.

Tom Donnelly was Callum Donnelly's brother. It's the first thing that went through my mind when I saw him standing there behind the trellis with that saw dangling in his hand. Tom Donnelly. *Callum Donnelly.* The boy who was murdered at the Shadowing Stones.

When Callum first went missing, everyone assumed he'd run away because his father, Jim, was a heavy drinker with a volatile temper. But his mother, Eileen, was different. A local girl from Marlborough. I remember watching her in the village shop one morning chatting away to Mrs Bussle, the shopkeeper.

Eileen Donnelly was vivacious and kind, a beautiful woman with long curly red hair and a singsong laugh. Callum had the same red hair and sensitive features. But unlike his mother he was shy and awkward, holding her hand and hiding behind her skirts while Tom, darker, bolder, stole around staring longingly at the various balls that Mrs Bussle kept on a spinner next to the stationery.

I remember one particular afternoon after school, watching him stealing one of those balls when he thought I wasn't looking. The two boys were a little older then and without their mother – it wasn't long before Callum vanished – and it was clear to me the latter was in the business of distracting the shopkeeper whilst Tom quietly slipped the biggest and most colourful ball into his coat pocket.

Except for his family, no one in the village took Callum's disappearance very seriously at first. But after the days stretched into a week and he was still missing, it became clear that he probably wasn't coming home. That was when the searches began in earnest.

How could I have forgotten all this? The whole episode was horrific and had been such a defining time in the lives of all us children. How could I have forgotten that long line of villagers spread across a ploughed field in winter, Isabel and myself in the middle? I remember my eyes meeting Tom's over the furrows and seeing his pale, bewildered expression. Hour after hour we searched; long, heavy steps trudging forward in our clay-laden wellingtons, the low sky over our heads. But thinking back now, I don't think any of us children understood what it was we were really looking for.

* * *

I've started spending more time with my mother – partly because I've grown bored of my damaged body, diminishing hormones and relentless introspection, but also because I know it's important to use this time wisely; that we may not get this chance to be together again. Who knows when I'm likely to return for another visit?

We spend many hours in the kitchen together, me sitting with my chin resting in my palms watching her prepare a variety of healthy meals and brewing those endless pots of tea. She'd never admit it, but I suspect she's quietly pleased my recent relapse has allowed her to take hold of the maternal reins once more.

Our evenings are spent sitting in the large, white-carpeted sitting room, or 'lounge' as she prefers to call it. She usually reads *The Times* as I watch television, or stare into the fire. Sometimes we'll attempt the crossword together with varying success.

The one thing we don't do a great deal of is talk – at least, not about anything important because my mother will happily discuss anything of no consequence. So most days I receive a running commentary on the lateness of the electricity bill, the incorrect number of delivered milk bottles and the idiosyncrasies of her new Ford Focus – that gold glasses chain always running back and forward between her fingers. But what really strikes me is the more she talks about trivial issues, the more I'm aware of how unwilling she is to touch on those subjects that actually matter.

For example, she never alludes to the consequences of my operation, even though her pity still cloys the air. I know this because I see the way she tries to avoid mentioning Isabel's children or referring to anything connected to pregnancy. One day she inadvertently refers to a friend's daughter in Calne who's just given birth to IVF triplets, and immediately I observe her cheeks and neck flush as she struggles to change the subject. I'm forced to give her an exasperated look over the kitchen table and snap, 'It's really okay, Mummy, you *can* talk about babies without my bursting into tears.'

But more than anything, I'm becoming increasingly aware of her unwillingness to talk about my father. I try to mention him now and then, but each time she stiffens and changes the subject and though I don't challenge her, because I don't want to upset her, this reticence after so much water's passed under the bridge, saddens me. It's not that I want her to 'get over it', but simply because I have memories of him I'd like to share with her; happy memories of holidays to France and Jersey, day trips out to London Zoo and picnicking on Hampstead Heath; memories of when we were a loving, thriving family. But it seems it's still too painful for her to contemplate, even after all this time.

When I was eight, Daddy had an affair with a crime writer called Linda Bell. At first, no one had thought it odd when Linda started spending a lot of time in our London flat having animated conversations late into the night washed down with bottles of Shiraz – or when she came down to stay for several long weekends at Fawley House. It was all normal practice in the literary world. So when Daddy suddenly announced he'd fallen in love and was leaving Mummy, the latter's sense of betrayal and her resulting breakdown was something quite dreadful to witness.

She didn't withhold our father access – she's not the type to bear grudges. So Isabel and I would go up and stay in London with him and Linda every other weekend. I wince inside now as I realise how hard this must have been for her, because Linda, despite what she had done to our family, was a vivacious and attractive woman and Isabel and I would return home fizzing with stories about the fun we'd had. And after Nicholas and Madeleine, our half-siblings were born, our talk would be full of them too.

Linda went on to help enormously with my own career, introducing me to her friend Amanda Reid, who was publisher of the *Lonely Traveller* series. She and my father also put me up during my time at university. Their house in Islington was so big that I had my own, rent-free flat in the basement. I could take my friends there and treat it as I liked, both during term time and the holidays. There was little need or reason to take the hour's train journey back to Fawley during my student days, so I rarely did.

* * *

One evening, when we're in the sitting room, I decide to ask about Tom Donnelly. It's been brewing for some days, my curiosity, encouraged by this slow illumination of long-forgotten memories. But it's strange, because the question feels like a weighty one and I spend several minutes trying to construct it, wondering simultaneously why I'm so apprehensive. Eventually I decide it's easier to let it go, switching on the television instead and flicking aimlessly through the Freeview channels with the remote control.

'Do you want to look at the *Review*?' my mother asks with mild irritation, her eyes rising over the top of the paper. She is sitting in her usual place – on her blue armchair next to the fire and wearing a dressing gown because she's recently got out of the bath.

I shake my head. I'm curled up on the sofa in my sweatshirt and jogging trousers, a blanket covering my lower half. Zola forms a tight black ball in the crook of my knees.

She straightens *The Times* and resumes reading under the soft light of the table lamp, turning her body to the side and crossing those slipper-covered feet in front of the fire, which occasionally spits and throws out smoke because it's raining outside. Several minutes pass before I finally accept there's nothing to watch and switch off the television. Then, resting my head back against the arm of the chair, I reach out to rub Zola's ears, and at the same time watch my mother's engrossed gaze moving down those columns.

'What's Tom Donnelly doing in Fawley? Is he living with his father now?' I venture suddenly, breaking the silence. 'I remember him going abroad after the business with his brother. I didn't know he'd come back.'

She glances at me over the top of the paper. 'He's only here for a visit.'

'So where does he live now?'

'In Australia. Jim's got cancer – he's not got long to live so Tom's come over to nurse him.'

I lean over the sofa's arm and lift the mug of tea from a side table. 'I'd completely forgotten about Callum, you know... Isn't that terrible? It only came back to me after seeing Tom. Did they ever find who did it?'

'No,' she says, shaking her head. She lowers the paper reluctantly and smooths it across her knees. 'No,' she repeats. 'I don't suppose they ever will now.'

'I remember the searches... And all the reporters hanging around. But I don't remember how he disappeared – just that it was a bit odd. Didn't the police suspect Jim for a while?'

My mother sighs, then leans forward and reaches for one of the logs she keeps in a wicker basket next to her armchair. 'A lot of people suspected him – it wasn't just the police.'

'Why?'

'Because he's the only one who *could* have done it.' But something in her tone tells me she's not convinced by this argument. 'Mrs Lane, the head teacher, saw Callum go straight home from school and go round to the back of the house to let himself in. It was the last time he was seen alive so the police concluded that whoever took him had to either already be in the house, or had access to it. Eileen was in Marlborough with Tom; and Jim was the first to arrive home after Callum. So I think the police suspected Jim came home that day and somehow ended up killing Callum, then hid the body – everyone knew he had a temper and was rumoured to take it out on his boys.' She winds her fingers together and stares thoughtfully at the carpet. 'But they couldn't prove it.'

'He came round here...'

'Who did?'

'Jim. He came round here the next morning looking for Callum.'

And suddenly I'm back there, sitting in the kitchen and hearing that knock on the porch door on a freezing morning just before Christmas. It had been the Saturday following the last week of term and my mother had gone to collect Isabel who'd spent the previous night at a friend's house. I'd opened the door to see Jim Donnelly standing outside in the snow, his chin tucked into his donkey jacket, his hands in his pockets as he stared at me warily. I'd felt a bit uncomfortable because I was still wearing my pyjamas.

'Morning,' he'd said. I remember how the cold had bitten sharply into my exposed neck and bare feet. 'We're looking for our Callum. You wouldn't have seen him, would you? Only he didn't come home from school yesterday.' I suspected he was a bit embarrassed because he averted his eyes as he spoke.

The telephone starts to ring and I watch my mother lever herself from the chair before going into the hall and picking up the receiver. From the conversation that follows through the half-open door, I deduce it's Isabel asking if she'll mind the children tomorrow.

'Of course, once Tom found the body, the gossip stopped,' my mother goes on, returning to the sitting room and letting herself back down into the armchair. 'Jim was volatile, but what was done to Callum... Not many people thought he was capable of that... And Eileen obviously believed he was innocent.'

I place my mug back down on the table and stare silently into the fire. That was something else I'd forgotten. We'd searched all through the Christmas holidays and then every weekend the following January and February. But it wasn't until the summer that Tom had discovered his brother's remains near the Shadowing Stones on Marlborough Down. I'd been away in France at the time; Daddy and Linda had taken me, Isabel, Nicholas and Madeleine for a long holiday to their chateau near Bordeaux. We stayed there for over a month so by the time we got back the media frenzy surrounding the discovery had subsided. I was only fourteen and my mother hid from me the more gruesome details of how Callum had died except to confirm he'd been murdered – that had been upsetting enough.

Later on I found out that he'd been shot and his body set alight beneath the stones. As a result, the police couldn't rule in or out any sexual motive. It must have been an appalling discovery for Tom, but by then I was ensconced in my new life at Marlborough College and I'm not sure I ever saw him again. A year or so after Callum's death, I heard that Eileen Donnelly had committed suicide – no doubt because of what had happened to her son – and two or three years after that Tom had taken off abroad.

Zola suddenly rises to his feet, arching his back in a knobbly stretch before dropping himself down onto the floor and going to sit expectantly at the sitting-room door.

'He wants his supper,' my mother says, getting up stiffly from her chair. She pads across the room in her slippers and opens the door to let him through before turning back towards me.

I stare up at her. 'What is it?'

She pulls the dressing gown around herself. 'Len Combstone told me something once.'

'What?'

Outside a blast of wind forces its way down the chimney, making the fire in the grate hiss and spit loudly.

'He said that some years before Callum disappeared, a young Irishman came into The Catherine Wheel. He told Len and some of the other regulars he was Jim's brother and that Jim had been involved in the murder of a young boy back in Ireland. Len and the others didn't really believe him at the time – the man was drunk and he obviously had it in for Jim. But when Callum disappeared, well of course they had to take it more seriously. Len told me about it because he was in a quandary as to whether to tell the police or not. I think he did in the end.'

I reach for my mug. 'He didn't think to ask Jim?'

'Len said he did the very next night but Jim just brushed it off and said that his brother bore a grudge against him marrying Eileen – because she was English. The whole family did apparently. Said his brother had come to make trouble on their behalf.'

'I wonder if Tom knows about it.'

She shrugs. 'I don't know, but Len said Tom also suspected Jim of killing Callum... that's why he left for Australia.'

'Really?' I stare up at her with raised eyebrows. 'It would explain why he's stayed away so long.'

She nods, slowly, in reply. 'Yes,' she says. 'It would. Is that finished?'

I nod then pass her the empty mug and watch her go into the hall, closing the sitting-room door behind her. Picking up the remote control once more, I go to press the on button, but my thumb hovers over it, withdraws. Placing it back on the arm of the chair, I turn to stare into the flames.

Though I'd been in a state, it was impossible not to notice Tom's thick jet-black hair, the buckled belt, leather boots and jeans. He looked like a cowboy or a gold prospector, only with the gypsy's face; kind, yet at the same time as rough-edged as the saw in his hand. Then I try to picture him in that house over the road, sitting with his father each night just as I'm doing with my mother, watching television and talking about day-to-day things. I think of the complex emotions he must be processing; how does it feel to nurse a man you suspect of killing your brother? And not just any man, but your own father, whom you might simultaneously love and respect, and know is soon to die?

It doesn't bear thinking about, and suddenly I don't want to think about it anymore. So instead, I push myself to my feet, and make my way to the kitchen to find my mother filling the kettle at the sink. Walking around the table, I take her arm and pull her towards me, putting my arms around her, feeling her small bones under the softness of the dressing gown.

Her body stiffens with surprise, then she places down the kettle and embraces me back. 'Oh Anna,' she says, 'it's going to be all right, really it is.'

And I want to tell her I know it will be, and that everything happens for a reason and I never wanted children anyway. But suddenly I'm too upset to speak.

7

ANNA

February's arrived before I'm ready to leave the house once more. It's strange that the thought of going outdoors should make me anxious, but I've never passed out before and it's made me lose confidence in my body. So I begin by treading up my mother's driveway, picking my way around the potholes and coming to a standstill at the gate. I do this several times before finally heading down our narrow footpath, turning at its end towards the village green. The latter feels close enough to home should anything go wrong.

If I'm to walk through the village then I have to pass the Donnelly's place. There's no way to avoid it unless I go up my mother's drive and double-back down round Soweton Road but it seems stupid to go so out of my way, and why should I want to avoid Tom anyway? Yet as I pass his cottage I find myself fighting a ridiculous surge of self-consciousness, wondering if his eyes follow me from behind one of its small windows. At the same time I'm faintly bemused, knowing how many times I've walked this way throughout my life – as child, teenager and adult – and never given it, or Tom, a second's thought until now.

There's no doubt their place has seen better days; the

window frames are peeling and chipped and its render is stained and blistered. An ugly gap, like a missing tooth, remains in the trellis from where I fell down that day, the broken panel propped against the sawhorse Tom was using that morning. Next to it a stack of logs lies under a blue, plastic sheet. From my bedroom window, I've noticed one particular car which is usually parked outside – a red Punto. Glancing discreetly through its windscreen as I pass, I observe spotless foot-wells and pristine upholstery – the tell-tale sign of a hire car. In front of it stands an old truck with deflated tyres.

Tom told my mother he was going to drop round to see me, so why hasn't he? Then I ask myself why I'm bothered and conclude it must be because of my boredom holed-up here in Fawley coupled with the need to distract myself from the situation with Kerem. But if I'm honest, perhaps there's something else fuelling this unexpected curiosity.

Because in much the same way as me, I realise, Tom's been forced back to here by adverse circumstances to spend most of his time confined indoors with an aging parent. We've both spent years carving out lives thousands of miles from this village where we were born. How has coming back here made him feel, I wonder? Is he impatient to return to what he's left behind in Australia, or has he, with so much time on his hands, also started to think about the past? And by the past, I don't just mean memories of his brother's death, but what came before it – our childhoods and adolescence spent around these sarsen-walled lanes. Has he also been visited by memories of tearing down Angel Hill on our sledges, or those evening games of rounders on The Green; a girl hanging upside down on a climbing frame, desperately trying to hide her knickers?

* * *

As my strength grows and my body heals, so I find myself increasingly drawn to the landscape around me and, before long, I'm straying past the village boundary and up the steep road that leads into Fawley Wood and the fields beyond, retracing the paths and tracks I once explored on horseback. And with each day that passes, I find myself venturing a little further than before. It doesn't seem to tire me – if anything it invigorates me – and I'm surprised at how well I'm beginning to feel. My skin looks clearer, my eyes brighter, and I realise that the operation is achieving that which the doctors promised: a steady return to full health.

These early February mornings start with iron-numb frosts and dense fogs, the latter which, over the course of each day gradually get thawed down by the sun, leaving trails of white mist lingering over the fields.

It's on one of these mornings that I fill a small backpack with sandwiches and a thermos, then put on my fleece and venture out of the village in a northerly direction, crossing the A4 and trudging up a steep concrete lane until I reach a farmyard. There I come to a halt and take a few moments to catch my breath from the steep climb before starting to descend down a grassy bridle path, each stride bringing the Marlborough Down further into view, until I find myself staring through those patches of fog at the same incredible landscape I remember riding through as a girl: acre after acre of sarsen-strewn hillside; a frozen wilderness of silent, wide-angled desolation.

The Grey Wethers Valley – named because of the hundreds of stones and boulders scattered across its slopes. The locals call them 'grey wethers' because from a distance they appear like flocks of dirty sheep. This area, I remember being told, was one of the 'workshops' used for the carving of the stones destined for Avebury and Stonehenge. Later on, communities would place their dead on the stones for the crows to pick bare. It's a dark image and would be hard to believe, except that all around, the landscape is studded with long barrows – the stone-age burial chambers suspected by some to be the resting place of peoples who were sacrificed at those two great monuments. The thought makes me feel exposed and uncomfortable, and for a second I'm tempted to turn back because, although beautiful, the place is also eerie and unsettling.

But I force myself to keep going and, for a while, head in the direction of the Ridgeway. My intention is to cross it and walk across the downs to Avebury, but after a mile or so I change my mind and head to the right where, several-hundred yards later, I meet a wide, chalk track which leads me onto a vast plain dotted with rowan trees and hawthorn, and shallow copses of thick gorse.

My boots beat a rhythm on the frozen earth, gloved hands pushed deep into my coat pockets. For a while I find myself following the smart, white-railed gallops which belong to Milbury Racing Stables before I take a left and start ascending an unfamiliar hillside, my feet treading along a narrow clay path beset by clumps of earth. The sun's fully out now, its rays illuminating the silver frost that still covers the grass. Above my head a red kite circles, its wings outstretched against an azure sky.

I walk all day, stopping only to eat the sandwiches and drink from the thermos. It's late afternoon when I finally turn in what I hope is the direction back to Fawley. Clambering over a gate and finding myself on another, wider chalk track, I stare at the horizon and struggle to work out my bearings because I've actually been lost for some time – whoever now owns the racing stables has changed the direction of the gallops' white railings. But it doesn't matter. There's something about the beauty of this day, of being part of this ancient, forgotten landscape that fills me with an exhilaration and clarity I'm not yet ready to have snuffed out by the centrally heated claustrophobia of Fawley House.

I walk for another forty or so minutes before I come to a Wiltshire gate. As I clamber over it, the chalk track in front breaks into a familiar fork and I suddenly get my bearings as I remember riding this way on Bella. From here, I know for certain that the right-hand path will eventually return me to the bridleway and Fawley, while the left path heads down though the Grey Wethers Valley, towards the Shadowing Stones.

I pause. Of course it would make much more sense to turn right. Firstly because I'm finally beginning to admit to myself that I'm getting tired and cold, and secondly because the light has started to fade. To go left will add another hour to my journey, leading me via a wide dog-leg through the hamlet of Milbury and leading me to Fawley via the back road. Yet my feet are already heading in that direction, drawn by curiosity and the tenuous excuse that it may be some time before I'm up this way again.

I cross the far brow of the hillside and immediately see the three stones. They stand about half-a-mile away, at the very end of the valley, fenced within a small meadow and swathed in a low mist that has begun to settle with the oncoming dusk. Great reaches of arable land rise to their left and right, and behind them stands that derelict barn, the contents of its forecourt spilling out and breaking the narrow hedgerow which edges the track leading to Milbury.

Resisting the temptation to turn back, I accelerate my pace, propelling myself against a current of irrational fear. It takes me around another ten minutes before I've reached the bottom of the valley but as I climb the stile and start approaching the stones, I'd swear that a hush has fallen over everything, as if the valley's holding its breath at my approach, and there's a sudden, steely coldness that seems to clutch at my skin. I'm aware of so much and so little at the same time. There's an aroma of smoky earth, of moist meadow grass and bitter, winter air. Above my head that same red kite still circles around me and the sheep wait like ghosts in the mist, their black faces watching as I plod over the freezing grass and finally come to a halt a few yards away from the stones' rubble-strewn base.

The light's falling fast now, but I resist the temptation to hurry past and instead force myself to linger, despite my unease at being alone at a place where a boy was once murdered, and I'm aware once again of the icy chill which has settled over everything.

I shudder, then instinctively turn to look around myself, but there's nothing except for the watching sheep; the barren hillsides. Telling myself to stop being so stupid, I rest my gaze on the patch of dark earth which lies beneath the stones and try to imagine Tom's thoughts when he'd stood here all those years ago, how he'd feel if he were to return here now with so many questions still unanswered. Had his father really murdered Callum? That business in the pub was strange – the drunken insinuation of another murdered child back in Ireland. I wondered if the police had ever followed it up. I remember the dark veil of suspicion which had hung over the village after Callum's murder; the sense of everyone checking each other out as the journalists looked on. That brief visit of Jim's brother's must have led to a multitude of finger pointing and hushed conversations over half-full tankards.

And if it *wasn't* Jim, how had whoever killed Callum known about the Shadowing Stones? It's a disturbing thought that his killer could still be living in the area, may even have been rubbing shoulders with Jim all these years. And why had Callum been brought *here,* of all places? Could it have been some kind of bizarre, pagan sacrifice? I remember that theory being mooted by the journalists with their constant questions about witchcraft and black magic. For a time, the village had felt like Salem and they'd homed in on us children, those reporters, because they thought that with our young imaginations we'd be more likely to spill the beans about any local cult activity, whether it existed or not. But all they managed to do was confuse and terrify us.

I jump as a pheasant darts from a thicket of gorse and launches itself clumsily into the air. Then, closing my eyes for a moment, I exhale, my heart drumming in my chest.

Tom had found the remains of Callum's clothes here at the base of the stones – and the police said this was where he'd been killed and set alight. But whoever had done it took the body and dumped it inside the old barn which still stands on the other side of the track. All those searches that winter, plodding our way over fields and woodland in our long lines. Did they come here and walk past the barn without checking it properly? How had the body been missed and why had Tom – then just a fourteen-year-old boy – managed to find it when so many others had failed? I turn my head and gaze through the mist at that decrepit building with its single metal-gridded window.

Deciding to follow in Tom's footsteps, I circle the stones and start walking slowly towards it, but my quest is interrupted by the sudden sight of a black Jeep parked in the barn's forecourt, its engine idling, fumes pouring from its exhaust into the dusk. Its headlights are switched off and I've been so distracted by my thoughts that I've not noticed it until now. Coming to an uncertain halt, my heart's quickening again because I've already recognised the number plate.

Then I slowly make my way forward, and as I clamber over the stile at the meadow's far end, see the back of two heads through the steamed-up rear window. They merge together for a few seconds, then separate. Behind the Jeep the barn rises in menacing form, its roof silhouetted against the evening sky.

I approach the driver's window and tap it softly. There's no mistaking the woman who sits inside. As she hears my knuckle hit the glass, her body jolts back, the wooden clip hanging precariously from a wave of blonde hair as she clutches at the open buttons of her blouse, struggling to cover a black lace bra. I raise my gaze to stare at the man who's sitting next to her, but do not recognise the defiant stare that meets mine.

Isabel lets down the window. Her expression is neither angry, nor defensive – just resigned. 'Anna,' she says quietly.

A few seconds pass as we stare at each other, our looks communicating our feelings in that silent way of sisters. Then, without turning her head. she says, 'Alex, this is my sister, Anna.'

The man nods at me but says nothing. I estimate him to be around my own age, perhaps a bit younger. Even in the half-light I can see he's good-looking, the face behind his large glasses is intelligent, sensitive. He looks like an artist or a writer. But his wide mouth's set firm and in his eyes a fierce light burns, although I'm not sure if it's anger at my interruption or something deeper and harder to determine.

He opens the passenger door and lets himself down to the ground. His clothes are scruffy, the elbows and collar of his corduroy jacket faded and worn. There are rips in the knees of his jeans, the bottoms of which are tucked into battered wellington boots.

I follow his gaze back towards the stones and the dusk-shrouded hillside, but there's something about the set of his jaw that tells me his concentration is internal rather than external, that at this moment the place in which we stand is entirely incidental to what's occurring in his head. I wonder if he's even heard of Callum Donnelly and what took place here all those years ago.

It's bitterly cold now. The man turns and stares at me for a few seconds, his gaze hardening. Then he sighs and walks round to the back of the Jeep to open the rear door. A black-and-white Border collie immediately jumps out and starts barking.

'I'm going to walk back, Iz,' he says, and something in the way he shortens her name, the implied intimacy of it, jolts me. He makes his way back round to the front of the car and leans across the passenger seat to kiss her on the cheek. But she reaches out a hand and cupping the back of his head, winds her fingers into his hair and kisses him passionately.

Eventually he extracts himself from her embrace with a dreamy, blissful expression. He half turns, nodding at me once more, before setting off down the track towards Milbury, the collie trotting at his heels. I hear his whistle on the clear, still air.

Trudging around the car, I climb reluctantly into the passenger's seat, pulling shut the door as Isabel winds up the window.

'So who in the hell is he?'

She's silent for a moment, following him with her eyes. Then she says, 'Alex Strong. He's a sculptor. Rents the studio up at Forest Manor.' She leans forward abruptly, pulling down the sun visor to inspect her face under the driver's light before taking hold of her hair and clipping it back into the comb. 'I bought a sculpture from him, if you must know. Because that's your next question, isn't it? How did we meet? And the next one will be "how long has it been going on?" More than a year,' she says, without waiting for me. 'And I have loved every second of it. Every single precious second. That man, Anna, is the–'

'And that's where you've been going, isn't it – each time you've told Bill you came to see me... That's why you kept rushing off after an hour leaving me to rot in that bloody bedroom.' And suddenly I'm shocked at the vitriol that's pouring out of my mouth. 'That's why you've been so out of it this last month, isn't it?'

'Don't be shitty.'

'Are you in love with him?'

But she leans back against the headrest and says nothing, her eyes following the silhouette of his back until it finally disappears around a bend in the track.

A bat streaks out of one of the barn's windows, circling the sky then darting back in again. I glance at Isabel, before turning and peering through the Jeep's rear window. The stones stand silently in the mist, their shape silhouetted against a sky streaked with yellows and greys thrown up by the sun's dying rays.

'So what about Bill?'

'What about Bill?'

'Are you going to leave him?'

She half smiles and closes her eyes. Right at this moment I'm fighting an urge to punch her, yet simultaneously I'm questioning why my sister's love life should elicit such a violent response in me. What is it I'm actually wrestling here – the green-eyed monster? Is it simply because she has the front to sit here enjoying the one thing that all long-term relationships are not supposed to deliver – *passion* – that great red flag the single like to wave smugly over the heads of their married counterparts? Because if I'm honest, right at this moment it seems to me Isabel has everything that I don't – money, children, security, and even that greatest jewel in the crown, *sex* – whereas here am I, deserted by my lover and sentenced to remain childless for eternity.

'No...' Isabel says eventually, and opens her eyes with a start, as if surprised by this answer. Then she says, 'Of course I'm not going to leave Bill – why would I?'

'Because you're in love with someone else.'

'Alex is poor.'

'So?'

'I can't live like that. You know I can't. Besides,' she adds, chaffing her hands together and frowning. 'Bill loves me – and he's the father of my children. I can't walk out on him just like that.'

'You can't have it both ways, Izzy. You can't have your cake and eat it.'

She turns, her eyes flashing though the darkness. 'And who says so, Anna?' she snaps. 'Tell me. Why can't I "have my cake and eat it?" You don't know what it's like, being married and bringing up children. It's not all *The Waltons* you know. You've no idea how it feels to wake up each day putting your own needs behind those of your family – running around fetching and carrying and organising this and cooking that. You wake to see the same tedious face every morning, hear the same tedious words and have the same tedious sex, knowing that you're trapped with him, that you'll never again know how it feels to have that first kiss, that first rush of feeling. They sell it to us like a fairy story, don't they? Only it isn't. A lot of the time *it's shit*. I was on anti-depressants most of last year but of course you didn't know that because you were thousands of bloody miles away having a ball with the sultans and pretending you didn't have a family back here with lives and troubles who might actually *need* you. I only came off the pills when I met Alex. He's my anti-depressant now.'

'But you're cheating on Bill.'

She snorts at this. 'What Bill doesn't know won't hurt him.'

'But he *will* know, Izzy, and it *will* hurt him. This place is much too small to have an affair. Look at what's just happened. I've just caught you together. What if it had been someone from the village? – it would be all over Fawley by tomorrow.'

'Well, we'll just have to be more careful – that's all. And don't think you're walking back in this dark, by the way – I'm driving you home.'

Reaching forward, she switches on the engine then pulls the Jeep into a violent three-point turn before heading up the track. As she forces her foot down on the accelerator, I find myself clutching at the seatbelt as the Jeep's four-wheel drive forces us through the track's deep ruts and puddles. I sense my sister's determination, that she's had enough of this conversation because it's taking her to a place she doesn't want to go, and her intention's simply to offload me as soon as possible. Eventually we reach the A4 and head towards Fawley. It's fully dark now and thin clouds partly obscure a full moon. Passing along the village high street, I notice Tom's red Punto parked in its usual place before we swing up Soweton Road and into my mother's drive.

'I won't come in,' Isabel says, drawing up at the house. 'I've got a parents' evening.' Then she adds, 'You won't say anything to Mummy, will you?'

I go to open the door, then pause, my hand still resting on the handle.

'Please, Anna. I'm not going to leave Bill so she really doesn't need to know.'

I notice my mother's anxious face watching us from the kitchen window.

'What? And risk losing that lovely house and all those designer clothes he buys you?' I retort. 'Of course you're not going to leave Bill. But you know what? In my book that just makes it worse. You want everything, don't you, Izzy? A good fuck and a secure marriage. Well you might think it's fine, but I don't. I think it's spineless – not to mention cold-hearted and downright selfish.'

She regards me coolly from under the overhead light.

Stepping down, I pull the passenger door wide open with the intention of slamming it in her face.

'I'm sorry, Anna.' She stares at me for a second and then drops her gaze and suddenly I realise what it is she's trying to say, that she understands the jealousy, or is it simply *injustice* that I feel.

'Yes, well you said it, Izzy... You're the one who's trapped... You're the one who's depressed, not me. I've never really wanted children. I mean, I keep bloody well trying to convince you and Mummy of that fact.' I'm vaguely aware that I've started shouting, that our mother can most likely hear everything I'm saying, but that doesn't matter to me right at this moment because I want her to hear. I want them both to hear. 'Does it threaten your great life-plan, Izzy, that there are women out there with better things to do than *breed* – that there might be more to life than marrying a rich man and changing his kids' nappies – oh, except you have a nanny to do that anyway, don't you?'

'Anna, I never...'

'You never needed to. I see it in your faces every fucking day. You and Mummy have some prehistoric notion of how I'm supposed to be reacting to that operation. "Oh look at poor, barren Anna going through early menopause. If only she'd found a man in time she could have had children and big houses like us and not ever have to do a real stroke of proper work in her life". Christ, it really bloody...' but as the expletive leaves my lips, I notice Isabel's gaze shifting over my shoulder.

I turn to follow it and my heart immediately jumps as I see him standing on the driveway against a silhouette of buddleia and the woodshed, a tall shape faintly illuminated in the darkness. He must have come up the footpath, but I've no idea how long he's been standing there.

An owl hoots from the apple tree in the front garden and

another echoes straight back. I hear the slow crunch of boots on gravel as he takes an uncertain step toward me, the orange tip of a lit cigarette rising to his mouth followed by an exhaled cloud of condensation and smoke.

'Hello, Anna,' Tom Donnelly says quietly. 'Came to see how you're going. Sorry it's taken a while.'

8

TOM

Anna takes a step back from the Jeep and turns, slowly, to face me. For a moment she doesn't say anything so I'm standing here on her mum's drive feeling like a bit of a twat, and for two reasons really. Firstly because I've clearly overheard that vicious rant she's just off-loaded on her sister, and secondly, because it sounds like I think she's been waiting for me to visit when she's most likely not given me a second's thought since that day she fell down on the pavement.

'Tom...' she says, sounding surprised, her eyes peering from under the woollen hat. She takes a step then sort of hovers, like she's not sure what to do.

I take a pull on the roll-up and glance over her shoulder at Isabel who's leaning across the passenger seat of her Jeep to get a better look at me, her face partially lit by the driver's light. 'Well, I can see this is my cue to get going,' she says, sounding a bit put out.

Anna mutters a quiet 'okay'. She pushes the door shut and Isabel throws her sister a frustrated look before reversing the Jeep sharply across the gravel in a sweep of headlights, leaving us facing each other in the darkness.

There's a full moon and a thin beam of light's being thrown over the drive from the kitchen window, but still I sense more than see Anna moving towards me, a small rucksack hanging from her shoulder. 'Thanks for coming round,' she says, and her voice is soft and a bit husky, like I remember.

'That's okay.' I drop the cigarette and crush it into the gravel with the sole of my boot. 'Sorry to leave it so long but Dad's not been great.'

'No, of course. I'm sorry, Tom... Mummy told me he was ill.' Her eyes hold mine through the darkness. 'Listen, it's terribly cold out here. Would you like to come inside?'

I glance towards that kitchen window with its undrawn curtains and for the first time notice Liz Carmichael's face watching us behind its latticed panes.

'I was actually on my way to the Catherine. Wondered if you fancied joining me...'

Fuck knows where that came from but thank God it's dark because I can feel my face turning red. Jesus, I mean, I only came round to see how she was, not to ask her out for a drink, and certainly not to the local boozer – this is Anna Carmichael, for Christ's sake – it should be Michelin stars for a girl like her, or a decent restaurant at the very least.

'Oh...' There's a short silence as she mulls the invitation over. Then she raises her face and smiles. Shifting from one foot to the other, she says, 'You know what? That sounds great,' and the mist rises from her mouth. 'Would you mind waiting while I get my purse?'

'Sure, no worries.'

She disappears through the gate and a few seconds later I watch her enter the kitchen. What looks like a heated discussion follows, with Liz Carmichael turning her face towards my form on the driveway, her fingers gripping a tea-towel. A minute later, Anna re-emerges minus the rucksack with a purse in her hand.

'Don't ask...' she says, rolling her eyes in the light of the window. I grin, then follow her round the back of the house and down the narrow footpath, stumbling along in the darkness as she strides confidently ahead, her head silhouetted by the street lamp at the path's end.

It's only six o clock and the pub's still pretty deserted. As I feel around for money in my jeans pocket, Anna rests her elbow against the bar's polished surface. 'You know, I honestly can't remember when I was last in here,' she murmurs, her eyes moving over the empty chairs and tables, the blackboard no longer wiped clean but now crammed with specials, chalked up in someone's sloping handwriting.

'It's changed a lot.'

'At least they've still got a fire.' She sniffs wetly and blows on her hands. In the lamp light I notice the pink flush of her nose and cheeks beneath the wool hat. 'Do you mind if we sit by it? I've been out walking all day and I'm absolutely freezing.'

A plump, blonde-haired woman I've not seen before comes to serve us. Anna requests a large glass of Shiraz and I order a pint of Carlsberg for myself. As I wait for my change, Anna carries her wine across the room and places it on a corner table before fetching a stool and putting it in front of the hearth. I watch her unzip her fleece then pull off her hat and shake out her hair.

I didn't take in much of her that day she fell down. It was hardly surprising given it happened so quickly – then all my concentration was taken up with trying to calm her down as we waited for the ambulance. Since then, I've seen her hurry past the house once or twice, but she always has her face lowered and that hat pulled down over her eyes and ears. So this is the first time I've had a chance to properly study her – this grown-up Anna – and I guess she doesn't look so different from how I remember her. She's still got that wide, determined mouth and steady green eyes, now faintly edged with crow's feet. Her hair's still brown and wavy, but shoulder-length now rather than right down her back, a few fine grey strands woven into the temples. Her figure – slim but solid-boned – still looks pretty good beneath the black jumper and Levi jeans.

'So you're completely recovered then?' I say, crouching on a stool next to her.

'Pretty much.'

'You were in a bad way that day.'

She nods and swallows a mouthful of her wine. 'I was. Thank you for calling the ambulance. They said I'd ruptured a stitch – apparently it hardly ever happens, only I've learnt if there's the slimmest chance that something can go wrong, then it's going to happen to me.' She smiles, and the rim of the glass has left a scarlet thread across her upper lip. 'So is Jim terribly ill?'

I reach down and shift a large log into the heart of the fire. 'Yeah. You could say that... He was in and out of hospital the last few weeks. That's why it's taken me a while to call round.'

'What sort of cancer is it?'

'Started in his lymph glands but now it's spread pretty much everywhere. Problem's the pain.' I shake my head. 'He's got morphine but it makes him dog sick.'

'It's good he's got you to look after him.'

I shrug. 'I guess.'

The bar door opens and a middle-aged couple enter wearing green body warmers. They walk over to the blackboard and start discussing the specials in plummy, self-satisfied voices, producing words I never imagined I'd hear in this pub such as, 'roulade', 'hollandaise' and 'pan fried'.

Anna pushes a hand in her coat pocket and pulls out a tissue. 'Mummy says you live in Australia now.'

'That's right. Adelaide.'

'How old were you when you went? I seem to remember you...'

'I was seventeen.'

She blows her nose, then says, 'It's terribly young... To go so far, I mean.'

'Is it?' I shrug and stare down at my pint. 'I never really saw it that way – it was just one big adventure at the time.'

'So what do you do there?'

I swallow a mouthful of lager. 'Run a haulage business. Started it up a couple of years after I got there.' And maybe it's because she's a Carmichael but suddenly I just can't resist giving myself a verbal chest thump. 'Yeah, it's a pretty big operation these days – employs around forty people. So I guess I've done okay for someone who left school without any qualifications. Got a big house with five acres of grounds, a pool – that kind of thing.'

She smiles and looks genuinely impressed. 'Really? Gosh. You must be very proud.'

'Well...' I say, trying to sound humble. 'These things don't really bother me. I'd be happy living in a hut, but Stella – my wife – she wanted a pool.'

'You're married?'

'Yeah....' I pause. Then, 'Yeah, I'm married. Got four children – all under twelve. They keep me busy.'

'That's nice.' She forces a small smile, then frowns slightly.

'And how about you?'

She screws up the tissue and chucks it into the flames. 'I'm living in Istanbul. Been there for six years now editing the Turkish edition of *The Lonely Traveller*. And I do a bit of English teaching on the side.'

I find myself looking at her with the same admiration she's just shown me. '*The Lonely Traveller*, hey? We've got a few of those on the shelves back home – they're great books. So I guess there's a Turkish man in tow?'

She nods, then looks away and pushes her hair behind her ear. 'Sort of. I mean, I live with someone. We're not married.'

'But?'

'What makes you think there's a "but"?'

'It sounds like there's one on its way.'

'Shit,' she says wearily, raising her eyebrows. 'That obvious, huh?' I watch her stare into the inside of the glass, swilling the wine around its base before releasing a sigh. '*But* he wants children.'

That middle-aged couple are ordering their meals and the pub's starting to get busy. A pair of beer-bellied men I recognise from drinking in here since my return enter and settle down on the stools at the bar and a family has just congregated around the large table in the pub's wide bay window. In the adjoining games room, I can hear the crash of pool balls being released followed by the sound of a girl's high-pitched laughter.

'Well I guess that's rubbed salt into the wound,' I say finally, hooking some tobacco and papers out of my jacket pocket. 'So is he calling it a day – or is he prepared to give up on the idea of kids?'

She pushes the tip of her thumb into her mouth and bites down on its nail. 'I don't know for sure,' she says, narrowing her eyes. 'But as he's not phoned for over two weeks, I'd say the writing's on the wall, wouldn't you?'

'Anna,' I reply, licking the cigarette paper and sealing it. 'If his way of finishing it is to stop calling you, then he's a spineless coward and you're well shot of him.'

I take the cigarette through the back of the pub and out into the car park, leaving her to mull this. But as I light up and stare out towards the garden's empty benches in the mist, the bare branches that reach up into the darkness against that full moon,

I'm wondering what kind of arsehole would let his partner go through the physical and emotional trauma of a hysterectomy and not be with her, whatever state the relationship was in.

I think back to the bitter words I heard just now on her old lady's driveway. Anna's heated insistence that she hadn't wanted children. But that day she'd fallen down, she'd started to cry and she'd carried on crying until the ambulance had appeared. I guess I wasn't thinking about it too much at the time, but I reckon it was a lot more than just physical pain she was feeling when they carted her off on that stretcher.

I return to find her staring contemplatively into the flames, the half-drunk glass of wine resting in the palm of her hand.

'Don't beat yourself up, Anna – all relationships have their problems.'

'Really?' She glances up at me. 'What, even ones where you share a lovely house, four children and a swimming pool?'

I sit back down on the stool. 'Yeah. Even ones like that.'

Her fingers tighten around the glass's stem. 'What makes you say that?'

Taking the poker from its stand, I reach down and start pushing the logs aimlessly around the grate. There's an obvious silence, and I feel her turn towards me.

'I think Stella's on a trick,' I say, finally.

'You mean she's having an affair?'

I nod, then squeeze the packet of tobacco back into my jeans pocket. 'Found out just before I got the news about Dad's cancer, so I guess in some ways the timing was neat. Came here to look after him... But it's given me a chance to chew things over, hey.'

And maybe it's because I've been cooped up with Dad for so many weeks and it's been a while since I last spoke to anyone of my own age, or perhaps it's just that curious look in her eyes and the fact she's clearly got her own shit to share, but suddenly

I'm telling her about it, that first day I'd started to suspect Stella was up to something – coming home late from a rare 'night out with the girls' and how quickly those nights out became a regular occurrence and once or twice there was a smell around her of aftershave and at the same time she'd pretty much stopped putting out in bed.

'And then there were the texts,' I say. 'Jesus, mobile phones have a lot to answer for. They make it all so simple and I don't only mean having the affair. They make it too damned easy to catch people out, too, even if you'd really prefer to keep your head in the sand and hope if anything *is* going on that it burns itself out. She always had her phone on silent but I'd see her in the garden when she thought I wasn't looking, you know, texting and WhatsApping and kind of smiling in that way people do when they're reading something nice about themselves. In the end – and shit, I hate doing stuff like this – but I got hold of it and read her messages.'

'And?'

I shrug. 'I can't be certain, but "*I can't stop thinking about you*" is a bit of a giveaway. And it was her who wrote that – not him.'

'Do you know who he is?'

I shake my head. 'It was a woman's name on the phone – not one I recognised which was odd considering the amount of texts she'd sent so I reckon Stella made it up. To tell the truth I've got a feeling it's one of my drivers. Fella called John. I've always thought he had the hots for her.'

Anna places her empty wine glass on the table and looks thoughtful. 'It's the worst thing with infidelity, you know. The suspicion... getting paranoid but never really knowing what's going on.' And something in her voice tells me she's had experience of the subject. 'So you think it's this guy because he obviously fancies her, but you're not sure. And then you'll think it's that good-looking bloke she knows from the so-and-so, and then another guy and so on until you drive yourself crazy. Have you confronted her?'

I shake my head. 'Not yet.'

For a moment she doesn't say anything, her gaze turned towards the fire. In the soft light of the flames I suddenly think how lovely she looks; the warm shadows filling the hollows of her cheekbones and accentuating the arch of her eyebrows under the brown hair. Beneath the wool jumper, her neck looks smooth and unblemished and I'm aware for the first time of a fine silver chain which rests in the dark hollows between her collarbones.

She turns her face towards me, and I wonder if she's sensed me staring at her because there's a flush of colour in her cheeks and she leans down and feels hurriedly around in her pockets.

'Do you want another one?' she says, standing up with her purse in her hand. 'Please say yes.'

'That'll be a "yes" then.'

She grins, then heads to the bar. I watch her chat easily to the barmaid as the latter pours our drinks, the gleam in Anna's eyes as she throws her head back and laughs about something, her hand coiling her hair to one side of her neck and her gaze occasionally sliding in my direction. To her right, those two men have gone silent, watching her.

'So where did you walk today?' I ask when she returns and hands me my pint.

She drops down onto the stool and something in her hesitation has me guessing what she's going to say before she says it.

'On Marlborough Down.'

'Oh yeah...? Did you go to the Shadowing Stones?'

She bites her lip, then stares at the laminate under her stool. 'I went past them, yes...'

'Much changed up there?'

'No. Sorry, Tom...' She shoots a sideways look at me. 'You know, I've been thinking about Callum a lot since, well... after I first saw you that day. It can't be easy coming back and facing all that on top of your dad's illness.'

I shrug. 'Yeah, well...'

But then I go silent because, to be honest, I don't really want to talk about it even though it was me who brought it up. And I know she gets me, because she's quiet too, but just for a moment I feel her hand brush my forearm before she suddenly places her glass on the mantelpiece and rises to her feet. 'Do you play pool?'

I look up, surprised at the invitation, aware at the same time she's trying to lighten things up. 'Yeah, a bit... Why, are you a hustler?'

'I might be.' She grins at me and cracks her knuckles by way of assent.

So we pick up our coats and hats and make our way into the other side of the bar where there's a pool table surrounded by pine benches. That crowd of teenagers have finished their game and now congregate in the car park outside the window smoking cigarettes. Anna inserts a pound coin and racks up the balls with expert hands.

'Yeah,' I say. 'You've definitely done this before.'

We toss a coin and she wins on tails and takes the break, firing in two reds immediately and then another before snookering herself.

'So have you been out much since you've been back?' she asks, stepping back. 'You know – reacquainting yourself with the area? I'd forgotten how beautiful it is here.'

'Yeah, a bit.' I lean down to double a yellow. 'Keeps you sane, doesn't it? – getting out. I've been up to the woods a few times, and I drove to White Horse Hill the other day. Jesus hey,

I'd forgotten how fantastic the view is from up there.' And as we start to chat it's good to see her face beaming at me over the cue, taking crack shots while barely interrupting her banter. And I do kind of get what she's talking about, not that I'm anything like as into the place as she is. I suppose I've guessed from the various times I've seen her pass the house in her hat and coat that she's a serious walker; it kind of seems a weird activity for the lively, sociable girl I'm chatting with right now – but as I picture her solitary figure climbing the hillsides with map in hand, well I guess it's not that surprising because it reminds me of the Anna I knew as a kid, only in those days she was always on horseback.

I buy another round of drinks and we go on to talk about the village and how we remember it as children – what's changed and what's the same, the people we knew then and what they're doing now; who we've seen since returning and how it's been to spend time with our folks again after so many years away. The talk's flowing between us and we keep erupting into laughter. I guess it surprises me, because I always reckoned Anna to be reserved and buttoned up like her mother. I never had her down as a pub girl.

She makes yet another winning shot, nominating her pocket and doubling the black into it like a pro, then patting me on the shoulder as she throws back her head with a peal of victorious laughter. We're four rounds in now and the booze and conversation seems to have ignited something in her. As I stare into those glittering eyes, Jesus, suddenly it's all I can do not to put my arm around her waist and kiss her, and as she sees me looking at her, she goes still, her laughter fading, and suddenly we're just standing there staring at each other and not saying anything at all.

At that moment, the bar door opens with a blast of cold air and Ray Curtis enters wearing a black woollen hat over his thick hair. He starts making his way to the bar but comes to an abrupt halt when he sees me, his gaze shifting and resting on Anna before swerving back to mine with a knowing, half-mouthed smile because I reckon he senses he's caught us having a moment.

'Tom,' he says.

'Evening, Ray.'

'How's Jim? I called by the other day but no one seemed to be home.'

'Yeah... he was in hospital, but he's rallied a bit now so come by.' I pause, then, 'Ray, do you remember Anna Carmichael – Liz Carmichael's daughter, from Fawley House? Anna, this is Ray Curtis – Ray used to be Dad's business partner.'

It's strange – but the second I say Anna's name I reckon I see a question mark pass across his eyes. I turn to look at Anna but she seems oblivious to his reaction, placing the cue in the rack before reaching out a hand and smiling at him.

'Anna,' Ray says, sounding a bit uncomfortable. 'I remember you. You used to ride around the village on a bay mare.' He stares at her for a few moments more, like he's seeking something in her face. Then he turns back to me. 'Can I get you both a drink?'

I glance at Anna, then shake my head. 'I should be getting back to the old man,' I say, and at the same time she goes to retrieve our coats.

We say goodbye to Ray, and leave the pub together, walking side-by-side in silence along the mist-filled road until we reach the end of the footpath.

'That was great, Tom,' Anna says, turning to face me under the street lamp. She wraps her arms around herself and shivers. 'Thanks. I really needed to get out – I've been going stir-crazy at Mummy's.'

'Don't I know it...' I reply, a bit clumsily. 'I guess we're kind of in the same boat.'

She smiles. 'We really are, aren't we?'

And then we're just standing there staring at each other again and not saying anything, just like we were in the pub when Ray Curtis came in.

The rest's a bit of a blur – I'm pissed, she's pissed and it's like something's taken us over because all I know is that she reaches out and touches my arm, then I feel her lips, soft against my cheek, and her hair smells kind of musky. At the same time, I put an arm around her waist and my free hand raises instinctively to stroke her face. A moment later we're kissing, our arms around each other, and then I'm pulling her by the shoulders into the darkness of the path.

Everything's gone deadly quiet. There's no sound of footsteps or approaching cars. Even the owls have stopped calling. My mouth's against her ear, and I can hear her breathing hard, her hands moving up inside my jacket, her warm breath on my face as she pulls back to stare at me with an amazed expression before kissing me once more, and at the same time I'm bewildered this can be happening, that I've flown halfway around the world only to find myself in the village where I grew up locked in a clinch with Anna Carmichael, my childhood crush.

The image of Georgia in our swimming pool abruptly floats into my mind, her eyes laughing as she flaps around in the clear blue water, her tiny arms almost swallowed by the red bands. The picture's so sharp it hurts. I see the scattering of tiny brown freckles across her nose, smell her skin and hair as I lift her out of the water; their combined scent of Johnson's shampoo and chlorine. Her small fingers pinch my cheeks as I raise her face to mine and press my nose against hers. It's early evening, but the sun burns down and from the garden comes the rhythm of crickets and the laugh of the kookaburra. Behind me, Stella lies stretched out, sanguine and bronzed in her red bikini reading a magazine, and I can hear the boys and Indiana on the veranda laughing as they tease the heelers.

'Jesus, Anna. I'm sorry...' I take a step back and taking her arms, press them against her sides.

'What is it?' she whispers. 'What's wrong?'

'Look, whatever I said about Stella... I'm still married.'

And then we're just standing in the freezing mist without speaking, the condensation from our breaths rising and meeting. Her confused expression is just discernible under the glow of that street lamp. She stares at me for a few seconds, then biting down on her lip, takes a retreating step along the side of the wall.

'I'm married...' I repeat, more quietly this time. 'I've got four kids. It's not fair on them. It's not fair on you.'

'It's okay. I understand.'

'Do you?'

She nods, then I feel her touch my cheek briefly with her fingers. I take them in my own and press my mouth into her palm before lowering her hand. Another long silence follows.

'Goodnight, Tom,' she murmurs finally, sounding like she wants to say something more.

'Goodnight, Anna. I'll call you, hey.'

'Please do.'

But she remains standing there for a few extra seconds, her eyes clinging to mine, and in the lamp's soft glow I can see the spirit's gone out of them, has been replaced with a troubled despondency. Then she turns, and with folded arms and bowed head, starts walking back up the path.

9

ANNA

The next morning, Kerem calls. His voice on the line sounds distant, but maybe because after last night he suddenly seems much further away. 'How are you feeling, *canim*?' he says. 'I spoke to your mother last night and she said you went to the pub with a friend. I think you must be better.' He laughs and adds, 'So when you are coming home?'

I try to picture him in our apartment, wearing his usual jeans and trainers and his blue Nike jogging top. He likes to dress casually when he's at home, being forced by his work to wear a suit and tie most of the time. He'll be sitting next to his tall bookshelf which is packed with titles by Orhan Pamuk and Yasar Kemal, and a litany of untranslated European and American works including *The Complete Works of Shakespeare*.

Kerem has a ferocious appetite for reading and I suppose that's one of the things I've always found most attractive about him – especially his ability to understand challenging literature in its mother tongue. Though not creative himself, he has a great appreciation for the arts. He also has a brilliant, lightning-quick mind and a razor-edged sense of humour which he chooses this moment to exhibit.

'Or are you having an affair?' he adds. 'Is that why you're taking so long?'

'Don't be stupid.'

'Well, you can't blame me for wondering. You haven't called me for weeks.'

But it's his turn to call, and he knows it. The last two times have been me.

'You mean *you've* not called *me* for weeks, Kerem,' I respond.

'Oh, we are keeping count? I didn't realise.'

There's a silence. Then I add, 'I'm being serious. How do I know you even want me to come home?'

This is followed by an immediate, and very audible sigh. 'Anna, I just want you to do what makes you happy.'

'What on earth does that mean?'

'It means I'm not happy if you're not happy.'

'You're talking in riddles.'

It's something he's always been good at – deflecting accusation and conflict into a wall of mirrors, leaving his opponent in the starting blocks while he's halfway down the tracks. He didn't achieve his first class degree from Boğaziçi University for nothing.

'Look,' he says, then pauses. He knows I'm familiar with his tricks and am not about to blunder after him on a game of verbal cat and mouse. And then for no reason at all he breaks into Turkish; '*Sevgilim nihayetinde eve geldiginde konusmamiz lazim,*' – 'Darling, when you finally do come home, we need to talk.'

It's the choice of language that troubles most. My Turkish is nearly fluent now, but still we tend to communicate in English most of the time, a language over which he has a terrifying command for one who has never lived in an English-speaking country. He's even been known to tease me for my occasionally lamentable use of it – sending up my mispronunciation of the *th* sound, something I have a tendency to do when I'm tired or distracted. 'Oh you *fink* that, do you?' he'll say with a grin. 'Sometimes I *fink* that too.'

But he hardly ever speaks to me in Turkish and I realise immediately it's his way of softening the likely impact of these words. Only it doesn't work, because I immediately know that what I'm listening to; it's tone of the executioner gently entreating his subject to approach the gallows, and I can guess what it is he's *really* saying – that when I do finally return our relationship will be over. Kerem will walk away a little sad but also relieved, while I will crash to the ground with an unbeating heart, my soul left raw because he's stripped from it everything he required.

Oh I know what to expect. I've been there many times before.

Christ, I can't face it yet. Not now, not again, and I'm hoping the longer I stay away and give myself time to adjust to this new reality, the blunter the blow of the axe will feel when it finally falls. But then I remember standing in the darkness with Tom last night and a voice in my head warns me I should leave Fawley as soon as possible because nothing good can come of this union either, and all I'm really doing is lurching uncontrollably from one unavailable man to another in order to put off the inevitable pain and loneliness to come.

Feeling like an animal caught between two trappers, I hear myself say in a brittle voice which is not my own, 'I'm sorry, Kerem, but I think I'm going to stay on here a bit longer. I just don't feel well enough to come back yet.'

* * *

The weather is drab and grey. Soon it begins to rain. It's too wet and miserable to go for a walk so I sit on my bed and flick with disinterest through the pages of a magazine, my eyes occasionally raising towards the window. From the distance comes the rumble of army guns on Salisbury Plain.

Beyond the school's black railings, Jim Donnelly's house stands in full view. The Punto is parked in its usual place outside the broken trellis, its red sides gleaming in the rain.

Last night keeps drifting back into my mind. Tom's face in the pub as he'd sat next to me drinking his pint, staring into the fire and mooning over his wife's suspected affair. His tallness; the steady movement of his body as he'd circled the pool table, chalking his cue as he considered each shot. Everything about this man is focused and methodical; from his meditative expression as he rolls his cigarettes to the way he speaks in that strange, gravel-toned Australian. He strikes me – though not in a negative way – as a man who puts a heavy emphasis on self-control.

Yet just for a moment he'd lost that control and I find myself shivering involuntarily, remembering the press of his hand against my neck, the hardness of his body against mine. I can still sense something of him lingering on me; his breath against my cheek, the scrape of his stubble, the masculine smell of sweat and leather that seems to follow him around. But I suppose the real shock is that something has *actually* happened between us after all these weeks of wondering about him in some kind of abstract way. It's not like I expected it. I'd not expected anything.

Tom Donnelly. The boy I briefly went to school with. What did I think of him when I was growing up? I suppose I noticed he was nice-looking – he'd inherited his father's striking black eyes and thick black hair – and I'd always suspected he had a bit of a thing for me because sometimes I'd catch him staring and he'd get a bit tongue-tied in my presence. But he was just the son of Jim Donnelly who delivered the wood. He wasn't anyone I'd particularly thought about – at least not until Callum died – and I'd certainly never considered him boyfriend material.

'I think Stella is on a trick,' he'd said.

On a trick maybe, but not enough of one to salve his conscience.

The days pass into a week, then two weeks. Despite his promise to call, I don't hear from him and don't see him around the village. I wonder if he's thought about me very much. It feels odd and maybe a bit sentimental to say it, but it seems to me there's a kind of intimacy about the way our houses are so close to each other, especially after what occurred between us that evening. It's strange to think if a plane flies overhead and leaves a vapour trail, we can both see it in the sky above our heads. If a horse whinnies in one of the village's many stables, we hear it simultaneously. We can smell the same plumes of smoke rising from bonfires in the gardens, hear the same shouts of the children as they tear around the playground. And one morning, as I wake up in the early hours, I wonder if he also suffers sleeplessness, is lying there right now in his bed, listening to the owls calling one another.

Before leaving Turkey for the operation, I cleared all my work, letting my publisher and students know I'd be away for several months at least and would be in contact on my return. I'm glad now that I made these arrangements because I'm beginning to realise I'm not at all ready to return to work, and for a while at least, can afford not to.

Because I've begun to understand that whilst physically recovered, I'm completely emotionally wrung out. At the age of forty-one, I have just lost the capacity to create a child, and as a result, have found myself in a relationship that's rapidly running out of its future in a country where I feel I no longer belong.

Because it's hard to admit, given it's been one of the central driving factors in my career, but I've become sick of being a foreigner. It's not that I don't love Turkey, or that I'm lonely. I have a large circle of friends in Istanbul – both Turkish and British – and my life is very much that of the freedom-loving expatriate. My weekends when Kerem is away working in his import-export business, are usually spent catching up with friends in restaurants, or cafes by the Bosphorus watching the fishermen and marvelling at the sights and sounds. Istanbul is a beautiful, ravishing city which, over the last six years, has seduced me time and again. But Istanbul is also a city undergoing a major social transformation. The rise of Recep Tayyip Erdoğan's repressive regime and the accelerated eradication of democracy and persecution of academics and liberal-minded thinkers – some of whom are my friends – has made me rethink my appreciation of it as a secular, forward-thinking country.

But more than anything, Istanbul is not my home and it's interesting that coming back to Fawley has made me realise there are many things I miss about being in England. Like reading the British newspapers – even the tabloids – and the humour and references that are so particular to my culture and history. I miss autumn, those fresh misty afternoons when the paths rustle with dry leaves, and oddly, being here at this time of year makes me realise how much I enjoy the English winters; the pleasure of sitting next to a pub's roaring log fire with the snow settled outside, a steaming mulled wine before me.

But most of all, I miss feeling that I belong.

It's the last thing that I expected, to feel this way. I suspected mine and Kerem's relationship was over from the moment I knew I needed the operation – he'd always been clear about wanting children – but I didn't realise I'd also fallen out of love with Istanbul.

* * *

My walking increases, becomes almost obsessive, taking me out each day, sometimes for five or six hours at a time. Fawley Wood is my favourite haunt. I used to ride there when I was a girl and then, as now, loved its thousand-strong army of beech trees fusing into a silver-beige horizon. In the summer, the wood becomes lush and dark under a canopy of lime-coloured leaves, but at this time of year the branches are naked and the tracks and paths are lit by a bleak light. There's little vegetation apart from the strands of ivy that wind around the tall trunks and some unidentifiable flora gathered around the occasional stump or lichen-covered rock.

But what really defines Fawley Wood in winter is its silence. There's rarely any birdsong or sound of wildlife apart from the occasional squawk of a pheasant or bolting of a startled deer. It's a strange, almost oppressive silence – some of the locals say they find it creepy and don't like to come here alone. I've discovered I'm the opposite, relishing the sense of aloneness – it suits my need to think things through and hush my mind's constant chatter.

Tom mentioned he'd been walking up here too but I tell myself that's not the reason I walk this way so often. Yet as I make my way along these deserted tracks, there's always a slight feeling of apprehension in my stomach, knowing there's a possibility I might bump into him around the next corner.

I've not seen anything of Isabel since I caught her at the

Shadowing Stones that evening – she's only been round a couple of times since our argument and on each occasion I've been out walking. But these trips regularly take me past Forest Manor and one drizzly afternoon, just as the light's beginning to fade, I'm walking towards its large wooden gates when I see a black-and-white collie trotting towards me followed by a familiar figure plodding along in a dark green coat.

'Good evening,' I say, coming to a halt. 'Isabel said you kept a studio up here.'

Alex Strong looks up with surprise – he's so engrossed in his thoughts he's not noticed me approaching. But as he recognises me, his eyes behind the large glasses take on that same studied defiance they wore when we met at the stones.

'Hello,' he says. He looks rougher today, his face unshaven. He stares down at the track and shifts from one muddy trainer to the other. 'Out walking again? It's not a great day for it.'

I smile. 'I try not to let the weather stop me from getting out. Otherwise I'd go mad.'

He nods at this, his eyes dropping back to the ground. 'I know what you mean.'

'So how's Isabel? I haven't seen her for a while.'

'Haven't you?' he says in an unconvincing voice, scratching the back of his head. 'She's fine. She was with me this morning.'

We stare at each other for a few moments, suddenly awkward, and I know he's waiting for me to make some kind of judgement about his affair with my sister but for some reason I feel no impetus to condemn him – he seems too sensitive somehow, too much a victim without me adding to his malaise. Besides, whatever I've had to say on the subject has already been aired to Isabel.

'Well,' I murmur, 'I suppose I'd better get on.' I push my hands into my pockets and go to step past him.

'I was just about to make some tea,' he says suddenly, at the same time withdrawing a bunch of keys from his jeans pockets and turning towards the gates. 'Would you like some?'

For a moment I don't move. I'm feeling a bit caught out and unsure of the protocol because I can guess his motives – that he wants to talk to me about my sister. But he pulls open the gate and turns to smile at me, all defiance gone, and as I stare into that restless, anxious face, I'm hit by an unexpected wave of sympathy.

'Come on,' he says. 'I'll show you my work.'

'Well, all right.' I bend down and pat the collie. 'But it's getting dark so I'll just pop my head in if that's okay.'

I follow him through the gates and wait as he locks them before leading me with cautious strides down an immaculate drive, his hands in his pockets, gaze lowered towards the gravel at his feet.

I've never been inside the Manor's grounds before but they look pretty much how I've always imagined; the main house's black-painted, studded doors set behind a pair of stone pillars on each side of a flight of stone steps, the latter leading down to the top of the driveway where a red Jaguar and black Mercedes stand parked.

'Who owns this place now?' I ask, following Alex past the tarpaulin-covered swimming pool.

'The Grahams,' he replies. 'They've had it for donkeys' years. Toby, the son, inherited it. He lives here with his wife. They're all right.' He wrinkles his nose and looks at me sideways. 'Kids are a bit stuck up.'

We stride past a hard tennis court and turn into a quadrangle of stables which sit around a circle of perfectly kept lawn, a life-size bronze statue of a rearing horse in its centre. Over Alex's shoulder, a pair of brown heads alight in unison over neighbouring loose-box doors, their ears pricking at the sound of our approaching footsteps. Alex clicks his tongue and moves towards them, stopping to stroke their necks as the collie crouches patiently at his feet. I come and stand beside him, running my palm down the nose of the first, slightly darker horse.

'That's Trojan,' Alex says. 'He's a champion three-day-eventer. And this is Eagle. Do you like horses?'

I nod. 'I used to have one when I was young. That's how I know these woods so well – only now I'm walking all the places I used to ride.'

'I had one too,' he says. 'We were in Devon then. There can't be a better way to spend your childhood than on the back of a horse. It gives you such a love of the countryside and solitude – I'm pretty sure it's what made me become an artist.'

I nod, surprised at this sudden candour, and wondering at the same time what this man can possibly have in common with my sister beyond physical attraction – Isabel with her love of fashion and all things material. Then I look down and smile as Trojan presses a velvety muzzle into my palm and slides a wet tongue between my fingers.

Alex leans down and murmurs something to his dog before straightening and walking on until he reaches a stable door at the furthest corner of the quadrangle.

'Come in and make yourself at home,' he says, sliding its bolts.

I move past him into a large studio. 'Gosh,' I say, turning in a circle. 'It's a good size, isn't it? Did they knock two loose boxes into one?'

He nods, then leans against the door frame and folds his arms. 'They converted this and built a fourth wing over on the other side of the block. There's another studio there as well but no one's using it at the moment.'

On one side of the room sits a potter's wheel and a steel kiln. Several shelves run along the wall to its right, displaying a variety of pots and other vessels. Underneath them lie a pile of old blankets covered in dog hair. A worn, dust-coated kilim has been thrown down in the middle of the concrete floor, on the other side of which rests a single mattress with a chequered duvet, and next to it a faded-blue armchair with stuffing bursting through its fabric.

'So are the Grahams okay with you living here?' I say, sitting on one of its arms and watching as the collie steals past his legs and lies down on the pile of blankets.

'I don't live here,' he says. 'I live with my mother, in Marlborough. She's got MS and early-onset dementia, so I'm her main carer.' He sighs and looks away. 'It's not easy, and I guess this is my escape from all of that really. I just use the mattress to kip on sometimes if I've been working late – or had too many at the Catherine.'

'Or when Isabel visits,' I add, eyeing that duvet.

That wide mouth tightens and a shadow of the old defiance darkens his face once more. Turning abruptly, he makes his way to the far end of the room where the wall is lined with more shelves. I rise from the chair and follow him, my eyes raising towards a thick oak beam that runs across the centre of the wooden ceiling above our heads. To its left, a rectangle skylight looks out to a scythe of moon.

'Well, this is my stuff,' he says.

His sculptures are moulded from clay and mainly depict human figures in contemplative repose. There are several studies of what looks like an Indian sadhu sitting crossed-legged, his head bowed, beard flowing over his feet. Another shows a mother staring devotedly at an infant she holds in her arms. But the two sculptures which stand out most are of a young woman; one depicts her in a chair, her thick hair tumbling back over her shoulders; the other has her lying supine on the ground, her head resting on her elbow. I immediately recognise his muse.

'They're beautiful,' I say, meaning it. 'You're very talented.'

'Thanks.'

'What does my sister think of them?'

He smiles and rolls his eyes. 'Oh you know Iz... She says she likes them but I'm not sure she really gets it, to be honest. Can I make you that cup of tea?'

I shake my head and take a step towards the door. 'No thanks. It's been lovely to see your work but I should get back before it gets dark.'

He sighs and stares at the floor. 'Right.'

'Sorry.'

'No. No I understand,' he says flatly. 'I just wanted to...'

I place my hand on the back of that armchair and turn to stare at him. 'You wanted to talk about Isabel? I don't blame you. It can't be easy being the other man.'

He throws me a sudden, savage look. 'Don't take the piss.'

'I'm not. Look, I understand. You want to get to know my sister better. But how can you do that when you're not allowed to meet her family – those people who've known her since she was knee-high; who'll let you into those secrets of when she was a little girl – the charming things she got up to? Because that's what you want to hear, isn't it? Now you think you've got the opportunity...'

I'm doing everything I can to communicate sincerity, but still his eyes smoulder. He takes a step away and turns to stare sullenly at his sculptures.

'Listen, Alex, I'm really not taking the piss. And I actually do know how you're feeling – I'm sort of in the same boat myself.'

He slides a curious glance towards me and at the same time I can't quite believe what I've just said.

'Look...' I go on quickly. 'There honestly isn't that much I could tell you about my sister even if I wanted to. I love her but we're not very alike and I've been away a long time. Even when we were girls – I mean, yes we were close then but we were still very different people. Isabel was always turned on by clothes and possessions. I wasn't.'

'I know that...' He pushes his hands into his pockets, his face darkening. 'I know she makes a big deal out of designer labels and shit like that. I'm not sure what it is – to be honest. I know we've not got much in common. In fact I think *we're* probably more suited to each other than she and I. You and me, I mean. Isn't that ironic?'

I stare back at him, surprised as I realise what it is he's saying; that we're around the same age and single, yet both futilely attracted to people who are unavailable. For a couple of moments I feel him staring at me intently – gosh, is he actually considering it? – and suddenly I'm experiencing a slightly distasteful sensation of smugness. Is he saying he likes me? Is he saying that *just for once I might be preferable to my beautiful sister?* I have to admit I find him attractive; his bone structure beneath those glasses is exquisite and he's definitely more my type than Isabel's. Just for a split second I'm astounded by my own fickleness as Tom's forgotten, Kerem's forgotten, and I'm thinking *well who knows, maybe at another time...*

But then he adds in a despairing voice, 'Do you think it's possible to be driven mad by love?'

His words deliver a wholly deserved punch into my solar plexus, simultaneously winding and humiliating me even though he's no idea what I'm thinking.

'Are you being driven mad?' I respond finally, because I have to say something.

He shrugs. 'I've never loved anyone the way that I love her.'

'It's only because you can't have her.'

He surprises me then, throwing back his head and laughing

in a manic way, then striking his forehead for effect. 'Oh right? Thanks. She told you that, did she?'

'She's told me nothing.'

'Come on, you don't expect me to believe that...' and his eyes abruptly narrow, holding me in their sights. 'After you caught us that evening – she must have said something about the way she feels.'

But it's easier to lie. 'Not really. I told you – we're not close. We used to be, but not now. Look, all I mean is that you can't have her now, at this time. I mean, *really* have her. She's got kids. She's married. You're just letting yourself in for so much hurt – can't you see that?'

'Yes,' he interrupts, roughly. 'I know. So what? I love her.' He places his hands on the edge of a shelf and starts slowly rocking back and forward.

'I really have got to go,' I say.

I hear him exhale. Then his hands tighten around the shelf and he stares up at me. 'Okay.'

'Thanks for showing me your work. It's very very good. You should concentrate on that – try to forget all this other stuff. It really doesn't matter, you know. The only thing that matters is doing what you want to do and trying to make a success of it. When you look back in years to come that's all you'll care about – you won't be thinking about Isabel, I promise.'

His body stilling, he gives me a strange look but doesn't reply. Then picking up the bunch of keys, he steps past me out into the yard. 'I'll need to let you out.'

I follow his hunched figure through the floodlit driveway. As we step out into the woods, the beeches tower above us like black sentinels.

'So what shall I say to Isabel?' he says when he reaches the gate. His hand's resting on its wrought-iron ring, his body almost silhouetted by the bright security light thrown from the house.

'That we met and you're worried if this continues, her perfect marriage will crumble and your nieces and nephews will come from a broken home? *He* will find out, you know.'

I'm aware of my brow raising, my lips unwinding into a cynical smile. I know he sees it too because he winces, even, though he's asked for it.

'No, it's okay,' I say. 'Just tell her I said hello.'

10

TOM

I wake to the sound of the Zoom ringtone and as I reach over the pillow for the iPad, I'm thrown into muddled disarray. It's usually me who Zooms, not the other way round, and in my hungover state, I'm struggling to remember how to pick up the call. Eventually I locate the green receiver icon and tap it with my finger.

Stella's face appears, looking stressed.

'Hey, what's up?' I say, leaning her against my upturned knees.

I'm lying in the same bed I slept in as a child, in the same small, oblong bedroom with its familiar chequered wallpaper, faded now and pocked with bits of ancient Blu Tack from where I'd once hung my Bowie posters. I'm surprised Dad even bothered to take them down. The few items of clothing I left behind all those years ago still hang in the wardrobe or lie folded in its cheap pine drawers – now faded and musty. It made me feel strange when I first saw them, like I'd come back to my seventeen-year-old self. My seventeen-year-old life.

Stella's in the office. I can see the notice board behind her, and the large door to the left which opens from the forecourt.

Through the sunlit glass I can just make out the blurred green outline of a *Donnelly's* lorry.

'It's that damned Hogarth's order, Tom. You said he wanted everything to go to the Sydney branch but their distribution guy's just said that's not right. Apparently they need five hundred units up at Brisbane. There's no mention of Brisbane on the system.'

I push myself into a sitting position and pull back the curtain to see a deserted playground. It's a different day to yesterday. A worried breeze stirs the tops of the sycamore trees and over the school's roof, a reddening dawn warns of rain.

'Yeah, that's right,' I say, my finger trailing along the window's chipped paint. 'Five hundred to Brisbane Wednesday latest. It's there in the email.'

'Well it's not on the system.'

'You're sure?'

'Yes.'

I stare at her for a moment, and she stares back at me. She's got a lot of make-up on – even more than usual. Her long hair falls loosely around her face and I can tell she's straightened it – something she usually only does when she's going out on an evening. She looks great – more great than I'd like for a working day and suddenly I wish I had the roster to hand to check if John's on a run today, and I'm just about to broach the question when I hear Anna's voice in the pub last night: *'It's the worst thing with infidelity, you know. The suspicion... getting paranoid but never really knowing what's going on,'* so I tell myself to pull myself together. Besides, like I've got a right to complain.

'Well it's no real problem,' I say after a moment. 'Just send another lorry and call back the extra units. If it leaves now there should be enough time.'

'There's no stock left at the depot. Everything's on its way to Sydney.'

'Shit.'

'What shall I do? Just ask Rick to turn and head over to Brisbane? It'll be late though – there's no avoiding it.'

'Yeah, do that. Offer Hogarth a free load next time, and some compensation to meet any losses. I'll write and tell him I'm sorry for the confusion.'

She watches me for a moment, then nods. 'It'll only be a few hours late if Rick puts his foot down and maybe does one overnight.'

'Tell him to do that and offer him a bit extra.'

'I will.'

There's a pause. Then she says, 'How's Jim today?'

'Don't know yet. I'm still in bed.'

'I can see. You look a state, hey.'

I hear the office door opening and then a shadow falls on the wall behind her. She glances to her right and I think I see mild alarm in her eyes.

'Who's that?'

She looks back at the screen. 'Just John come to hand in his time sheet.'

'How come he's not on the Hogarth order?'

'How come you're not on the Hogarth order, John?' she echoes, turning back to her right.

John Harris suddenly leans down into the camera and grins widely over her shoulder, displaying his tanned face and impressive row of teeth. 'G'day, Tom, how're you going? I've just finished the Jameson's run, that's why.'

'Hi, John,' I reply, and raise a hand slowly in mock salute. I force myself to smile and strain inwardly to mute the resentment from my voice.

'How's life with the poms? Stella says you're...'

A moan rises up the stairs, and I can hear Dad's weak voice calling my name. This is followed by a loud crash.

'Gotta go, guys,' I say quickly. 'Dad needs me. I'll call you later, Stel.'

I tap the red receiver icon and place the iPad back on the bedside table before throwing the duvet aside and rushing downstairs to find my father face down on the floor, the blankets piled across his middle. The drip stand leans over him, its line still attached to his cannula.

'Jesus wept, Dad.'

I pull the blankets off him and lift him in my arms as you would a child. He feels lighter than Indiana, my five-year-old. I lay him gently back down on the couch and pull the duvet over his legs and feet, noticing with distaste the purple vine of varicose veins that run behind his knees, the yellowing, thickened toe nails and the deep parmesan crusts of his heels.

Placing a pillow under his head, I return the stand to its usual position.

'Need ... a crap ...' he says.

'Why didn't you call, hey? I'll get the pan.'

'I did ... call.'

I go to the kitchen and fetch the bedpan. 'Sorry, Dad,' I say, trying to suppress the agitation in my voice as I hold my breath against the inevitable stench which follows. After all, it's not his fault he's old and ill. And it's not his fault what's happening with my marriage either. 'I was talking to Stella. Want some breakfast?'

But he shakes his head and looks towards the window with moribund eyes.

'You in pain?'

And I know that he must be bad, because usually he denies it but this time he closes his eyes then gives me a very slight nod.

I check the morphine bag to find it half full, then press the dispenser twice to give him a hefty dose. 'You'll feel better in a bit, hey. I'll just go and get some clothes on and then I'll be with you.'

I empty his bedpan into the toilet before heading back up the stairs to take a shower and dress. I return to find him drowsing, his eyes half closed, his breathing slow and heavy.

I tidy around him, straightening his sheets and putting a fresh box of tissues on the table. Then I go outside into the overcast morning and chop some logs from the almost-depleted pile, placing them in a large wicker basket that I heave indoors before building a fire. Once that's going, I go to the kitchen and fix myself a coffee which I carry outside with me.

As I lower myself onto the doorstep and roll my first fag of the day, I'm still smarting over that Zoom call. That look in Stella's eyes when John had first entered the office. Had I imagined it? And if I hadn't, what had it meant?

It's fully light now, but the mild, cloying air is very different to yesterday's crisp chill, and in the distance I think I can hear a rumble of thunder – although it may just be the guns from Salisbury Plain. I used to hear them all the time as a child and it was always difficult to tell the difference.

What are you doing? I told you not to come in here while I was talking to Tom. That's what Stella's look had meant.

I know I'm right.

I also know I'm being a hypocrite.

And at last, just for a moment, I allow myself to remember last night and Anna, the brightness of her eyes as she'd circled the pool table; the slimness of her body when I'd taken her into my arms; the hungry press of her lips against mine. The whole thing had come out of nowhere, but I'd reacted like a moth irresistibly drawn into a flame. I'd pulled back just in time, but my wings were still singed.

The sound of an engine jolts me out of my meditations. I turn to see a truck laden with logs backing slowly into the yard.

'Morning, Tom,' Ray Curtis says, jumping down from the driver's seat and slamming the door behind him. He's wearing the same hat he had on in the pub last night, but the usual buckskin jacket has been replaced with a grey Arran coat. 'Brought you some logs.'

'Cheers, Ray, that's good timing – we're nearly out.'

'I saw.'

He raises the lever and the truck spills its goods with a loud clatter over the driveway. I crush the cigarette under my heel, then together we gather armfuls of the wood and stack it under the blue tarpaulin.

'Good night last night?' he ventures cagily as we work. He's looking at me sideways and his lips wear a knowing smile.

'Yes, thanks,' I say. 'Hey, Anna and I just went for a drink, that's all. We used to know each other a bit as kids.'

'She's an attractive girl.'

I shrug. 'I guess she is.'

He looks as if he's contemplating asking more, but in the end remains silent.

'Stay for a coffee?' I ask when we're done. 'Dad'll be pleased to see you. He's been asking where you've got to.'

'Sure,' he says, swiping his hands against his thighs.

I push open the front door. 'Come on through.'

We enter the sitting room to find Dad awake. His face is turned towards the door and his eyes flicker with sudden light as he sees Ray.

'Hallo, old friend,' says the latter, taking off his coat and laying it on the back of the sofa. 'How're you keeping?'

'Ray...' Dad stretches out a hand and for a moment they wrap fingers. He stares up at Ray with a steady, unblinking gaze.

'Good to see you, Jim. Sorry I've not been round but I thought you'd want to spend some time with your boy.'

'Aye, but still no need for you to be ... a stranger.'

'I shan't be after today.'

'How do you take your coffee, Ray?' I ask, moving into the kitchen.

'Just black, thanks,' he replies. 'No frills.'

I go into the kitchen and fix him a mug of instant. When I return, he's perched on the arm of the chair and staring into Dad's face. Dad's murmuring something to him but I can't make out his words. Then Ray slowly nods before turning to take the coffee from me.

He doesn't stay long. Just enough to give Dad an update on the business and the various goings-on in the village. Apparently Mike, like many other landlords in the area, is thinking of quitting The Catherine Wheel. The brewery have put up his rent for the third time and he's had enough.

'As soon as a pub does well,' says Ray, 'this is what they do. It's a travesty.'

'Won't be any pubs ... left ... soon ... after covid and this inflation crisis,' Dad replies, but his words taper off and I realise the morphine is kicking in.

They talk a little more. Then Ray stands and hands me his half-empty mug. 'Well, I'd best be off. Got a lot of orders today. Good to see you, Jim. I'll pop round later in the week.'

When we get to the front door, Ray turns and lowers his head in a confidential manner. 'He's not looking good, Tom. Use the time you've got left, my friend. Seriously – take it from one who knows.'

He says this in a weighted tone and I think suddenly of his parents, killed in that car crash when he was just in his twenties. Then he raises a hand before turning and tramping his way across the gravel back to the truck.

I close the door and return to the sitting room. Dad's eyes are closed but his lips are moving.

'You okay, Dad? Need anything?'

He shakes his head.

I stand and watch him for a moment, then turn away. I'm about to go back upstairs to email Hogarth's, when I feel his fingers touch my hand.

'Did I tell you about ... the barbecue?' he says.

I stare down at him patiently, sensing more morphine-induced ramblings coming my way.

'What barbecue, Dad?'

His fingers wrap around my wrist. 'The barbecue with Wendy and Ian. You remember!' he pants. 'The couple at the ... campsite. You went shopping.'

I open my mouth to speak, then close it, mystified.

'You bought chicken and came out of the shop ... in Buncrana. You saw me.'

The room is suddenly shrouded in darkness and rain begins to pepper the window panes. I glance through them to see a massive black cloud swelling over the school's roof.

'I told Father Crotty ... about you.' His eyes are still closed. He looks as if he's asleep. Perhaps he is. But somewhere deep inside, and no doubt fuelled by the morphine, the cogs of his mind are busily working.

'Told him about what?' I say slowly, because I'm only just cottoning that he thinks he's speaking to my mother.

'About *you*,' he retorts in an insistent voice. 'I told him I was sleeping with ... you.'

I'm silent for a moment, considering. Then I say softly, 'Why did you do that, hey?'

He opens his eyes at that, and glares at me. 'My da ... I told you ... Eileen. Don't you remember? My da told me to confess.'

I drop onto the same arm of the chair where Ray was sitting just a minute ago and watch him in silence. I can't work out if there's a thread running through his words, or whether he's just throwing out isolated snatches of memory.

'I was with O'Malley. You saw me remember ... in Buncrana with the ... chicken? I didn't speak to you and Jesus ... you were so angry.' He pulls his hand from mine and rests it on his stomach.

Outside the window a woman passes by. For a moment I think it's Anna. She wears a maroon coat similar to the one Anna often wears. But when I look closer I see she's older than Anna, and her hair is fair, not brunette.

'Who's O'Malley?' I say.

He raises the hand from his stomach with its cannula and line, and scratches awkwardly at his neck. A minute or so passes, then his eyes suddenly open and he thrusts his body forward with a surprising strength. 'No!' he says. 'Oh Jesus ... no! What in Christ's name did you do that for you stupid ... bastard!'

I take hold of his shoulders and try to push him back down, but he struggles frantically against my hands and nearly falls off the couch in his effort to push me aside. 'Jesus ... I can't see. We've got to get out ... of here!' he yells through gasped, snatched breaths. 'Help me, Sean! I can't ... see ... a thing!'

'Dad!' I shout, forcing him back against the couch. 'Dad, wake up...'

'Aaaaghhhh!' he wails, and I've never heard a sound like it. It rises from his throat, strangled and drawn out. Pushing against me with his hands, he flings himself back against the couch, his breaths coming fast and hard.

Then abruptly he turns away and folds his head into his arms.

'Dad,' I whisper eventually. 'Dad, it's Tom. Try to wake up.'

A minute or so passes. Then an arm slowly lifts and his eyes are open. 'Tom?' he whispers.

'Yes, Dad?'

'Tom. Is that you? Are you ... home?'

'Yes, Dad, it's me. I'm home. What were you dreaming about?'

He stares at me, then his eyes sweep downwards. 'Nothing,' he says. 'You're not to worry.'

I'm silent, staring down at him and fighting my frustration that none of this is making any sense and I really need to get on. But then I remember those words of Ray's just now when he left, and I remind myself that no matter how confused I feel about this man and the litany of question marks he's left over my life, that soon these incoherent ramblings won't be possible any more. He won't be repeating himself any more. He won't be speaking of his life with my mother any more – because he won't be here.

His body abruptly buckles, then he kind of convulses and half-rises in the bed. 'You must know love ... Tom,' he says, with sudden urgency. 'You must know ... love in your ... life.'

'I do know love, Dad,' I say. But as he drops back down, something in his eyes as he stares up at me tells me that he doesn't believe me.

'I mean *real* love ... like the love I knew with ... your mother.'

'I know what you mean.'

'Do you?'

'Yeah.' But even as I say it, I can hear the shadow of uncertainty beneath the word.

He turns his face away.

'Dad I...'

'I really loved your mother. I loved her blue eyes ... the way they creased when she laughed. I loved her voice. Remember her soft ... voice? She was strong ... magical, brave. When she walked into a room everyone felt better. She was ... like a warm light. I was a better ... person ... with her. She completed ... me.'

'I know that, Dad.'

'Falling in love with her was like ... jumping from a plane ... without a parachute.'

'Dad, you're not looking well. Should I call an ambulance?' And he's not. His pupils are dilated, and there's spittle all around his lips, the latter of which are as white as his skin. As he speaks, I can hear phlegm blocking the words in his throat and he shifts constantly from side to side as he speaks.

He gasps, then lets out a long moan. I rise up and pull my phone from my jacket pocket to dial 999. The service controller quickly agrees to send out an ambulance.

He's silent throughout the call, but when I put the phone back in my pocket his face slowly swivels and his eyes seek me out.

'I found her,' he whimpers. 'I found her, you know, Tom. I– It was me.'

I reach over and pull a tissue from the box. 'Found who? Who are you talking about?'

'Eileen. Did you know I found her?'

I'm silent for a moment. Then uncertainly, 'You mean you found Mum's body? Yeah, Dad, I knew that.'

I *did* know it, but for some reason I'd chosen never to think about it, and he'd never attempted to speak to me about it before. Mum had woken up one morning, about a year after Callum's death, and after sending me off to my grandparents for the day, had swallowed a bottle of sleeping pills.

'Came back for my lunch to find her ... lying there on the sofa.' He turns his face to the side and there's a long, smothered retching sound before, 'I-I ... never thought she would ... do that, Tom. Why in Christ's name did she do that? She was the strong one. I was the one ... everyone blamed ... Not her. She said it was ... her fault. But it wasn't.'

Gently, I wipe the spit away from around his mouth and,

taking a deep breath, fight to quell the panic inside my chest. Then I say, 'What was her fault, Dad?'

He closes his eyes and slowly shakes his head.

'Dad?' I repeat. 'What was her fault? You mean Callum?'

'He put out her flame. He took away her ... hope.'

'Who did, Dad? *Who* took away her hope?'

Outside the rain's coming down hard. It slams against the window panes and the cottage seems to creak under its weight.

'I didn't mean. I didn't ... It's me who should be sorry...' and tears are suddenly winding their way down his face. They drip from his nose onto the pillow's white cotton.

'You didn't *what*? Dad, please try and explain. You're not making any sense.'

But he turns his head away and several minutes pass before he suddenly moans and his body curls up, braced against the pain. I pull out my phone to check the time, and at that moment hear the ambulance drawing up outside, followed by footsteps and a hard banging on the door.

'Thanks,' I say, opening it to the paramedics – a man in his forties whose smiling black face fleetingly reminds me just how stubbornly white Fawley has remained, and a younger, blonde woman. Their jade shoulders are sodden with rain. 'It's my father,' I say. 'He's really bad and he's up to the limit with morphine.'

The woman nods and moves towards the sitting room like she knows the place already. I follow her in and watch her lean over Dad as her colleague brings in the stretcher. I hear Dad mumble something, and then utter another cry of pain as they gently lift him onto it.

I step back as they wheel him out. His eyes are still open and they lock into mine as he passes. I grab an ancient golfing umbrella from the hallway and hold it over his face as they raise the stretcher into the ambulance.

'I'll follow you in the car,' I call to him, but my words are lost in the thud of the rain against the umbrella and at the same time his face becomes obscured by the male paramedic who's leaning over him and feeding a line into his cannula.

Eventually the man steps back and my father raises his head slightly to peer at me over the blankets. His lips move but I can't make out the words so, closing the umbrella, I climb into the ambulance. I lower my head towards him.

'What's that?'

He makes that chewing motion again then reaches for my hand. 'Speak to Ray... ask... Ray,' he mutters.

'Why? What does Ray know?'

His gaze holds mine, blinking hard. There's a short silence, then he whispers, 'I'm frightened, Tom.'

I hear the paramedic moving around impatiently behind me. 'I'm sorry, Mr Donnelly, but we really need to close these doors,' he says.

I nod briefly over my shoulder, then turn back to my father. I clutch his fingers in mine. 'I know, Dad,' I say helplessly. 'But it'll be all right. I promise.'

'Will it?' he responds, then he looks to the side and another tear winds down his face. 'Do you think Eileen will be there ... in heaven?' he adds. 'Do you think she's waiting for me? I hope ... so. But I told God to burn in hell after ... Callum. What if He doesn't let me ... in now?'

Hearing one of the doors slam shut behind me, I straighten and release his hand. 'He'll let you in, Dad, I promise,' backing away from him. 'Of course he'll let you in.'

He mutters something in reply but I don't hear it because I'm halfway down the steps and the paramedic's pulling the other door to, shutting me out before making his way to the front of the ambulance. A few moments later, the engine starts and I watch in silence as it heads off into the rain.

11

ANNA

The following Sunday afternoon, I arrive back from a walk to find Isabel's finally shown her face, turning up unannounced with Bill and the children 'for a quick coffee' on their way home from a matinee showing at the Marlborough Palace cinema. I feel a surge of irritation as soon as I walk through the kitchen door to see them all, knowing she'd do exactly this, use her family as her decoy to ward off further confrontation after our row on the driveway. I stare at her as she stands by the dresser, looking elegant in a cream silk blouse and green linen skirt.

I greet them with a quick 'hello' before going to hang my scarf in the utility room.

'Long time no see, Anna...' says Bill as I return, leaning back in his chair and eyeing me up and down. 'You're looking well.'

I fetch a glass from a cupboard and go to the sink without looking at him. 'I'm feeling it, thank you,' I reply, filling the glass with water and gulping it down.

'I expect that means you'll be heading back to Turkey soon?'

'Yes, I suppose it does.'

There's no room at the table as Bill and the children all sit around it, the latter's heads pressed together, engrossed in a colouring book.

'So, big sister, how long's it been since I last saw you?' I say, leaning against the sink. 'Two, three weeks?'

From the corner of my eye I see Bill raise his head and give his wife a look.

'I've been over,' Isabel retorts defensively. 'You know I have. But you're always out bloody walking.'

This, I know, is true. But I also know that phone calls to my mother have preceded these visits – calls which I suspect have been made to establish my absence.

Isabel takes a step forward and ruffles Nathaniel's hair. 'That's a lovely tractor, darling,' she says. 'Why don't you draw some cows and sheep next to it, then it'll be a proper farm.'

Nathaniel grabs a crayon and begins scribbling with long, erratic strokes.

'So what happened with Tom Donnelly the other night?' she says, returning her attention to me.

You mean, how much did he hear of our argument? is what I'm tempted to reply, though, of course, I don't. Something about meeting Alex Strong in the woods has remained with me, but it's not just about pity, it's also to do with the sense of a connection being made between us. Because in those tortured eyes of his I've seen something I recognise – something that's open, torn and raw – and in this reaction I'm sure I'm not being selfish or driven by envy of my sister, but by a genuine fury that she can be so disregarding of another person's vulnerability in order to fuel her own emotional needs.

'They went to the pub together,' my mother interjects. 'She didn't come back for hours, and she was rather sloshed when she finally swayed through the door.'

'Oh *yes*?' Isabel says and gives me a knowing look.

'I had a couple of glasses of wine. So what? It's been long enough.'

My mother hands a crayon to Ella. 'That reminds me,' she says. 'I bumped into Tom this morning. He said for you to pop round.'

'Oh really?' I reply, fighting to keep the eagerness from my voice and sensing Isabel watching me keenly. 'Where did you see him?'

She bends down and points out something in the picture to Ben. 'At the garage. He's looking terribly tired – it sounds like Jim's nearing the end.'

I take a slow breath, then swallow another mouthful of water and turn to my brother-in-law. 'So how's business, Bill?' I say brightly, changing the subject.

As I listen to my brother-in-law lament the effect of Brexit on his company's turnover, I'm dimly aware of the children's heads still bent over that colouring book and Zola sliding in cautiously through the cat flap, but all the time I can feel a growing tingling in my hands and wrists, a dryness in my throat.

Eventually they all rise and there's a scramble of coats being pulled over arms. I hear myself, as if from a distance, saying 'Goodbye' and am aware of Isabel coming up and giving me a brief hug. 'I've left some wine in your bedroom,' she whispers. Then, 'Anna, I'm so sorry. Please let's talk...'

After they leave, it's just my mother and me picking up broken crayons and pencil shavings, and putting away papers and colouring books. But still I wait until I've emptied the dishwasher of last night's crockery and the table's been wiped clean, before I finally go into the utility room and put on my coat.

'I'm just popping round to see Tom then,' I say, sticking my head through the lounge door. My mother's sitting with *The*

Times' crossword spread out across her knees and a dictionary in her hand. 'Won't be long.'

'All right, darling,' she murmurs, without looking up.

I open the back door and make my way down the footpath, turning at its end to see the red Punto parked in its usual place. It's five thirty and though chilly, the village is bathed in a sharp, golden light and the air smells faintly of manure – they must have been muck-spreading the fields. As I walk towards the Punto and turn into the small driveway to make my way around the sawhorse, it feels a little strange to have Tom's permission to finally approach the house rather than head on past it as I usually do. Because during these last weeks, I've felt that kiss has made it, and him, entirely out of bounds.

I come to the front door and ring the bell, but it does not seem to be working. In the end I rap the letter box and wait, but I there's no sound from inside. A minute or more passes. I rap it again then bash the door's peeling paint hard with my knuckles.

Eventually I hear approaching feet, a voice yelling, 'Yeah coming,' before the door opens abruptly to reveal a dishevelled Tom. He stares at me from the darkness of the small hallway. 'Anna.'

We stand in silence for a few moments, absorbing each other. His matted black hair falls across rheumy, red-tinged eyes. I wonder if I've woken him up.

'Hello,' I say awkwardly, and my limbs are suddenly feeling cold. 'Mummy said she saw you this morning – that you said for me to come round.'

I'm waiting for him to invite me in but he doesn't move and his gaze travels languidly over my shoulder in the direction of the school.

'Yeah... I did,' he says, after a long moment. Then he sort of straightens and shakes himself. 'It's good to see you, hey. Come on in. Ray's here.'

He steps back and I find myself following him through the narrow hall into a narrow, damp-smelling sitting room where Ray Curtis sits in a brown armchair before a fire, a tumbler of whisky balanced in the palm of his hand.

'Hi,' I say.

'Hello there,' Ray replies, after a moment, before raising the glass slightly and taking a mouthful of the whisky. His mouth twitches as his eyes rise like two blue shards and take the measure of me.

He'd worn a woolly hat that time we'd met him in the pub, so it was hard to get a gauge on him. But today his hair's loose. It falls over the collar of his buckskin coat in a thick, grey-peppered wave and his chin is lined with fine grey stubble. He's not a very tall man – perhaps five foot ten at most. But he's got broad shoulders and a wide chest, and there's an undoubted intelligence burning in his gaze. It hits me that Ray Curtis is very attractive, yet there's something I find a bit odd about him. He seems defensive in my presence – I noticed it in the pub and it's evident again now. The feeling's reinforced as he suddenly swallows the rest of the whisky and rises.

'Well I'd better be off,' he says, handing the glass to Tom.

'You sure, mate?' Tom replies surprised, taking the glass from him. 'You're welcome to stay.'

'I've had quite enough, my friend. I've got to get that delivery up to the Manor and then I need to do some paperwork.'

Tom shrugs. 'I'll see you out then,' he says.

'Nice to see you again,' Ray adds, his gaze briefly meeting mine before swerving away.

'You too.'

Several minutes pass as I hear the two men talking quietly in the hall, their conversation inaudible. Hanging my coat over the back of a chair, I turn to inspect this room I've walked past so many times, always wondering what mysteries lie behind its small windows. In the far corner lies a fold-out couch with sheets and blankets piled neatly at its end. A stainless-steel drip holder stands next to it and there are assorted boxes and bottles of medicines on the shelf above. I stare at them for several seconds, then force my gaze away towards the peeling wallpaper and worn carpet, the ancient-looking brown sofa and twin armchairs. It's a different world to the one I've just left, and I wonder how Tom must have felt when, as a boy, he'd accompanied his father to Fawley House with its cream-carpeted rooms and immaculate lawn.

There are no ornaments, which is not really surprising in the home of a male widower. But on the far wall next to the window hang two large paintings of what must be Fawley Wood in bluebell season. The room's only other personal effects are a row of framed photographs which stand propped in a line along the narrow mantelpiece. There's a large one of Tom's parents on the day of their wedding, embracing outside Soweton Church and looking very much in love. I recognise Eileen Donnelly's auburn hair, her pre-Raphaelite features. Then with a slight jump, I find my eyes settling on two smaller, school photographs of Tom and Callum.

I step towards them, with my arms folded, enjoying the warmth of the small fire which burns in the grate at my feet. The pictures must have been taken around the time that I attended Fawley Primary – in fact, my mother has one of me and Isabel with the same blue-wash backdrop. Tom looks just as I remember him that first day; simultaneously dark and bright, the Artful Dodger, while his younger, more sensitive brother stares out of the picture without smiling, his pale-blue eyes uncertain.

There's the slam of the front door, then I hear Tom come

back into the room. I turn to see his gaze moving over my shoulder towards the picture of his dead brother.

'Do you remember him?' he says, after a moment.

'Of course I do.'

A muscle twitches beneath his right eye. 'What do you remember?'

I shrug. 'Mainly at school – you know, that term. And also seeing him with you in the woods sometimes when I was out riding. The two of you always had a wheelbarrow.'

He smiles briefly at this, his eyes moving towards me then back towards the photograph.

'Where's Jim, is he in hospital?' I ask. It's a stupid question.

He nods. 'Yeah, but he's picked up a bit so they're bringing him home again tomorrow. Saying it's likely to be the last time.'

'Oh Tom... I'm sorry.' Then I go silent, unsure of myself. Taking a step back, I slowly let myself down onto the sofa, feeling its ancient springs press into my thighs.

He moves to the other side of the fire and begins smoothing a cigarette paper on the mantelpiece. 'Like I said, it's the pain which makes it so hard...' As he licks the paper and seals it around the tobacco, I notice for the first time the yellow nicotine stains on his index and middle fingers. '...You know, with Dad. Watching him being so stoic and trying not to bother me with it. But all the time I'm watching him fighting and losing and getting more and more tired and uncomfortable. It's like it plays with him hey, blows life into him then sucks it right back out again. The morphine makes his mind weird, too.'

He lights the roll-up and takes a long drag before walking to the small window and opening it slightly. Outside, twilight has started to settle over the playground and the air is punctuated by the coos of a wood pigeon, that hypnotic sound so acute to memory, which seems to contain all of rural England.

He stares through the grimy glass for several long seconds.

'But you know what? At the same time, it isn't so hard. Because maybe the wanker deserves to die.'

I pick up the poker and prod at the fire. 'That's a bit harsh.'

He turns round to look at me. 'Come on, Anna,' he says finally. 'You know why I left. Everyone knows.' His brow furrows under his unkempt hair as he sucks on the cigarette, the smoke drowsing out between his lips. 'The other day he was off his head on morphine, and he started saying loads of weird stuff. He said Mum had felt guilty about Callum's death, but that it was him who should really be sorry. Why would he say that unless... you know... he'd had something to do with it? And the thing is...' He smiles grimly and suddenly his eyes are filled with confusion. 'He might have done it. He really might. When he was drunk he could be a right bastard. But to actually *kill* his son? Anna, I just don't know and I've lived with not knowing since I was fourteen years old.'

Closing the window abruptly, he makes his way back across the room towards me, coming to a halt by the fire and leaning forward, one hand gripping the edge of the mantelpiece 'Shit,' he says. Then again, '*Shit.*'

It suddenly hits me – he's drunk – no wonder he was looking so puffy-faced when he opened the door, no wonder this candid talk. Now he's closer, I can smell the beer on his breath and clothes and I wonder how long he's been putting it back. Judging from its acrid smell, the smoke from his roll-up clearly holds more than just tobacco and at the same time I notice several roaches scattered across the hearth.

'I thought he had, you see,' and suddenly now he's forcing his sentences out between choked breaths. 'But I hadn't got any proof... and I couldn't be certain. He was my dad for fuck's sake. I'd been proud of him until Callum... for all his drinking and his temper, he was like a giant to us. And I knew Mum thought he was innocent, so that confused me even more... But after she did away with herself I became convinced he'd done it – why else would she have done something like that? Course, I couldn't ask him back then... I just couldn't let him know what I was thinking because if he *was* innocent it would finish him – and if he was guilty he'd have probably killed me too. In the end the whole thing started making my head explode – I felt like I was going insane, and that's why I left. Left, and got as far away from Fawley as the planet would allow.'

As he breaks off to fling the half-smoked joint into the fire, I find myself recalling that story which Len Combstone told my mother; the mysterious uncle and the dark rumour he'd spread about another dead child in Jim's distant past.

Tom's not mentioned it and the omission makes me realise he probably doesn't know about it. I suppose I should tell him now, but it feels wrong. I'm only just getting to know him and somehow having this knowledge just seems too intimate, and potentially too damning when it's based purely on hearsay.

Tom's eyes rise and hold mine. 'You see, the trouble is ... now I've come back I'm not so sure. I left an ogre and I've come back to a dying old man, a sickly, old white invalid. I just can't find the will to hate him anymore, Anna, and I wasn't expecting to feel like this. I wasn't ready for it and I can't... I look into his eyes and all I can see is happiness that I've finally come back so he can prattle on to me about Mum and Ireland and, you know... all his old man's memories. But nothing else. There's no shiftiness, no guilt. Just pain and...'

'Love?'

For a moment he doesn't move. Then he nods and presses his face into his hands, and I'm rising from the sofa to go to him, my hands stroking his hair. He grips my shoulder and presses his forehead against mine. I can't explain the absolute closeness I feel with him at this moment, the ease with which this is happening, and it's as if he's thinking the same thing because suddenly he says, 'Jesus this is strange, isn't it...?' then his arms are around me and his mouth's on mine, and I taste tobacco and lager on his lips before he pulls back slightly, but only slightly, to look into my face.

'Anna, we mustn't,' he says,

'We won't,' I whisper, staring up at him.

12

TOM

I lie on my side, listening to Anna's breathing; soft and regular, like a contented cat. She sleeps on her side with the length of her body pressed against mine, my arms wrapped tightly around her.

I've no idea what time it is – six maybe, seven? Through the undrawn curtains a yellow ribbon of dawn rises over the school's pitched roof and I can hear the milk float's bottles clinking as it stops and starts along the high street. I've been awake for ages – came to in the darkness with that lurching feeling you get after you've had a load to drink and realise you've done something really fucking stupid.

Random images stumble across my mind as I lie here trying not to wake her, my limbs stiff and numb from keeping still. Dad lying in bed in that hospital ward; the unblinking, hollow and hopeless eyes of the skeletal patients in the beds opposite him. He's only one away from the window bed now; it's got a view of the fields that run down the valley to the M4 and the hills in the far distance. He calls it the 'death bed' because it's the one they put you in when you're about to die.

Then my thoughts flip over to Stella. I spoke to her

yesterday for the first time in a week and let her know his time was near. Of course, she immediately offered to fly over knowing full well there's not a cat in hell's chance she can leave the kids for that length of time. Jesus, she didn't fool me and I could already guess her thought processes – the first was her conscience kicking in – *I offered to come so at least he can't throw that one back at me* – and the second was the knowledge that his death will trigger my return to Australia.

Am I being too hard on her? Of course, my instinct now will be to defend my own infidelity especially when I've no concrete proof of hers. *I can't stop thinking about you* – it still doesn't mean she's actually done anything. The mind's one thing, the body another. Innocent until proven guilty, and all that.

But if I'm honest, Stella's not the only reason I feel like crap. It's also to do with being an out-of-control moron because I've woken up knowing Anna came to the house last night to find me steaming drunk and leery.

After I'd left Dad at the hospital, I'd called into the garage on my way back to get petrol – that was when I saw Liz Carmichael. Then I'd stopped off at the Catherine and stayed there till late afternoon, sinking pints and chasers with Ray Curtis and rapping about the old days before inviting him back here, but all the time I'd kept thinking about what Dad said as they'd lifted him into the ambulance.

We'd already smoked several reefers and sunk another three or four tinnies and I was just about to hit Ray with that question, when Anna appeared at the door and after that it all gets a bit vague. All I can remember is that Ray left and I started going on to Anna about Dad and the next thing we were kissing and my hands were all over her.

I must have dropped off again because I wake to find the room's filled with sunlight and there's the sound of birdsong, footsteps skipping along the pavement outside and women chatting as they drop their kids off at the school.

Anna mutters something in her sleep and turns away from me. I lift my arm to release her, at the same time turning my head to study the strands of dark hair that fall across the white curve of her shoulder. Her back's pressed against me now, and her skin against mine is velvet-soft and smells of musk – the same smell peculiar to her that I noticed that night on the path. I lift a hand and very gently stroke the nape of her neck, allowing myself for a few seconds to forget Stella as I consider this girl who lies besides me and who, if I'm honest, has started occupying my thoughts more than I'd like these last few weeks.

Yawning silently, I slowly push myself into a sitting position. She's lying with her face pressed into the pillowcase. I can just about see the profile of her open lips, the soft curve of her eyelashes. Her breathing stays deep but there's something that makes me wonder if she's feigning it, is lying there playing possum as she also wonders what she's done, because those kids and their parents are being pretty loud. Somehow she's *too asleep*.

I raise myself quietly from the bed, pull on a dressing gown and make my way down the narrow stairs to make a coffee and roll myself a cigarette. Then, picking up an ashtray from the mantelpiece, I go to watch the headmistress lining the children up from the sitting room's small window, my eyes squinting beneath the sunshine's glare.

'Tom?'

I turn to see her, barelegged and shivering, standing at the foot of the stairs. She's wearing the blue denim shirt I had on yesterday, her arms wrapped around herself, her hair hanging untidily across her face as she watches me, wary of my response now that it's morning and cold reality is upon us.

She looks so vulnerable standing there and her eyes are sort of entreating me not to reject her again as I did that night on the path. At the same time, it occurs to me that she wasn't drunk last night and still chose to sleep with me in my inebriated, sleazy state. The look in her face right now, it's like she thinks I'm about to slap her or something, and immediately I'm stubbing out the fag and moving towards her, coming to an uncertain halt in front of her. We stand and stare at each other for a few seconds, searching each other's faces. Then I wrap my arms around her, pulling her shivering body against mine and stroking the back of her head.

'I'm sorry,' she whispers, into my shoulder, her voice muffled by my dressing gown.

'What for?'

'Because you're married. I don't want to cause you any trouble.'

'None of this is your fault, Anna.'

She tightens her grip around my waist. 'You were looking really down just then. Were you thinking about Jim?'

I lean my cheek against the crown of her head. 'No. I was thinking about you.'

There's a silence as neither of us moves. Eventually she steps back and stares up at me for several long moments. The song of those children's voices rises from the playground and the sun seems to blast through the windows even more brightly. She takes my hand and leads me back up the stairs.

Last night we made love in the dark. It was frantic and passionate – but also clumsy, drunken and confused on my part. This morning I seek to correct that; touching her face, her neck and breasts, first with my fingers, then with my mouth. I hear her sigh as I feel her hands moving over my neck and shoulders. I move further down her body, dusting her stomach with kisses. At this point she stiffens and her hands press down on my back, imploring me to stop, but I already know what's troubling her, that hard welt of skin left by the surgeon's knife. Last night, I skirted over it to save her discomfort, but this morning I linger, my lips tracing the wound from end to end.

Afterwards, we lie in each other's arms, listening to the sound of birds and the occasional footsteps of people walking past on the pavement.

'I wonder why Ray left like that,' I say eventually. 'I thought he was in for the long haul – he likes a session, does Ray.'

Anna's quiet for a moment. Then, 'I don't get the impression he likes me very much.'

'He doesn't know you.'

'He seemed to know me better than I know him – you know, when we met him in the pub. He remembered me riding around on Bella all those years ago.'

'Ray never misses a pretty girl.'

I feel her mouth smiling into my skin, then her arms press around me more tightly.

'Would you like it if I told you more about Callum?' she says finally, breaking the silence which follows. She raises her head to look at me. 'You know – stuff I remember about him.'

For a moment I don't answer. I guess I'm a bit taken aback and maybe even a bit moved. Then I nod, slowly. 'Yeah, that would be good.'

She sinks her head back onto my shoulder and I feel her breath drifting over my chest. 'When you were children you were always together. He was always behind you, wherever you went. Like your little red shadow. I remember you both when Jim used to come round and deliver the wood. He always used to hide around the side of the shed, or behind your dad's truck. You were much more forward than him – you'd come into the kitchen with Jim sometimes and kind of wander around looking at everything. I have a feeling that when we were quite small we used to play together a bit. Didn't we climb Mummy's apple tree together? Do you remember? Callum was there too but he was too young so he waited at the bottom for us.'

I turn and kiss her forehead. 'Yeah. Of course I remember. We could see Marlborough Down – once we got to the top.'

'That's right. You don't realise it's that high until you're up there – how funny, I wasn't sure if I was imagining we did that...' She looks toward the ceiling, blinks hard. 'What else? You and Callum looked quite different from each other, didn't you? He looked like Eileen and you looked more like Jim – all dark and dour and on the lookout.'

'Callum was shy. I was always the one in trouble.'

'Tell me about it. I saw you steal a power ball once in the village shop.'

'I stole a *what?*'

'A power ball. Don't you remember – those small, colourful balls that bounced for miles? You thought no one was looking, but I was. You put it in your pocket while Callum distracted Mrs Bussle.'

I hear myself laugh but inside my chest my heart's accelerating. 'Shit. Saw that, did you? Of course I remember. Callum dared me to nick it – it was the only time I nicked anything and I got caught. After we'd gone, Bussle noticed it missing and caught us playing with it on Soweton Road the next day. She came round to tell Dad and he had my hide for it.'

The sun's bright rays flood the room once more. For the first time I notice the thick cobwebs strung across the ceiling's dust-ingrained coved corners; the smears on the window panes, and resolve to clean this room and the rest of the house before Dad returns from hospital.

I feel Anna raise her head, wondering at my silence. 'Was Jim very violent?' she says, after a moment.

I shrug, then shift up the bed slightly. 'Depends what you call violent. Like I said, he could be a bastard when he drank but most of it was verbal... I dunno, he used to smack us around the head now and then for saying things out of turn, but he never actually beat us except that one time – that's why I was surprised, you know, about you being in the shop that day, because Jesus, he really lost it over that ball. He'd been boozing down the Catherine and after Bussle left he took a belt to me. Thinking back, I suppose he was mad because he thought Bussle would be spreading it to all her customers that Jim Donnelly's sons were no-good tea-leafs.'

'It's what some people thought – that Jim killed Callum and your mum knew it. That's why she committed suicide.'

It's difficult to know what to say to this so in the end I stay silent, my gaze levelled at those cobwebs.

'How did she do it, Tom? It's so long ago I can't remember.'

'Overdose.' I reply bluntly. 'Sleeping pills. I was staying in Marlborough with my grandparents. She'd been nagging me to go and see them – kept saying I wasn't seeing enough of them and they weren't going to be around forever.'

'She planned it?'

I sigh. 'Yeah. Set the whole thing up so I wouldn't be here to find her. Guess she didn't want me to go through that a second time...

'Dad found her when he came home for his lunch. They reckon she'd taken the pills straight after I'd left that morning.'

At that I go silent, recalling the second time in my life when the world had stopped. I'd been splayed out on my grandparents' large sofa watching *John Craven's Newsround* when the phone had rung. My grandfather had answered it. I remember hearing his cheery, 'Afternoon, Jim, what can we do for you?' and after a minute or so I'd started to wonder at the silence, eventually turning to see him just standing there, tears dribbling into his grey beard.

'Jesus, I'm not being much of a host here, hey,' I say

suddenly. 'Can I get you some tea or coffee?' But I'm already rising from the bed and pulling on the dressing gown.

She asks for coffee. When I return with a mug of instant she's sitting up with the duvet pulled around her, biting down on her lip and watching me intently. I place her mug on the window sill then sit down next to her.

'I wonder what made her do it,' she says. 'While she still had you, I mean.'

I shrug. 'She didn't leave a note, so we'll never really know. But I guess she was way more depressed than anyone realised.'

She blows on her coffee, then sips at it.

'Do you remember the snow on the day Callum disappeared?' I say suddenly. 'Jesus – it was some of the heaviest I've ever seen.'

She lowers the mug to her chest and nods. 'I remember.'

'It was the last day of term. That morning, I promised him we'd build a sledge to take on Angel Hill.' I lean over her and open the bedroom's small window. 'It was the last thing I ever said to him...

'Then I went to school. It snowed all morning and eventually they closed the building but it was too late. One of the buses ended up jack-knifed across the access road, blocking the way for the others, so I had to walk down into town and wait for Mum to come and fetch me. She left Callum a note telling him where she'd gone and that she'd be back soon...'

'Isabel got stuck in Marlborough that night – Mummy said she'd never seen the roads that bad.'

I nod. 'When we finally got home Dad was already back – he'd packed up early because of the weather – but there was no sign of Callum. At first we thought he must have gone sledging, or to a mate's. But when teatime came and went and, you know, still no Callum and no phone call – well, it was obvious something wasn't right.

'Dad called the police around nine. It took them several hours to get to us and Mum was going out of her mind. To begin with you could tell they thought he'd run away, even though my folks went out of their way to convince them Callum was a happy kid, you know... Mum kept insisting there weren't any problems and also, well why would he run away in weather like that? He hadn't even taken his coat. Besides, Christmas was coming and he was really looking forward to it.

'A few days went by – including Christmas Day – then a few more, and I could see the coppers were finally waking up to the facts. On the afternoon he'd gone missing, he was seen leaving the school and going around the back of the house – so we know he'd got home, and the thing about the hat and the coat... Well it was unlikely he'd gone out again – least not of his own choice. Trouble is, by then the snow had thawed so they never knew if there'd been other footprints on the driveway or in the garden at the back. That was an almighty, unforgivable fuck-up on their part.

'Dad had been working on his own that day. He always did Fawley, Milbury and the south villages, and Ray covered Soweton and Avebury. Dad said he'd packed up just after four and came back to an empty house. Didn't think much about it – assumed Mum had taken us Christmas shopping and was having trouble getting home because of the snow. He was lighting the fire when me and Mum came in – only without Callum.'

I close my eyes for a second and picture it. Walking into the sitting room ahead of Mum to see Dad kneeling at the hearth, snapping kindling over his knee. He'd turned and looked up at me with a weird look in his eyes. He'd been wearing this look since the episode with the belt but I couldn't work out if it was shame at what I'd done, or what he'd done to me.

Over my shoulder Mum had said, 'Where's Callum?' and

he'd replied, 'I thought he was with you...' followed by a silence before he'd shrugged and said, 'Well he must have gone round to Paul Combstone's house,' only by then Mum had stepped back into the hallway. 'But his coat and hat are here,' and she'd called his name up the stairs and Dad had stood up to pull back the curtain and was watching the flakes drifting down under the street lamp. And after that it was just one slow drip after drip of cold realisation, landing minute after minute, hour after hour, day after day, until there was no getting away from the truth of it – my little brother wasn't coming home. Not then. Not ever.

I'm aware, suddenly, that a long silence has passed. I turned to see Anna watching me, that mug of coffee cupped in her palms, her body pressed back against the headboard. 'Go on,' she says softly.

I sigh and lean forward, placing my elbows on my knees and winding my fingers together. 'The police kept taking Dad in for questioning. Then they came to see me and Mum. They asked us if he'd ever hit us. I didn't tell them about the belt incident but Jesus, if enough fingers are pointing... You're different when you're fourteen – you just feel this blind emotional shit. I guess I just started to think, "They obviously think Dad did it so it must have been him" – plus he was the next one in the house after Callum so at the time it did seem *kind of* obvious. It's only later you start to rationalise. There were no witnesses, no sign of any attack. They must have thought he'd got pissed and lost his temper but they never found Callum's blood on his clothes, or around the house. Plus he didn't keep guns – Callum was shot. Why would Dad do that? And you know what?' I raise my hands in the air. 'Looking back, he just didn't act like a man who had killed his son. Every time I come back to it I remember the look in his eyes that day we came home and Mum had asked where Callum was, and there was nothing there but true concern, you know, at that moment...'

I drop my head and stare at the floor, my hands hanging between my knees. What I'm not telling her is that these observations are actually pretty new to me too – it's not stuff I'd really thought about back in Australia. Over there, I was convinced Dad was guilty and was sitting here in this cottage day after day rotting in the cancer brought to him by divine retribution. What I'm telling her now... Well, I've only really just started to consider it myself.

A sudden breeze lifts the faded curtains. From next door's garden comes the blast of a lawnmower's engine starting up.

'Then he probably didn't do it, Tom,' Anna says. 'It doesn't sound like he did...'

But immediately I rise to my feet and walk across the room, coming to a halt at the doorway. Pressing a hand against its frame with my back to her, I rest the other on my hip and stare down at the carpet.

'What is it?'

'There's something else – something the police don't know.'

I hear her place the mug back on the sill. 'What?'

Leaning back against the door, I stare at the back of my hand for a moment before returning reluctantly to sit back on the edge of the bed. 'It's something Dad said on the day of the funeral. We'd just got back from the wake – him, Mum and me. I went up to use the loo. When I was coming back down the stairs I overheard them talking in the kitchen. Dad was saying, "I've got to tell them, Eileen..." and Mum replied, "Don't you dare, Jim. What good would it do? They'll put you in prison and then what would become of me and Tom?"

'Later I asked her about it, but she insisted they weren't talking about Callum – she said it was something to do with the business and money, and I guess that's what I wanted to believe too, so for a while I did. It wasn't till after she died that it started to bug me, that bit of eavesdropped conversation. And I guess it's gone on bugging me ever since because neither of them were ever the same again after Callum died and it's hard to, you know, know what was grief, or something else. Looking back, I just have this really strong sense that Mum knew something. That they *both knew* something. And that stuff he said to me the other day, about them both feeling guilty. Well that just confirms it, doesn't it?'

I take a deep breath, turn to look at Anna. She's watching me intently, her brow knotting beneath the long fringe, her skin almost translucent under the bright sunshine which pours through the window. Then she shifts herself down the bed slightly, the duvet still wrapped around her. I feel her fingers folding themselves softly around my wrist. 'Tom, how did you know Callum's body would be at the Shadowing Stones?'

I rise abruptly back to my feet, pulling my hand from her grasp and walking to the far side of the room. I stand with my back to her, my arms folded, staring at the wall before me. Then, closing my eyes, I let my forehead fall against the faded wallpaper and take several long deep breaths before shaking my head. 'I don't want to talk about that.'

But in my mind's eye that scene's playing itself out once more, like a cine reel on my retina; waking up in the early hours with an acute instinct; walking through the darkness along the lane to Milbury, before crossing the A4 onto the track as the sun rose on a brilliant mid-summer dawn. Climbing over the stile into the meadow as the cries of sheep echoed up from the Grey Wethers Valley. Then walking through that sea of blood-red poppies with dread weighing down my heart, the cries of those sheep seeming to increase in volume as those three silhouetted stones rose out of the mist – as if they were waiting for me. Jesus, that's exactly how it felt. *They were waiting for me.*

Outside, the sound of that mower ceases, followed by a relief of silence; a second later there's a banging sound as its user empties its drum of grass. I feel Anna come up behind me and put her arms around me, her face pressed against my back.

I turn and she's standing before me naked, her dark hair hanging over her shoulders, her gaze holding mine. Then she unfolds my arms and, holding my hands in hers, leads me slowly back to the bed. Taking off the dressing gown, I climb under the duvet next to her and pull her against me.

'He was only eleven years old,' I whisper.

And I hear her say, 'I know.'

'How scared must he have been? He was just a kid...' then my voice chokes and I can feel her lips brushing the tears from my cheeks as outside that school bell rings for first break and the song of the children's playing fills my head.

Closing my eyes, just for a second, I imagine I can hear Callum's voice among them and he's shouting, 'I'm over here, Tommy,' and I'm turning around to watch him leaping out from behind a tree in Fawley Wood. We're playing hide-and-seek to break the tedium of collecting the windfall; there are bluebells everywhere, my mother used to call them 'the flowers of optimism', and the sun's out. It's May – his final May on this earth – and he's grinning because just for a moment he had me going there, thinking he'd vanished. He's my brother and he's just eleven years old, and his eyes are shining with the promise of the life he'll never get to live.

13

ANNA

After we've risen from the bed and dressed, I follow Tom downstairs into the hallway. For a second we stand facing each other wordlessly before he lifts my coat down from its peg and places it around my shoulders. He leans forward and kisses me lightly on the lips. 'Thank you for a great night, hey,' he says, at the same time dropping his arms to his sides and taking a slow step backwards.

I hover on the driveway, unwilling to leave just yet. 'So when do you think you'll go back to Australia?'

His gaze lowers to the carpet and it's hard to read his expression in the dull light. 'You mean after Dad dies? Soon as I've organised the funeral and sorted out his stuff.'

'You'll sell this place...' and as I say it, I'm already struggling to imagine Fawley without the Donnellys. The house will remain of course, but the people who'll buy it will be strangers – new people who will have surnames I won't recognise and, as a result, won't concern me. They'll most likely be wealthy because you need a fair bit of money to buy a house in Fawley these days. Half the village seems to be second homes now, owned by London people, although I know it's ripe for me to think that. No doubt they'll do a tasteful job on it; they'll sort out the roof and re-render the walls; the wood pile will be removed and the front yard covered in fancy paving, or a well-trimmed patch of lawn, and the broken trellis will be replaced without a thought ever being given to how it got torn down in the first place.

The next moment, Tom's stepping forward and pushing the door open for me in a way that feels definite and irreversible. But there's an air of uneasiness about him as I step onto the drive and squint into the bright morning sunshine, the breeze sending my hair in a bang across my face. I turn round to stare at him with something approaching panic; unwilling to say goodbye just yet and at the same time feeling horribly aware he's not asking to see me again.

I don't blame him. Looking at him standing before me now, his eyes staring at something beyond my right shoulder, I can almost see the weight of his responsibilities lowering back onto his shoulders. Of course it's no use, yet I linger, because there's still so much I want to say. All those nuggets of shared experience, the people we both knew as children, the places we've both been and the things we've done since leaving this village. We've barely touched on any of it. And maybe it's because I'm lost and hurting from Kerem, and losing him and Istanbul is forcing me to turn to the only real home I know – I don't know – but Tom's the one thing in my life which makes sense right now. Finding him's been like coming across a life raft in the middle of a vast, unnavigable sea, but how can I tell him any of this when he isn't mine, and when in the playground the children play and the windows of the houses opposite overlook us, and if we're not careful last night's liaison will be the talk of the village?

So instead I step back, and clutching my pride to my chest like a well-worn toy, say decisively, 'Goodbye, Tom.'

And without a flicker he replies, 'See you.' But just for a moment his gaze moves back to mine and he stands there with an unreadable expression. The sunlight's blazing down on his face, accentuating the shadows under his eyes, the fine fray of broken veins around his nose and cheeks. Then, sighing heavily, he reaches out a hand to squeeze my shoulder. 'Take care of yourself, hey.'

* * *

I make my way home and enter the kitchen to find my mother standing against the dresser with bowed head, her pale lips pursed and brow knotted, running her thumb and index finger back and forward along that gold spectacles chain.

Bill's sitting at the table, his body slumped forward like a limp reed, face pressed into his forearms. When he hears me enter he lifts his head and struggles to compose himself, taking off his glasses and wiping them on his jumper. But he doesn't smile or rise to peck me on both cheeks, which is his usual way.

'Hi, Bill,' I say. I watch him for a moment then, at a loss for what to say or do, step past my mother towards the kettle.

'Where on earth have *you* been?' she hisses under her breath.

I glance at the clock above the dresser. It's gone eleven. 'At Tom's. Sorry – we sat up late talking and I ended up crashing out on his sofa.'

'The door was unlocked all night. Anybody could have walked in.'

'This isn't Peckham, Mummy. They were hardly likely to, were they?' I turn to my brother-in-law. 'I'm making some proper coffee, Bill. Would you like one?'

He stares back at me without smiling, then slowly shakes his head. I notice for the first time how wretched he looks: his face blotchy and swollen, and his hair uncombed and swept up into a strange wave. He's usually impeccably turned out, with creased trousers and crisp white shirts, but the tie-less suit he's wearing this morning looks soiled and crumpled. Fine bits of fluff cling to his collar and sleeves.

'Bill, are you okay?' I say, coming to a standstill.

'He slept in his car last night,' my mother says. 'At the end of the drive. I found him there when I took the recycling bin down this morning.'

I stare hard at my brother-in-law, trying to absorb this information through a smog of tiredness and confusion. I've entered the kitchen with a head full of Tom; the enormity of what took place between us last night and that final, impassive farewell. I didn't come home expecting to find a family scene and my brain's finding it hard to adjust.

'You knew about him, Anna, didn't you?' Bill says suddenly, pushing a hand through his hair and altering the slant of that strange quiff.

I pour boiling water into a cafetiere. 'Knew about who?' I say.

'This Alex Strong bloke.'

I look across at my mother who raises her eyebrows and glares at me as if to say, *Go on then, tell him to stop being such an idiot*, but instead I sigh, then shake my head. I haven't got the energy to lie. 'Izzy didn't tell me about him. I caught them together once in her car and I told her to finish it. We had a massive argument – in which I took your side, by the way – and I'd not seen her till she came here with you yesterday.'

'So I gather.'

I shrug and slowly press the plunger into the cafetiere, cursing under my breath as brown froth overspills onto the sideboard. Out of the corner of my eye, I'm aware of my mother's arms dropping slowly to her sides, her eyes narrowing with disbelief.

'That's why I was shouting at her the other night, Mummy,' I add. 'I'm sorry, but she begged me not to tell you what it was about.'

Christ – am I actually *enjoying* this? I'm aware of just how easily these words seem to be galloping off my tongue. But what's bothering me more is just how unconcerned I feel about betraying my sister.

A couple of seconds pass, then Bill leans forward, placing his elbows on the table and cornering me with a look of wounded rage. 'Tell me about him,' he says.

Rinsing through a J-Cloth, I mop up those spilt grinds. 'Tell you about who?'

'Cut it out, Anna. What does she see in him? Is it because he's younger than me? I know he's not much over thirty.'

'Come on, Bill...'

'Is he handsome? Sexy? Is that what it is?' he says, rising to his feet and gripping the edge of the table. The movement makes me jump. 'Anna, I want to know. You've seen him. Tell me what she likes about him.'

Outside the strange, unsettled weather continues – the breeze gusting across the windows as the sun bursts through the windows to illuminate the whole kitchen one minute, then throwing it back into dullness the next. I'm aware of my mother stepping back, her head lowering as her fingers tighten around the edge of the dresser. For a moment I'm silent, my heart beginning to thump as I finally realise the depth of my brother-in-law's anguish and the ease with which I've fuelled the flames.

This time I decide it's wiser, and kinder, to lie. 'Look, Bill, I only met him that one time and we probably exchanged two words. If I'm honest I'd say he was rather scruffy and he clearly hasn't got two bob to rub together – I certainly wouldn't say he was Izzy's type.'

'Then what in the hell does she see in him?' he shouts, smashing down his fist and making us both jump. 'She says it's been going on for more than a year so she must *see something*.'

As he spits those last two words a fine spray of saliva coats the table's wooden surface. The sight of it seems to sober him slightly – evidence of his own lack of control perhaps – and he slowly lets himself back down into the chair and stares at the wall opposite with an agitated expression, his eyebrows lifting and falling in response to his thoughts, his fingers splayed along the edge of the table in a way that, ironically, reminds me of Alex Strong in his studio that evening.

I pour the coffee into a mug, then go to the fridge to get some milk. As I pass my mother, she throws me a pointed 'What on earth are we going to do?' look. I shake my head but inside my heart's racing. I've never known Bill behave like this before, never knew he *could* be like this, and suddenly I'm feeling terrible for the way I've always written him off as shallow and entitled – for never seeing the vulnerability beneath the sangfroid.

I place the carton on the table. Then, pulling out a chair, sit down opposite him, stirring the milk into the coffee and blowing on its surface. 'How did you find out?'

He's silent for a second, his eyes shifting back and forward, skirting the plates and mugs along our dresser. 'Actually it was you, Anna.'

'Me?'

He nods. 'When we last came here yesterday, you said you hadn't seen Isabel for weeks. But she told me she'd been coming here every afternoon. She'd even been giving me daily updates on your recovery.'

'Oh.'

'So when we got home I got hold of her handbag and looked at her phone – and that's when I found his texts.'

Phones... What was it that Tom had said about them? *'They make it too damned easy to catch people out, too, even if you'd really prefer to keep your head in the sand.'* What had he meant by that? Did he suspect that Stella actually *wanted* him to catch her out?

Had Isabel wanted to be caught out too?

'Have either of you any idea what this has done to me?' Bill whispers as his gaze sweeps from me to my mother. *'Have you?'*

We stare with dismay at the tears which are running down his face, lost for words at the sight of his anguish. As I reach out a hand and press his forearm, the sun goes in once again and I'm just about to tell him he really needs to be talking to my sister when I become aware of the sound of wheels skidding against gravel. Raising my head to stare out the window, I sigh with relief as I see Isabel's Jeep pulling up next to her husband's Mercedes. The next moment she's slamming the car door and charging across the drive through the garden gate, the latter clanging hard against the wall.

'For God's sake, Bill!' she cries, charging into the kitchen without bothering to shut the door behind her, and turning wildly from her husband to our mother, and then to me. Her gaze holds mine for a second, simultaneously questioning and defiant and I know she's wondering how much I've told them. Then she swings back round to Bill, who's risen to his feet and is hurriedly swiping the tears from his eyes with his shirt cuffs. 'For God's sake...' she repeats, her tone weakening. 'You didn't have to involve Mummy and Anna. This is our business, not theirs.'

Her hair, matted, unclipped, falls down on either side of her face and her make-up is smudged beneath her eyes, giving them a hollow, skull-like appearance. She looks pale and exhausted, and for once she's wearing old clothes, a faded pilled blue jumper hanging loosely over washed-out jeans.

'Did he stay here last night?' she says, turning towards our mother, who stares at her narrowly for some moments before slowly shaking her head. 'I found him asleep in his car this morning – at the end of the drive.'

On hearing this, Isabel's lips begin to twitch uncontrollably. 'Oh Bill, that's just ridiculous...' She reaches across the table to take his hand, but he snatches it away and goes to stand at the kitchen sink, his back turned to us.

A few moments pass, then his shoulders sag. 'Actually, Isabel, as I'm sure your mother and Anna will want to know the reason we're divorcing,' he says, bowing his head, 'it seemed only right to involve them.'

'Oh Bill, no!' my mother exclaims with hands clasped tightly together as she stares first at her son-in-law, and then at Isabel. But the latter's gazing at her husband with a horrified expression, and I realise that for all their arguing this is probably the first time he's mentioned ending the marriage.

'I really hope he's worth it,' he adds.

'How could you be so bloody stupid, Isabel? What on earth were you *thinking*?' my mother abruptly snaps, surprising us all. We all turn to stare at her, caught out by this unexpected display of anger and at the same time I realise that it probably comes straight from the wound of her own betrayal by our father. I wonder if Isabel realises it too.

'Please, Mummy...' Isabel says, 'not while–'

But our mother's in full flight now, her arms crossing as her small, grey eyes pin themselves to her daughter's face. 'Haven't I always told you marriage is something you have to work hard at. It's not all that "being in love" stage, you know. I tried to tell that to your father and he didn't listen, and clearly neither have you.

What on earth is wrong with people these days...? Everything just seems to be about sex sex sex.'

'Mummy I–'

'I mean, do you *really* want Nathanial, Ben and Ella to feel like you and Anna did when Daddy left us? *Do you?* Did you think about that at all when you started mucking about with this boy?'

'Bill, how many times...' Isabel beseeches weakly, her eyes returning to her husband because it's clear nothing is going to subdue our mother. 'It was just... a bit of fun. That's all. A bit of an escape. Call it the ten-year itch. I won't see him again.'

But my brother-in-law remains with his back turned. As I stare at those tensed shoulders, I find myself recalling Alex Strong in his studio, the tortured look in his eyes as he'd said, *Do you think it's possible to be driven mad by love?*

'I mean it, Bill,' Isabel rushes on. 'I've never had any intention of leaving you or the children for him. If you don't believe me, ask Anna–'

At that her husband rises to his feet and turns to face her. 'Well that's unfortunate, because you're free to see him all you like from now on.' And suddenly he's side-stepping past her towards the door. 'I'm sorry, Liz,' he adds, turning apologetic eyes towards my mother. 'Isabel's right. I shouldn't have brought this to your house.' And then he's closing the door behind him, softly, respectfully.

The next thing I'm hearing is my sister screaming his name before she rushes after him.

I'm about to follow but my mother's hand is on my arm. 'Leave them to it,' she says in a low voice, 'don't get caught in the middle.'

So instead we watch through the porch window as Isabel grasps her husband's elbow, tugging him round to face her and forcing him to listen as she goes into a long, tearful rant, the words of which neither of us can hear.

The next thing he's pushing her away so hard she nearly falls, and storming determinedly across the grass towards the apple tree as she staggers after him, her heels sticking in the grass. When he reaches the tree's thick trunk he turns to face her once more. I hear my sister's voice raising, becoming hysterical, and I can just about make out the words, '...spend all my time... looking after your bloody children... I don't know who I am anymore...' when he leans down to say something and before my mother and I have time to register what's happening, she delivers him a stinging slap across the face.

'Bloody hell,' I say, elbowing my way through the door and rushing across the lawn to find them staring at each other with stunned expressions.

'Izzy...'

My sister turns towards me, her hands clasped together, her tear-streaked face beneath the scattered hair almost unrecognisable. Behind us I'm aware of my mother slowly picking her way over the grass. She comes to a halt about five yards away under the shadow of the branches, her eyes fixed on Bill who stares at his wife with numb eyes, his palm cupping his left cheek.

'Izzy, why on earth did you do that?' I say, reaching out to touch my sister's shoulder. But she jerks her body away from me with such a savage look I think she might strike me too.

Bill lowers his hand to reveal a smarting red welt across his left cheekbone. 'I'm going,' he says flatly. Then he straightens and I realise I'm watching his military training come into play as he attempts to assemble himself amidst the emotional chaos. 'I would suggest you stay here until you've calmed down, Isabel, and then you need to come home so we can discuss our future.'

And with that he nods to me and my mother before making

his way across the grass with precise strides, his hands in his pockets and chin jutted forward. We watch him carefully close the gate and get into his Mercedes.

'He's in shock,' I say.

My mother nods. Isabel just stands there, her hand covering her mouth as she watches him accelerate slowly down the drive.

'Come inside, Izzy,' I say, putting my hand on her wrist. She glances at me for a moment, then nods, allowing me to lead her back into the kitchen, our mother traipsing behind.

As I close the door, Isabel immediately slumps into the same chair in which Bill has just been sitting, her face buried against her outstretched arms, her blonde hair trailing over her shoulders.

'Oh Christ,' she moans, her voice muffled by her skin and the table. 'What have I done?'

A silence follows as Mummy and I stand there watching her.

'Why did you hit him, Izzy?' I ask eventually, because someone has to. 'He didn't exactly deserve it.'

She shakes her head. 'I don't know.' A few moments pass, then she raises her chin slightly and blinks hard. 'Honestly, I don't. I just get so frustrated when he starts going on about how much he's done for me and how other women would give anything to have my life–'

'Well he's right.' That's our mother. She's standing opposite Isabel with arms crossed and lips pressed tightly together, her upright stance communicating acute disapproval of the behaviour she's just witnessed.

'Don't you think I *know that*, Mummy?' Isabel snaps, rising and fetching some kitchen roll from the dresser. She presses her face into it and blows her nose loudly. 'Can't you see that's why I'm so frustrated – it's with myself, not Bill. I just don't understand why I feel this way when I look around me and see everything I've got and–'

'You're spoilt,' my mother interrupts. 'That's the problem. We spoilt you – your father and I after we parted. It was guilt I suppose – and now Bill's done the same. You've never learnt to appreciate the value of things.'

Isabel shrugs, then slowly sits back at the table.

'But you should at least...' Suddenly Mummy's voice begins to wobble and she's pressing the back of her hand against her mouth and blinking hard. '*You* of all people should at least appreciate what it means to come from a broken home.'

'Mummy, I–'

'*I mean it.*'

'I know you do,' then Isabel's pressing her face into the kitchen roll and the hands which grip it have started to violently shake. I find myself surprised by the profundity of her despair, just as I was by Bill's just a few minutes earlier, and again realise with some guilt just how little time I've spent trying to understand these two people.

'Mummy, you've got to believe me, this isn't like you and Daddy. I *really* don't want to divorce Bill...' Isabel says, lifting her head to stare at our mother before releasing a fresh deluge of tears. 'Honestly. I do love him ... and I love the children – you see ... I think deep down it's actually *me* I don't like so much ... I don't know whether Anna's ... told you but I've been ... taking anti-depressants. Bill doesn't know ... I know I should have told him but ... well I just didn't want him to know how wretched I've been feeling.'

Whether it's intended or not, I can't help but notice how this sudden outpouring serves a dual purpose; the first seems to be a genuinely raw communication of Isabel's unhappiness; the second is to quietly extinguish our mother's rage. As with most parents, the sight of her child in distress has an immediate, pacifying effect and she's staring down at Isabel now with a face full of concern as she pulls up a chair and folds her hand in her own. 'Oh darling,' she whispers. 'I'm sure Bill will come round. You just need to have a very long talk with him and apologise for everything. And then you need to explain how you feel. Maybe it's postnatal depression? Have you considered that? After Ben, I mean. Perhaps Bill can arrange for you to see somebody – a counsellor, or someone like that?'

Isabel's pale fingers press around my mother's bony ones. She nods, then buries her face into the crook of her arm. But as her sobbing grows deeper and more wretched, I'm beginning to wonder, despite the flippancy of her earlier assertion that her dalliance is over, for what – or whom – it is she's really grieving. The loss of her husband and emotional security, or of her lover? Because I suspect my mother's right – that if Isabel goes to Bill with enough contrition, he might yet forgive her – it was made very clear to us today just how much losing her will devastate him. But there's no doubt in my mind that today's events will signal the end to her affair with Alex Strong.

14

TOM

After Anna leaves I take the opportunity to call Stella at the office, but Paul the logistics manager, picks up the phone and tells me she's gone home. We chat for a bit, and I let him know I'll most likely be heading back soon. He assures me there's no hurry as Stella's running things just fine, and there's really not much to report except that John Harris has just handed in his notice with no explanation. Which I guess only serves to further fuel my suspicions. Not that there's much I can do about it right at this moment.

After that I try to Zoom Stella, but there's no answer, so I call the kids on Reef's smartphone. He tells me they're at home with the au pair, watching TV, and their mum's still not back yet even though it's nearly their bed time. They all chat to me briefly in turn, but I can tell they're eager to get back to their programme, so I let them go.

I put down the iPad feeling hollow.

When afternoon arrives, I go out to the front yard and saw some logs before building a fire and putting fresh sheets on Dad's couch. Then, true to my vow of this morning, I take it on myself to clean the house, hoovering up those cobwebs and wiping the surfaces with a damp cloth before taking an ancient carpet shampooer around the edges of each room. I even find a dusty bottle of Windolene and clean the worst of the smears off the windows. Dad probably won't even notice, and most of what I've done he won't even see, but I don't think anyone should die in a dirty house.

The ambulance turns up at five. I watch a different pair of paramedics wheel him down the ramp with his nurse, Iona, behind them. His skin in the evening sunshine looks chalk-white against the red blankets. They push him though the hall into the sitting room and lift him onto the couch.

As they adjust the drip, Iona, takes me to one side. 'He's really on borrowed time now, Tom,' she says, placing her hand on my arm.

A few minutes later, I stand on the pavement and watch the ambulance drive off. Then I go back into the house.

'Good to be home, Dad?' I say, kneeling to light a firelighter with my Zippo.

He's silent, his hollow eyes following its flames as they rise and catch newspaper and kindling. Then he yawns. 'Aye, but I'm ... tired ... son. Bit of a journey ... they kept me in that corridor for over an hour. Need sleep...' and his head's already sinking to one side, paper-thin lids sliding down over his eyes.

I rise and lift his head gently, placing a cushion under his cheek to support him. His pink scalp and wisps of white hair feel softer than a baby's against my palm. He's out for the count, his mouth fallen open, exhaling small, wheezy snores. A string of spit drips from his chin onto the cushion and there's a rancid smell of sickness about him – I've noticed it before but now it's almost overpowering.

Taking a tissue and wiping his chin, I stare down at him and think, *One day, this will be me. I am forty-one years old and I've probably lived more than half my life, so it won't be so long before*

my own sons and daughters are looking down at my sick,
wizened face and contemplating their own mortality.

I place the guard over the fire then move into the hallway.
Shit, I really need some air and to get away from that foul smell
so taking down my coat, I walk round to the front of the house
and roll myself a cigarette.

Outside the light's falling. I can hear boys shouting and a
football being booted around next door's garden. There's a peal
of laughter followed by a loud shriek. It's a different family to
the one who lived there when I was small. He'd been a
decorator, his wife an invalid. They'd had no kids. This lot look
like professionals – teachers or the like, and they don't seem to
be there all the time – city people no doubt, driving out the
locals as usual. I've watched their two boys from the window on
several occasions. It's weird to think that once it would have
been me and Callum making that noise as we kicked our ball
around behind Dad's house.

I light the cigarette, the heady petrol fumes from the
firelighter still clinging to my fingers. As I exhale a long trail of
smoke, my gaze steals across the empty playground towards the
school's high spruce hedge and the Carmichael's house. Its
upper storey is shrouded in the twilight and though the lights
are not on yet, I know the spread of its windows well. Of the
two bedrooms which are regularly occupied at night, I've always
suspected Anna has the one on the corner, nearest to the school
– and nearest to me – because that's where the light usually
stays on late. Sometimes, when I've not been able to sleep or
risen to take care of Dad, I've found myself staring out towards
those illuminated panes wondering what's keeping her up.

But after the events of last night I've resolved to stop
thinking about Anna. Instead I struggle to replace the soft
intensity of her face with my wife's tanned, animated one. Then
I make myself think back to my first memory of Stella, all those

years ago, coming into my office for an interview in her short skirt, her golden legs crossed before me. I'd made a comment about not expecting to employ Jerry Hall as our receptionist. She'd responded by throwing back her head and letting out a ringing laugh.

I reckon I've never believed in types and it's always fascinated me how different the people can be that we're attracted to. Brash, confident, and overtly sexual in a way no man can miss, Stella barged into my stoic world and filled it with laughter, lust and excitement. As well as fancying her like mad, I immediately liked her straightforwardness, her sense of purpose. Stella doesn't think too much, she's more of a doer, a person with endless energy who's ever on the go. A loving, if occasionally domineering mother, she's always making sure the kids are occupied in some worthwhile activity and keeps their TV time to a minimum. She can also cook like a celebrity chef and I've never known her look anything less than fantastic – going out without make-up on would be like going out without her skin.

And as for last night, I tell myself I regret what I've done because I've no concrete proof of Stella's unfaithfulness – whatever my instincts and John Harris's resignation might be telling me – but who knows, maybe I'm just in denial because, let's face it, that text was pretty conclusive.

My eyes wander back to that unlit bedroom window. I wonder what Anna's doing right at this moment, what she's feeling. It's weird to know that now and then she's got to be thinking about me. Does she feel happiness, regret? Or is she angry with me for the way I said goodbye to her this morning? I just hope she understood why I had to be like that. After all, she too, is in a relationship, even if it's running out of steam. She too, has betrayed someone.

But to be honest, I think I'm really just in shock. It's not just because Anna's someone I used to fancy. I know it's shallow, but I can't help thinking it kind of reflects where I've got to in my life because never in my boyhood dreams did I believe a girl like her could ever be interested in me. How did I see myself in those days, in comparison to the daughter of Stephen Carmichael, the wealthy owner of Fawley House? I was just the son of a paddy wood seller; a rough kid who went to the local comprehensive and left school at sixteen with no qualifications, whose prospects were to be a factory worker or bricklayer, or a craftsman at best. Yet here I am, twenty-something years later, owner of a seven-bedroom house, a successful business, married to a beautiful woman and a father of four amazing kids. Shit, how did I manage all that?

And suddenly, my adolescent self wants to yell, 'Guess what, Callum! Guess who I got off with? Only Anna Carmichael!' and I'm laughing out loud into the evening air.

And you know what? I'm not ready yet to go back into that fusty room with its stench of smoke and death. I don't want to sit there listening to Dad's wheezing while I sweat guilt over Stella. So instead I walk up the road to The Green and sit down on the bench under the beech tree.

Shit, I just can't seem to get Anna out of my head. Everywhere I look, memories of her lurk. From the games of rounders we used to play on this green, her slim frame running barefoot from base to base with bat in hand, her face bright with laughter; to the wheat field on my right which reaches up to Fawley Wood, the same field I'd once seen her standing in, gazing intently at me across the furrows as we searched for my missing brother.

The minutes pass and night steals over the hedgerows and gardens, and the field of sarsens behind me. I stare into the darkness and roll myself a small joint with the grass Ray Curtis gave me yesterday. I take a draw on it and savour the dope's slow climb up through my veins, the exhalation followed by inevitable elevation. It's nice stuff – skunk, but not the type which blows your brain out – and quite honestly, I could happily sit here all night watching the bats dart over the tree tops as the dew gathers on the grass. But I've got to get back – I don't want Dad waking up alone while he's so close to the end. So I reluctantly throw the joint onto the damp grass and, rising from the bench, start walking back down the high street.

When I re-enter the house, Dad hasn't moved but he's awake and lucid. I feel his eyes following me as I kneel to place another log on the fire.

'Are you okay ... son?'

'I'm okay, Dad. Just popped out for a fag and to stretch my legs a bit. Are you hungry?'

He nods, but that hollow gaze stays fixed on my face and there's a look in his eyes I can't quite read.

I go into the kitchen and heat him up a tin of Heinz tomato soup. When it's ready, I pour it into a bowl and bring it back into the sitting room before propping myself on the arm of his chair and ladling it into his mouth with a teaspoon. It's a slow and laborious process, this reversal of roles. As I pause to scrape the soup from around his lips, I think with irony how he probably once did exactly the same with me when I was a baby, sitting in this same chair with me on his lap, spooning mush into my mouth.

He manages only half-a-dozen spoonfuls before raising his hand and pushing the spoon away. As he does this, the blanket lifts briefly and I notice his other hand clutching some sort of book.

'What've you got there, old man? Secret reading?'

For a moment he's silent. Then, 'Just something of ... your mother's. A book of her sketches. Ray came by while you were out. I asked him to ... fetch it for me. She always kept it in her ... bedside drawer.'

'Oh yes?' And once again I'm feeling that same, irrational irritation that Ray Curtis should get to share such intimacies with my father rather than me. 'Can I see it?' I add, picking up the bowl.

He stares at me for a moment then shakes his head. I notice his arms tightening around the book's cover, pressing it to his stomach. 'Not now, son. Maybe ... later.'

I shrug inwardly, and realise I'm becoming inured to his strange behaviour. I take the bowl back into the kitchen and rinse it before making make myself a sandwich and carrying it back through to the sitting room.

We sit in silence as I eat, our eyes on the fire, and I find myself wondering what makes people want to paint or write. It's not an urge I've ever really had – to express myself creatively. But I guess that's just the way I'm wired. The thought automatically leads me back to the image of Anna, frowning at her computer screen, busily writing up travel notes from some trip she's taken, and suddenly I'm considering that inevitable question.

'Hey, Dad, do you remember Anna Carmichael?' I say finally, between mouthfuls. 'The girl who fell down outside the house the other week, I mean.'

That same, slightly vacant stare. But then he raises his brows and he nods his head slightly. 'You mean Liz Carmichael's daughter. Aye, I remember. There were ... two of them. Isabel and Anna.'

'You've got it.' I put the plate down on the carpet. 'Isabel's a few years older.'

'You liked Anna when you were small. Used to gawp at her ... when we took the wood round to her mother's.'

'Did I?' I shake my head. 'I don't remember.'

He tries to smile. 'Aye so you do. Liz ... was nice-looking too. Bit too classy for me, mind.' He pats the sketchbook beneath the blanket. 'Anyway, Eileen was always ... my number one.'

'I know that.'

'I loved that ... woman ... like no one else.' He shakes his head and I think, *Off we go again.* 'Not that I'm regretting ... any of it, of course. But it's hard ... leaving your land, your own flesh and blood and not being able to go back. It's hard, not being where ... you belong.'

I find myself recalling Anna's face in the pub as she'd played pool, her visible excitement about being back enmeshed in the landscape of her childhood.

Rising to my feet, I stand over him and wrap my hands around his spindly shoulders. 'You've been in Wiltshire much longer than you were in Ireland,' I say, lifting him into a sitting position and placing another cushion behind his back. 'You must feel Wiltshire's more of a home to you now than Donegal ever was.'

But he shakes his head once more and grips the arm of the chair. 'This was your mother's home, son. It was your home. But it was never ... mine.'

I can hear his breathing, harsh and hollow.

'So why didn't you go back there, hey?' I ask, resting back in the chair. 'You know, after Mum died and I'd left for Australia. There was nothing to keep you here after that.'

'Aye. Well you ... saw to that,' he says. He stares at me for a few moments and I see that same strange look in his eyes before he turns his head away, weakly. Then he adds, 'But there was never any ... going back to Ireland, son. Not then, not now.'

'That's ridiculous.'

But he shakes his head and doesn't attempt to answer. His eyes are fixed on my mother's bluebell paintings. He often does this when he's mulling stuff – but I guess it's because they're kind of peaceful, those paintings, and maybe also because they came from a time when Callum was still alive and the world was still a pleasant place to be.

I've looked at those pictures myself many times since I've been back here and come to realise that they're actually pretty good – even with my limited knowledge of art I reckon I can tell by Mum's sense of colour and the way she's used the texture of the paint to bring the trunks into the foreground, well they're not your run-of-the-mill landscapes.

Looking back, Mum's creativity was always something she kept very much to herself. She'd got a degree in fine art, which was unusual for women of her generation. She even had her own studio up at the Manor in exchange for cleaning the place – and she was adamant that we were not to visit her there. Maybe it's the thing all artists share, the need to seek that private place inside themselves, like a potting shed of the mind. Maybe that need for mental isolation is even more important than the art it creates.

The fire spits loudly, making us both jump, the ember falling within the hearth. I sit and watch its orange glow gradually die.

'It ... wasn't me,' Dad says suddenly.

I look up. He seems to have sunk even more deeply into his chair, his body almost submerged under the blankets, as if hiding from his own words. But those simian eyes fix me with a look which is thinly defiant; challenging but not quite angry, reminding me of the man he used to be.

'I didn't–' He coughs, and a chill runs through me as I realise I'm looking into the face of a person who knows they're going to die. Then he whispers, 'That morning I came into your room. You'd gone. Your things had gone. You didn't even leave me a note. It was like Callum ... all over again.'

'I phoned as soon as I got to Sydney.'

'As soon as you were far enough ... away.' He shakes his head. 'It doesn't matter now. Tom, I know why you left but you ... were wrong.'

My heart leaps in my chest. I somehow never expected him to be the one to raise it.

'I didn't ... kill Callum.'

Once more, the fire spits, but this time a larger ember lands on the carpet at my feet. I don't move, despite the circle of black spreading around its orange orb and the stench of smouldering nylon setting off that unwanted image reel, sending me straight back to that mid-summer dawn, the cries of the sheep rising from the hillside as I'd waded through that scarlet river of poppies until I finally reached the stones. Coming to a halt, and staring down at the mixture of ash and earth at their base, wondering at the same time at their blackened insides and the smell of burning that hung around the place. I'd squatted down, my elbows resting on my knees, my eyes drawn to something in the dirt.

'Then who did?' I say, turning to face him.

And there it is. After so many years the question's finally been asked. But how different this scene is to the one I'd always imagined. In my mind, because I haven't been here to watch my father grow old, I'd always pictured the two of us squared up face-to-face, fist-to-fist, roaring at each other like two titans. Never had I imagined myself sitting here half-stoned, delivering the question to a feeble, defenceless invalid.

There's the sound of running footsteps along the pavement outside, then a woman's voice calling her child. Anna's face suddenly floats into my consciousness, her skin beneath mine as we were fucking in bed this morning, sweat-soaked hair stuck to her brow as she'd moaned my name.

Dad turns his gaze towards the fire.

I stamp my boot onto that smouldering ember, rub it violently into the carpet.

'The other day, you said you and Mum felt guilty over what happened to him. After the funeral I heard you telling her you wanted to go to the police. She told you not to. Said it wouldn't do any good and that they'd put you away. She was *begging you* not to tell them whatever it was, Dad... What was all that about? When I asked her she said it was the business but you know what, I didn't believe her. Mum wasn't any good at lying, was she? She couldn't look me in the eye when I asked that question. And now all these years later, you're not looking me in the eye either.'

He glances at me, then quickly turns his gaze away again, his atrophied features making his expression hard to read.

'What did you want to tell the police?'

'I don't know ... what you're ... talking about.'

'Yes you do. I can see in your eyes that you do.'

Silence.

'Mum topped herself. Why did she do that?'

Those paper eyelids press together and his bird-claw hands begin to shake.

'Because she knew it was you all that time and she realised she couldn't live with it anymore? Is that why?'

He twists his face further to the side.

I refill my glass then turn to stare at him and hear myself suddenly say, 'You took that belt to me, Dad. Just for stealing a ball. You nearly killed me. How do I know you didn't take it to Callum that day? Did he somehow piss you off when you came in from the snow? Had you been down the Catherine at lunchtime knocking it back with your cronies, hey? Were you knackered and cold and angry because you couldn't deliver any wood, and he was badgering you to make a sledge for him like he'd been doing with me in the morning?'

'No... No, Tom, you've got it so ... wrong.' And now he's shaking his head from side to side, and I'm watching his eyelids rise, then fall, and that same deep shame burning in them I remember from all those years ago when we'd first asked where Callum was and he'd looked up at me from making the fire. Then he adds, the words coming out through harsh breaths, 'I can't tell you how sorry I was for belting you. It was just... Aye, far too much to drink and business was bad. But it wasn't deserved and I despised ... myself for it afterwards. I still ... despise myself.'

'And Callum?'

He shakes his head. 'I never hurt ... Callum.' His body explodes with dry, rasping coughs which go on and on, and with a shock I see thin tears begin to trickle down his cheeks – and all the time he's sinking down and down like he wishes those blankets could suck him beneath them and bury him forever.

'The other night when you were out of it on morphine, you told me to ask Ray about it. What does Ray know?'

He blinks at me.

'What does he know, Dad?'

'I don't know what you're ... talking about.'

'Yes you do.'

He shakes his head. 'Ray's got nothing to do ... with this. I don't know what I ... was saying.'

'You know what you're doing, don't you?' I tell him. 'You're condemning me to spend the rest of my life tortured by a question I can never answer. Is that what you want?'

'Sometimes ... questions are ... easier than answers.'

I move to stand over him, placing a hand on each arm of the chair. 'Don't you reckon I should be the judge of that? Who are you to decide what's good for me to know and what's not?'

'Tom, please...' He's reaching his hand towards my face, and struggling to rise. Tears still run down his cheeks but there's no self-pity in his voice, just a terrible urgency. 'You've got to believe me. I didn't kill Callum. I know I drank ... too much. I'm so sorry for belting you. I don't ... know what got into ... me.' He sinks back into the blankets and covers his mouth with his palm as another coughing fit erupts, though now I'm not sure what's coughing, and what's sobbing and all I can see is his absolute desperation to make me believe him before it's too late. 'I didn't kill Callum,' he repeats. 'He was my son. I loved him. I loved you both so much...' And as I hear him exhale that final sentence, the realisation runs through me like a sword.

He's telling the truth.

I straighten and stare down at him, blinking hard, my arms fallen by my sides. He looks up at me through his tears and I know he sees he's finally got through to me. But immediately I turn away and, resting my elbows on the mantelpiece, press my face into my hands, because just at this moment I can't face him. Yeah, maybe he knows something – I reckon he's keeping something back, just as I thought Mum was keeping something back all those years ago when I asked her about that overheard conversation. What did he just say about questions sometimes being easier than answers?

But he didn't kill Callum.

And if I'm to be completely frank, this conclusion isn't just a result of what he's just been struggling to tell me. It's also because I've kind of got to know my dad again these past weeks and now his volcanic temper's been diluted by a mixture of sobriety, ill-health and old age, other, better memories of him have begun to break through the layers of bitterness, anger and blame.

Because gradually I've come to remember the fiery, but ultimately honest patriarch of my childhood, who loved and protected his family like a lion and of whom I was in awe. He was a difficult, troubled man – probably, I now realise, because his parents had disowned him and he felt himself to be in permanent exile from the country and people he loved – but he was also a man people liked and wanted to spend time with, even if he had a reputation for drinking too much and having a temper. It didn't stop the other regulars surrounding him in the Catherine to hear his stories and laugh at his jokes, and drink the countless rounds he bought them.

And as I finally come to understand these things, I have a terrible sense of the time I've wasted, of the lie I've sold myself over the years that was probably just an excuse to run away from what happened to my brother and mother, and yes, from *what happened to me*, and as I realise this my head drops into my arms because it's this knowledge that's killing me – that he may not blame me but that doesn't mean I'm absolved. After all, it was me who stole the life he gave me and gave him nothing in return. It was *me* who was the one person left on this miserable earth that could have helped him and given him comfort and a reason to go on living. But no, instead like the selfish seventeen-year-old prick I was, I left him alone to cope with his loneliness and grief while I ran away to the other side of the world to grow an orchard in paradise.

'I'm sorry...' I mutter suddenly, collapsing to my knees and pressing my face into his lap. There's a long silence, then I feel his hands slowly rest on my head.

'It's all right, son. It's not your fault. None of it was ... your fault.' A long silence, then, 'I need you to ... understand that.' He coughs weakly and I hear the phlegm gurgle in his throat. 'And I'm glad you made ... a life for yourself. You're better off in Australia away from ... all this.'

I shake my head, press it into his spindly knees. 'I'm a coward.'

'No, Tom. You were brave. You deserved ... a life. What your mother did... There's never been anything for me after that. Don't you see? I died that day ... too. Since then, I've just been going ... through the motions. So I'm glad you went away, even though I've missed you. There was no life for you ... here.' His voice grows fainter, as if he's physically drawing away from me. 'Just a man ... who was already dead ... inside. I love you, Tom. And I'm proud of ... you. Don't you ever forget ... that...'

After this he goes silent, those hands still resting on my hair. I close my eyes tightly, trying to hold in the tears, but they seep between my eyelids and into the blanket's soft wool.

The minutes tick by, the only sound the soft crackle of the flames and his ragged breathing.

* * *

I must have fallen asleep because when I wake and raise my head, the fire's gone out and my body's stiff and cold.

I fall back on my knees, my boot heels digging into my arse. His head's slumped to one side. One arm rests on the arm of the chair – beneath it lies the sketchbook. His skin looks like chalk under the lamp light and there's a long thread of spit dangling from his chin. I can hear him wheeze.

'Dad?'

The slightest of movements – the half opening of an eye, a small smile before a raising of his head.

'I'm all right ... love. We'll be out of here soon. They can't catch us now we're on ... the ferry.'

His eyes roll back in his sockets and I realise he's delirious again. He must have given himself a shot of morphine while I was asleep. I'd stupidly left the dispenser on the table next to him.

'We're safe now, Eileen. Here, take the tickets and go on ... inside. I'm worried about you and the baby in this ... rain. Don't want you to get ill now. I'm going ... to stay up ... on deck for a bit, love.' Then he grins. 'They're playing the Beatles ... can you hear? *We can work it out.* That's ironic because ... we'll be in ... Liverpool, in eight hours.'

With an accelerating heart, I rise to my feet and go to stand above him. Then, softly I say, 'What baby, Dad?'

He's silent for a moment, taken aback by the sudden sound of my voice. Then he laughs. 'What do you mean, you silly woman. I'm talking ... about our baby.'

There's a chill at the back of my neck.

After this he goes silent, his head settling back into the pillows. I watch him for many minutes as his breath becomes ever deeper and hollower. It rasps in his chest like a file.

'Dad?'

Just for a moment, both eyes open wide and he stares at me. Those eyes hold mine and then he smiles. I realise I've woken him from wherever he's been.

'I'm all right ... son,' he whispers.

Then his head slumps to one side and my mother's sketchbook slowly slides from under his arm, hitting the floor with a dull thump.

15

TOM

I stand on the pavement with my hands in my pockets, watching the paramedics lift a blanket over Dad's face before carrying the stretcher up the ramp and closing the ambulance's doors behind them. Then they drive him away for the final time.

Several minutes pass but I don't move, my eyes fixed on that empty road until I gradually become aware of voices. It's morning break time and behind the school's iron railings I turn to see three children watching me. I smile at their solemn expressions, then make my way across the road towards them.

'Hello there,' I say.

They gravitate towards me like nervous calves, their faces bright under the morning sunshine. The taller of the two boys has straight dark hair, the smaller one's freckled with a mop of golden-red curls. The girl is pale-skinned and pretty with brown hair pulled back tightly in a gold and glitter comb similar to one Indiana wears.

'Was that your daddy?' It's the girl who speaks. She considers me with large, grave eyes, her head tilting to one side.

'Yeah,' I say.

'Is he gone to heaven?'

I find myself nodding, unable to speak, a bomb exploding in my throat. Suddenly my hands are on those railings and I'm closing my eyes and pressing my forehead against them, the cruel, too-late sunshine leaving a commotion on my retina.

Through the spiral of light and dark comes the sound of other voices followed by the shriek of a whistle and a teacher's voice saying, 'Come away now, children, come away,' and a car horn sounds to my right – someone's trying to get past me but I'm blocking the road, then my knees are buckling, my palms sliding down the cold iron bars.

'Tom.'

The car horn sounds again. There's another whistle, the teacher's voice rises, 'Peter, Cal, Joanna – please *come away*.'

I hear the little girl saying, 'I only asked him if his daddy is gone to heaven,' and again 'Tom!' but I'm too busy thinking, *Cal? That red-haired boy is called Callum...* as I feel a hand on my arm and realise it's Anna's voice saying my name, and her shoulder's pushing up under mine, prising me away from the railings.

Wrapping an arm around my waist to support me, she says, 'Tom, come with me, come inside.' Then I'm staggering next to her like a blind man, aware of our feet crunching on the gravel, the door slamming out the sunshine. A moment later, I'm collapsing against her in the hallway.

* * *

I sit in Dad's armchair as Anna moves around the room, re-stoking the fire and straightening the furniture where the paramedics pushed it aside to make way for the stretcher. She says little, but each time she passes I feel the soft press of her fingers on my shoulder. Eventually I slump back in the chair and, closing my eyes, listen to her in the kitchen as she tidies and does bits of washing up, knowing that the most important thing that she can be for me right now is a presence.

Then, just for a moment, I imagine it's no longer Anna but my mum out there, preparing supper. Me and Callum are on the sofa and we're just about to settle down and watch *Grange Hill* before going out to kick a ball around the garden. Dad's not back in yet; he's rarely in before six, but we're expecting him soon. It's just an ordinary weekday for our ordinary family – there's no reason to think anything's about to change. In the autumn, I'm going to go to the comprehensive while Callum will stay on at Fawley for another two years until he's old enough to join me. I'm feeling a bit apprehensive about the change of school, but excited too about getting out of the village and making new friends. Dad wants me to study woodwork – he reckons I could be a carpenter if I put my mind to it because I'm pretty good with my hands and making stuff. Myself, I'm not so sure, but there's plenty of time to decide.

The door shuts, cutting short the memory, and I turn to watch Anna enter the room with two mugs in her hand. She passes one to me.

'It's black,' she says. 'I couldn't find any milk or sugar. Sorry.'

'No worries. I ran out of everything yesterday – too busy looking after him.'

She bends down to pick something up from the floor. 'What's this?'

I look up to see her holding the sketchbook. I stare at its cover for a moment, then say, 'Drawings of my mother's. He had it with him all day yesterday.'

Letting herself fall back into the other chair, she casually lifts the cover and stares at the first page. 'Gosh – it's dated July 1983.'

'Hand it over.'

As she passes it to me, two bits of paper fall from beneath the pages onto the carpet at my feet. I reach down and pick one of them up.

It's part of a newspaper page, its torn, yellowing columns folded in half, its top half with the paper title and date missing. I unfold it and smooth it across the arm of the chair.

LONDONDERRY MEN ARRESTED ON SUSPICION OF ULSTER BANK BOMBING

Three men have been arrested on suspicion of carrying out last month's Londonderry Ulster Bank bombing after the RUC carried out a raid in the city. The men, who have been named as Sean O'Malley (25), his brother Bryon O'Malley (23), and Fergal Leahy (23), were arrested at a flat in the Rosemount area at 4am on Thursday.

They are being questioned in relation to the notorious Ulster Bank robbery which took place in the city's protestant Waterford district.

During the robbery, customers were held up by gunpoint as four men with sawn-off shotguns and wearing balaclavas demanded more than £40,000 from cashiers.

On leaving the bank, witnesses reported that the leader of the group threw a grenade back into the foyer, killing three people, including a British soldier, and seriously wounding five others.

The dead have been named as Brenda Sweeney (52) a housewife from Londonderry, David O'Connor (35) an electrician from County Antrim, and Second Lieutenant Mark Wright, from Solihull, Birmingham.

Two other men believed to have taken part in the robbery – including the getaway driver – have not been found.

I read the article twice, wondering why my mother kept it. She must have picked it up when she was in Ireland, but why this particular story? Or had she simply torn a strip off out of the newspaper to use as a bookmark?

But as I turn the page over, the reason for keeping the clipping becomes obvious and suddenly I'm smiling as I recognise the picture of Kris Kristofferson and Barbra Streisand in a clinch and above it, 'Returning to Buncrana Odeon soon: *A Star is Born*'.

'What is it?' asks Anna, dropping her head into her palms and fixing me with her steady gaze.

I hold it up it up to show her. 'It was their favourite film,' I say. 'He took her to see it on their first date.'

She blows on her coffee and prises herself back against the chair's arm, pushing her feet up against the other as she smiles then stifles a yawn. 'That's so sweet,' she says.

'What's that other thing that dropped out?'

She reaches down again to pick up a scuffed cream envelope, its seal stuck down with aged Sellotape. As she goes to pass it, her hand pauses as she reads some writing on its front. She's still for a moment, her brow twisting, then she passes it to me.

I immediately recognise my mother's handwriting.

For Jim
(This letter is not to be opened or read by anyone
else but my husband after my death.)

'Jesus...' I say.

My eyes trace the curve of my mother's handwriting, the neat loop of her vowels and carefully slanted consonants. It's been a long time since I've seen it but it still feels so familiar that it makes me shiver – like her scent, or the soft touch of her fingers.

'Are you going to read it?'

I turn the envelope over and my finger smooths the Sellotape. Underneath it I can see a line of small, soiled tears in the original seal. It's pretty clear that this envelope has been re-opened many times in the past.

'I don't know,' I say finally, and my skin feels cold and clammy. 'No, I don't think so. It's not what she wanted, is it?'

'Come on, Tom,' Anna says gently. 'You've got to read it. There may be information about Callum in it. Don't you think that's why your dad had it with him – because he wanted you to read it? I'm sure the police will want to see it, too.'

I shrug. 'Dunno,' I say finally. 'I need to think about it.'

I turn back to the sketchbook and flicking through it, find myself studying numerous rugged waterscape and landscape sketches depicted in my mother's familiar sweeping strokes. Most are clearly of Ireland, but one or two at the end are Wiltshire scenes – the Silbury Hill and Fawley Wood, and a detailed sketch of the stone bridge over the River Kennett. Occasionally I stumble over one or two of a young man's grinning face who, from the black hair and dimpled chin, deduce must be my father.

There's a long silence as I slowly flick through the pictures. I feel Anna watching me.

'So what time did Jim pass away?' she says eventually. 'I woke up at some point and noticed the light was still on.'

I place the sketchbook and envelope onto the arm of the chair, then swallow a mouthful of the coffee. 'Around 6am. We finally talked yesterday evening – you know, about Callum and what happened. He got pretty upset trying to persuade me it wasn't him... And then he just kind of faded away over the next couple of hours. We both fell asleep for a bit, and when I woke I thought he'd maybe already gone, but then he started talking again and saying a load of weird stuff about Mum and leaving Ireland and ... and then he kind of smiled at me then let out this sudden breath.'

After that I go silent.

'Tom,' she says. 'Are you okay?'

I shrug and look away from her, my eyes closing, my forehead pressing in my palms. In my mind, those children's faces drift into focus, their curious expressions as the paramedics wheeled Dad up the ramp. The image is slowly replaced by the faces of my own kids, and it hits me for the first time that Reef, my eldest, is the same age as Callum was when he was murdered. Fuck, I can't believe this hasn't occurred to me before – how would me and Stella feel if Reef were to disappear. If he were to be taken away from his home and murdered in some remote spot – how would we ever recover from that?

'Tom?'

I nod. 'I'm okay.'

'No, you're not.'

There's a silence. I stare at my hands, wrapping them together and unwrapping them.

'I don't think he killed Callum,' I say suddenly. 'I've spent all these years blaming him and hating him, and now I don't think he did it.'

I lift my head to see her gazing at me with such intense sympathy it makes my chest hurt. Not just because I can see she doesn't blame me, and she's letting me know I should forgive myself, but because it's reminding me of something – except it takes a moment to realise what it is. She must have seen the ambulance from her window and, somehow guessing, rushed over because she's not wearing any make-up and right at this moment she looks so young and untouched and suddenly she's not forty-one years old anymore, she's just fourteen, and the face I'm looking at is the same face which once gazed back at me across that field of ploughed furrows, an angry grey sky stretched out behind her as the wind blew up the hood of her duffle coat.

Immediately I rise and move across the room towards her, holding her face between my hands. 'There's somewhere I've got to go,' I say. 'And I need you to come with me.'

* * *

We drive along the back road to Milbury and park the Punto in the centre of the hamlet, leaving it in a verge next to a field of ponies. By now, it's early afternoon. The sun's shining and the sky above us is cornflower-blue, its surface streaked with stratus cloud. For the first time, I notice how the verges have become thick with dandelions and in the hedgerow the hawthorn's about to blossom.

It seems extra cruel to me, for Dad to die now – particularly in this freezing fucking country. If he'd lived for just one more day I'd have carried him out to the driveway so he could feel the sun on his face and hear the birds singing. I'd have sat next to him and talked with him about the old days and all my memories of when me and Callum were kids. I'd have let him rattle on about how he met Mum and I'd have told him about Adelaide and shown him pictures of the kids (why didn't I bring any with me, and why hadn't I Zoomed them with him so they could have had at least one conversation with their granddad before he died?).

I'd have talked to him about the problems with Stella and

maybe even asked his advice on what to do. He's my dad, after all, and it's his job to guide me through this shit. I might even have mentioned Anna, although I reckon the glint in his eye last night told me he'd kind of guessed – what had he said when I pretended I couldn't remember liking her as a boy? *Aye so you do.*

We follow a road shaded by chestnut trees, their branches ending in sticky buds like miniature toffee apples, before crossing a small bridge which rises over the Kennett, and finally the A4. We walk along its grass verge until we see the small lay-by opposite, and beyond it the track that leads to the Shadowing Stones.

The traffic's heavy – there's a tailback behind a tractor – and it takes us a while to cross the road. Anna moves in front of me and goes to open the gate. It seems surreal now as we stand with the sun pouring down on us and flies swarming around our heads, remembering how on that bitter December day I'd pulled in here on my way back from the airport to stare at the frost-coated fields, my limbs shivering as I'd contemplated seeing Dad again for the first time in a quarter of a century.

'Are you really sure you want to do this?' Anna says, resting her hand on the gate's catch. 'You've just lost your father, Tom. It's a lot to face in one day.'

The concern in her voice makes me hesitate. We turn and look at each other, the breeze sending strands of her hair across her face. Then I raise my gaze over her shoulder at the track beyond, the distant shape of those three stones.

'Yeah,' I say. 'I'm sure.'

Pushing the gate out, she lets me through first. We make our way forward in silence, the sound of traffic fading until all we can hear is the rough beat of our feet on chalk, and the song of skylarks and curlews. The hedgerow is thick with blackberry bushes, nettles and tall cow parsley. To our left and right, the hillside stretches out in a hazy green sweep which seems to be awake and listening.

At first, the going's easy, the track's white grooves are filled with chalk and flint which glint in the sunshine. But after a few hundred yards we come across deep ruts swollen with clay-filled water and thick mud. February's deluge has left its mark, despite today's warmth, and neither of us have decent footwear. Anna's wearing a pair of high-heeled leather boots under her jeans and I'm in canvas brogues, so I struggle up the right-hand bank and reach out to haul her up behind me. Together we edge along its thin causeway, trying not to slip on the muddy grass, our hands clutching the barbed wire fence for support.

Eventually the ground below rises slightly, the water receding into its sides, and we drop back down to ruts which are filled with wet, chalky clay. It sticks to our feet in heavy clumps, weighing down our steps and slowing our progress. There's a smell of stagnant water and the air's filled with stinging flies which follow us in determined swarms.

'You asked me how I knew Callum would be at the stones,' I say suddenly – although I've been considering my words for some time. I glance up at Anna, who's walking in front of me with folded arms.

'Go on,' she says.

'I guess it sounds a bit crazy, but it came from a dream.'

She swipes at a fly, then swings her head round and gives me a curious look.

I shrug and release a long sigh. 'I dreamt I was on one of the searches. We were walking in a line across the Grey Wethers Valley. Everyone else was looking towards the Ridgeway and Avebury, but for some reason I kept turning my head back towards the stones. I thought – and I know it sounds crazy – but in my dream, because I kind of *knew* I was dreaming, I could hear Callum calling me.

'And the next thing, I woke up with this feeling in my gut, you know. So I got up and walked to Milbury while it was still dark. I didn't wake up my folks to say where I was going. The irony is, it was actually kind of beautiful, you know, and it's always stuck in my mind because it was a hot day, like this one, only it was mid-June. I was heading up this track and the sun started rising. Everything was pink and gold, and there was a mist lying over the fields.'

It's warm walking in the sunshine and Anna takes off her coat, tying its arms together around her waist. I know she's waiting for me to go on, but for a moment I pause and swallow heavily because I've realised we're getting close. She turns to look at me again, but I keep staring straight ahead.

'There were poppies...' I say. But then I go silent, my stomach pitching into a tailspin as we round the bend in the track and suddenly they're no longer small black specks in the distance but solid structures – the near-side of that old barn simultaneously rising before us and beyond it, in the fenced-off meadow opposite, the three stones silhouetted against the sky.

'Tom?'

I nod but say nothing.

'Tom?'

I stare at her, confused, and wonder why she's come to a standstill, why she keeps saying my name.

'I'm all right.'

Only I'm not all right. Suddenly, I'm going to be sick.

'Sit down for a minute,' she says.

But it's too late. I'm doubled over, my hands on my knees and that coffee she made me this morning is splattering over the nettles leaving dark splashes on my brogues. I'm aware of her hands clutching my shoulders, but she says nothing, waiting

227

patiently as I vomit several times, then slowly, with her support, lower myself down onto the ground, feeling the firmness of the bank beneath my legs and the warm grass under my palms.

'Here... Take some deep breaths and rest for a bit,' she says. Her fingers squeeze my wrist and I let her hands and words give focus to my mind's disarray. Those flies still dart around us and the silhouette of her face eclipses the blinding sun.

Minutes pass. Turning away and closing my eyes, I concentrate on the sound of the skylark, the drone of a microlight in the sky, the cries of those distant sheep – anything but what lies at the end of this waterlogged track.

'I think we should go back,' Anna says.

'I threw up that day, too,' I reply, pushing myself forward into a sitting position, letting my head drop between my knees. 'Jesus, I feel bad...'

'Tom, this is too much.'

Wrapping my hands together, I cup them around the back of my neck, sinking my face more deeply. 'I'm going on, Anna. I've got no choice.'

'Of course you've got a choice. We can come back any time. Just wait a few more days – at least until...'

But I shake my head. 'No, it's got to be today.' Thrusting myself forward into an upright position, I turn to stare at the stones. They're only fifty metres or so away now, that barn standing halfway between me and them. But even from this distance I can feel whatever it is that hangs around them. I felt it back then, too, like some kind of mild electric charge in the air, something almost intangible, but fuck, it's there all right.

'Anna, you've got to understand... I've spent all these years hiding on the other side of the world blaming Dad for what happened here. I've had my head in the sand all this time living the fucking Australian dream. Even when I found out he was dying, you know, I didn't want to come. But Ray kept calling and piling on the pressure and Stella was banging on that I'd regret it if I didn't – so in the end I came because… well I guess I thought, well, I owed it to Callum, you know, to try and find out what really happened. And on a practical level, I reckoned I'd need to be here anyway to sort out the old man's estate. But what I didn't know was how I was going to feel when I walked into the room to see him like that, so weak, so diminished…'

My voice falters and I take a step back as she goes to wrap her arms around my neck. '*Don't*… I don't deserve it, Anna. I really don't. You know what? It only occurred to me today that Reef's the same age as Callum was when he was killed, and I thought to myself, what if Reef was murdered? What if they did that to Reef, and then all the rest of my kids just fucked off to the other side of the world and never wanted to see me again for another quarter of a century because they thought, "Well maybe Dad did it because the police were a bit suspicious and we overheard something we maybe shouldn't have," but they didn't really know and didn't bother to ask…'

Anna takes another step towards me, but this time I crush her hands inside my own and hold then against my chest as I turn my gaze towards that barn, half-pulling her with me. 'Don't you see? I've spent all these years avoiding this place, burying my head in the sand and not wanting to think about what happened here. I owe it to Dad, and to Callum. Otherwise what else do I deserve?'

'You were just a boy,' Anna says urgently, pulling me back towards her. 'Stop punishing yourself like this.'

'I'm not a boy now.'

I release her hands and continue up the track. At the same time, the nausea's beginning to rise again and my head's pounding like a drum, and I'm sure if I stop once more then my fear will get the better of me and it'll all be over. My response is to accelerate my pace until I'm almost running.

Behind me, I hear Anna telling me to slow down but by now I've reached the barn and immediately it's obvious that nothing's changed. Even the rotting doors look the same, crudely held together by those same two planks nailed across them, their lower slats rotten and broken and the metal, gridded window at its front is still there, its missing glass now crudely patched up with black plastic. A random iron bar swings loosely from its sill.

There's a sudden scrabbling as a pigeon flies from the window and tries to launch itself into the sky, but a piece of wire has somehow got caught around its leg. It pulls the bird up in mid-take off, sending it sailing upside down, its wings flapping in panic as it swings crazily from side to side, its body bashing the brick wall.

Climbing the stile, I stride across the meadow which, that day, had been covered in a scarlet sea of poppies but is now thick with clover and white dandelion spores which rise in front of my feet like soap bubbles. I can hear Anna still shouting my name as I cross those last twenty metres to the base of the stones.

Then, leaning forward, I close my eyes as I fight to get my breath back. My body's shaking and the grass beneath me feels as if it's about to fall away in some mighty tremor. I'm aware of so much, and so little, all at the same time. My heart's still pumping like a piston and my skin prickles as if bugs are crawling in and out of its pores. The drone of that microlight, now directly above me, is like a huge hornet inside my head.

Ten, maybe twenty seconds pass before I slowly straighten, my eyes rising with something like dread towards that henge.

'For God's sake, Tom...' Anna gasps as she stumbles up behind me. 'For God's sake...'

I glance round at her. She's breathing hard and her face is flushed scarlet from running in the heat. She bends over for a moment, legs astride, her hands on her hips before collapsing down on the grass.

I turn my gaze back to the stones. Up close like this, they seem unremarkable, an anti-climax even. The ground at their base is thick with nettles and weeds. Thistles shove their heads between the smaller boulders and directly under the dolmen, the dry, clay-coloured earth dips into a concave bowl. Flints and smaller sarsens scatter its surface; a lollypop stick and a crumpled Tesco's bag lie at its mouth and I can see the remains of someone's picnic strewn carelessly on the grass behind it. There are a couple of crushed Heineken cans, a half-drunk plastic bottle of Pepsi Max and the remains of a sandwich carton. It's typical display of human selfishness which, in another place, and another time, would piss me off but which today seems to offer a comforting mundanity. A family came here and sat beside these stones, eating and drinking. No one was hurt and as far as I know, nothing extraordinary happened. They finished their food and drank their drinks; they left their litter, and went home.

My heartbeat's slowly returning to normal and the nausea's subsiding. I take deep breaths, my hands resting on the inside of the two upright stones as I lean between them. Then I take a few steps back and sink cross-legged onto the grass beside Anna.

A silence follows. I lift my face upwards and, just for a moment, enjoy the feeling of sunshine warming my skin. With the waterlogged track now behind us, those infuriating flies have dispersed and have been replaced by midges and the occasional early bee. A yellow butterfly tumbles across the grass, settling on a thistle flower; the song of the skylark has been joined by the call of a thrush and the clicking of grasshoppers' wings, and behind it all, the constancy of those sheep's cries echo across the hillside like the sighs of ancient ghosts and I'm thinking it's ironic that throughout my life, I've always connected their sound to Wiltshire, because listening to it now, I'm suddenly thinking of Australia.

Australia... Jesus, I wish I'd taken Dad there. It will be autumn there now and in the bush the ground will be brittle dry and thick with dust. In Adelaide, the water on the River Torrens will be low as it gets, and the last of the beach-goers will be packing up their towels and surfboards.

Stella will be putting away the garden furniture and covering the pool. She'll be asking the gardener to start cutting back the vines and climbing roses for the winter, and maybe to put some more bulbs in – that southern-most flowerbed's looking pretty thin.

The days will be drawing in, the sun lying low in the sky, the evenings at their most cool and pleasant. It's my favourite time to be there, a catharsis after the months of oppressive heat. It would have been a perfect time for Dad to sit out on the veranda with a beer and spend time with the kids when they get home from school. They'd have crowded around him and he'd have told them all about Mum, and me and Callum when we were kids, about Fawley and his family back in Ireland. And maybe he'd have taken the boys fishing like he used to with me and Callum, or played Hungry Hippos with Indiana – she'd have loved that.

'What are you thinking about?'

I turn to see Anna staring up at me, her hand raised across her forehead to shield her face from the sun.

Slowly I withdraw the tobacco and papers from my jacket pocket and begin making myself a cigarette. 'I was thinking about Australia.'

She watches me for a moment, surprised by my answer. Then she frowns. 'You mean you were thinking about Stella.'

I glance towards her, a smile spreading across my lips.

'What is it? Why are you smiling?'

'Nothing.'

'I can always tell when you're thinking about her. Your eyes kind of get closer together, and you start looking really cross without realising it.'

'Is that right?'

She nods. 'You need to get it sorted out, Tom. You need to talk to her and find out what's really going on. You might be here trying to face what happened to Callum, but you're also using this trip to hide from your relationship.'

'Reckon I could say the same about you.'

Her brow raises. 'Sorry?'

'Well, I notice you're still here. What's Mr Turkish Delight been saying recently?'

She looks down at the ground. 'I've told him I want to stay in England for a bit longer. He's okay with it.'

'You mean you've not found the guts to finish it yet and neither has he. One of you is going to have to get off that fence at some point. And while we're on the subject, tell me something. Is it because of your dad, do you reckon – that you're not married and have no kids. Is it because he left you all?'

'I *beg* your pardon?'

I give her a long look, then light the cigarette. She glares back at me, her eyes fizzing.

'Come on, Anna, don't take it the wrong way. I just don't understand why someone as good-looking as you hasn't got herself hitched, that's all.'

'You make it sound like there's something wrong with me.'

I shake my head. 'That's not what I'm saying. I'm just trying to understand. I want to know what's happened to you during all these years we haven't seen each other. Because I'm getting the impression you're a bit troubled.'

'Oh right. And *you're not*?'

I open my mouth to say something, then grin and close it again.

She sighs and drops her head. A long silence follows as I watch her, aware that I have steered this conversation and wondering why I've chosen this moment and setting to do it.

'It's just that I've watched Isabel do everything by the book,' she said finally. 'Having lots of doting boyfriends then meeting Bill and having his kids – while I've simply ricocheted from one let-down to the next. Each new man comes into my life promising everything but then seems to end up delivering nothing. And the only common denominator seems to be me.'

'By making the wrong choices?'

She glances at me. 'You mean it's subconscious? Maybe. But I never see it when I first go for them. On paper they always look fine, and everything they say is initially fine. But they always turn out to be either commitment-phobes or, you know, ruminating on past girlfriends. Or simply "not looking for a relationship right now". How often have I heard that one?'

I release a lungful of smoke. 'And the Turkish man? What about him?'

'Kerem's different. I already knew him because he used to travel to Oman on business when I was working there. So he called me when I came to Istanbul and we went on a date, and it just kind of went from there. A couple of months into it I moved in with him and everything was great at first. He's a clever guy, and funny, and we were having a really good time.'

'Except?'

She shrugs. 'He kept putting off talk of children and marriage. And I knew he was trying to keep me away from his family. They are practising Muslims – they observe Ramadan and his father and brother always attend Friday prayers – and okay, I knew they weren't terribly happy about us even though they always made me welcome when we did go and visit them.'

'That's a quite a few red flags.'

She sighs, and the corners of her mouth crease down. 'I know. But enough of me, that's not why we're here.'

I take another drag and continue to watch her as she leans forward and lets her chin fall into her palms.

'So what was it you were saying back there on the track? You started talking about poppies – and then you were sick... What was that all about?'

'It doesn't matter.'

She raises herself back into a sitting position and wraps her arms tightly around her knees. 'It *does* matter, Tom. If you can start psychoanalysing me, then surely I have the right to do the same to you? You ask me to come here with you and you want me to help you face this thing. Well don't you think actually *talking about it* would be a good way to start?' She pauses. Then, 'I just want to know what happened that morning. That's all – so I can understand what you're going through.'

I stub the cigarette into the ground then, dropping my head and pressing my hands into my face, take a deep breath. 'It's just that this field was full of them. Poppies, I mean. It's one of the things I most remember about that day.

'The thing you need to understand is... I didn't really expect to find anything... I hadn't taken it all that seriously, you see, the dream, just kind of thought I was kidding myself and I was actually thinking about turning back when I noticed something odd.' I point towards the stones. 'You see the lichen there, that flaky looking stuff? It's kind of creamy-yellowish now. But that day it was blackened and scorched. And just when I was thinking that... that's when I saw it. I hadn't noticed it before because it was lying next to my trainers.'

I pause, aware my voice has gone up an octave. 'It was a bit of a red sleeve... It was badly scorched but I knew straight away it was from Callum's jumper. The next thing I knew, I was over there by that stile being sick.

'Once I'd calmed down a bit, I came back and started combing through the poppies, all around the stones, walking in wide circles looking for more signs of him, but it was impossible looking for red in a sea of red, if you know what I mean.

'So I decided to head back. I climbed over that stile feeling so relieved that I was about to get away – because even though I knew it'd happened months before, there was still this feeling, you know, that whoever did it might still be around, might even be watching. I knew it was stupid, but you don't really think rationally in a situation like that. And that should have been it, especially, you know, considering the way I was feeling right at that moment, just totally freaked out. Only then, as I was passing the barn, I saw another bit of red wool caught on the gate...

'Fuck, Anna, I still don't know why I went in there. I should've just gone straight home and shown my folks what I'd found, but it still felt like Callum was here somehow and directing me, just like he'd been in my dream.

'The barn's doors weren't locked and they opened easily. The light was bad but I could see there wasn't a lot in there – just rusted old farm machinery. But what I noticed immediately was the smell.'

I feel Anna's hand on my shoulder. 'I walked around the tractor and noticed an old skip standing behind it. The smell was getting stronger with every step – I knew pretty much immediately where it was coming from. So I made myself walk towards it... I stood next to it for ages, trying to work up the guts... Anyway, eventually I made myself lean over its side – and that's when I saw what was left of my little brother.'

My body has begun to shake. At the same time, I'm aware of Anna's arm moving across my shoulders.

But I can't deal with sympathy right at this moment. 'Fuck it,' I say, rising to my feet. 'Come on, I need to see this thing through.'

I pull her up beside me, then turn to stare at those stones for a few final moments. That microlight has moved on at last, its drone fading as it draws away over the Grey Wethers Valley. The sun's directly above our heads now; it's a beautiful, fresh spring day.

Together, we turn and walk back to the stile. Anna climbs it first, and I follow. We head back down the track until we reach the gate to the barn's rubbish-strewn, wired-off enclosure, our arrival prompting a panicked commotion as that pigeon, still hanging on its piece of wire, tries to escape our approach, only to find itself swinging futilely back and forward again, its breast rebounding against the barn's brick wall.

'Poor thing,' Anna says, staring up at it as she pulls open the metal gate and lets me go through. 'How on earth did it manage to tangle itself up like that. Is there any way we can cut it down?'

'Not unless you've got a ladder and wire cutters to hand,' I say, walking towards the barn because I've got more important things on my mind than rescuing a dumb bird.

Once again my heart's hammering in my chest but I try to ignore it as I concentrate on finding a path around those piles of boulders and bushes of thistle. When I reach the barn's far end, there's a second set of doors, this time chained and padlocked; but the chain's loose and there's a wide gap between them. 'This is where I got in last time,' I say, mostly to myself. I kneel down and push my shoulder against the wood to force it open a few more inches, then shove my head through as Anna's footsteps crunch up behind me.

Dropping onto all fours, I force my way into the gap until I'm staring into the semi-darkness, noticing the broken glass which lies on the ground between the nettles and rubble. I shout a warning to Anna to mind her hands and knees. The next thing, I'm forcing my way between the doors and standing upright, the smell of musty straw and rotten wood thick in my nostrils. Immediately I'm aware of that same unnatural chill I felt back at the stones. It's pressing in on me from all sides. Goose bumps rise on my arms beneath the leather jacket.

Anna crawls through behind me. 'Gosh it's cold in here,' she says, pushing herself up. We stand in silence for a minute or so, allowing our eyes to adjust to the dimness, aided by the wide slat of sunlight which falls across the floor from the doors and another, thinner ray, thrown by that metal-grated window. 'It *really is* cold,' she repeats, staring up at me. 'I'm not imagining it, am I?'

'No,' I say, shaking my head. 'You're not.'

She turns a circle, then wraps her arms around herself.

'Look,' I say. 'All that crap... it's still here.'

And it is, even down to the same tractor and bits of broken machinery. That old plough still rests in the corner, the broken spokes from a combine harvester piled up next to it. The straw bales have been replaced with sacks which have grain spilling from their rotting hemp – and near the doors stands a familiar blue builder's skip with the faded white words, *Bin it, Skip it*, still visible on its side. As I start walking towards it, I feel like I'm heading against an inverse current.

'It's not the same one, is it?' Anna mutters through chattering teeth as she comes up behind me. 'They *can't possibly* have left it here.'

I walk straight up to stare over its edge to study its rubbish-strewn innards, the cold metal pressing against my chest. Then I turn round and lean back against it, pressing my shaking hands into my pockets and closing my eyes. At the same time, I'm aware of Anna hooking herself up by her elbows and peering in.

'Things are just things,' I say, after a moment.

'What?' Her voice reverberates around the skip's hollow base.

'Don't, Anna. There's nothing to see in there.'

She hangs poised on the edge for a couple more seconds before slowly sliding back down. 'What do you mean – "things are just things"?'

'Just that. It's only what we connect to them that matters. Those stones out there are just stones. People visit them every day without anything ever happening. I mean, the stones have got nothing to do with Callum – they've been here for thousands of years. So what if this is the skip I found him in? I couldn't expect the farm to bury it, could I? Or melt it down? They'd hardly have expected me to come back here. It doesn't look like they've ever come back here either and I mean, this was where it was kept, so why move it?'

'But it's about respect...'

I shrug. 'What difference does respect make now? He was lying face down in it and his body was black and covered in flies. You know...' I break off. 'Oh Christ, don't!' I say, though I'm not quite sure what it is I'm actually saying, because she's just standing there wordlessly and hasn't moved.

'Don't...' I repeat.

I'm aware of my body heaving; the sweat covering my face and palms despite the chilling air; the nausea in my gut. Suddenly I'm about to gag again. 'Can you feel it?' I say roughly, and now I'm stepping backwards towards those doors.

'I just feel cold, that's all.'

'That's what I mean. There's something in here.'

'Tom, don't be...'

'I can't stand this. Come on. Let's get out of here.'

She steps back, watching me punch my way back through the doors on my hands and knees. But I'm in such a panic to leave I forget about the glass until I feel a shard enter my palm, then a soft trickle of warm blood running down my fingers. I suck at the wound as I launch myself back into the sunshine, stumbling over the rubble as I push the gate open and try to ignore the panicked flapping of that pigeon's wings.

The next moment Anna's beside me and we're hurrying up the track, swiping our way back through the swarms of black flies and wading through those sluices of muddy water until the sound of traffic finally rises up from the A4 and I can see the roofs of cars and lorries moving beyond the hedgerow. The chill's lifting with every step we take, and the sun's warming my face once more.

We're drawing close to the A4. I let Anna go ahead because I need a few minutes to come to terms with what's just happened; plus I don't want her to know that with the relief of getting away from the barn, I've started to relive another set of memories; memories of that fourteen-year-old boy who staggered down this same track all those years ago with a scrap of red jumper in his hand.

After I'd blurted out my discovery to Dad, I'd barely spoken to anyone for the next year. I skived school and stopped caring about exams – not even the woodwork GCSE I'd worked so hard for. Eventually I was referred to a child psychiatrist because I was in such a bad state; I couldn't sleep or eat, and I felt like I had this lump in my throat the whole time which the psychiatrist told me was called *globus hystericas* – my body was so tense that I couldn't swallow because the muscles were knotted so tightly together. I was having constant flashbacks and I guess that was the beginning of the reel; repeatedly picturing myself here on that dawn morning, a river of blood-red poppies endlessly carrying me towards the Shadowing Stones.

I was put on medication and prescribed counselling. The psychiatrist was good; she helped me cope with the flashbacks and the anxiety they were causing. She reckoned I had survivor guilt that it was Callum who'd been snatched instead of me and that these things were normal and natural to feel in such circumstances. Then, just as I was beginning to get better – to be able to speak, sleep and eat again – Mum went and topped herself.

A few months later I turned sixteen. I immediately left school and started working as hard as I could – sometimes around the clock. It was partly to block out the pain of losing my mother so soon after Callum, but also because a survival plan was beginning to form itself in my mind. I slogged like a bastard, doing nights in the tannery in Marlborough and dayshifts at the creamery in Devizes, and using my bike to get everywhere. I also helped Dad deliver the wood when time allowed (paid this time), whilst never allowing him to know my plan or letting on that I'd started suspecting Callum's death might actually be his handiwork. I had no intention of confronting him about it back then – all I wanted was to get as far away from him, and Fawley, as possible.

In less than a year, I'd got the money together and secured a temporary work visa, and without saying goodbye, I took a coach to Heathrow and boarded a plane to Sydney. And then, for a long time, I guess I managed to stuff it all away into some dark drawer in my mind. I met and married Stella and got residency, and busied myself with building a successful business, in living a gilded life with my attractive wife and four beautiful children. I actually, for a while, even came to believe that the bubble I'd created would protect me forever. But, Jesus, who was I kidding? Because I've learnt it doesn't matter how far you go, you can never really escape the things that happen to you, and for the rest of my life that cine reel on my retina is set to run and run.

Because when I started up this track on that brilliant June

morning, I was an energetic fourteen-year-old boy with my whole life lying ahead of me. I walked into that barn of my own free will, just as that pigeon flew in to it of its own free will. And you know what? It suddenly occurs to me that I'm maybe not so different from that poor bird. Because I also have a wire around my leg, and no matter how hard I beat my wings, can never fly away.

16

ANNA

It's late afternoon by the time I get home. As I walk around the side of my mother's house, I notice Isabel's Jeep in the driveway and at the same time hear children's laughter. Turning to look down the lawn, I see Nathaniel and Ben charging behind a large red-and-white football, their little sister tottering behind them.

I open the metal gate between the two sarsen walls to find my mother and sister sitting next to each other on the wooden bench, their hands clasping glass tumblers. Though the day's cooling, the sun still pours through the budded branches of my mother's apple tree, scattering a tapestry of light and shade on the lawn around them.

'You've been a long time,' my mother remarks, her eyes rising over Isabel's shoulder as I wander across the lawn with folded arms. 'How's Tom?'

I shake my head. 'Not good.' I look down at their nearly-finished drinks. A wooden chopping board sits on the grass at their feet, its concave base home to a pool of sliced lemon, pips and juice. 'Is that G&T?'

My sister nods. 'Peace offering,' she says quietly. 'Help yourself.'

'Thanks. Think I will. Anyone want a refill?'

They shake their heads. I go to the kitchen and fetch a glass, filling it with Gordon's gin, Schweppes tonic and ice before returning to the garden. I lower myself into a cross-legged position on the grass and, taking the board, slice myself some lemon.

'So what time did Jim pass away?' my mother asks.

I drop the lemon into the glass then swill the drink around, listening to the soft popping of the ice. 'About six o'clock this morning.'

'Poor Tom. How's he coping?'

'Not very well. He'll be better when he's had some sleep.' A shadow passes across my mother's eyes. At the same time her lips reduce to a tight knot and I realise I'm observing the fear which comes with the autumn years – that knowledge of the random fall of the dice and the inevitable stacking of the odds. This time it's Jim with the losing throw, but she knows she won't be able to avoid it forever. I think of Tom breaking down at those school railings this morning and a black heaviness settles on my chest because one day, I'm going to lose my mother as Tom has just lost Jim and when I do, I'm not sure I'll be able to bear it.

'Well, Big Sister,' I say, pushing the thought away and turning towards Isabel. 'Have you come to stay with us?'

She takes a slow sip of her drink then turns towards her children. 'Not just yet.'

My mother rises abruptly to her feet, the empty glass in her hand. 'Think I'll go and trim a bit more of that hedge while we've still got the sunshine.'

We watch her carry the glass back to the kitchen before re-emerging to pick up the shears she's left leaning against the porch wall. She looks frailer than ever today, walking with her back bowed, her thin frame clothed in dark-blue corduroy trousers and a turquoise pullover. Making her way through the gate and onto the front lawn, she pauses to speak to the children, pushing a stray hair behind her ear before moving determinedly down the drive towards the tall hedge where the wooden stepladder stands.

'This place is getting too big for her,' Isabel says, and I sense her attempt to postpone any interrogation about the scene that took place here yesterday. 'I keep telling her she should sell it and get something more manageable.'

'It's her home, Izzy – it's all she's known for the last forty-odd years. Things aren't that simple.'

We watch her adjust the ladder then slowly climb it, looking increasingly insecure with each wobbly step, her left hand gripping the hedge for balance, the other dangling the shears.

'Honestly. Does she *really* have to do that?' Isabel exclaims. 'Why on earth can't she get a bloody gardener? It's not like she's short of money.'

'Because she's stubborn and likes to be in control. Len Combstone said he'd come round and offered to do that hedge with his strimmer but she told him he wasn't to bother. She said it rather impatiently too – like he was implying she was incapable of doing it herself.'

Our mother reaches the top of the ladder and starts trimming the hedge with short swipes of her elbows. As I watch her work, I think of the regrets Tom's suffering now it's too late to turn back the clock, and realise that in the years to come, how mine and Isabel's most vivid memories of our gentle, long-suffering mother will be of her in this garden. One day she'll sell this house, or Isabel and I will sell it when she's passed away, and then, in that unwelcome future, we'll only have each other and our memories to remind us of how as children we'd follow her around, sidling up behind her and popping snap dragons with our fingers while around us fat bumble bees would climb into the purple cones of foxgloves and a hundred wasps would settle on countless fallen apples.

'Bill's forgiven you then?' I say, sipping the gin and tonic and eyeing her over the rim of the glass.

Her cheek twitches as she considers the question. A moment passes before she releases a resigned sigh. 'Yes, he has. Well sort of. He says he's willing to give us another chance if I agree to marriage counselling.'

'That's good.'

'I can't believe I did that, Anna. Hit him I mean... I've never done *anything* like that before.'

I shrug, unsure what to reply.

'And Alex and I are finished.' She glances down at her drink, then slides her gaze back towards our mother. 'Obviously.'

'It's for the best, Izzy.'

She bites down on a lip. '*Is it?* After I left you yesterday, I went straight up to the Manor to tell him it was over. What else could I do – I have to put the children first, don't I? I mean, Bill might be willing to try and forgive but he's still furious and I'm not sure he believes I've really ended it. The kids keep asking me why Daddy's in such a bad mood... I'm honestly not sure if we'll get through this, Anna. He wants to know where Alex lives – he says he won't rest until he's swung for him.'

'He'd have Alex for breakfast.'

'I know.' She suddenly presses her face into her palm and goes silent. At the same time the corners of her mouth turn down and a single tear begins trickling down her wrist.

'Oh Izzy...' I push myself onto my feet and go to sit on the bench next to her. 'I really don't know what to say. How did Alex take it?'

'Not at all well.'

I clutch her free hand in mine. But as I wait for her to pull herself together, I'm thinking about the day I'd caught her with her lover up by the Shadowing Stones, the flushed, euphoric look in her face after she'd kissed him, and the bitter words she'd spoken in the car that night about her marriage.

There's a chatter of magpies from the top of the apple tree. I turn my face up to see a pair flapping their wings as they chase each other from branch to branch. At the same time, there's a growing chill in the air. It's gone five o'clock now, and the sun's starting to sink behind the tall chestnuts and beeches of Soweton Road, silhouetting the long line of pylons that reaches up the Kennett valley and sending shadows across the lawn. My mother takes another step up the ladder, so she's standing on its very top. She reaches forward and starts clipping at the hedge's far side.

'Did Alex tell you we bumped into each other?'

Isabel slowly straightens, her hand dropping from her face into her lap. 'By Forest Manor?' she says. 'Yes, he did.' She delves into her handbag, pulling out a tissue and blowing her nose. 'What did you think of his sculptures?'

I nod. 'They're very good – especially the ones of you. He struck me as pretty sensitive. I think he could be *too* sensitive, you know, and maybe even a bit unstable... He's very in love with you.'

'I'm in love with him too. It's not a one-way street.' But then she breaks off, her eyes lowering to the grass at her feet.

'What? What is it?'

She turns to look at me and I watch her weighing up whatever it is she's unwilling to tell me. Then, 'He came inside me, Anna.'

'He *what*?'

'Yesterday, when I told him it was over...' She pauses, looks a bit ashamed. 'You know those sort of women... who think a relationship's on its way out so they get themselves up the duff on purpose? Well I think that's what he tried to do – you know, to me.'

'He tried to get you pregnant?'

'I know it sounds mad. Of course we were both desperately upset... and... well one thing led to another – and it's not as if I've gone off him, if you know what I mean. Then, right at the last moment, he said, "You're going to have my child," and he came inside me.'

'Bloody hell, Izzy. Could you be?'

She shakes her head. 'I got the morning-after pill,' she says. 'Anyway, I'm nearly forty-four years old – he'd be lucky...'

'God, he sounds desperate.'

'I know. And I suppose that's why I'm telling you – because it's so... messed up. He kept saying he wanted children one day – it's all rather sad, isn't it?'

We lapse back into a troubled silence, her hand still resting in mine as she wipes her eyes before placing the tissue back in her handbag. I stare up once more at those restless magpies then turn my head towards the top of Fawley House, its three chimneys standing against a pink-blue wash of evening sky. From somewhere comes the smell of barbecue smoke, and I can hear laughter and children's shouts rising from next door's garden.

'So how's Tom?' Isabel asks eventually.

'Well, his father's just died, so he's actually not so good.'

'I didn't mean that.'

I swallow the rest of my drink. 'I know what you meant.'

'So?'

'So what?' I turn towards her, but she's looking past me, distracted by something.

'Oh bloody hell – sorry...' but she's already up and moving towards the gate. I run my finger around the rim of the empty tumbler, as she sweeps down the drive, her impression one of carefree elegance, dressed in loose, white linen trousers and a tan-coloured silk blouse. I watch her scold Nathaniel before swooping down and lifting Ella from the lower rungs of the ladder.

My mother pauses her clipping and looks down, unaware that Ella's been attempting to climb up to her. Observing this everyday scene of parent–child interaction, I feel an unexpected heaviness in my heart as I find myself picturing the same situation taking place in other countries – Tom raising strong arms to lift his daughter down from a tree in the blazing heat of Australia; Kerem on our roof terrace with an unknown female figure behind him, his hands holding two nut-skinned toddlers away from its rail.

Once Ella's been safely lifted to the ground and propelled back into the care of her siblings, Isabel returns through the gate and makes her way back across the lawn.

'Bloody Nat,' she snaps. 'He egged her on to do that.'

I smile but say nothing as she lowers herself back down on the bench. 'Well?' she says, after a moment.

'Well what?'

'You were talking about Tom. Mummy says you didn't come home the other night. I'm not sure she's terribly convinced by your explanation that you fell asleep on his sofa. She's no fool, Anna – even if she doesn't like to confront things. She says Kerem's virtually stopped ringing and you won't talk about him or when you're going back to Turkey. You're not working and seem to spend most of your time wandering the countryside like some kind of hobo, and well... quite frankly she thinks you seem depressed. As much as we love having you here – and I'm so glad Mummy's got company... But it's not like my jet-set sister to be hanging around the family home for months on end. What is it that's bothering you – is it the operation? Did Kerem want children that much?'

I'm about to issue a snort of indignation; but stop myself, knowing that the force of my denial will be a confession in itself. Then I shrug and lean forward, placing the glass at my feet before resting my jaw on my upturned palm.

'Did... and does,' I say miserably.

I close my eyes, and within the muddled walls of my skull the sounds of the garden seem to heighten and intensify; the commotion of those magpies; the excited shrieks of my nephews and niece coming up the drive, the *thump-thump* of the football against the sarsen walls.

'I can't see a future, Izzy.'

'But that's so silly, Anna – the world's your oyster. You can do any–'

'*No*, that's the whole problem, don't you understand? I'm sick of having so many choices. I'm sick of travelling and being a stranger, and upheaval, and men who don't stick around.' And this time it's Isabel's turn to put her hand on mine. I look up to see her eyes filling with concern as I finally hear myself admit it.

'I know Kerem doesn't want to be with me anymore but it's not just that. I don't want to be in Istanbul anymore either – I think I've decided to leave but I don't know what I'm going to do next... where I'm going to go... I don't know where I want to be and that's the problem. It's like I've got no foundations, no support column. I just feel frightened and lost...'

'And this honestly has nothing to do with Tom?'

'No, of course it doesn't. Why should it?'

Isabel lets out a sigh. 'Come on, Anna. If you were in a better frame of mind I'd talk about the pot calling the kettle black.'

I drop my head and stare down at the grass. 'Yes, all right, we slept together.' I turn to gauge her reaction, but those blue eyes hold mine with their steady gaze and she says nothing. 'But he's going to go back to Australia. Once he's had the funeral, that will be it. He's got a family there.'

'So where does that leave you?'

I shrug. 'Nowhere. It leaves me nowhere.'

'Has he got feelings for you?'

'I've no idea. Yes, maybe. But I don't think he wants them. I don't think he's the kind of man who has affairs.'

'So why's he having one with you?'

'Because his marriage is in trouble. He thinks his wife's seeing someone else.'

'He's got kids, you say.'

I nod, resignedly. 'Four of them – all quite young.'

'So he's got to go back, no matter what.'

'*Of course* he has to go back, Izzy. Not just for the children – he's got a successful business there as well. There's no question of him *not going back* so I don't really know why we're even discussing this.'

'Don't be so defensive,' she says softly, lifting her glass and eyeing me over its rim. 'It sounds like you're in love with him.'

I sigh and stare down at my feet. 'I know... And I know it seems crazy after just one night but it feels like it's been building up you see, ever since we went for that drink in the pub, maybe even before that. I started thinking about him a lot after he called the ambulance for me that day... And yes, I do feel quite strongly about him. I mean... I'm actually *a bit frightened* of how I feel.'

I watch my sister absorbing these words, her gaze lowering as she swirls minute slivers of ice around the base of her glass. 'Well I can understand it,' she says eventually. 'I mean, Tom's a bit of a kindred spirit, isn't he? You knew him as a child, and now fate has brought both of you back to–'

But she breaks off as the garden gate slams open and the kids charge through it and go straight into the kitchen. Our mother walks up the drive behind them and closes it with a weary face, the shears dangling heavily in her hand. She smiles and waves before following her grandchildren indoors.

'I'm really sorry, Anna...' my sister says quickly, and I realise that this is the real reason she's come round and now intends to rush out the apology while she still has the chance. 'I really should have been here spending time with you instead of using you as an excuse to see Alex. I suppose it's my karma, that Bill's found out. It serves me right.'

I stare at her for a moment, then sigh and turn towards the apple tree. 'I'm sorry too.'

'What on earth have *you* got to be sorry for?'

'Losing my temper – because I was jealous.'

Her eyebrows raise. '*Jealous*? What have *you* got to be jealous of?'

I shrug. 'Watching you experience passion while having children and a stable marriage with a good man who loves you? That evening I felt like you'd got all the chips while I was left with nothing.' I drop my head. 'It's pathetic, I know. I'm not proud of how I behaved.'

'Anna, do you honestly think I'd be having an affair if I was happy?' Isabel retorts in a low voice. 'Do you really think that's what I want for my children and Bill? It's the worst thing, you know, because Bill's done absolutely nothing wrong. He gives me everything I want; he's not violent or bad-tempered. He loves me and provides me with a beautiful house and wonderful children. And yet most of the time I just feel so bloody empty...'

I'm silent for a moment, considering these words. Then I say quietly, 'Have you thought that Mummy might be right – about the postnatal depression, I mean?'

But she shakes her head, lifts her face to the sky and says in a high, fragile voice, 'No, it started before the children. Anna, if I'm entirely honest, I'd say it started the day he proposed.'

I stare at her, my mouth fallen open. 'You're joking,' I say finally.

She shakes her head. 'Dreadful, isn't it?'

'And you've never said anything to me about this? Over *all this* time?'

'I've not said anything to anyone. Maybe I've been in denial but I don't think I really understood it myself at the time. I just remember staring at that ring and wondering why I didn't feel over the moon, why I had this cold feeling creeping into the pit of my stomach – I suppose you'd say it was a "gut reaction".' She lets out a brief, dry laugh.

'Anna, please don't look at me like that. I really did like Bill a lot at the beginning. I remember when we first started seeing each other that I couldn't believe such a lovely man could be interested in me. But the next thing there he was asking me to be his wife, and even though I had that bad feeling I thought, "Well it's probably just because it's such a big decision and I really can't say no, can I? I mean, I'm hardly likely to meet anyone better than him at the age of thirty-two."

'And Mummy liked him so much and I knew how disappointed she'd have been if I'd, well you know, turned him down. Especially after Daddy – she kept saying how happy it would make her to see me settled down and you *know* how persuasive she can be...'

She pauses at that, then turns towards the house. I follow her gaze and watch the shape of my mother through the porch glass as she leans down to take off her gardening crocs.

'Mummy's always banging on about how hard he works to provide for us all,' she goes on, 'but that just makes me feel even worse. I know it's like she says – that there are women out there who'd give their right arm to be in my place. So why is it that most of the time I just feel this... I don't know how to describe it.'

'Try.'

She drops her gaze to the grass, her eyes narrowing. Then she raises her head and her gaze meets mine in a kind of anguish. 'I suppose it's just I look ahead at the years to come and think, *So that's it, is it*? Ludicrous, isn't it? There's you talking about being fed up to the back teeth with upheaval and desperate to have some routine – well I'm the opposite. Don't get me wrong, I mean I'll never regret my children. But it's the *certainty* of everything that depresses me. The truth is, for me getting married felt rather like walking into palliative care. All of a sudden I knew exactly how my life was likely to be in ten, twenty, thirty years' time – right down to the finishing line. And that's how I've felt ever since we tied the knot. It's like something inside of me died the moment I said, "I do".'

'You feel trapped.'

She sniffs. 'Trapped and empty. Poor dear me, the girl who has to suffer having everything she ever wanted. What is *wrong with me*, Anna? How can I be so selfish? – not just to him and the kids, but to you as well... Honestly, how am I going to feel when you've gone back to Turkey? We see so little of each other and we used to be so close, didn't we? I was hoping we'd get that closeness back again while you were here but all I've done is spend this precious time moping after Alex and used your being here as a ruse to keep on with him.'

'We've still *got time*, Izzy,' I interject quietly. Then edging my body towards hers, I put my arms around her shoulders. 'I promise I'm not going anywhere, not for a while.'

She looks down at the bench, pressing the back of her hand against her mouth, and I can see she's fighting tears again. Then she turns swiftly, and places both arms around me. As we embrace, I close my eyes and wonder how wretched Bill must be feeling, unable to make his wife happy no matter how hard he tries, and then I think about the various people I've known who conveniently met and got hitched in their late twenties and early thirties – the perfect baby-breeding age – and who, on the surface, appear perfectly content. Is it really always the case, or do the same feelings of disappointment and anti-climax lurk behind many of those tightly closed doors?

Had it been the same for Stella, I wonder? She'd met Tom in her late twenties. Was she also feeling like Isabel – sick at the certainty of her future but too scared to do anything about it, knowing she was unlikely to find another man as good as him? I picture the latter over in his father's cottage, just a hundred or so metres away from where I'm now sitting. As he dropped me off at the end of the path, he said he'd call me. But once again, despite hugging me goodbye, I sensed the barriers rise as he'd dropped his arm and leant back against the driver's door to stare at the road ahead.

Several minutes pass before Isabel straightens and reluctantly loosens her arms. 'I should be going,' she says. 'I only meant to pop in and Bill will be home soon. He'll go mad if I'm not there. But, listen, please come over soon and have dinner with us. And I'll come and see you tomorrow and every day after that. I promise.'

I nod and push a strand of her hair behind her shoulder. 'We're a pair, aren't we?' she says with a smile. Together we rise from the bench and make our way across the grass, Isabel's handbag thrown over her arm as I carry the tumblers and chopping board.

'Are you off, Isabel? Don't forget the millionaire's shortbread,' remarks my mother, going to the dresser and lifting down a biscuit tin. I carry the board to the sink and rinse it off under the tap.

'Thank you, Mummy,' Isabel says, brushing the damp from her eyes with her wrist. If our mother notices her tear-stained face then she chooses not to comment on it. 'Say "thank you" to your grandmother, children. Look at the yummy–' But she's interrupted by the buzz of her mobile phone.

'That'll be Bill...' she murmurs under her breath, rummaging into her handbag. 'Checking up on me, no doubt.'

'Oooohhh, look, Nanna's made us millionaire's shortbread!' Ella and Nathaniel shout in unison, crowding around my mother as she peels off the lid.

'Excuse me, sticky fingers... now hands off...' the latter admonishes as they take a dive into the tin, but her voice is gentle, amused, and I have that same painful sensation I'd had earlier watching her in the garden, only instead of Ella and Nathaniel, it's myself and Isabel pressing in against her apron and staring longingly at the thick golden brown slabs that, as kids, we had so loved but were not allowed to eat until after our supper lest it spoilt our appetites. Overlooking the scene is my father. He's standing in the porch smoking a Silk Cut, his grey hair and distinguished, handsome face illuminated by the evening sun.

'Oh for fuck's sake, no,' Isabel says, staring at her phone.

'Isabel!' my mother exclaims, horrified. 'Not in front of the children.'

But my sister's oblivious to her, to all of us. 'Oh fuck, Alex, no...' and her hand is lifting to her mouth as her eyes widen with horror. 'Oh God no, no. *Please no.*'

17
———

TOM

After dropping Anna at her footpath, I drive straight to the undertakers in Marlborough and start going through the paperwork with them. Then I shoot into Waitrose to stock up on provisions. I return to chop some wood in the front yard before building a fire. Pulling the shopping out of the bags, I stare without enthusiasm at the various tins and packets scattered across the work surface before me. I know I should eat; I've not eaten since this time yesterday but I've got fuck-all appetite.

Instead I crack a tin from the fridge and collapsing into an armchair, stare into the flames.

Christ, what a day.

After Dad breathed his last this morning, I sat with him for an hour or so, trying to work out what in the hell I was feeling. I guess it was partly shock at seeing death occur at such close hand; the actual desertion of the spirit from the physical body. And I suppose I was wondering where we actually go when we die because if there's one thing I'm sure of, it's that he wasn't in there anymore. Yeah, that was his skin, his hair, and his eyelashes – but he'd clearly left the show. And apart from that? Well maybe I felt a kind of relief that it was finally over and he was no longer suffering and I could go home now and not have to worry or feel guilty about any him anymore – even if I'm still no nearer to knowing what happened to Callum.

But if I'm to be completely honest, most of all I reckon I just felt numb.

It's early evening now, and the room's shrouded in darkness. I turn to switch on the lamp, then realise I should probably let Ray Curtis know what's happened even though I'm really not in the mood to see him.

His response on the phone is unsurprised, kind of flat. But an hour later he appears at the door with a six-pack, tugging two cans from the plastic rings and handing me one before letting himself down in the other armchair.

We sit together in silence, drinking lager and smoking our way through his packet of Benson & Hedges.

'You know what, Tom,' Ray says eventually, pushing his fag into a saucer and staring into the fire, 'and I feel bad saying this... But I was almost relieved when he told me he'd got the cancer. He didn't want to live anymore. He hasn't really wanted to live since Eileen died.'

I turn my head to stare at him but he keeps his gaze concentrated on the flames, finger and thumb stroking the stubble on his chin, the other clutching his can.

'How do you think he kept on going?' I say. 'He didn't really have much to live for, did he? Why didn't he take the easy way out like Mum?'

Ray shrugs, then pushes back his thick hair. As he does this I notice the tattoo on his hand – the hand-drawn anti-apartheid slogan and the three letters across his knuckles; ZEN. He'd had it done when I was a kid – I remember him holding it out to me and Callum and trying to explain about South Africa and white people hating black people. I remember Callum's bulging eyes as he'd carefully stroked Ray's hand with his finger.

'Jim never had any self-pity,' he's saying now as I observe those strange black-and-white swirls. 'It's something I always admired about him – that he suffered so much tragedy yet managed to bear it.'

'It's like he saw living as a way of punishing himself.'

'Maybe it was.'

'But why would he want to? If he was innocent, I mean...'

Ray fires a look at me. 'He *was* innocent, Tom.'

I hold his gaze for a moment, then rest forward on my elbows. 'He seemed to think you knew something about that, Ray.'

I feel him turn towards me. 'What makes you say that?'

'Something he said just before he went into hospital that last time. He was rambling on about him and Mum feeling guilty but he wouldn't say why. When I pushed him he said, "Ask Ray". What did he mean by that?'

'I've no idea.'

'So why say it?'

He shrugs. Then in an exasperated tone, 'I don't know, Tom. Probably because I was here. I saw how it was and how responsible they felt. *Of course* they felt guilty. Callum was their son and he was murdered. They weren't there to protect him when he needed them most. Any parent would feel guilty in that situation.'

I continue staring at him and I think about my mother's unopened letter. Does he know about that, too? But somehow I suspect he doesn't, and even if he does, I just can't face it now because I know he'll just go off on one like Anna and tell me I should take it to the police. Besides, I'm whacked and to be honest, starting to wish Ray would piss off home and leave me alone.

I bow my head and go silent. A few minutes pass, and then I know he's got the hint because he suddenly stands up. 'Think I'll head off. You need sleep, my friend.'

And then of course I feel like shit. Shit, because Ray was my father's best friend and did more for him than I ever have. Shit, because he obviously needs to talk and to grieve too. But still I say nothing, rising to my feet and patting him on the arm. 'It's been a long day, mate.'

He nods. 'I understand.'

'Come round tomorrow and we'll have a proper session.'

Ray leaves, but I don't go to bed. Instead I return to my place in the sitting room and fling another log on the fire.

Hours pass. There's a police helicopter in the sky. It keeps going over and over, passing up to the woods and back again. I guess they must be looking for someone but its incessant drone starts to wind me up. Just when I think it's gone for good it returns once more, flying so low over the roofs and treetops I swear it's going to hit something. But then, after about half an hour, the sound abruptly dies away, and silence returns.

It occurs to me it must be early morning in Australia so I get up and phone Stella before she leaves for work – phone rather than Zoom this time because I know I must look a wreck. Of course she's sympathetic and makes all the right noises – lots of 'I'm sorrys' and all that shit. I don't ask to speak to the kids because I know if I do the sound of their voices will break me and I don't want to put them, or me, through that.

'So when do you think you'll be home?' she asks eventually, and I catch the agitation in her voice.

'When I've got everything sorted out here, I guess. Couple of weeks at most.'

'The kids will be happy.'

'And what about you? Will you be happy?' I hear my voice

echo back down the long-distance line; *And what about you? And what about you?*

There is a too-shrill laugh. 'Of course I'll be happy, Tom. We all miss you, honey.'

But I can hear it now for sure and know if it wasn't for the bleakness of the occasion she might be telling me much more. And suddenly I won't let it go.

'Tell me about him.' Only my words are followed by a silence – too much of a long, fucking silence.

Then, cautiously, she says, 'Tell you about who?'

'You know who I'm talking about.'

My chest's aching now. I'm waiting for denial, anger, astonishment even – feigned or otherwise. But all I get is more of the same. And then the words I really don't want to hear: 'Let's talk about this when you're back.'

'No, Stella. Let's talk about it now.'

'You've just lost your father, Tom. It's really not the right time to be doing this to yourself.'

'I know you're fucking him. It's John, isn't it? Is that why he's just handed in his notice? So he doesn't have to face me?'

And still there's no denial. In the distance, behind her words, I can hear Indiana's voice asking excitedly, 'Is that Daddy on the phone?' and the tears well up in my eyes as I hear Stella telling her to go and wait in the kitchen.

Then she says, 'Get your stuff sorted and come home, Tom. We can talk then. You don't need this on your plate right now. And get some sleep, hey – you sound done in. I'll call you in a couple of days.'

The line goes dead before I can reply.

18

ANNA

Soweton Parish Church stands on top of the hill which rises between Fawley and the village of Soweton in the neighbouring valley. The church was built to serve both communities and, as a result, isn't geographically part of either. A tall, rather imposing building, it stands isolated and alone, its grey stone walls exposed to the elements, its rambling, yew-dotted graveyard overlooking the valley of the River Kennett and beyond it, on the other side of the A4, the vast, sarsen-scattered expanse of Marlborough Down.

There's no more than thirty people at the funeral. It seems a small congregation for a man who'd lived in the village for more than forty years. When my father died ten years ago, I remember people having to wait outside the church because it was so crowded – but then I suppose he lived in London, where he was well-known professionally.

Standing with my mother and Isabel in the middle rows, I feel a bit like an intruder. My mother knew Jim well enough but though I remember him from those wood deliveries, I was only a child so we'd never really spoken apart from that morning he'd come round looking for Callum.

As I strain to reach the notes of the various hymns, I find myself studying the back of Tom's bowed head. I wonder how he feels knowing he's about to bury his father before flying to the other side of the world, leaving his grave, and those of his mother and brother, untended. Apart from his short telephone call to invite us to this service, I've seen nothing of this man who was briefly my lover.

We start singing 'Jerusalem'. I glance at my sister who stands to my left, her whole being livid with emotion. She wears an expression of indelible shock, her hair scraped back tightly into a ponytail, revealing a waxen complexion. Shadows circle her bruised-looking eyes, their lashes intermittently beaded with tears. I'm not sure why I'm surprised at her grief – or is it, in truth, a combination of grief and remorse? – but maybe I've never really seen my sister experience acute anguish or pain before, except perhaps, after the death of our father.

Since receiving that text from Alex warning her that he was going to kill himself, and then learning from the police that his body had been found hanging in Fawley Wood, she's been staying with my mother and me, unable to cope with Bill or her children.

After the hymn, Tom rises to say a few words about his father. They're delivered in a quiet, monosyllabic tone which betrays nothing of his feelings. He pays tribute to Jim's wood deliveries to the community over the years, then jokes lightly about him keeping the pub in profit during his younger days and expresses hope that he's now reunited in peace with his mother and Callum. As the latter's name is mentioned, I notice a scruffy-looking man in the pew to my right scribbling shorthand in a notebook. A journalist. Callum's death had been national news once.

A few minutes later, we're shuffling out of our pews and walking out of the church. Though the air's clear and the sun's shining, it's a restless, chilly day. I button up my coat as we take our place in the row of mourners, each one shaking hands and offering a few words of condolence to Tom. He moves slowly down the line, reaching my mother first. I watch him smile as she chats to him about the days when Jim used to come round to the house to do jobs for her.

Isabel follows, putting her delicate hand in his large one and squeezing it before suddenly bursting into tears. 'Oh Tom, I'm *so so terribly* sorry,' and I watch him straighten, his brow lifting in surprise at this unexpected outpouring.

Finally it's my turn. He takes both my hands in his, gripping them hard for several long seconds as his gaze penetrates mine. Then he leans forward, pressing his cheek against my ear but saying nothing. I feel his warm breath under my hair and, closing my eyes for a second, shiver involuntarily as I inhale his familiar aroma of soap and rolling tobacco.

'I'm surprised Jim didn't have a Catholic funeral,' my mother remarks as we make our way over the grass to the newly-dug grave which lies under a low sarsen wall. To its right, interspersed with other graves but within sight of this one, stand the two stone crosses which mark the final resting places of Eileen and Callum Donnelly.

'He was lapsed,' I explain. 'Gave it up after Callum died apparently. Anyway, the nearest Catholic church is in Marlborough.'

We reach the edge of the grave and stand listening with bowed heads as the vicar commences with his final oration. 'In sure and certain hope of the restoration to eternal life through our Lord Jesus Christ, we commend to Almighty God our brother Jim, and we commit his body to the ground...' As his voice drifts through the gravestones and down into the valley below, I surreptitiously inspect the mourners who surround the grave; my gaze travelling quietly from Tom's lowered, meditative stance, to my mother's stoic, respectful one, her eyes pressed tightly shut, hands folded over her black handbag; then my focus swerves round to Isabel who's standing beside me, only she doesn't appear to be listening to the vicar at all. Instead she's upright and rigid, her eyes fixed on the group at the opposite side of the grave. I follow her gaze to see Ray Curtis staring straight back at her.

'...earth to earth, ashes to ashes, dust to dust. The Lord bless him and keep him, the Lord make his face to shine upon him and be gracious unto him, the Lord lift up his countenance upon him and give him peace. Amen....' then Tom moves forward to scatter a handful of soil across the coffin's polished lid.

A minute later and it's all over. The attendants move forward with their shovels and start showering earth onto the coffin. Tom steps back and puts his hands into the pockets of his suit, then walks with bowed head towards the sarsen wall.

'The wake's down at the Catherine, isn't it?' I hear someone say. To my left I'm aware of my mother chatting to an old man with a large bald head and missing teeth. Isabel remains rooted to the spot, her eyes following Ray Curtis as he joins Tom.

'Izzy,' I whisper. 'What on earth's going on?'

She shoots a quick glance at me and then returns her gaze to Ray. 'What do you mean,' she whispers back "what on earth's going on?"'

'Why are you staring at Ray like that?'

'*Ray–*' She turns towards me. 'Do you know him?'

I shrug. 'Not really. I've met him once or twice with Tom. His name's Ray Curtis – he was Jim's business partner.'

'He's from Fawley, isn't he? I remember seeing him around the village when we were children.'

I nod. 'Yes he is. Why?'

'Because that's him.' She takes a sudden, determined step in his direction but I grab her arm and bring her to a halt.

Then shaking my head, I say in a mystified voice, 'That's who?'

'The man at the river. Look at his hand.'

I turn to watch Ray Curtis as he comes to a standstill in front of Tom. The former says something then sits down on the wall, withdrawing a cigarette from a packet and lighting it. As he does so the back of his palm is laid bare – he's four or five yards away from us but I can clearly see it – the three letters spelling out ZEN on his index, middle and ring fingers; the black swirl of the Yin-Yang on his knuckles.

'Shit, Izzy.'

As he takes a drag, Ray's gaze moves over the graves before rising surreptitiously towards Isabel. But when he spies us watching him, he immediately drops it to the ground and there's something in the way he does that, and the uncomfortable working of his jaw, that tells me my sister's right.

To our left, people are making their way out of the gates and getting into the various cars which line the road. My mother's finished talking to the man with the bald head and now winds her way between the graves towards us.

'Isabel, you look terrible,' she says when she reaches us. 'You should take yourself home.'

'I'm okay,' Isabel replies stiffly, her gaze following Ray Curtis as he and Tom rise from the wall and start heading side-by-side towards the cars.

'Well, you don't look it.'

'Honestly, Mummy, I'm perfectly fine. Come on, let's get to the pub. I don't know about you two but I need a drink.'

* * *

The Catherine's busy, the mourners milling with the pub's regular drinkers around the bar, which is heaped with plates of ham and egg sandwiches, crisps and sausage rolls. Neither Isabel nor I are hungry, so we fetch ourselves two large glasses of white wine and go to sit together in an alcove at the end of a long table. The sunlit high street through the window behind us is lined with cars from the congregation. Our mother sits down opposite with a cup of tea and starts chatting animatedly to Len Combstone. There's no sign of Ray Curtis.

I watch Tom hang around the bar, shaking hands with the various people who approach him, noticing how he keeps each exchange short before giving the person a cursory nod and a thanks. Once or twice his gaze raises to meet mine over their heads, but he offers no smile or acknowledgement.

'So what are you going to do?' I say, turning to Isabel.

She shrugs, then frowns into her glass. 'What can I do?'

'You should go to the police.'

'And tell them what? That when I was twelve I was coming back from the river and a man grabbed me and told me I was beautiful and that I ran away and never saw him again until now. And besides...' Her voice falters and her hand around the glass begins to wobble. 'I've got too much on my plate at the moment. I honestly don't think I can take any more... I still can't believe it, Anna... How could he have done that, especially to his poor mother? I mean, okay, so he felt hurt and rejected, but he always knew I was married. I honestly never led him on that I was going to leave Bill. I've got three kids for Christ's sake...'

It takes me a moment to realise she's talking about Alex. Reaching out a hand, I press her shoulder. 'He clearly had a lot of problems, Izzy. You weren't to know that.' I watch her run her thumb and forefinger against the edges of her mouth, then she closes her eyes. Across the table I notice our mother turn to watch her older daughter. Isabel's distress is impossible to ignore

– as is Bill's complete absence, although Rachel, their nanny, has brought the children over several hours each day. All my sister seems to want to do is lie on her old bed staring into space, or sit in front of my mother's upright piano and run through the hundreds of scores she learnt as a child. This would be pleasant if it were not for the endless repetition due to her almost obsessive determination to iron out every mistake, despite not having played for years.

Isabel did her best to hide the worst of things – initially telling our mother that she and Bill had had another huge row and needed some space from each other. But in the end she felt compelled to confess that the young man who'd so tragically hung himself in Fawley Wood last week had been her jilted lover.

'Izzy,' I say now, 'have you thought, I mean... well what if Ray's done it to others? And what if he actually... got somewhere. You know? If you come forward then maybe they might too. You know how it is now with DNA.'

'I'm not going to do anything, Anna,' Isabel hisses. 'So please don't keep on at me.' She raises the glass and swallows the rest of her wine. 'Besides, I absolutely don't want Mummy to know and if I go to the police she's bound to find out and she'll get terribly upset about it, especially as I didn't tell her at the time.' Wiping her face with the cuff of her black jacket and sniffing, she rises to her feet. 'Want another? I'm going to get pissed.'

Tom glances enquiringly at Isabel's strained face as she approaches the bar. Then he turns in my direction and I watch him considering her vacated chair. His gaze meets mine then he starts making his way through the crowd of mourners towards me, a pint of lager in his hand.

'How're you going?' he says, sitting down beside me.

'I'm okay.' I smile at him. 'More importantly, how are *you*?'

He swallows a mouthful of lager and stares at the table. 'Oh

I'm just bonzer, mate – it's been a bloody fantastic week, even by my standards.'

'Oh Tom.'

He shakes his head but under the table I feel the rough skin of his fingers close over mine and squeeze them hard. 'Sorry I haven't called.'

I shrug. 'It's okay. You've had a lot to deal with.'

'Yeah, you can say that again. There's other stuff that's happened too.'

I stare at him curiously but he forces a smile and stares down at the table's polished surface. From the other side of the table I feel my mother watching us. I realise Tom feels it too because he suddenly lifts his head and looks straight at her. 'How are you going, Mrs Carmichael? Thanks for coming today.'

'I'm very well, thank you very much for asking, Tom. It was a very moving service.'

'Thank you.'

'I expect you're terribly relieved it's all over.'

'You can say that again,' he replies quickly, then stares back down at the table.

My mother watches him for a moment, her eyes narrowing behind the varifocals before turning to resume her conversation with Len Combstone.

When he's certain she's not watching us any longer, Tom leans in towards my ear. 'Will you come back to the house with me when this is over?'

I pull back and stare at his entreating expression, at the same time noticing the booze on his breath and the exhausted gaze which is accentuated under the window's bright sunshine. He's clearly not at all together and if I had any sense at all I would stay well away from him today.

'All right,' I say.

* * *

It's gone five by the time we leave the pub and head down the high street towards his father's cottage. Tom walks beside me, his hands buried in his trouser pockets, looking absurdly handsome with his hair falling in loose waves over the collar of his suit.

'There's something I want to talk to you about,' he says, staring hard at the ground. 'And I need to show you something.'

When we reach the front door he opens it with a Yale key and gestures for me to pass before closing it behind me. I walk through the narrow hall and enter the sitting room, which feels cold and bare under the bright glare of a naked bulb. His mother's bluebell paintings have been taken down from the walls but the accumulated dust and grime on the latter have left pale squares clearly indicating where they'd hung for so many years. The centre of the room is stacked with books and boxes of ancient-looking kitchenware, topped with the room's dirt-encrusted, ancient floral lampshade.

'You've been busy,' I say, my spirit deflating at the sight before me, the reality of his imminent departure.

'Yeah,' he says, his eyes resting on the boxes, his mouth colliding into a grimace. Then, 'Take a look at this.' He straightens and I watch him make his way through the kitchen and disappear into his father's office. A minute later he returns with a long fold of dusty green tarpaulin which he places on the sofa and slowly unrolls, bit by bit, to eventually reveal a dust-coloured rifle. 'Found it up in the loft.'

'Crikey.' I take a step towards the gun and, reaching out a hand, run a finger along its steel barrel, leaving an s-shaped trail in the dust.

'I googled it. Apparently it's an AR-18 Armalite rifle. Made in the USA and used widely by the American, Japanese and

British military in the 1970s – so not your standard piece for shooting game. There was some ammunition as well.'

'So Jim *did* have a gun...' I take a step back then let myself slowly down into a chair. 'You've *got to* tell the police about this, Tom. And you need to tell them about Eileen's suicide note. Have you read it yet?'

'No,' he says. 'And I won't. Neither will they. Those were her wishes. I can't just ignore them.'

'So you'd rather torture yourself with not knowing?'

He nods. 'Than betray her? Yeah, I would.'

'That's crazy.'

'No it's not. That note was written for my father. No one else. I think you'd feel the same in my situation. As for this...' He lifts up the gun. 'I'm taking it down the station tomorrow. I only came across it yesterday morning so I've just not had time with organising the funeral.'

'But why would he have it?'

He shakes his head. 'Fuck knows. I asked Ray to come over to look at it. He said he never knew Dad had a gun. But I dunno – he didn't seem so surprised, actually.'

He turns and places both elbows on the mantelpiece, resting his forehead on them. 'Anna, I don't know what to think any more. My head's mashed. I guess that's why I asked you over because I needed someone else's view.'

As I hear these words, I'm aware of my thoughts abruptly swerving from his dilemma back to myself, my heart sinking as I absorb the truth of his meaning – the realisation he's only really brought me back here because he needs someone to talk to, and while, deep down, I know it's the wisest course for both of us, I'm simultaneously fighting a wave of disappointment at this abrupt demotion from lover to sounding board – even though I know it's foolish to expect anything more.

'Look, do you want something more to drink?' he says

suddenly, lifting his head from his hands and turning towards me, as if reading my thoughts.

I rise from the chair, shake my head. 'I should go home. Sorry, but it's getting late and I'm worried about Isabel. She's not in a good place at the moment.'

'Right... Okay.'

He's resting back against the mantelpiece and looking at me in a disorientated way, but there's something else smouldering in his eyes and I recognise it immediately – a look of surprised dismay, of repelled expectation and rejection, which exactly mirrors my own feelings. I stare back at him without moving. Then simultaneously we both step forward and I feel his arms close around me and pull me against him, his mouth crushing the side of my neck, my cheek, my mouth, before he steps back and, taking my hand, leads me up the narrow stairs.

* * *

Anaesthetised by the three large glasses of wine I drank in the pub, I must have crashed out soon after making love, because the next thing I know I'm waking to find the room shrouded in dusk with Tom's naked body next to mine. Lifting my head, I expect to see him sleeping, but his eyes in the half-light are open. I feel his soft breath warming my face, the damp tickle of his chest hair against my collarbone. Under the duvet, his wrist moves to rest casually over the bare skin of my hip, then he reaches forward and his mouth presses wetly against my cheek. He murmurs my name.

A little later he rises and starts searching around in a drawer before sitting back on the edge of the bed and building a joint. I watch him surreptitiously, listening to his heavy breathing and feeling his concentration as he heats the resin up under the flame and crumbles it onto the tobacco. Then, climbing back under the blankets beside me, he flicks the Zippo and a few moments later the heady smell of cannabis drifts over me.

'Sorry to keep you from your sister, hey.'

I smile up at him, then stroke his arm. 'That's okay. Mummy's with her.'

'She was having an affair with that Alex bloke, wasn't she?' he adds casually, inspecting the joint before licking at a loose edge of paper and sealing it with his fingers. 'He sent her a text telling her what he was going to do, didn't he? Len Combstone said she called the police and they spent most of the night looking for him. I heard the helicopter. Poor guy. What did the text say?'

I push myself up onto one elbow. 'It was a quote from a novel.'

'Oh yeah – what?'

'"He had really forgotten and overlooked one little circumstance in life – that Death would come and end everything, so that it was useless to begin anything, and that there was no help for it."'

'Jesus.'

'It's from *Anna Karenina*.' I reach up and prise the spliff from his fingers, take a long drag from it. 'By coincidence one of my favourite books. Poor Isabel, she's in a terrible state.' I pass the joint back to him. 'So when are you going back to Australia?'

I sense him deliberating his answer, the effect it may have on me. 'Pretty soon, I guess. I've instructed an estate agent and I should finish sorting out his stuff in the next week or so. There's not much left to organise really. I miss the kids, hey.' He feels around in the gloom then flicks the ash into a saucer. 'By the way, you'll be pleased to know I followed your advice,' he adds, glancing at me over his shoulder. 'I had it out with Stella and yeah, she's definitely fucking John.'

I stretch an arm across his belly and press my face against the damp skin of his shoulder.

'That's all I know,' he adds. 'I asked her and she didn't deny it. But she's refusing to talk about it until I get back.'

'What are you going to do?'

He shrugs. 'No idea. If it wasn't for the kids I'd probably be telling her to sling her hook, but I've got them to think about. Oh yeah, and then there's the small problem of the business I spent years building up – she owns half of that as well.'

I stroke his bare stomach with my fingertips. After a minute, he turns and presses his lips against my forehead, his hand travelling through my hair and down between my shoulder blades. Then he rises naked from the bed once more and switches on the small bedside lamp before leaving the room without putting on his dressing gown, the joint still in his hand.

As I wait for him to return, I consider this revelation and wonder how long he's known about it. It's been over a week since we went to the stones and I've not heard from him at all apart from that brief phone call inviting me to the funeral – a message my mother took because I was out walking. But at the same time, I'm strongly aware of the shift in his attitude towards me today, of a new openness and the sense he's no longer trying to push me away or suffering a conscience about being with me.

He returns a few minutes later, entering the room with a can of lager in each hand, the joint dangling from his lips.

'What the hell,' he says, handing me one of the cans. 'Let's have our own private wake, hey. It's not every day you get to bury your dad and find out your wife's been having it away behind your back.'

'It's good you can laugh about it.'

He sits on the side of the bed and stares morosely at the carpet. 'Fuck it, we should get divorced,' he says. 'We've been dead for a long time and it's probably my fault just as much as hers. I guess we've drawn away from each other, but her more than me if I'm honest. I've received more affection from you these last few weeks than I've had in years from her.'

'But what about your children...'

'Oh yeah, that's right, the children.' He opens the can then raises it to his lips. 'Oh yeah...' he repeats, more slowly this time and with greater emphasis, wiping his mouth with the back of his hand. 'She made sure we had *them* all right. But you know what, she's always turned it on and off like a tap. Each time, the moment she discovered she was pregnant, it was like someone had super-glued her legs together for the next two years, or at least till she was ready for the next one.'

'You sound like you regret having them.'

He shakes his head vigorously. 'Of course I don't regret having them. They're the best thing that's ever happened to me. But I can't ever leave them, can I? Because of them I'm trapped in Australia forever.'

This last sentence of his makes me sit up abruptly and stare at him. He's still looking down at the floor, his brow furrowed under the long dark hair, the can resting in his hand. We're silent for some moments, the question remaining unaired because there's no use in asking something that's already been answered. At the same time, I'm becoming aware of the sound of ticking, and glancing towards his bedside table, notice a small travel clock. Its black-and-white face seems to glare back at me defiantly, that minute hand continuing its determined journey around the dial, counting off the days and hours we have left together.

Winding my arm around his naked waist, I press my face against the coolness of his back. 'Aren't you cold?' I whisper. 'You must be.'

He shakes his head, cups his free hand over my elbow, his fingers stroking its skin. That soft *tick tick tick* of the clock is the only sound. Then taking several swift mouthfuls from the can and staring up at the ceiling, he says, '"Sometimes questions are easier than answers". That's what Dad said – just before he died. It didn't hit me at the time – but since I found that gun it keeps coming back to me. What do you think he meant?'

I'm silent for a moment, considering his words and simultaneously struggling with myself because the last thing I wanted was to raise it on the day of Jim's funeral. But now I feel he's left me no choice.

'There's a couple of things that have been troubling me,' I say finally. 'I was planning to tell you but not...'

'What?'

I stare down at the duvet, contemplating the question and the effect it may have on him. 'Tom, do you remember an uncle coming here to visit? When you were young, I mean.'

He raises his head, looks at me oddly. 'Yeah,' he says slowly. 'Patrick. He only came the one time. Dad and him had a row and he ended up driving off in the middle of the night. How did you know about that?'

I slowly relate to him the story which my mother had told me. When I've finished Tom's silent, his face chewing it over.

'A murdered child in Ireland?' he says finally. 'Len's never mentioned this to me.'

'Maybe you should ask him. It sounds to me like your uncle was out to cause trouble – but all the same...'

'Yeah, maybe I will.' But he sounds unconvinced.

'Also, it's not connected, but there's something else. Why wasn't Ray at the wake this afternoon?'

He shrugs. 'Dunno. He said he was going to come down a bit later – guess he got held up but yeah, it's a bit weird now you come to mention it. Seeing as he was Dad's best mate.'

'Did he have a key to this house?'

He throws me an odd look. 'I've no idea. But Dad left the

door unlocked most of the time so Ray and the nurse could get in and out as they needed. Least he did towards the end.'

'I don't mean now. I mean when Callum went missing.'

'I don't... Well, yeah, he did, because he used to...' And then his eyes widen as he finally understands. 'Come on, Anna. Jesus, you *can't* be thinking that...'

And suddenly he's rising, almost violently, from the bed and shoving my arm away. Taking his dressing gown from the hook on the door, he wraps it around himself.

I swing my legs out of the bed, holding the duvet across my chest. 'Look, Tom. I didn't really want to tell you all this today, but I do think you've got the right to know.'

'Know what?'

'That Ray assaulted Isabel.'

'He *what*?'

'It was when she was twelve years old. She was down at the river, you know where the stone bridge is? The water's deep there – she and I used to go swimming under the bridge in the summer.'

'Yeah, Anna. I swam there too, remember.'

Ignoring his sarcasm, I describe to him what occurred between Isabel and Ray Curtis on that mid-summer day. For a moment he says nothing, his hand reaching behind him for the dressing gown cord. Then he frowns and shakes his head. 'Why haven't you told me this before?'

'Because she didn't know the man was Ray until she saw him today at the funeral. She recognised his tattoo – you know, that weird anti-apartheid thing he's got on his hand.'

I watch Tom's eyes slowly fill with cold disbelief.

'Look, I know it wasn't a serious attack compared to other stuff you read about. But he still *groped* her, you know, and terrified her. He was a grown man. She was only twelve years old. It affected her badly at the time.'

Tying the dressing gown around him, Tom slowly lowers himself back on the bed, but he's a foot or so further away from me now. Taking a Rizla paper, he smoothes it on his knee, then places a trail of tobacco along its spine. 'Yeah, he had a key,' he says eventually. 'Dad kept some of the paperwork here. Sometimes when we came home from school Ray would be in the office doing the accounts. He was better with figures than Dad – don't think Dad's schooling in Ireland added up to very much.'

'So Ray had access to the house. He could've been here waiting when Callum came home that evening and that would explain why there were no screams or signs of a struggle – because Callum would have trusted Ray, wouldn't he? Ray might have asked him to go somewhere with him, cooked up some kind of story about a surprise Christmas present for you or Jim he wanted to show him.'

'Is she really sure it was Ray? Jesus. A lot of people have tattoos like that...'

'Come on, Tom...'

He lifts the roll-up to his mouth and lights it. 'You know, when Callum and I were kids, Ray always had a string of girlfriends. They buzzed around him like bush flies. And these women were *mature*, of a legal age. I don't remember him ever showing an appetite for children.'

'Well, he'd hardly advertise it, would he?'

His mouth presses into a grimace. 'So what's Isabel planning to do about it?'

I raise my hands. 'What can she do? It's her word against his, isn't it? And, it was decades ago. But I still think she should tell the police so they can look into him a bit more. He might have a record of this kind of thing for all we know.'

'So let me get this straight. You're saying that if Ray could grope Isabel, he could do the same to Callum? There's just one important detail,' he adds. 'In case you haven't noticed.'

'Callum was a boy. But he was also beautiful and very sensitive. Lots of paedophiles abuse both sexes, Tom, you read about it all the time.'

'Yeah but...' He relights the roll-up, which has gone out, and his eyes betray the conflicted workings of his mind.

'You know Ray had guns,' he muses after a moment. 'At least he did, back then. I remember him showing them to me once when I was over at his place – he was always bringing over braces of pheasants he'd shot up in Fawley Wood. Dad used to hang them in the backroom.'

'I had to tell you, didn't I?'

'Yeah – you had to tell me.' But he says it in a dead voice. A coldness settles on him and though he doesn't move I can feel him mentally withdrawing from me, a crevasse splitting the ground between us. 'You realise what you're saying, don't you?' he says finally. 'Ray was Dad's best mate. He's *my* mate. He's done a lot for our family, helped us through what happened to Callum, then looked after Dad when he was ill and now he's helping me deal with him. For Christ's sake – and now you're implying... no, I don't believe it....'

'It might explain why Jim was protecting him – why he said that thing about questions being better than answers.'

'Now you're just being stupid. If Dad really thought Ray'd killed Callum there's *no way* he would have protected him, even if he...'

'He what?'

But he stops, then shakes his head. 'It's just something Dad said before he died – that I should ask Ray, that *Ray* knew why he and Mum felt so guilty over Callum. So I did... and Ray said it was because he was here when it all happened and that they were parents and no wonder they felt guilty. It kind of made sense.'

'But anyone would say that, wouldn't they? It's not rocket science. Do you think Jim was hinting at something?'

He shrugs and then looks pointedly down at the watch on his wrist.

Feeling stung, I stare down at the floor, a coldness gripping my throat. 'Look, I'm just telling you everything I've learnt since I've been here, Tom. I don't know what any of it means.'

The can crushes in his hand. 'Yeah, well. Thanks, Miss Marple, but I'd prefer you to keep the village gossip to yourself from now on.'

'Okay, okay. I'm really sorry I brought any of it up, I really am.'

I rise from the bed and reach for my pants and skirt, yanking the latter up over my hips, almost splitting the zip in my rush to get away. He nods, almost absently, then tales a drag on the roll-up and eyes me through the smoke.

Outside the small window over his shoulder, the dusk has turned to darkness and condensation's begun to cloud its panes, signalling the freezing temperature outside.

'You're shooting the messenger here, you know that,' I mutter, fumbling with a button.

He doesn't reply. My chest aches as I stand there waiting for him to say something, anything, to stop me leaving, and at the same time becoming horribly aware that this may be the last time we will ever see each other.

But he remains silent as I finish dressing with my back to him, buttoning up my black blouse, then pulling up my tights and hurriedly tying the laces of my boots.

I turn, once more, to face him. He's still sitting there on the side of the bed, watching me coldly. 'Don't look so upset, Anna.' He leans over the bed and stubs the cigarette in the saucer. 'I'm no loss to you. You're out of my league now just like you were then.'

'That's rubbish.'

'No, it's not. You're just a bit lost at the moment, that's all, and you need a bit of rough to see you through this dry patch. You're at a crossroads, between boyfriends, between lives, and I just happened to roll up at a convenient time. But don't worry, before you know it you'll be living in some city in sub-Saharan Africa, shacked up with the next Mustafa.'

Staring down at him, mouth slumped open, his words splitting my heart like an axe. 'Fuck you,' I say.

He raises his eyebrows.

'Fuck you, Tom... Christ, what is this bollocks? You've wiped Kerem off the map, don't you realise? Why the hell do you think I'm still around? Because I don't know where to go next?' And as I say it, I realise suddenly how stoned I am, the dope gone straight to my head from standing up so quickly.

He throws back his head and laughs, but I can tell by his demeanour, by the slightly crazed look in his eyes that it's hit him too and now it's hard to determine what's really meant and what's emerging out of the stress of the day and all the new information that's suddenly surfaced and all the shit that, one way or another, he's been putting in his mouth to help him cope with it.

'Yeah, Anna. You've got it in one. *Because you don't know where to go next.* Don't think I don't remember you and Isabel at school.' He reaches down to the carpet and picks up that crushed can, then swigs the rest of his lager. 'Don't think I don't remember how the local kids all homed in on you because you were the posh Carmichaels, come to deign us with your presence for a *whole* term. How privileged we all felt for that, hey. I remember you standing in the playground in your pretty clothes and thinking how untouchable you both seemed back then. And you know what? Nothing's changed except that now you've got letters after your name. I was watching you both in the pub today – you and Isabel, and your old lady, sitting there like you'd somehow arrived by accident. Someone even asked how I'd managed to get royalty to the Wake.'

'Jesus, Tom. What kind of stupid, fucked-up attitude is that?' I put my hand on the door handle but for some reason I can't make myself go through it just yet. 'How in the hell can you be so small-minded to blame me for the one thing I've got absolutely no control over? I can't help it if my parents were wealthy and yours weren't, and yes, I'm sure there are lots of differences between us because of it... *Letters after my name?* So I went to university and you didn't... Well that's clearly an insurmountable obstacle for us, isn't it? I mean, if you want to insult your own obvious intelligence by smashing yourself over the head with that massive chip you carry on your shoulder.'

'Don't patronise me.'

'*I'm not* patronising you. It's *you* who's patronising you. It makes no difference to me at all that we have different backgrounds – if you must know, I really admire you for what you've achieved, especially after everything you went through with Callum and your mum. Can't you see? I couldn't give a shit if you went to university or not, it doesn't change the way I feel for you.'

At that, he reaches forward and places the can on the bedside table, then drops his head into his hands and sighs heavily. 'Yeah? And what exactly is it that you *feel for me*, Anna?'

I gaze down at him, the words gathered like dice in a fist; words that, once thrown, can never be taken back and, right now he doesn't deserve to hear. Then I close my eyes and visualise it, the fist opening, the dice scattering, the ball rolling round and round and round the roulette wheel and no idea where it will finally come to rest. 'I love you,' I say bluntly. And then, just to make absolutely sure he's got it, 'I love you, Tom. I love you.'

The declaration is followed by a stony silence. I hear him breathing heavily and try desperately to remind myself that he's drunk and angry, and I'm also drunk and stoned and will no doubt live to regret this admission, and what's worse, I know it's all my fault for agreeing to come back to this house with him when I could see he was in no fit state for anything but sleep.

He places his elbows on his knees, wraps his hands together. 'You don't love me, Anna,' he says quietly. 'I'm not even sure you know how to.' He raises his gaze to meet mine. 'Come on. When's the nearest you've got to loving anyone? Because I'll tell you something for nothing. From where I'm standing you're choosing this lonely road of yours, these men who can't commit.'

'*You're* not a man who can't commit.'

He laughs at that, then adds with cruel irony, 'That's right – just a shame it's to someone else.'

And as he says it, and even though I know he's being unnecessarily cruel, I feel myself buckling helplessly under the truth of his words. Like one of those irritating digital photograph frames, one by one, each lover's face flashes slowly before my eyes. Even Kerem, during our first month together, told me he wasn't sure he could marry a non-Muslim and the caveat had sat snugly between us ever since, despite moving in together, despite pretending to have a committed relationship the word 'marriage' had rarely been spoken since that day because I knew instinctively what would follow, could already hear him saying, '*I warned you from the beginning. I warned you.*'

Even the issue about having children had been a sham – Kerem had always been careful, constantly saying that the time was not yet right and now I wonder if he'd ever really planned to have them with me because in reality, the implications of the operation were most likely just an excuse for him to nail a final full stop on the relationship he never really saw lasting the course.

And I'd let him do it, I'd let him steal my chance to have children as he used me to fill time, to bulk out the years as he'd put off the real commitment that would have to take place, marriage to a good Muslim girl, just as his parents wanted. Because I'd known it too – or had at least suspected it all the way through the relationship, but because I didn't want to be alone, I too had chosen to live in a state of cosy self-delusion. It had been a mutually convenient arrangement from which he was sure to emerge as the chief beneficiary.

I turn away and as I reach for my coat I feel my head beginning to reel, not just at the double humiliation of Tom's harsh words and obvious refusal to reciprocate my declaration, though that feels bad enough. No, what's upsetting me most is the awful realisation that he's probably right; that I *have* always been the architect of my own loneliness and this attraction to him, yet another man who'll never be able to offer me any kind of a future, is just an extension of the same negative pattern of behaviour. What had he said to me at the Shadowing Stones about my choice in men really being about my father leaving us? Could he be right?

Without saying another word, I yank open the door and send it smashing against the wall with a bang that makes the whole house shake, then charge blindly along the corridor towards the stairs. But before I'm halfway down them, I'm finding it hard to see because of the tears that are pouring down my face. My legs have started giving way beneath me, my head spinning in a confused spiral of dope, booze and humiliation. I grasp the wooden banister to stop myself falling and at the same time hear the smack of bare feet behind me then feel his arms lifting and half carrying me to the hallway below. When we get to the bottom I lash out at him, my hand slapping his cheek hard before he catches it in his own and holds it.

'Fuck off you wanker. Just fuck off!'

'Anna. Listen.'

I struggle against him in the darkness, my other fist flailing against his chest, my feet kicking at his shins.

'Anna, for Christ's sake, take it easy... Please, just hear me out.'

'I don't want to hear you out, you moron. Just fucking well let me go.'

'I'm sorry, I feel terrible about what I just said.'

'So you should, you fucking piece of shit. You *fucking dickhead.*'

His hands grip my shoulders and I can feel his breath hot on my face. 'I know. I deserve it. I'm angry with Stella and my folks and I'm taking it out on you, but if you're going to go, I mean, if this is the last time we ever see each other then I want you to know how important it's been to me that you've been around these last few months. But that's not all. Anna, *stop it*! Please, listen... The difference is... well, the way I see it I'm just someone you've latched onto while you're going through this blip in your life. Anna, don't you understand? The point is, I've *always* loved you.'

His body's trapping me against the banister and his mouth's almost on mine. I use all my strength to push against him, but it's like trying to shift a wardrobe.

'I remember the very first day I ever saw you. You were hanging around the side of your mum's house watching Callum and me delivering the wood. We were really young then – seven or eight at the most.'

I hear his heavy breathing in the darkness, the fresh sweat on his skin beneath his dressing gown. 'I remember you on The Green swinging upside down on the climbing frame, trying not to show your knickers.' He chuckles, and there's a pause as a hot disbelief steals over me that he too, recalls that day. 'And when we were on the searches, you were standing in a field with your wellies covered in mud, and you stared across at me and I remember feeling... Jesus, just so *moved* that you were there. Do you remember that day?'

I nod into his chest without moving. We're still for a moment, then I feel him kiss my hair and my neck.

'I remember watching you ride your mare in the woods. You were older then, you'd turned into a woman. I went home and lay in that same bed we've just been lying in and I...' I hear his breathing start to quicken, the hard stubble around his mouth travelling across my cheek. 'Since I came back I've spent so many hours staring over that playground at your mother's house, staring into those windows and wondering about you. I've spent hours walking around these roads, thinking about you.'

I hear myself saying like an echo, '*I know I know I know,*' and there's only the sound of our quickening breaths before he says, 'And now I've got you I'm being a total arsehole because I'm scared, *I'm scared*, Anna...' and then, 'But please don't think I don't love you,' and I begin to cry once more as he says it again, 'Please don't think I don't love you...' before he gasps loudly, pulling me hard against him, almost crushing me as he cries out my name.

We remain locked against the banister, our bodies pressed together in the darkness, our shallowing breaths the only sound.

19

———

TOM

The following morning I take the gun to Wiltshire Police Headquarters in Devizes. The constables on duty leap out of their bored, rural skins the moment I place it on the counter and tell them who I am and where I found it, crowding around it with greedy eyes.

I ask them if they ever knew about Patrick's accusation in the Catherine, but of course it would have been before their time. They promise that they will look into it and someone will get back to me.

I leave the gun with them and go to buy some tobacco in Morrisons.

Anna was right though. A good night's sleep has provided a bit more emotional equilibrium and now I'm not feeling so sure. It's all down to one thing really – the look in Dad's eyes on the night he died; that final declaration.

But why the need to keep a gun?

Two days later I get a phone call from an elderly-sounding man who tells me he'd worked on my brother's case as a young constable and remembers it well. He offers me his condolences for Dad – he's just read about his death in the *Gazette and*

Herald – before telling me he's had the gun checked over by a ballistics expert who'd confirmed my diagnosis of its make and military heritage. But it was not the same gun which had been used to kill Callum. That, he explained, had a plain old 12 bore; a type of gun used for shooting game and which many people in the countryside had kept during the seventies and eighties.

As for Patrick's accusation; yes they had looked into it. The Irish police had even gone to speak to my family in Donegal. No one there knew of any murdered child and Patrick had flatly denied having ever visited his brother.

* * *

Most afternoons, I take a break from sorting out Dad's stuff to phone Anna and we go out for a walk or drive. We find enjoyment in winding together threads of separate parts of byways and bridle paths, completing our shared knowledge of the landscape around Fawley, and as a result, doubling it.

These walks usually last for several hours and, as a result, it's taking me longer to sort out the house than I'd originally planned. I know I'm prevaricating – putting off the inevitable because I want to spend a bit more time with Anna in this place where my roots reach deep beneath the earth before I leave it forever – but I reckon that's my choice, so fuck Stella because she'll just have to wait. Besides, I figure I've got the rest of my life to be in Australia.

We usually finish with a drink at the Catherine then come back here so I can carry on sorting stuff out. Anna will watch me go through a box of photographs, or a pile of books, sitting and listening intently as I burrow down and attempt to uncover each forgotten memory.

Dad had kept the best of my mother's clothes; he'd covered them in polythene to keep out the moths and kept them in two long drawers at the bottom of the wardrobe. I tell Anna to go through them and choose anything she likes. Mum had good taste and she'd only been thirty-five when she died. Some of this stuff wouldn't look out of place on the high street now – particularly the long suede coat I remember her buying from a vintage shop in Bath and hooting with delight when she'd got it home to notice the *Harrods* label inside.

I make Anna put it on and tell her to twirl around – she looks gorgeous in it, her dark hair tumbling over the beige collar, its suede bottom reaching the tops of her high-heeled leather boots. I find it comforting to think of her wearing these clothes and reckon it's how I'm going to picture her in my mind after I've gone – wandering through some bazaar in one of Mum's floral dresses. The image makes me smile.

* * *

Predictably unpredictable, after several weeks of breezy sunshine, the weather suddenly turns milder and dampens into late April showers – or April storms, if I'm to be precise. Day after day, heavy grey clouds climb determinedly over the tops of the chestnuts on the Soweton Road before spilling their load on the village.

The Kennett bursts its banks, flooding the fields to the south of the village and making some of the smaller lanes impassable. The weather makes walking a chore – though Anna doesn't seem to mind – so I'm forced to get down to finishing sorting stuff until the house is more or less cleared, the only exception being the small office where Dad's old pine desk still stands along with its matching chair and a shelf full of mouldy lever-arch files.

It's the last room to sort and I guess I've been putting it off because I've been quietly worried about any potential legal or financial stuff that might be waiting inside those drawers. It's not that long since Dad gave over the business to Ray and I'm aware there may be unfinished accounts and other stuff to go through – things he probably hadn't put his mind to once he'd been diagnosed with cancer.

So one morning, after Anna's left for her mother's, I decide to sit down and confront it, at the same time aware the heavy feeling in my chest's probably more to do with knowing this is the last job and there will be nothing left to prevent me leaving once it's done rather than any real dread of what the accounts might throw up. And in the end my fears are unfounded – there's very little left here from the business bar a few receipts and some ancient sales ledgers.

Most of the desk's drawers are empty except for the bottom one, which seems to be either jammed or locked. I search around the room for the key but there's no sign of one and eventually I lever it open with a hammer. It gives easily and I pull it out to reveal what seems to be a pile of newspaper cuttings sheaved in a cardboard folder, and a couple of faded yellow Kodak wallets containing some old photographs.

I switch on the desk's small lamp and, letting myself down slowly in the chair, realise the cuttings all relate to Callum's murder. Dad seems to have kept everything ever written about him; the folder contains articles from both the national and local press; some are headline news, others appear in later pages, the font size and application of bylines appropriate to where the piece figured in the unravelling of the story, starting from Callum's disappearance in the December (small, single column pieces, appearing on page 5 or 6 of the *Gazette and Herald*), to the mounting police search and the rising speculation that he'd been abducted or murdered (headline font, five or six columns, front-page matter for both red tops and broadsheets), to the dwindling hope of finding him (back to a single column on page

5 of the nationals) and finally, to my discovery of the body at the Shadowing Stones the following summer (back to headline font, 6 columns, front-page of the nationals). And then the ensuing investigation (smaller but still impressive font, 3 columns, probably on page 2 or 3 of the nationals, but front-page of the *Gazette*) which threw up few, if any suspects, although many of the articles report that Dad was questioned repeatedly throughout – and finally just a few paragraphs on page 7 of *The Daily Mail* announcing the police were winding things down but keeping the case open.

Putting down the cuttings, I turn to the first wallet of photographs. There aren't many – perhaps ten or so. This lot are in black-and-white and their age has brought a sepia tint to their edges. The first one depicts a fierce-looking man with wild, dark hair and a beard, who bears a strong resemblance to me and Dad. He stands on top of a hill against a backdrop of rugged-looking land, and in the far distance I can just make out a lake. This has to be my grandfather, Michael Donnelly, on his Donegal farm.

Another shows him standing with his arm around a sharp-featured woman. On the back I recognise Dad's spiky, semi-illiterate writing: *Mum and Dad, September 1975*. The photo's followed by a face I recognise – those familiar Donnelly dark features and dimpled chin; Patrick. Shit. I wonder where he is now, what he's doing. Does he still remember the events of that night? Does he remember going to the Catherine and drunkenly accusing Dad of being a murderer?

The next one's of Dad, only here he's maybe twenty-five at most. He's sitting next to another man with short brown hair and a pinched-looking face, and they're both clutching pints of Guinness and smoking fags. I turn the photo over: *With Sean O'Malley, O'Ryan's bar, 1976*.

There are more photos of other, younger people – Dad's

other siblings I guess – boys and girls with the same black hair and toughened faces, standing around various decrepit outbuildings or sitting on stone walls, that same bleak landscape spread out behind them. Most have names written on the back: *Margaret, Siobhan, Darragh, Anne, Seamus.* A roll-call of the lost.

Have I ever seen these pictures before? Had Dad shown them to me during my childhood? I don't recall them. He'd often talked about Donegal and his family, but I've no memory of these faces. It would be hard to forget this unkempt-looking lot, but I'm pretty sure that, up to this moment, I've not had any idea of how any of my Irish kin actually looked in the flesh.

The second wallet holds more recent photographs, this time taken in colour on a Kodak Instamatic. These appear to be related to the business – there are five or six faded snaps of smallholdings and barns around Marlborough and I wonder if at some point Ray and Dad had been considering moving it to commercial premises rather than storing the wood at Ray's. Towards the end of the pile, I come across a single shot of me and Callum laughing together as we push the wheelbarrow down Ivy Lane, the piles of kindling almost reaching our chins as we fight to stop the whole thing from toppling over.

I place the picture to one side, deciding to keep it to show the kids – I'm not sure what it's doing in this wallet, and reckon it probably got put in here by accident because it's followed by one of another outbuilding, only it takes me a moment to recognise it, and then, with a chill creeping up my back, I realise I'm staring at the barn on Marlborough Down. I close my eyes for a moment, aware that my hand's begun to shake as I place it slowly down on the desk, aware too that there's a final photograph lying beneath it. My heart's accelerating and I force myself to take several long breaths before lowering my gaze.

It's a picture of Ray Curtis and Callum standing in front of the Shadowing Stones.

The wind blasts around the house and suddenly I hear the back door slam. Anna must have left it on the latch when she let herself out this morning. At the same time, I notice the curtains shivering slightly against their frames and feel a coldness closing in around me. It's as if my brother's ghost has suddenly stolen into the house, as if he's been waiting all these years for me to find this photograph.

My thumb and forefinger squeeze its corner. When was it taken? There are leaves on the trees on the line of hedgerow and what looks like young corn on the western field. So I reckon it had to be late spring. Ray and Callum are standing next to each other with Ray's arm wrapped casually around my brother's shoulders. Callum looks around eleven years old – the age he was when he died. They're smiling into the camera and both appear relaxed. There's no one else in the picture.

The phone rings, making me jump and reminding me I need to get it cut off before I leave. I rise quickly and make my way to the sitting room, the photograph still in my hand.

It's Anna.

'Hey you,' I say, fighting to keep my voice calm. 'What are you up to?'

I hear her breathing into the receiver. 'Not much – I was thinking about going for a walk even though the weather's awful – I've got cabin fever and Isabel's driving me mad murdering Bach. Want to come with me?'

I slide my thumb back and forward over Ray's face. 'Mind if I duck out this time? Don't really fancy getting soaked and I'm almost done sorting out the office. How about I meet you in the pub later, hey – say around six?'

'All right. Are you okay? You sound a bit strange.'

'Me? No, I'm fine, just a bit tired. Have a good one, hey. Don't get too wet now.'

My hand still holding the photograph, I put down the phone then head upstairs to take a slow walk through the empty rooms, stopping to peer out of each window, either across to the empty playground or the small patch of lawn that rises up behind the house. It needs mowing – I was hoping to get it done before I leave but it's not going to happen if this rain keeps up.

I check my watch and realise with a shock that it's already gone noon. Pausing to stare out of the small landing window, at last I see what I've been waiting for; the sight of Anna clad in jeans and trainers making her way past the house and heading in the direction of the woods, the coat hood shielding her face from the buffeting wind.

Only when I'm convinced of the direction she's taking do I make my way back down the narrow stairs into the sitting room. Then I pick up the phone, and with a shaking hand, dial Ray Curtis's number.

20

TOM

I reach the Shadowing Stones before him but my timing's deliberate – I meant to get here first. I need some time to gather my thoughts before we meet and – I dunno, maybe it's like I want to draw the battle lines or something.

Putting a foot on one of the bigger boulders, I grasp the edge of the top stone, its surface under my hand rough with flaking lichen, before hauling my myself onto the roof of the stones and swinging a knee up behind me. Then I pause for a moment to catch my breath before pushing myself up to a standing position and waiting with folded arms for his arrival, my gaze fixed on the barn and the end of the track which leads to Milbury.

It's just a few weeks since Anna and I came up here on that bright morning – the same morning my father passed away. It's weird to think now about the panic which overwhelmed me back then on first seeing the stones. At that moment, I'd thought I'd never be able to come back here – yet here I am and this time alone and without any anxiety or fear. I reckon I owe that to Anna.

It's a very different day today though, weather-wise. Although it's mild – you could almost call it humid – the sky's heavy and grey and a vicious wind whips through the valley, the threat of rain in its fists. To the east, another black mass of cloud is rising, casting a wide shadow over the valley.

Ray's late. But I could've guessed that. Dad always used to moan about his lack of punctuality – it was one of the reasons he kept losing his girlfriends, because he kept standing them up. If he does that to me today I'm going to kill him. But after another five minutes, his blue Land Rover finally emerges around the track's nearest bend and begins bumping its way towards me. I take off my jacket and place it beneath my feet before lowering myself down and briefly closing my eyes.

It's a weird sensation, but sitting here alone in this ancient landscape, I've the feeling that I've somehow become an actual physical part of it. The cold sarsen beneath my thighs; the hypnotic swathe of the valley as it winds down to the watchful black eye of that barn; the cries of the sheep on the hillside and the wind that pummels the back of my neck. It's as if I've finally established a permanent assimilation with this place which has haunted me for most of my life and, whatever happens and wherever I go, there will always be a part of me left here watching over my little brother; as permanent as these three stones, as permanent as time.

Where are you, Callum – are you here? The air's humid and cloying and there's no sense of the icy chill I felt back in the barn that day I came up here with Anna. But still, I kind of sense you're here.

Jesus, when you were brought up that track all those years ago, how silent it must have been. It was the deepest of winter days, the ground covered in heavy, unforgiving snowdrifts. Even though you were nearly twelve, you still greeted snow like an excited kid, marvelling from our sitting-room window at the gleaming white playground beyond the school's railings. To you, snow had only meant one thing – fun, excitement, wonder and pleasure. But on that day, for you, these downs must have been more silent, more ghostly than a moonscape. There could have been no movement, no sound beyond that of yours and your murderer's footfall, the snow's deathly quiet as oppressive as a straitjacket.

I hear a door slamming. Opening my eyes, I see the Land Rover pull up at the end of the track. Then Ray alights from the driver's side and stands there for a few moments before turning and moving slowly in my direction, his stocky legs carrying him easily over the stile. As those blue eyes settle on my shape sitting cross-legged on the dolmen, his approaching figure gradually slows until he comes to a halt a few metres in front of me. He lifts a hand in salute. 'Tom,' he calls into the wind. 'You've picked a good day for it.'

I dunno. I guess he's trying to be funny and yeah, maybe I'm imagining it, but it seems to me there's something a bit guarded in his manner as he stands there with his boots planted among the thistles. But then I reckon I've asked a pretty strange thing of him, to meet me at the place where my little brother was murdered.

Staring down at him, I withdraw some papers and tobacco from my jacket pocket. His smile fades at my lack of reaction.

'So why are we here?' he says. 'Please, enlighten me.'

I watch him carefully as I roll the cigarette, but his expression seems genuinely perplexed.

'Well, Ray...' I say, lighting the fag. 'I suppose I just wanted to see you one more time before going home. And, you know, rap about it a bit – Callum, Dad – all that stuff I've been avoiding. I don't really feel I've properly dealt with it – and I wanted to try, you know. There won't be another chance.'

'I see.' But his voice is unsure. Then, 'I'm not sure what to say, Tom, but fire away. Say anything you like but come down first – it's difficult to hear you from up there.'

Pushing my arms back into the jacket, I press the packet of tobacco into its inside pocket and lever myself across the rock before leaping and landing hard onto the turf below. I straighten and face him, the wind battering my face. My heart's pumping hard, but outwardly I reckon I'm betraying little of what I'm feeling.

But I know he's guessed something's up, because his eyes suddenly narrow with mistrust. Taking a step back, he shifts slowly from one foot to the other. Placing his hands in his coat pockets, he raises his gaze and studies the stones behind me, the skyline I've just vacated.

'Creepy old place this,' he says. 'Supposed to be some kind of ancient timepiece, isn't it? I've always thought it looks more like a sacrificial altar myself – the way that top stone is so wide and flat.'

The wind stills and even those distant sheep seem to go silent.

'It sounds like you know, Ray.'

But he shakes his head. 'It's just my opinion – that's all.'

'You've clearly given it a lot of thought.'

'Not for a long time, but yes, I suppose I did for a while – after Callum.' Then he shrugs. 'But I haven't thought about it for years. I can't even remember when I last came up here.'

'How about the winter of 1994?'

The words delivered, I wait for him to crash to earth like a bird shot in mid-flight, but instead his jaw opens and he says, 'Why would I have...?' and then he gets me and his eyes seem to shrink with a combination of shock and deep offence – something I've not really been expecting, and haven't prepared for.

Cutting to the chase, I slide my hand into my back pocket and retrieve the photograph, holding it out towards him.

He hesitates, then reaches out and takes it, lowering his

confused gaze towards his and Callum's grinning faces. I feel a surge of irritation as I watch him wipe the dust off its surface with his thumb.

'Where did you find this?' he asks.

'In Dad's office.'

He glances up at me, then back at the photograph.

'Well?'

'Well what, Tom? It's a photograph of me and Callum. Your father took it. He'd spoken to somebody at Milbury Racing Stables about renting the barn for the business and we came up here to take a look at it – but it was too rundown, even then. After we'd finished we came over to look at the stones, as anyone would. I think it was during the school holidays and that's why Callum was with us. Maybe you were too – I don't remember. Do you?'

'Why didn't you come to the wake, Ray?' I say, ignoring the question. I place a hand on one of the Shadowing Stones, as if testing it with my weight, then kick a flint hard across the grass. 'Well? He was your business partner – your best mate. So why weren't you there?'

This sudden shift in interrogation wrong-foots him. He passes the photograph back to me, then turns, with clenched jaw, towards the stones. I can see his mind turning over and at the same time notice a flush of red spreading across his cheekbones.

'Nothing to do with Isabel Carmichael, was it?'

Like a reflex, his hand shoots into his jacket pocket to withdraw a packet of Benson & Hedges. Reaching out, he offers me one without looking at me, and for some reason I take it. He takes another for himself then, cupping the lighter against the wind with a visibly shaking hand, lights mine before raising it to his own.

'Anna told you,' he says.

'That you tried to assault her sister? Yeah, mate, she did.'

The hand on the lighter goes still. He raises his face and stares at me with incredulity. 'Bloody hell, Tom. That's how she described it – as*sault*?'

'She said when Isabel was twelve you came up behind her while she was walking by the Kennett and you grabbed her breast.'

A fine drizzle's begun peppering our faces, coating our skins and hair in a greasy film.

'She was *twelve*, you say?' He lights his cigarette, then his eyes briefly settle on his knuckles as he blows the smoke in my direction. 'Shit.' He shrugs and half laughs. 'Look, my friend, all I can say is that she may have been a child in years but that's as far as it went. I can assure you she didn't look like one – or act like one for that matter.'

'So you're not denying it?'

'I'm not denying anything, except that I assaulted her.'

'Come on, Ray. Don't try to spin me a–'

'Look, I'm no pervert, Tom – come on, I don't believe you think that. I had no idea she was underage until I saw her in her college uniform in Marlborough a few months later. Even then, I'd never have guessed she was *twelve*.

'Look, I was a hot-blooded guy in my twenties back then. I was cutting back over the fields from the Catherine to my folks' place and I'd had too much to drink and I was feeling horny as hell in the sunshine when I saw this goddess walking along in a scarlet swimming costume. That girl looked at least eighteen – she had this walk, you know... swung her arse like she knew she was the best thing since sliced bread. She had blonde hair down to her waist and... Jesus Christ, I didn't *assault* her. I just lost control and caught hold of her for a second in a clumsy way – I honestly didn't mean to touch her there though and as soon as I realised what I'd done, I pulled away.

'I still don't know why I did it. I've never done anything like that before or since. But she was so beautiful Tom – she still is. When I saw her at the funeral, I couldn't take my eyes off her.' He pauses to take a drag on the cigarette, then stares down at the ground. 'But when I saw the looks she was giving me, I felt ashamed because I knew she'd realised and yes, I'd been well out of order that day – and you're right, that's why I didn't come to the wake. I'd actually like to apologise to her, Tom, if you'll help me. I'm not proud of what I did that day.'

He turns and takes a couple of steps across the grass before pausing, his gaze fixed on the barn.

Then, as if on cue, he straightens, then swerves back towards me, his gaze narrowing with a slow comprehension, that curtain of greying hair billowing around his face. 'You think what happened with Anna's sister, you think I did that to Callum as well?'

I throw the spent cigarette to the ground. 'I dunno, Ray. Let's just say I just thought it was a bit of a coincidence – your grabbing a kid around the same time my brother was murdered. Scared the old man would find out, were you? Did Callum threaten to spill the beans on you?'

'Callum was like a nephew to me. So were you. I'd never have hurt either of you.'

'Yeah – but it's usually someone they know, isn't it, hey? A step-parent, or friend of the family. You had a key to our house, mate. *And* you had guns.'

'Come on, Tom. Don't you think the police questioned me at the time? Don't you think they knew I had a key? That I kept firearms? None of which, by the way, matched the one which was used to kill Callum. And just for your information, I had an alibi for the day he disappeared – I was delivering wood in Soweton. About five different people saw me during the course of that afternoon. People tend to remember when you're going out of your way to deliver an essential provision in waist-high snow.'

I raise the photograph. 'Did the police know about this?'

He throws the cigarette to the ground and stubs it out with his foot. 'You know what? I think I've had enough.'

But he can't move because my hand's on his arm, my fingers sinking into the flesh beneath his coat. 'You think *you've* had enough?'

Without warning, he's grabbing my jacket collar in his fists and hauling me up to him so our faces are only inches apart. He might be fifteen years older than me, but he's still pretty strong. 'I didn't kill Callum, you stupid fucking prick...' he hisses. His grip's like a vice around my neck and I feel his breath hot and moist against my skin. The rain's coming down faster now; it sprays us and the wind rushes up the valley sending my hair across my face.

I'm caught out by the force of his anger which, for a second, overwhelms me and at the same time it's like I'm weakened by the uncertainty of my accusation in the face of such indignation and rage. But then I close my eyes and recall Dad's sickly face staring back at mine, hear the same tired indignation in his words just before he died, '*I didn't ... kill Callum,*' and suddenly I'm struggling against Ray's grip, forcing him round in a circle, placing my foot behind him and hooking it under his ankle, tripping him backwards, his shoulders crashing down on the sharp flints and sodden clay beneath the Shadowing Stones.

The next moment his hands are hauling my body down with him into the darkness, and I hear my voice echoing off the stones' enclosing walls, 'Well who the fuck did kill him, Ray? Because if Dad didn't do it, I reckon he knew who did. I overheard him and Mum talking after Callum's funeral. He *knew* something, Ray... they both did. I told you what he said,

"Ask Ray". I never did believe the bullshit answer you gave me to that one.'

Ray's body slowly stills, his chest heaving as he struggles to regain his breath. Slowly he raises his face, and I can see from the look in his eyes that something in what I've just said has knocked the fight out of him. We lie there motionless, on the same soil where more than a quarter of a century ago, my brother's body was covered in petrol and set alight, listening to the endless sigh of the wind over the hillside and the splatter of the rain against the sarsen canopy above our heads.

His grip on my collar remains tight and unrelenting, and I can feel his chest pressed against mine. 'I'm going to let you go now, Tom,' he says quietly. 'And then we can talk. But if you try to hit me, or make any other ridiculous accusations, I'm going to walk away and I'm never going to speak to you again. Do you understand?'

I lie there saying nothing, my gaze turned up to the stone ceiling. Slowly his hands loosen their hold on my collar and I feel the leather slacken around the back of my neck. Then, in unison, we lever ourselves up into a sitting position, pressing our spines against the stones and staring at each other like a pair of exhausted warriors.

'You do know, don't you, Ray? I can see it in your eyes.'

He leans back and, withdrawing the box of Benson & Hedges, hands me one, lighting it first before taking another for himself. Then his head falls back against the stone and he closes his eyes. He takes a long drag before giving me the very slightest of nods.

An icy feeling creeps into my arms and shoulders, passing into the base of my neck. It's the reason I asked him to come here – because I reckoned either he killed my brother, or knew who had. But I wasn't counting on being right.

He shakes his head, then rubs his knee. 'But I can't tell you, Tom. Jim made me swear that I wouldn't.'

There's a sound of voices over the wind, car doors slamming, and I'm aware suddenly of a flock of sheep appearing over the hillside and pouring along the far side of the barbed wire fence that separates us from the next field. Ray and I turn, simultaneously, to see a blue estate car pulling up behind them and the distant shapes of men alighting from its doors. There's a loud whistle and then a collie leaps out of the car's boot.

I turn back to Ray. 'I'm not prepared to accept that, Ray, and you know it. You know what he said when he was dying? "Sometimes questions are easier than answers". What did he mean by that?'

Ray's left cheek twitches.

'Jesus. Are you really going to make me go back to Australia still wondering and guessing and never really knowing what happened; whether it was Dad, whether it was you or some other fucker down the Catherine? Combstone perhaps? I'll go to the police if you don't tell me. I'll tell them about Isabel – and I'll make sure I show them this...' I hold up the photograph. 'Then maybe they'll *have to* get the truth out of you.'

Those blue eyes travel from my face to the picture in my hand and I realise how lame the threat sounds. I can see he knows it too because he half smiles, but still appears to be considering my words, weighing up his loyalty to Dad against my desperate need to know.

'So what *did* you overhear him and Eileen saying that day?' he asks finally.

I stub what's left of the cigarette and close my eyes because for some reason I can't look at him as I relate the conversation I overheard on the evening of Callum's funeral.

'And you never asked them what it was about?'

I shake my head. 'Didn't take it in at first... There was so much going on with the media circus coming to town – remember all the TV reporters camped out in the pub car park, hey? Christ, I was only fourteen and suddenly Fawley and my family were on national television.'

His voice is gentle now. 'Of course I remember it, Tom. Everyone in the village does.'

'They were bastards those journalists.' I open my eyes again, stare straight at him. 'Do you remember how they used to make up bits of crap to get people talking? There would be some rumour circulating around the village and they'd try and turn it into fact. I'd forgotten all that, you know – but then I found a load of press clippings this morning – Dad kept everything. Did you know the reporters used to put down flowers outside the school gates with messages they'd written themselves? I used to watch them doing it from the kitchen window – then they'd photograph people reading them and I'd see those messages on the front pages the next day.'

'That's the red tops for you.'

'And the police tape? You'd see it wound around the gates and the hedges to show where they'd been searching. I'd see it for months afterwards in the weirdest places – up by the dump in the woods. And all down by the river – there was tons of it down there. Not nice for the kids when they were swimming...'

'Tom...'

I don't know where I'm going with this – I seem to have lost track of the reason we're here. But now I'm finally talking about it, it's haemorrhaging out of me. 'Remember the sniffer dogs? You'd see them with their handlers all over the place, up at the woods and all over the fields all that winter and spring. Must've cost a fortune, that search. *How the fuck* did they miss him, Ray? All that time, all that money, police and media coverage, and in the end it was still me – it still *had to be me* – who found him.'

He stares back at me in silence, his forearms resting on his knees.

'Anyway. So that was why, like I said, it didn't really sink in at the time – what I'd overheard. And when it finally did, I asked Mum about it but she insisted her and Dad had been talking about something else, something to do with the business. I know I should've pursued it but I guess I just wanted to believe her. But later, with all the finger-pointing at Dad, I'd remember that conversation and start thinking about what exactly she'd meant and I was going to ask her again, only then she went and topped herself... And after that I couldn't see what else she *could have meant* except he'd done it, most likely in one of his tempers – and I kept thinking that must have been why she killed herself, you know, because she'd protected him and couldn't live with herself anymore. She was strong; as much she loved him she couldn't have gone on harbouring him over something like that.'

I let my head drop into my arms. All I can hear is the falling rain and the panicked cries of the ewes as they try to evade that circling collie.

'What did you and Jim talk about all those days when he was sick, Tom?' Ray eventually asks. 'I take it you asked him some of this stuff?'

I slowly raise my head. 'We talked a bit but he was out of it a lot of the time. Couldn't make sense of most of what he said.'

'Did he tell you anything about when he and your mother met in Ireland?' He regards me cautiously, elbows resting on his knees, the cigarette dangling from his fingers.

'Yeah. But it was mostly stuff I already knew. Mum went there to paint and they met and fell in love. He kept talking about it.'

'That's all he said?'

'Pretty much. Oh, and he got her pregnant while she was

there – with me, I mean – and that's why they had to leave. Guess that was one revelation I'd not expected.'

'Seriously?' Ray shakes his head. 'He never told me that.'

'Yeah, well. I don't expect he was very proud of it.'

'Maybe it explains a few things.'

'Like what?' I raise my hands. 'What exactly does it explain, Ray? That he blamed his kids for making him leave Ireland?'

'No, *no... Stop* this, Tom,' Ray snaps, exasperated. 'Can't you see he loved your mother? He chose to do the right thing by her, that's all, and you should respect him for that. *Honestly...*' He cups his hands around his forehead for a moment then lets his palms fall outwards. 'Come on, Tom. Think about it. Why do you think Jim chose to move to a place like Fawley – in the back of beyond, where people were likely to leave him alone? And why did he never go back to Ireland, despite being so homesick for the place?'

I shrug. 'Mum's parents lived in Marlborough, that's why he moved here. And his family disowned him. There was nothing for him to go back for.'

Ray turns his gaze towards the barn and the wind simultaneously moans, tunnelling its way between the three stones, lifting his hair and sending a fresh spray of rain across his mud-splattered coat.

'All right, my friend,' he says wearily, sounding kind of reconciled to his task, like he's had enough and now just wants to get it over with. 'I'm going to tell you what I know.' Withdrawing a tissue from his coat pocket, he blows his nose, wipes the dirt from his forehead. Then he raises his gaze back to mine.

'Not long after you left for Australia – me, Len and your father were all drinking in the Catherine. Jim had more than a skinful and he suddenly started telling us about his past – I mean, his life before he met Eileen and moved to Fawley. He'd never said much about it before and after that night, I understood why. But I think with Eileen and you gone he felt the need to finally get it off his chest. After he'd finished, he swore us both to secrecy and until now I've kept my word. I'm pretty sure Len has too.'

He squeezes the tissue hard before pushing it back into his pocket. 'Tom, I don't know how much you know about your father's life in Donegal, but it was a very poor county back in those days – the poorest in Ireland. There were very few jobs and a lot of frustrated young people with few chances in life. Many of them had to emigrate to find work and the ones who stayed had to scrape a living any way they could.

'Buncrana, the town where Jim grew up, is just across the border from Londonderry, which in the seventies had been flooded with British troops. The government said they'd sent them in to calm things, but their presence still created a lot of bad feeling. Jim told us that in the year or so before he met your mother, he and his brother Patrick had started working for a gang based in Londonderry. It was mostly politics which motivated him to get involved – your grandfather had brought all his kids up to believe in a united Ireland so Jim wanted to help the cause as well as make a bit of cash. At first it was small-scale; smuggling – mainly cigarettes, booze, maybe some firearms. But as time went on he found himself getting roped into heavier, more violent stuff – extortion, protection rackets, that type of thing – he wouldn't go into it that much except to say he was already in way over his head when the gang's ringleader, a man called O'Mallin, told him they had a major operation coming up, something which–'

'It was O'Malley,' I interrupt. 'Not O'Mallin.'

Ray raises his head. 'Sorry?'

'I read it in a newspaper article among Dad's stuff. That was his name – least I'm pretty sure it was – if it's the same guy.' As I say it, I'm thinking of that folded-up newspaper article that had fallen from my mother's sketchbook. I'd been looking at it again just the other day and something about it had started to bother me – the exact way the page had been torn around the border of the bombing article while a corner of the *A Star is Born* advertisement on the other side had been missing.

Ray rests his chin across his knuckles. 'Sean *O'Malley*. Okay.' He drops those hands and kind of rouses himself. 'Well around that same time, Jim met your mother. You know the rest. They fell in love and Jim went to your grandparents to tell them he'd met an English woman and wanted to marry her. I wonder if he told them she was pregnant as well. Given their Catholic beliefs, that would have been incendiary. Anyway, your grandfather wasn't having any of it and Jim was given an ultimatum – it was his family or Eileen.'

'O'Malley held up a bank in Londonderry,' I say. 'As they were leaving the bank, he threw a grenade over his shoulder and three people were killed – including a British soldier. Christ... so Dad was in the IRA?'

I know how slow I'm sounding, but it's taking me a bit of time to take all this in, like a delay on a satellite communication.

Ray nods. 'O'Malley *and Jim* held up that bank, Tom. Along with Patrick and the others in the gang. Only Jim never expected O'Malley to throw the grenade. These men were extremists. Jim said he'd watched them threaten people and beat them half to death just on the basis of a rumour. We thought those days were gone, but it's not looking good for Ireland with what's happening at Stormont right now and these border issues after Brexit. It's a time bomb, and if we're not careful, we'll find we're right back where we were in the seventies.'

He picks up the packet of tailor-mades and holds it out towards me.

'It's your last one,' I say. My voice sounds distant and weak, like someone else is speaking the words for me.

'Have it.' He lights it then passes it to me. I raise it to my lips and take a long drag.

'So that explains how he got the gun.'

Ray nods. 'Jim must have smuggled it over from Ireland for his own protection. Of course he felt wretched about what happened. He thought they were going to rob a bank to raise funds for the cause – not murder innocent people in cold blood. He went straight to Eileen in a state, and confessed everything to her. He promised her he wanted out and that night, they fled to England in her van.'

I watch Ray for a moment, the inevitable question turning itself over in my mind. 'But I still don't get it,' I say finally. 'I mean, what's any of this got to do with Callum?'

Ray presses his eyelids together and nods, as if expecting the question and wondering why it's taken us so long to get here. 'After Jim left, everything went quiet for a while. He didn't contact his family, so he assumed O'Malley didn't know where to find him.

'Then a year or so later, he read a newspaper report – most likely the one you found. The RUC had carried out a raid on the gang's flat in Londonderry. There was a messy shootout in which two civilians got killed. It caused a stir in the British press at the time because memories of Bloody Sunday were still raw and a lot of journalists and politicians felt unnecessary force had been used. There was an enquiry, but it found in favour of the soldiers.

'Ten months later the case went to court. O'Malley and two other men were found guilty for robbery and murder. They got life sentences – ended up serving ten years each. Patrick got two for driving the getaway car.'

A fresh downpour begins drumming the earth around the stones, followed by another blast of wind.

'Jim said that Patrick turned up once in Fawley. Do you remember that? You would have been very young.'

I give him the slightest of nods.

'Jim never knew how his brother had tracked him down and it came as a massive shock. Anyway, Patrick had just come out of prison. He warned Jim that the gang knew there'd been a tip-off about who was responsible for the robbery, and by a process of elimination they'd worked out the informer had to be your father. Who else could it be when everyone else had been sent down? Patrick warned him that O'Malley wanted revenge. The two people who got killed in that RUC raid – Jim hadn't realised you see but one was the wife of one of the gang. The other was O'Malley's seven-year-old son.'

I stare at him, my mouth fallen open. Suddenly everything's beginning to swim. The charging wind and driving rain, the cries of those panicking sheep, it's all melting into one great nauseous whirl.

A kind of blackness passes across my vision. I'm aware of that same chill I felt in the barn that day folding itself around me, its steely fingers worming under my jacket sleeves and across the skin of my arms. The words ricochet inside my skull. '*And there it is. There it is. There it is.*'

Dropping my face into my hands, I'm already imagining the scene; soldiers in fatigues bursting into some unknown flat; the smothered cries behind the door; the blast of the gun, followed by panic, shouting, and then the terrible realisation.

These images are followed quickly by another, equally brutal one – of O'Malley and his men snatching Callum as he'd walked around the house to the back door, his satchel over his arm, then somehow bundling him into a car without anyone noticing. How long had the men been watching the house before they chose their moment? Why hadn't anyone noticed them in a quiet village like Fawley? They must have watched Mum drive off to fetch me from Marlborough, then seen Callum leave the school and make his way over the road. Were they waiting around the back of the house? Or did they knock the back door and grab Callum when he opened it? Fawley wasn't the kind of place where you warned your child not to open the door to strangers.

'Jim thought O'Malley must have planted someone at Milbury Racing Stables,' Ray goes on. 'They employ a lot of Irish lads there. He said it would have given them time to do a reconnaissance of the area and plan the operation. They'd soon have learnt that the barn wasn't used and it would make a good place to dump the body – knowing it wouldn't be found for a while. Plus by using the Shadowing Stones, what better way to make it look like a local person had done it, even Jim himself?'

He pauses, presses the back of his hand against his lips. 'I mean, of course, the bastards could've just grassed on Jim, but that wasn't their way. They were more likely just to kill him – he said that's what he wished they'd done – he said that's what *he thought* they were going to do when they phoned to say they had Callum. But killing him obviously wasn't cruel enough in their eyes. After all, they'd had plenty of time to plot their revenge while they sat around playing cards in the Maze prison, hadn't they? No, their intention was to give him another kind of life sentence – one that comes without any hope of parole.'

There's a sudden roar of wind and the rain's begun pelting down like bullets against the stones. I stub out the cigarette and, clamping my palms together, realise they're hot with sweat. And as I stare out from under those stones into that fog of water, a new memory's slowly coming back to me. It was one of those curious incidents that had stuck in my mind for a bit, might have stayed there for longer if Callum hadn't disappeared soon after.

I'd been in one of the Marlborough pubs on an evening – back then, there were a couple of landlords who turned a blind eye to underage drinkers. I was with some school mates but they were playing pool in the backroom. I was standing at a fruit machine with a pint of lager in my hand, when two Irish men had come up on either side of me. 'Good evening,' one of them had said, 'you're Jim Donnelly's boy, aren't you? Tom, isn't it?' I assumed they drank in the Catherine and that's how they knew me – they'd seen me in there with Dad, although I didn't recognise them. They were around Dad's age but still small and lithe in build – and said they worked up at Milbury Racing Stables. I'd not been particularly troubled by them; we'd passed the time of day and one of them had even bought me a drink. It was only when they left that one of them said something I thought was a bit strange – but it was more the tone he used than his words. 'Well, Tom, maybe we'll be seeing you again, or maybe we won't.'

When I got home I told Dad about it. He asked me to describe the men but he couldn't place them. He'd seemed unsettled by it and kept asking me what they'd looked like and where they said they knew him from.

Five days later, Callum had disappeared.

I turn to Ray. 'But it wasn't that simple, was it?' I wait for him to reply, but he's silent, eyes pressed shut and face averted so I can't read his expression. Beyond him, I notice that estate car bumping away over the grass, the lambs left pressed fleece against fleece in a pen, waiting to be collected.

And suddenly I'm scrambling to my feet, pushing myself into the rain and wind. I hear Ray shout my name and it seems to echo back in a voice higher than his own. From across the valley, the cries of the ewes reply to the panicked bleating of their young – the sound rises and fills my head, spiralling outwards, pressing against the edges of my skull.

I feel Ray's hand grasp my arm but tear myself away, screwing up my eyes and stamping blindly across the grass, away from the barn and the stones, making my way up the valley towards the distant horizon of Ridgeway. I can hear his boots thumping over the thistle-covered ground behind me, his voice bellowing my name. But I keep going, my breath tearing from my body before I swerve around so quickly he almost crashes into me. I grasp him hard by the shoulders, shove him backwards.

'They made him witness it, didn't they? They made him watch – O'Malley saw those soldiers shoot his own kid and he wanted to do the same to Dad.'

But he lowers his head and won't look at me, and over his shoulder I suddenly noticed a maroon shape hurrying up the valley towards us, hooded head bowed against the rain, a figure that I had last seen heading in the opposite direction from the Shadowing Stones, towards the woods.

Anna.

I swing back to Ray. '*Admit it.* They made him watch while they shot my brother – didn't they?'

He's still for a few moments, then he gives me the slightest of nods.

'Oh Jesus, Jesus Christ...' I close my eyes and try to picture the horror of it; O'Malley's face as he'd raised the gun and pointed it at Callum; his eyes narrowing as he found his target. How had Dad felt? What had gone through his mind as he stared into the terrified, pleading eyes of his child knowing he could do nothing to help – and Callum, rigid with fear and, not understanding anything, knowing it too. Imagine if it were me standing there staring at Reef or Indiana, unable to protect them and knowing it was my fault that they were there? The thought is incomprehensible; nauseating.

I open my eyes, stare at Ray. 'But there's something else, isn't there? Something you're *still* not telling me.'

He shakes his head numbly.

My fist comes out of nowhere, surprising me, surprising him. It smashes against his jaw, sending him sprawling across the grass. I haven't prepared for this, I'm not a violent man – I've never started a fight or been in one and I'm not prepared for the rage that's suddenly boiling out of me. Abruptly the image comes into my mind of Dad yanking his belt from his jeans and throwing me down onto my bed, that satanic spirit burning in his eyes. I'd never felt it before but now finally recognise that same capability for cruelty has probably been there in me all along, and like him, I've not finished yet – a well-aimed kick into Ray's belly follows and I hear him groan, then his arms fold over, curling up into the foetal position.

'Tell me!'

But he shakes his head and shifts his body, and still he doesn't speak and though I sense he's still trying in some absurd way to protect me, right at this moment I detest him for it – him and Dad too. All the months I've been here, all that time either of them could have told me the truth and I could've made either my war or my peace with it – and even though I know it's irrational and maybe what I'm really feeling is years of pent-up anger and confusion and grief releasing itself all in one go but before I know it my eyes are seeking out a sarsen boulder which lies under the branches of a nearby yew tree. Suddenly I'm moving through the rain towards it, placing a hand on each of its sides and hauling it up to my chest. I turn and stagger back through the rain.

Ray Curtis lies with his back turned to me as I lift it skywards and shout, 'I don't care what you promised, you bastard – it's not Dad who's suffering now. You've got no right to keep the truth from me anymore...' and at this he raises his gaze and his eyes bulge with horror as he spies the boulder, and now he's sliding wildly to one side like a panicked snake and I hear him shout, 'No, Tom, no...' then, his fists clinging to tufts of thistle and levering himself backwards, he yells, 'It was your mother who grassed on O'Malley... It was *Eileen*... not Jim,' as I feel something crash against me and hear Anna scream my name, the combined force of her body with the weight of that huge sarsen sends me staggering sideways onto my back, crushing her beneath me.

The boulder drops from my hands and hits the earth with a dull thump.

* * *

When Callum and I were kids we used to play a game. We'd take some toys and place them on the edge of an imaginary cliff (usually the end of one of our beds or the arm of a chair). We could only save one toy – that was the rule – and would have to give a detailed justification for our decision. The remaining toys would then be shoved over the edge to what we imagined was certain death on the rocks below. We would spend hours deliberating over which toy we would save and why, basing it on various factors including the amount we played with it, its financial worth, where it had come from, and so on. Mum hated that game; she said it was cruel and told us off whenever she heard us playing it.

What had made those men choose Callum instead of me? Because he was closer in age to O'Malley's son? Because he was smaller and weaker so easier to grab, easier to hide? Or was it because he was the 'little one'? Where had I read that the mother always turns to her youngest first in a situation of crisis, the infant least able to protect itself? Had they settled on him because his death would be even more painful for my mother than my own? In hindsight, that last, faintly menacing statement they'd made in the pub implied they were in the process of making a choice.

* * *

I lie on the grass with the wind knocked out of me. I'm soaked from head to foot as the rain, though thinning, continues to spray my face and neck. I feel it dripping off my jacket zipper and trickling across my collarbone. Coughing hard, I turn my head and find myself staring at those three stones in the distance; dark, still, as unconcerned as ever against a backdrop of slate-grey sky. We're higher up the valley now and those lambs' cries are more distant but still distinct and urgent, carried towards us on the wind.

I become aware of a voice speaking my name, feel a hand thumping my back. With what feels like superhuman effort, I raise my body to release Anna before settling back to the sodden ground. A few moments pass, then I'm distantly aware of her rising to her feet, her hand pressing my shoulder. But I shake my head and keep my gaze turned towards the stones as I listen to their voices, hers and Ray's.

They talk for some minutes. 'It's up to Tom to tell you. Ask Tom...' I hear Ray say.

Eventually she returns, her fingers closing around my wrist. 'Come on,' she whispers. 'Let's get you home.'

The three of us make our way back down the valley in silence, our feet following a groove of chalk which winds its way between mounds of warren-riddled turf, yew trees and gorse bushes. The sun, a livid white eye, glowers through the clouds above our heads.

Ray walks ahead, his hands in his pockets, his eyes on the ground. As I follow him I stare at his soaking hair and find myself wondering at his and Len Combstone's loyalty to Dad – to have kept such an explosive secret to themselves for so long, when so many would be tempted to spill the beans down the Catherine, or to journalists, after a few too many. I guess it would also explain the change in Combstone's attitude towards Dad since I'd left.

I stumble slightly, my foot catching a clump of thistle. Anna takes my hand and squeezes it in response. I open my eyes and turn to look at her. Seeing my expression, she slows, then attempts to pull me towards her into an embrace – but I swerve away because I know if I let that happen I'm going to break down and maybe she knows it too because she doesn't push it.

We carry on heading downhill towards the three waiting stones and those lambs. Their bleating increases in volume as we grow closer and I watch them press against the far side of the pen, their panicked heads raised as they push against one another to try and escape our approach. Ray draws further ahead, as if wishing to rid himself of our presence. Above our heads, that sun finally pierces the cloud and a bright shaft steals across the dark brow of Fawley Wood on the opposite hillside, turning its branches into a blazing bronze which begins stealing its way along the valley towards us.

When we reach the Shadowing Stones I call to Ray. He turns and looks at me warily, then walks towards us, coming to a halt next to the three stones. Letting go of Anna's hand, I take a step towards him until we're facing each other. 'Have you still got that fag packet?' I say.

He stares at me blankly, his brow furrowing under the long hair because I know he was expecting something else – an apology, maybe. He'll get that in time, but I'm in no mood for it right at this moment. Then he shrugs and fumbles around in his pocket before offering up the empty packet.

I take it from him and it sits in my hand, its cellophaned

sides slivering wetly under my fingers. Turning towards the stones, I duck my head beneath the top stone and run my hand along its base, scooping a small amount of the soil into my palm before funnelling it carefully between my thumb and index finger into the box. Pressing down its lid and placing it carefully into my jacket pocket, I straighten and turn towards the barn and Ray's Land Rover.

'Let's head back,' I say.

21

TOM

My dearest Jim

Writing this is the hardest thing I have ever done.

I pray that it is you who find me here, and that you find me at peace, because peace is what I crave more than anything now. If I cannot have our son back, then I cannot have peace in my life, therefore, I would rather be dead.

I am so sorry that it is you who has to find me this way, and that I have had to leave you and Tom to face this cruel world alone, but I feel that I have been given no alternative because I'm sure if I continue living, that I shall go completely mad.

Please understand, I don't regret any of it. I don't regret making that call because those poor people in that bank deserved justice and O'Malley needed to pay for what he did. We cannot be cowards in this life, we cannot allow fear to prevent us from doing what is right. Otherwise, what kind of world do we deserve to live in?

But most of all, I do not regret you or our life together. Ours was a real love, wasn't it? It began like a thunderclap neither of us was expecting, and the passion that fuelled it never depleted. All these years later, I still have the same rush of feelings for you I experienced when you first approached me on your father's farm. But it was more than love at first sight for us. We have a connection, don't we? Something vital and deep and lasting, something neither of us can quite explain. We are part of each other and we've been so very lucky to experience such a thing.

And now I have to take that part of you away and I feel so terribly sorry for this because I don't want you to be alone, my love, I truly don't. But at least I know you'll have Tom.

Please look after him and guide him well. I chose his name when we were on the ferry home. I never told you that, did I? It's strange, but I knew he was a boy, and when I watched you through the window, standing with your hand on the rail watching the Belfast docks fade away into the horizon, I named him Tom and told him that his father was a good man no matter what he had done, and I assured him that even though he wasn't planned, he was wanted so very much. He's strong, our boy — despite everything he has been through, and he's a survivor like his father. I know he'll make you proud.

Oh Jim, I'm so exhausted by the workings of my mind, I'm so exhausted by going over and over and over what happened to Callum and the knowledge of the pain and fear he must have suffered. And though I don't regret my actions, I still know they directly brought about our son's death and for that I suffer terribly and I just hope you understand why I've had to do this. I'm so terribly sorry.

Jim, please promise me that you'll destroy this letter and never tell Tom what really happened to his brother. He must never know the truth of your past and what you did in that bank, even if you never intended for it to end as it did. We cannot risk that he will one day want to take revenge.

Neither can I bear for him to know my part in this wretched story, because I fear that one day he'll blame me for what happened to Callum and that is another thought I simply cannot bear.

I must leave you now. The house is empty and it's time. I say I'm not a believer, and I don't believe in heaven. It's still true. I had my heaven with you here on earth.

Travel safely, my love.
Eileen

I place the letter down on the floor, then my head falls forward. Pressing my fists into my eyes, I take long, steady breaths.

Upstairs, Anna's asleep, exhausted by the day and night that's just taken place.

After he dropped us back at the village, Ray headed for home with not so much as a goodbye while Anna and I came back here to my father's cottage. We sat for hours drinking coffee and talking it all over, me in one armchair and her in the other. At some point her head slumped forward so I picked her up in my arms, undressed her, and laid her down on the bed. She didn't stir she was that bushed.

Then, finally understanding why my mother didn't want me to read it, I went to fetch this letter.

But at least I know you'll have Tom.

Jesus, what had she understood about my mind during that time? I guess she'd been so wrapped up in her own anguish and so unable to think straight that she'd never contemplated the fact that for me, her suicide would be the final straw and bring about my own form of absolute desertion. She'd also never realised that the idea of *blaming* her would have been total anathema to me when she was the one thing holding me together after the trauma of discovering my brother's body.

My mother's death had been one of silence, one that had left a dull edge to the air and life itself. She hadn't said goodbye. She'd barely said anything. She'd simply packed me off to my grandparents' with a quick kiss on the cheek followed by a pat on the back, understanding that I was now a self-conscious teenager who'd got into the habit of flinching from her hugs. 'Be a good boy,' she'd said, staring out of the front door as I'd traipsed across the drive and climbed into my grandfather's car. I'd raised a thumb without looking back. I'd been feeling cross because I hadn't wanted to go and didn't understand why I was being made to go.

One hour later, she was dead.

I'd stuck up that defiant thumb and walked away not knowing, not understanding that when I was still just a tiny cluster of cells she'd already named me; already guessed my gender. That in the tumult of her confusion and fear on that ferry ride home, she'd reached out to me, her unborn child, as she desperately sought reassurance of a secure and happy future. I think of her now, of Dad and the unbelievable change that occurred in both their lives as a result of their meeting on that Donegal hillside, and then my body buckles as the first sob explodes out of me and the tears finally begin to flow unchecked down my face, soaking my hands and smudging the ink of her words.

* * *

Many minutes pass. Eventually I force myself to rise and pad unsteadily to the kitchen to get a tin before returning to the armchair. God knows what time it is. The fire's almost gone out and the road outside is deathly quiet.

I swallow a mouthful of lager then close my eyes, my thoughts shooting between random images like a pinball. Stella, with John Harris's hairy arse between her thighs; my children sitting in front of the television and fighting over the remote control while I tried in vain to talk to them; my father and mother strolling through those golden rays of sun in Fawley Wood, their arms wrapped around one another. Then O'Malley's face in that faded sepia picture, his cruel, soulless eyes staring out at the camera. How much had this man stolen from me without even knowing me? And much more importantly, how much had he stolen from *Callum*?

My brother would have excelled at school – the teachers had already labelled him as 'very bright' – and he'd have probably gone to university on the back of my mother's and grandparents' encouragement. He would have been married now, and no doubt he'd have made a better fist of it than me. I'd have had nieces and nephews who would have been cousins for my children.

If O'Malley hadn't turned up in my father's life, my mother would still be here and Dad probably wouldn't be dead because he'd still have plenty of reason to live.

I must have fallen asleep because suddenly I'm waking up in the armchair with a half-smoked roll-up between my fingers. Outside the window, a robin's solo scale kicks off the dawn chorus and a fine ribbon of yellow slashes the sky above the horse chestnuts on Soweton Road. I think about joining Anna in bed but I've got a sudden tightness in my gut and I'm feeling a bit heady and weird.

For a few minutes, I'm not sure what's happening: my heart's thumping, there's a prickle of pins and needles in my wrists and fingers and nausea's rising in my gut. They're the same feelings that floored me when me and Anna were walking up to the stones – the same symptoms they treated me for all those years ago and warned me could return with the right triggers. Yeah, well I guess I've had quite a few of those all right.

But I need to do something because it feels like my heart's about to explode it's pumping so hard and I can feel the sweat gathering in my palms. So hurriedly grabbing my coat, I leave the house and take myself off in the direction of Fawley Wood.

As I walk through the deserted village trying to shake off my panic attack, the dawn chorus reaches a crescendo, the hedgerows alive with wood pigeons, chaffinches, doves and cuckoos so different to early mornings in Australia where the gardens resound with lorikeets, rosellas and warblers. Eventually I reach the woods' empty car park and walk towards its large wooden barrier. Then I turn and rest against it, my gaze on the wheat-thatched and slate-tiled roofs which sit in the valley below me, the cut-throat dawn slowly forming above them. Though the veiled, grey circle of the moon still hangs above the trees, it's semi-light now, the sun's emerging rays stealing across the pylon-lined, mist-covered fields.

As I duck under the barrier and start heading down the main track which leads into the heart of the wood, I'm numbly aware that tears have started trickling down my face. I recall again mine and Callum's trips up here to collect the windfall – or 'loads' as Dad called that particular chore – and how we dreaded being told to do it, particularly in the winter when we would traipse up here in the rain and snow.

But there were also poignant bright spring mornings like this one, when the dawn was breaking through the trees, its rays illuminating the fat white blobs of cuckoo spit which cling to the branches of saplings. And suddenly I'm grateful the old man made us do those loads in the months leading up to my brother's death. Though only a handful of years apart in age, me and Callum were at very different stages in our young lives. While I was going through puberty, he was still a boy. We were at different schools hanging out with different kids and during those last few months of his life, those journeys were the only times we were properly together and able to forget our differences, where we were able to play and laugh together as brothers.

After Callum died, the old man didn't make me do loads anymore.

There's a sudden, loud crash. I turn, and through a blur of tears, see a stag and his hind leaping away from me between the trees, disturbed by my approach. After fifty metres or so they slow to a standstill in the mist, turning their heads towards me. I stop to watch them and for a moment none of us move. Then I slowly lift my hand, in salute. The gesture causes the stag to raise its head slightly, its antlers breaking the dawn rays which pour through the trunks behind it. Then they're off once more, white tails bobbing up and down until they gradually merge with the trees, and are gone.

I don't want to go back to Australia.

The thought comes from nowhere. *I don't want to go back to Australia* – no matter how good the weather and lifestyle, or how beautiful and varied the landscape. I don't want to go back to a land which is not my home and will never be my home. I don't want to go back to a marriage that's over; to a life that will always be half of what it was without my wife in it; to an existence of paying through the nose to watch my children grow up under the care of another man.

And despite everything that's happened here, despite the losses I've suffered; as I head away from the track and begin winding my way between the silent trunks with tears still sliding down my cheeks, I'm beginning, at last, to understand why Dad longed to return to Ireland. Because it was in these woods that my parents used to walk together hand-in-hand and where Callum and I gathered the windfall and chased each other. It was on the village green that I learnt how to hit a ball with a cricket bat and watched Anna laugh as she ran from base to base. And it's in this valley that my father's body will rest next to my mother's and my brother's; where the ghosts of my family walk beside me; where each track and hillside is mine because I claim my right to it from birth; where a woodpigeon's cooing brings back memories of warm, sunny evenings with my brother and friends spent out on our bikes and the shape of a girl on a horse reminds me of dark nights pulling myself off between the sheets as I changed from a boy into a man.

I stagger backwards abruptly, my back slamming against a beech trunk. Pressing my face into my hands, my body releases a long, drawn-out howl which echoes hollowly around the depths of the forest. It's immediately followed by a mass flapping of wings as a flock of sparrows rise in a panic from the treetops. For a second I'm motionless, shocked by this unexpected and wholly uncontrolled exorcism of grief.

Then I turn and repeatedly dash my fist against the trunk, my chest heaving as another anguished cry blasts the silence, only this one is livid with fury and rage, like the sound of a wild beast being cornered with spears and slowly goaded to death.

I picture O'Malley's pale face in that photograph staring back at me. *How could you have done that?* I'm thinking. *How could you kill a child who has had nothing to do with you or with the evils of this world, who has had nothing to do with any evils done to you? Your son was killed in the crossfire. It wasn't what my father wanted, or planned. It was a tragic accident, that was all. Surely you knew that? But of course you knew that. You just didn't care.*

I punch the trunk seven, maybe eight more times until my body abruptly slumps against the tree and goes still. Dropping my head, I stare wonderingly down at my right hand, the knuckles a mulch of blood and moss.

'Dad, I'm sorry...' The words spill out of my mouth as I groan loudly, my back sliding down the tree, my legs giving way onto the grass. I picture my father's fragile, shrunken face against those blankets and I know despite his final words of reassurance, that I will never, ever forgive myself for going to Australia and leaving him here alone.

The grass's morning dew seeps into my jeans and as the forest's arms seem to close protectively above my head. I close my eyes and await my punishment, my body braced instinctively for that reel to continue its endless trajectory – the inevitability of the Shadowing Stones rising in the mist from a sea of scarlet poppies, that dreaded scrap of red wool appearing on cue beneath my feet. But oddly the image doesn't come, even though this time I'm actively fighting to conjure it. Beyond my harsh breaths, all I can hear is the forest's silence, and on the dark surface of my retina, there is just a soft, receding light – and then nothing.

22

TOM

I hand the estate agent the house keys and watch him drive away, then spend the next half an hour packing. I've organised for a couple of crates to be shipped on with the stuff I'm keeping – it's not a lot, given it represents a family's whole existence. There are photo albums, Mum's paintings, and her sketchbook of course. Then there's her jewellery box, plus her remaining clothes, the ones which Anna didn't want. I don't know what to do with them, but I don't want to chuck them. I'm not keeping much from Dad, just those photos of his family and the one of O'Malley in case I decide to take action from the relative safety of Australia – that's something I'm going to need to carefully consider – and his whisky tumbler, plus an ancient, broken watch I remember him wearing when we were young.

When I've finished packing, I close the cases and carry them to the car, then return to make a final patrol around the house. Everything's done; the rooms are all cleared and clean; the house-clearance people have taken the bigger furniture and his old truck's been towed to the breakers yard. Any items of use have been given away to the local PTA and various people around the village – but there wasn't much because his stuff was so antiquated.

Ray Curtis has sort of forgiven me – well, if not forgiven then he's at least accepted that I lost it for a bit and am no longer about to murder him.

It's been six days since I confronted him and he's been round here several times since then to help fill in the gaps. He reckons Dad and my mother guessed O'Malley and his men had kidnapped my brother soon after he disappeared but hadn't been able to tell the police for obvious reasons. Callum had been held captive somewhere over the Christmas period – probably in the barn – and O'Malley had phoned Dad on New Year's Eve to tell him to meet them at the Shadowing Stones the following morning. Any word to anyone, and that would be the end of his son, he warned. But if he followed their instructions, they'd let Callum go.

Dad knew O'Malley's son had been shot during the raid in Derry – Patrick had told him that when he'd come to visit. But he still assumed they were going to exchange his life for Callum's and for that reason he hadn't told my mother he was going to meet them.

Fortunately, I'd already been sent to stay with my grandparents in Marlborough over the rest of that Christmas. Mum had been desperate to shelter me from the media and her and Dad's deep distress, so I was out of the way and didn't get to witness the terrible scene that was to take place in our house on that bleak New Year's Day.

Dad knew his best and only hope, was to try to persuade O'Malley it wasn't him who'd tipped-off the police. He'd even prepared an impassioned speech about his deep Republican loyalties which he insisted hadn't faded despite his devotion to Eileen, but he wasn't holding out much hope. He knew there was nothing concrete he could say to prove it and for them to be taking such decisive, risky action meant they must be pretty determined. So he was prepared for the exchange knowing the responsibility he held, and went to meet them resigned to the fact he was probably going to die, *accepting* that he was going to die. But what they'd planned for him and my mother was a thousand times worse.

There were three men present – the same ones who'd carried out the bank robbery. Patrick wasn't there.

After they'd killed my brother they made Dad walk away at gunpoint – back down the track to Milbury. One word to the police, O'Malley warned, and they'd be taking out the rest of us at the first opportunity, starting with my mother. But if he kept his mouth shut then they'd leave him alone to live with the consequences of his actions.

He returned to Fawley a man destroyed, to collapse at my mother's feet. Telling her what they'd done was as hard as watching his son die.

Only then she'd abruptly broken down too, and through her grief had finally confessed she'd been the one who'd tipped-off the police. If he hadn't told her about his involvement in that robbery... she'd sobbed. If he'd just kept his mouth shut and kept her out of it altogether. It had been too much for her conscience to carry – *all those poor, innocent people murdered.*

Eventually she'd decided to make a short anonymous call to the police telling them what she knew – which wasn't much, just that the man behind the Ulster Bank robbery was called Sean O'Malley and that he came from the town of Buncrana in Donegal.

In hindsight, my father reckoned the men already knew it'd been an English woman who'd called the police. The IRA had enough moles in the RUC who would have been able to provide this information at some point during their incarceration, and that was why they weren't ever likely to be convinced by the impassioned speech he'd delivered on the silent snow-covered Grey Weathers Valley that New Year's afternoon. O'Malley even said that if it wasn't him who'd grassed, then it had to be Eileen, at which Jim had scoffed, and that was the exact moment O'Malley had shot his son.

Dad hadn't known what they'd done with Callum's body but it was an obvious bet that it was probably somewhere around the Shadowing Stones and he didn't let on and neither did Mum in case they drew fingers towards themselves. And this is something that, looking back, I find hardest of all. The memory of those searches, the two of them sitting there giving every appearance of waiting anxiously for news as the police and villagers searched the fields, day after day, week after week. And all that time, they both knew exactly what had happened to Callum and where his body was likely to be.

I move over to the sitting-room window and open it to reveal a cloudless blue sky. Outside it's a hot day – the first properly hot day since I arrived. My eyes follow a grey squirrel as it scurries along the school railings and leaps into the branches of a sycamore tree. The air's moist and pungent with the fragrances of spring; a heady blend of moist cut grass, cow parsley and blossom. I close my eyes and enjoy the warm rays on my face, the drone of lawnmowers in nearby gardens and that ever-present cooing of the wood pigeons. Then, because I can't help myself, I open them to stare, one final time, over the playground towards Liz Carmichael's house.

'It's like the story of Abraham and Isaac, isn't it?' Anna had said to me when we were sat at home drinking on the evening after my confrontation with Ray at the stones. 'You know, when God asks Abraham to sacrifice his son. Jim had to sacrifice Callum in order to save you and Eileen.'

'But God let Abraham sacrifice a sheep in the end,' I'd

replied, staring into my can. 'There was no reprieve for Callum, was there? Or Mum for that matter.'

Anna has barely left my side since that day. I've grown so used to her being with me she's become like an extension of myself. Her patience seems to know no bounds as I work it all through, nodding or shaking her head as each question comes her way – 'Do you think that...?' and 'If he had, do you think he would have...?' and so on. Most of the time she bats it back to me, recognising it for what it really is, a question I'm asking myself. 'I'm not sure, Tom – what do *you* think?' she'll reply, so allowing me to explore further the maze of motives and emotions, and the terrible regrets, that made up the story of my brother's death.

But she also tries to buoy me up, getting me out of the house and walking, whilst telling me stories and making me laugh, or going for a drink or a night out, like the evening she took me to the cinema in Marlborough for my birthday. Other times she takes me by surprise, like when she turned up at the door last night – *our last* night – with two tickets in her hand.

'There's an Abba tribute band playing in the village school this evening,' she announced. 'It's in aid of Fawley Church roof. Let's go – it'll be fun.'

Initially I'd shaken my head and held my hands up in horror. 'You must be fucking joking.'

But she'd shaken her head and laughed. 'Oh come on, Tom, don't be such a stick-in-the-mud. We don't have to dress up if you don't want to. Even Isabel's going – and so's half the village apparently. It'll be a nice way for you to say goodbye.'

And in the end I gave in, and was glad I did because we had a gas. The organisers had really gone for it with the best of seventies kitsch; putting silver streamers around the place and disco balls and coloured lights. There was a bar of course, and a prize for best fancy dress, and the villagers had made a massive effort – you'd have thought they'd had nothing else to do all year but work on their white capes, wigs, huge platform heels and silver jackets. Anna and I went in our jeans and T-shirts, but Isabel wore a long grey dress with a small sequinned cap on her head – no doubt to look like the blonde one. Ray Curtis turned up in a silver suit and a fake beard and ended up winning best male fancy dress. A bit later on I noticed the two of them – Isabel and Ray – having an intense conversation by the bar, seemingly oblivious to how ridiculous they looked.

It was good to see so many familiar faces, even if they were hidden beneath such crazy garb – I'd seen some of them in the pub, or at the funeral, but others I hadn't met since coming back here.

These were the boys and girls I'd gone to school with; their children were now attending Fawley Primary in their places. And their parents were there too, people I remembered waiting at the school gates to pick them up – now in their sixties and seventies, grey-haired and retired. Many of them recognised me, if I didn't recognise them, and asked after my life in Australia – noting with surprise, and visible pleasure, that I was clearly involved with Anna although I didn't attempt to explain us and batted away any enquiries towards that end. One or two mentioned Callum, but in general people kept away from the subject. Pretty much everyone offered their condolences over Dad.

The band were brassy and upbeat, if not massively talented, but Anna got a few pints in me and then had me dancing to all the old cheesy classics. And once up, we didn't sit back down until the end, twirling and turning each other clumsily under our arms, catching Anna's waist and pulling her against me, going round and round until we almost fell over with dizziness, our bodies hot and covered in sweat and our faces bright with laughter.

It wasn't quite the final night I had planned for us – not that I'd given it much thought beyond maybe taking her for a quiet dinner in Marlborough or Devizes – but in the end I'm glad that's what we did because it's given me some pretty good memories.

When the disco finally finished and the bar closed, we said goodnight to the other partygoers, then walked hand-in-hand over the road to enter Dad's place for a final time. And then we said goodbye – if you can call sitting for hours in the lamplight on the edge of an airbed borrowed from her mother with the sweat drying on our faces, if you can call that a goodbye. We talked about everything and nothing; we talked about Callum and Dad, and Alex Strong and her sister's intention to return to her unhappy marriage; we talked about Stella and the kids and what I'm going to do next. Problem is, I've no idea about that one. Am I really going to leave Stella and does she want me to leave her? Is this affair of hers just a result of being a bit bored with the way things are, or is it more than that?

I'm not going to know until I get back. It's easy to think we can separate while I'm looking at it from the other side of the world with this lovely girl sitting beside me, but it'll be another story when we find ourselves looking at our kids and all we stand to lose. I'm old enough to know now how life goes and how Stella sets store in security and things like having a nice house and shit like that – stuff I can provide that John Harris most likely can't.

So I guess I need to know how serious she is about this arsehole and try and work out just how angry I really am about what she's been up to and what role I might have played in driving her to it, and then I reckon I'll have to tell her about Anna, and after that, well maybe we'll know how the cards are really set to fall.

But I couldn't really say any of this to Anna so I just told her

I didn't know what I was going to do and I was going to wait until I'd spoken to Stella. After that we changed the subject and I let her chatter on about the times we've shared together these last few weeks and how, in her opinion, it's been... I dunno, like some kind of intense, midlife thing we were both meant to experience to... what? Set us back on the right path? Show us how love can be? Make us understand the value of our roots?

As usual, she's over-thinking things but I'm not going to point it out to her because I know it irritates her to fuck when people say that. 'It's like saying I've got size five feet,' she says. 'Of course I over-think things. That's the way I am. Better than *under-thinking* them, don't you think? – like most of the morons in this fucked-up world...'

No, unlike Anna I don't really need to look for the reasons. All I know is I'm going to miss her like hell once I've gone because it's like – I dunno, she's kind of a part of me now, knowing Callum, remembering it all as I remember it all, and remembering each other as we were before life began chipping away at our soft edges. I know I'm going to be lonely without her, even if Stella stays – it's not just Anna's company, but the feel of her touch and her constant warmth that makes her so easy to be with. It's been so long since Stella and I were this intimate – if we were ever this intimate – I'd forgotten how it can be.

But I don't know how to say this stuff, it sounds sentimental, and maybe she thinks I'm not really feeling all that much because when we finally lay down I told her I didn't want to make love, I just wanted us to hold each other and be as close as we could because we only had those last six or seven hours left together in our whole lives, but maybe she didn't understand because at some point in the early hours I woke up in the darkness to hear her crying and it sounded like the tears were being wrung from the depth of her soul.

I immediately tightened my arms around her and told her I loved her but her response was, 'I know you're thinking about her, not me, I know you're thinking about Stella...' and when I tried to persuade her I was thinking about everything, and it was all so confusing I didn't know where to start, she said, 'It's like you've always been in my blind spot. I feel like I've spent my whole life searching for you, only to find you've been here all along,' and, 'I wish I could just lie here being held by you until we both die because nothing's going to mean anything without you in my life...'

And I wasn't sure what I was supposed to say in return except, 'I wish I didn't live so far away,' and, 'You could come, you know... at least for a visit...' But she just laughed out loud into the darkness, shook her head and cried some more, and said, 'You'll be back with Stella the second you hit the landing strip and a week later it'll be like we never happened. You're going to forget me, Tom, I guarantee it. I'll fade from your memory so quickly it'll take your breath away.'

Another surprise. When I woke up this morning she'd already gone. Her parting gift was an empty hollow in the pillow filled with the scent of her hair and a single blue forget-me-not.

I stared at that flower for a very long time.

That was three hours ago. Now I take one last look around and breathe in deeply, inhaling them all and, closing my eyes, attempt to hold them inside me forever; Dad, Mum, Callum – and Anna.

Then I lock the door and get into the car, letting the engine run for a minute as my eyes travel along Fawley high street.

At that moment the school bell suddenly rings for morning break and I turn to watch the kids charge out into the playground one final time; the two girls running ahead, the younger one in a yellow dress and brown sandals, slightly apart from the others, her pretty face friendly but anxious under a sweep of long dark hair.

The older girl is taller, blonde, and surrounded by a circle of admiring boys. At the other end of the playground, a black-haired boy stands watching them, distracted for a moment from his game with his younger brother who's rolling around on the grass knowing he won't get told off for being out of bounds. In those days you weren't allowed to go on the grass until after the Easter holidays. I smile at the unexpected memory of being able to lay my feet on soft turf after months of being confined to concrete; of knowing the spring had finally arrived.

Then I slowly lower the handbrake and pull away from the curb, leaving the school and its children behind me forever. Heading up the high street, I pass the red-brick Victorian houses to my left and the older, thatched cottages with their ancient lintels, on my right.

When I come to the end of the Carmichaels' footpath, the place where I first kissed Anna, I pull into the side and stare down it, hoping in vain for a final glimpse of her striding towards me between the wall and the tall hedge. I even think about getting out and going up to the house because suddenly I want to tell her that leaving her feels like my heart's being slowly torn in two and that I'm going to feel wretched without her in my life, and how wrong she is because to forget her would be like forgetting myself.

But I don't go up the path. Instead I push down the accelerator and drive on past The Catherine Wheel and on up Angel Hill before accelerating over the small bridge that crosses the Kennett and bearing right up the hill towards the A4 and the great watchful sweep of Marlborough Down.

But at the same time I'm trying to ignore the deep wrench in my stomach, a lurching emptiness I've not been expecting, and though I know it'll pass I've got this really shitty feeling that I'm driving towards a vacuum, a chasm where nothing of any meaning exists as I leave behind everything that's made me who I am – and it's funny, but I'm thinking that maybe this is what the Buddhists mean when they talk about the inevitability of change and loss; the loss of Anna; of my mum, my dad and brother; of the child in me I must abandon here forever.

But at the same time another voice comes into my head and whispers that soon the emptiness will be filled with the faces of my children, and later, their children, and I wonder if Dad felt something of the same when he drove away from Donegal with a heart weighed heavy with grief, Mum sitting beside him as he said goodbye forever to the people and land that had given him his blood and his soul and headed towards an unknown future, guided only by the strength of his faith, and his love.

EPILOGUE
ANNA

May arrives and the fine weather has turned into a protracted, early heatwave. The countryside hums with new life; cabbage-white butterflies flutter between the wildflowers in the meadows; black stag beetles and red ants scuttle across tree stumps and under rocks, and spiders sew fine webs which, on early mornings, gleam between the branches of saplings. To the north of the village, the fields reaching towards the Marlborough Down are luminous with yellow rape and blue linseed and the vast, cloudless sky is filled with swifts and migrating swallows.

I've decided to stay on in England for a bit longer. There's been no hurry to get back to Istanbul since I made the decision to leave it, and I feel I need a bit more time to consider what I'm going to do next. I also want to enjoy this glorious spring now I'm fully recovered because it's only in these last few months that I've realised just how badly the endometriosis had been affecting me. For years, I'd suffered horrific periods. I'd also been wiped out by anaemia and fatigue without ever really knowing it. Now my health has returned and the HRT has taken effect, along with the fitness gained from so much walking, I possess an energy that would have been unthinkable six months ago.

The good weather has brought an army of walkers and tourists to the village and the Catherine's garden has become home to large, rowdy families who, having returned from walks into the woods or across the Ridgeway, sit around its wooden benches wolfing down baguettes and baskets of chips. The area has become almost irritatingly busy; the woods' tracks and paths are full of mud-splattered kids on off-road bikes spewing petrol fumes into the lilac and pollen-filled air, and the downs are littered with groups of ramblers with colourful rucksacks on their backs, their hands clutching maps and walking sticks.

Yet despite this invasion of civilisation, to me Fawley has never felt emptier.

Since he left for Australia, I've been working hard to maintain the illusion that Tom's somehow still in the village. At first it's not too difficult – after all, most of the time he'd kept such a low profile his presence could only be detected if you were actively seeking the red Punto parked opposite the school, or the glow of his cigarette lighter outside his father's house at night. So for the first week or so, it's easy to believe he's still around and the part of me which quickly grew used to our daily routine still listens out for his phone call or his hard double-knock on the door.

But then, even though I think I've prepared myself for it, the FOR SALE sign appears outside the house, plunging its stake straight into my heart.

He's gone.

Despite the sunshine, I feel his loss almost as if he's died. In fact, it might actually be easier if he *had died* because it's hard knowing someone you've come to care for deeply is continuing with their life only without you in it. I know I sound ridiculous and melodramatic. I know it's stupid to feel this way after being with him for such a short time – after all, I've survived without him perfectly well until now – but I now realise there's always been a sense of emptiness, or incompleteness in my life until Tom, and over the last month or so we spent together I'd become more and more convinced of something between us that felt integral and destined, something *right*.

I miss him. God how I miss him... He was illuminated, concentrated, intense and sincere – so different to the other men I've known – and without him, the sunshine and beauty of the spring means nothing because he's not here to share it with me. The freshness is gone and now everything feels empty and dull. Like TS Eliot on those Margate sands, I connect nothing with nothing.

He doesn't text me – he's not the kind of man who texts – and I resist the temptation to text him. But at the end of May I receive a letter. It comes with an address in Adelaide and a landline telephone number.

Anna

How are you? I'm okay – well, actually I'm not so good. I've moved out and I'm staying with a mate for a while. Stella and I talked things through and she says she wants to start a life with this guy. I'm not sure how it's going to pan out with the kids – we're talking about joint custody and she says she's okay with that – which is a relief. The finance and business stuff is going to be a lot more tricky.

I'm not sure how I feel. One moment I'm relieved, the next a bit upset – mostly because of the kids. They've not taken it well but then I guess it's not surprising, their dad goes off for five months and comes back and immediately moves out.

I keep thinking about everything that happened with Dad and Callum. It's still a lot to take in and there's no one here to talk to about it to.

Like I said, I wish I didn't live so far away. Keep thinking about you and what you're planning next. I always picture you in Fawley, but I guess you must be back in Istanbul by now. Maybe you've decided to stay there after all and work things out with your man? If not, I guess your next letter will be from Brazil or somewhere crazy like that. Or maybe England – you kept saying you might move back to Wiltshire. Maybe it's a good idea.

Anyway, I miss you.

Tom

For some reason this letter really upsets me. Even though I know he's not a man of words, I feel especially stung by the monotony of his tone in those last few sentences – 'You kept saying you might move back to Wiltshire. Maybe it's a good idea'. I know he's not good at expressing his feelings but I needed something more than this and it feels like an anti-climax, like the obligatory postcard after a pleasant holiday romance. To me, he sounds lonely, distracted; writing partly because he's got nothing better to do but also – I suspect – to offload his upset over the break-up with Stella. I sense he's shocked – as if he never really thought it would happen.

'A bit upset – mostly because of the kids...' Christ, he's such a master of understatement – why can't he just tell me that now he's back in Australia the reality's hit and he's devastated. I've not replied and I'm not sure I'm going to because I don't want him to spoil the illusion of our love – and I'm beginning to suspect an *illusion* is all it was, for him at least. Well he can do and think what he likes, but I'm always going to cherish my memories of the short time we spent together, even if I'm condemned to spend the rest of my life suffering its loss.

Because I know I'll never forget those first weeks after I'd realised he was also back here in Fawley and the time I spent walking by his house wondering if he was watching me pass. I'll never forget the days and weeks I spent rediscovering those various tracks and paths and the memories they brought with them and speculating whether if he too, on finding himself back in this village where he grew up, had immersed himself in discovering those same tracks and paths, those same memories – only to find that *he had* – although I hadn't known it until that night on the staircase after we'd rowed over Ray Curtis. Those words had been like a meteor blasting away the walls of my heart.

In those last weeks after he'd confirmed the truth of Stella's affair and was free to act without a conscience, we were finally able to share the stories of our childhoods as we wandered together like two errant school children around Fawley and its surrounding countryside. We talked and talked, sharing our memories and our reflections, uncovering and relishing the most innocent and beautiful times of our lives.

Then, as dusk fell and the hedgerows were shrouded in mist and the air was full of evening birdsong, we'd turn and head hand-in-hand back to the village, stopping briefly to share a drink in the Catherine before returning to make tired love in the small bedroom where he'd slept as a child.

* * *

The time to leave is approaching. This holiday from my life, which was supposed to take six weeks but has actually lasted six months, is finally drawing to a close.

I telephone Kerem and inform him it's obvious from our lack of communication that our relationship's over and as a result I've decided to leave Turkey – so I've awarded myself that last bit of dignity.

He can hardly pretend he's surprised – he knows we've both just been using the distance between us as an excuse to avoid confronting the inevitable – but he puts on a good show of hiding his relief and even sounds a bit sad. He asks me what I'm planning to do once I've collected my things and I reply that I've no idea, although that's not entirely true.

Tom was right in one thing in his letter. For some time I've been quietly considering settling back in Wiltshire although I've not thought about what work I'd do here. But my mother's not getting any younger and I don't like leaving her to look after Fawley House on her own even though, for the moment, she remains able-bodied and frustratingly determined to carry on with things the way they are. I also recognise I can't be with her for twenty-four hours a day and nothing Isabel and I can do or say will ever persuade her to stop climbing up ladders or mowing her oversized lawn.

But if I leave England, I know I'll miss her and my sister in a way that I never thought possible six months ago. A combination of the illness and hitting my forties perhaps, plus my growing sense of estrangement from Turkey, has made me finally appreciate what's important in life: my family and my roots; time spent alone; the simple beauty of nature and the rhythms and moods of the seasons.

But why this sudden desire to come home? Is it simply because I'm scared? Or is what I'm feeling just the need to clutch on to something permanent and secure in a world which feels increasingly fragmented, hostile and violent? To do so seems crazy, and not to mention a terrible waste. Of course it's good I've come to appreciate Fawley and my family. But I also believe that to stay well we need to keep moving and growing – mentally as well as physically – and I'm not sure how I'd be able to do that if I came back here to live. Yes, I'd be secure, but I'd also be betraying that other Anna I've worked so hard to become. The years of study; the decades of travel and adventure and widening my mind and learning languages and absorbing new cultural experiences; the time spent mastering the arts of good teaching and writing. Has it all been for nothing?

It's these issues that are on my mind when I finally call Amanda Reid at the *Lonely Traveller* offices to discuss my situation. She says she accepts it's time for me to leave Turkey – that she's actually surprised I've stayed so long given the situation there – and she assures me there'll be work for me wherever I wish to go next unless it's the UK as they don't do a UK edition. But they publish annual editions for most countries and, she tells me, they now have a new online service which requires constant updating, so there's plenty of work. She even goes on to hint that there may even be vacancies coming up at a Commissioning Editor or Publisher level for certain regions, and to let her know if this might be of interest because my experience would be highly valued. Such work would be office-based within the relevant country and would offer a major new challenge.

It seems the world's still my oyster, whether I want that oyster or not.

* * *

My mother and I do not share a tearful farewell; I'm only going back to Istanbul for a couple of weeks – principally to box up

347

my stuff and get it shipped back here to put in storage until I prepare for my next move – and to say goodbye to colleagues and friends, and Kerem of course.

But still, there's something significant in my leaving. I know it and she knows it. The long holiday is over and when I come back I'll be the old Anna, map in hand, in transit to somewhere exciting and exotic. Another page turning, another chapter of my life beginning.

So we hug each other in the warm sunshine and I hold her close for a moment, my hand moving up and down that curved spine as I breathe in the combined scents of her Pears shampoo and the lavender fabric conditioner she uses. Over her shoulder, Zola leaps softly from one sarsen wall to the other and begins to wash himself, his black coat gleaming in the sunshine.

'Take care of yourself, darling,' she says. She's silent for a moment, then stepping back and gripping my hands, she adds something which is totally out of character, something that my father might have said, but I'd never have expected from her. 'I am terribly proud of you, you know, Anna, getting all those qualifications and writing those books. Life isn't just about getting married and having babies – not for all women. I *do* understand that better than you realise.' Then she narrows her gaze and her voice lowers to a whisper. 'So please don't think about staying here on my account – you need to spread your wings and learn to fly again. Don't you understand? They're not broken any more.'

And as the tears well up in my eyes, she lets go of my hands and I can see what she's doing, the symbolic releasing of her child back into the world after nursing it through illness; the silent message that she knows I have to go and that, as my mother, she doesn't expect me to stay.

But as I climb into the car next to Isabel there's a lump in my throat, and by the time we pull out of Soweton Road and pass the FOR SALE sign outside Jim Donnelly's house, the tears are streaming down my cheeks.

'Come on, Anna...' I feel Isabel's hand pat my knee. She glances round at me. 'Come on, don't be silly,' she says again. 'You'll be back in a couple of weeks.'

'But then I'll have to go again,' I say. 'And start over in another place. In another country – where I don't know anyone.'

We pass the Catherine Wheel. Mike the landlord's outside, chatting to the postman as he waters the hanging baskets. They both smile and raise their hands as we raise ours in return. The next moment, we're crossing the bridge that leads out of the village and I'm turning to look one last time down at the thin stream that, only four weeks ago, was the swollen Kennett, its banks spewing water over the road and fields.

Inside my chest my heart tears and tears.

'But that's what you do, Anna,' Isabel says.

'No.' And I shake my head. 'It's what I *did*. I told you before but maybe you didn't believe me. I'm burnt out, Izzy, I don't want to travel any more. I want to settle and feel rooted and know I'll never have to pack my bags again.'

'Then come home.'

We're pulling out on to the A4 now. Isabel accelerates and as the village falls behind us a familiar emptiness fills my soul.

'But what would I do for a living? I'm a travel writer; an English language teacher. What could I possibly do if I came back here permanently?'

'You could marry a rich bloke and be fucking miserable.'

I turn to stare at her. She returned to Bill two weeks ago and I'd assumed things were going better, but as I see the ironic smile on her face, her lips pressed tightly together as her gaze remains fixed on the road ahead, suddenly I'm not so sure.

'I thought the counselling was helping.'

'It is.'

'Then...'

'It's no magic cure. All it's doing is showing me how unfulfilled I am with my life and how powerless I feel to change anything. I know I need to find some kind of purpose – get back some sense of my own identity beyond being a wife and mother. But how? You see, I know you and Mummy think I don't appreciate everything I've got – well I sometimes feel the same about you.'

'What on earth can...'

'I mean, at least you're *your own* person, Anna. You can go where you like and do what you like. I'm so envious of that, you wouldn't believe it. Really, just to be able to do something as simple as earning your own living and not rely on a man to put food on your table. I know it's my fault I messed up. I should have stayed at Oxford and got my degree – but *please* don't tell me to go back and re-train. I'm in my mid-forties and it's just not that easy. I don't care what anyone says.'

'That sounds like the depression talking.'

'Maybe.'

'At least you've got the children.'

'I know,' she says, sounding unconvinced.

'Don't sound so bleak, Izzy. Those kids are your roots and your future. They're what will bind you to the world and give your life meaning. Tom had to go back to Australia because that's where his children are – so that's his home, whether he likes it or not. But at least he's *got* a home. I've got nothing to bind me to anywhere except Fawley and once Mummy's gone even that won't be there anymore. Don't you see? The older I get the more lost I'm going to feel. It's like I'm held up by these fine strings which could break at any second and then there'll be nothing to support me at all.'

Isabel frowns and bites down on her lip. 'You've got *me* to support you, Anna. I'm not going anywhere. And you mustn't think having children is some kind of guarantee you're not going to be lonely. Look at Jim and Tom... Look at you – you've barely seen Mummy these past fifteen years. It's the risk you take when you have kids – I'm quite aware there's nothing to stop mine from moving to the other side of the world once they've grown-up and I'll have no right to stop them. And please don't forget that having children makes you very vulnerable. Awful things can happen to them – things you never get over, like with Callum. So please stop torturing yourself with these thoughts, Anna. Let them go, once and for all.'

Placing both hands on the steering wheel, she lapses into silence, her gaze narrowing as she brakes to let a tractor out of the Milbury junction. Swiping the tears from my cheeks, I turn to stare down the track, its hedgerows thick and lush with nettles and cow parsley. The fields to each side are ablaze with rape and I can just about make out the Shadowing Stones drowsing in a haze of heat at its end. Suddenly it strikes me that today's date is June twenty first – the summer solstice. This evening, their broken shadows will point directly south, just as they have done for thousands of years.

I stare at those stones for several long moments before the tractor crosses, and we slowly drive on.

Our goodbye at Heathrow is hurried. The set-down is busy and Isabel has to double park next to a coach full of disembarking pensioners. I tell her not to bother getting out, but as I'm hugging her I become aware of her phone on the dashboard silently flashing, then the words, 'Message from Ray Curtis' appear on the screen. As I pull back from her I open my mouth to say something, then close it again.

It's her business, her life.

* * *

And before I know it, I'm back in that enormous junction which over the years has become so familiar; wheeling my suitcase determinedly across the grey tiled floor of Terminal 3, my gaze rising over the heads of the other passengers toward the *Departures* board, the smell of filter coffee, aviation fuel and hot conditioned air filling my nostrils.

There's a game I've always enjoyed playing at airports, ever since I started travelling in my early twenties. I invented it to help pass the time. Once I've found my flight and checked it's on time, I like to look down the list of destinations and try and imagine which one I'd choose if I could go anywhere I wanted. It used to thrill me, the endless possibilities held on a single Departures board and I'm glad to find that today, despite the shock of being back at Heathrow and the emptiness in my heart, that my eyes are, once again, inadvertently wandering down that list:

INSTANBUL, JAKARTA, MILAN, PARIS, TOKYO, ADELAIDE, LOS ANGELES, SINGAPORE, DUBLIN...

But eventually I turn and, with a heavy sigh, start wheeling my case towards the Turkish Airlines check-in desk.

In five or so hours I'll be back in Istanbul. It will be baking hot there now and the scent of jasmine will sweeten the breezes that sweep the Bosphorus. Kerem and I will sit together and enjoy those last balmy evenings on his roof terrace as we debrief each other on everything that went wrong between us before toasting the end of our relationship with cold Çankaya wine.

I will listen to, and try to impress on my memory forever, the blasting of the tankers' horns as they slide up and down the glittering water and the song of a hundred mosques at sunset echoing between its seven hills, and the shouts of children playing football on the street below; and I will say my final goodbyes to that most beautiful of cities, giving it the respect and time of mourning that it, too, deserves.

I swerve round, my gaze raising back towards that board. Then my hand slowly unzips my handbag and starts rummaging through the rubbish at its bottom until it closes around a soiled envelope, its seal torn open. I pull out the letter and unfold it.

Like I said, I wish I didn't live so far away.

And suddenly I'm reading it for the first time.

So typically paranoid and insecure. So immediately suspicious and quick to look for hidden meanings, have I missed the blindingly obvious?

Keep thinking about you and what you're planning next.

He's not good at expressing his feelings. These words, I know, are as much as he's prepared to bare of his soul. Of course, we never really discussed it that night. But then the distance was so great and he didn't know how things were going to pan out with Stella. He had to give his marriage a chance for the sake of his children, I understand that. So there were no promises to be made then and it's not like I asked for any.

But now, is it such an impossible idea? As a journey, it wouldn't be straightforward. I'd need to organise a visa, and it might be tricky at my age to get a work permit. It's not like I can just get on a plane and go there.

Anyway, I miss you.

But as I stand in that terminal surrounded by the clamour and mayhem of international travel, I have a strange sense of everything suddenly going silent, as if a glass jar is slowly lowering around me, its walls cutting out the sounds of the people hurrying here and there with their cases and trolleys, the computerised voice in this post 9/11 world warning over the loudspeaker about leaving unattended luggage.

It couldn't happen straightaway. First I need to make a phone call – because I might have got this completely wrong. Then I'll need to speak to Amanda Reid to see if there are any work possibilities. She said there were jobs going in 'various regions' but she didn't say which ones. I've got Istanbul to sort out and Kerem to say goodbye to. And then there's Fawley – the family and home I've become so deeply reattached to these last six months. I'd be so far away from them and that's something I'm going to have to think about very carefully, even though I know what my mother will say – because she's already said it.

And maybe she's right. Because as I stand here in the silence, my eyes arrested by that single word which seems to glow back at me in bright neon, I feel my heart accelerate and at the same time a delicious sense of anticipation is stealing through my limbs, filling the emptiness at last.

ADELAIDE.

THE END

ACKNOWLEDGEMENTS

It is not often that I have a book published (it took eight years to write *Broken Shadows*), so I want to take the opportunity to thank some people who have helped me on my creative journey.

Firstly to everyone at Bloodhound Books for their dedication and professionalism, and to Jane Gregory and Stephanie Glencross at David Higham Associates for their belief in this novel.

For their encouragement in all my literary endeavours: my family, Sarah, Ann and Ciara Moncrieff, Ronnie Goodyer, Helen Holwill, Philippe and Dominique Ullens, Sammy-Jane and Amy Ryan, Alex Aisher, and Neil and Kate Goodwin. For going above and beyond in providing invaluable feedback on early drafts of *Broken Shadows*: Emily Johnstone, Tara Wynne, Alison Baxter, Matt Dickenson and Claudia Bufton. Thank you also to the people of Buncrana, Ireland, who took me under their wing when I visited for research.

To Adrian Ward, Vince Bell, Nick Beere, Pat Ward, Ben Borrill, Tom Harris and Stuart Cluny for nurturing my song-writing abilities. Also to Richard Beauvoisin who changed my life by teaching me to dance, and my wonderful extended family at Ceroc.

To the people of Lockeridge in Wiltshire, the village where I grew up. I returned home in turmoil and the seeds of *Broken Shadows* were sown.

And finally, thank you to Warwick Dufour, for being the real and very happy ending to this story.

ABOUT THE AUTHOR

Sorrel Pitts grew up in the ancient English landscape of Wiltshire, which is a strong presence in her writing. She worked as a magazine editor before moving overseas to teach English in Turkey and Spain. On her return to the UK she became Commissioning Editor for Macmillan Publishers and Editorial Manager for Oxford University Press. She is now living back in Wiltshire and is a freelance editor and writer.

Sorrel's debut novel *The River Woman* was published in September 2011 by Indigo Dreams Press. Sir Michael Parkinson called it, 'a fascinating story told by a very promising writer'.

A NOTE FROM THE PUBLISHER

Thank you for reading this book. If you enjoyed it please do consider leaving a review on Amazon to help others find it too.

We hate typos. All of our books have been rigorously edited and proofread, but sometimes mistakes do slip through. If you have spotted a typo, please do let us know and we can get it amended within hours.

info@bloodhoundbooks.com

Milton Keynes UK
Ingram Content Group UK Ltd.
UKHW010920110224
437550UK00005B/210